Kandy Shepherd swapped a career as a magazine editor for a life writing romance. She lives on a small farm in the Blue Mountains near Sydney, Australia, with her husband, daughter and lots of pets. She believes in love at first sight and real-life romance—they worked for her! Kandy loves to hear from her readers. Visit her at www.kandyshepherd.com.

USA TODAY bestselling and RITA® Award–winning author **Marie Ferrarella** has written more than two hundred and seventy-five books for Mills & Boon, some under the name Marie Nicole. Her romances are beloved by fans worldwide. Visit her website, www.marieferrarella.com.

STRANDED WITH HER GREEK TYCOON

KANDY SHEPHERD

AN ENGAGEMENT FOR TWO

MARIE FERRARELLA

MILLS & BOON

® and TM are trademarks owned and used by the trademark owner and/ or its licensee. Trademarks marked with ® are registered with the United Kingdom Patent Office and/or the Office for Harmonisation in the Internal Market and in other countries.

First Published in Great Britain 2018
by Mills & Boon, an imprint of HarperCollinsPublishers,
1 London Bridge Street, London, SE1 9GF

Stranded with Her Greek Tycoon © 2018 Kandy Shepherd
An Engagement for Two © 2018 Marie Rydzynski-Ferrarella

ISBN: 978-0-263-26469-2

38-0218

MIX
Paper from
responsible sources
FSC® C007454

This book is produced from independently certified FSC™
paper to ensure responsible forest management.

For more information visit: www.harpercollins.co.uk/green

Printed and bound in Spain
by CPI, Barcelona

STRANDED WITH
HER GREEK TYCOON

KANDY SHEPHERD

To my dear friend Anne Yeates and her clever boys,
for introducing me to the historic university
town of Durham in Northern England—
the inspiration for my hero and heroine's past.

CHAPTER ONE

CRISTOS THEOFANIS HAD made such a monumental mess of his own marriage, he found it impossible to share in the joy as he watched his favourite cousin and his wife renew their wedding vows. Seeing their happiness in each other, the intimate smiles shared by a man and a woman deeply in love, made him fist his hands at the memories of what he had lost.

But he was careful to keep in place the mask he chose to present to the world—happy, without-a-care Cristos, unaffected by the losses that secretly haunted him. His pain was his own to keep all to himself.

The renewal ceremony had been held in the tiny white chapel perched on the edge of a cliff overlooking the turquoise waters of the Ionian sea on his cousin's privately owned island of Kosmimo. Now the happy couple was flocked by joyous well-wishers as they spilled out of the chapel. Cristos stood alone by a stunted cypress tree, marooned on his own black cloud of dark thoughts, his face aching from the effort of forcing smiles he didn't feel.

Of course he wished his cousin well, but Cristos was haunted by memories of his own wedding five years ago in a register office in the medieval city of Durham in the north of England. He had looked down at Hayley, his bride, with pride and adoration and a wondering disbelief that such an amazing woman had agreed to share her life with him. In return, her eyes had shone with love and trust as she'd offered him both her body and, more importantly, her heart. A priceless gift. *One that had been wrenched away from him.*

Remorse tore through him like a physical pain. He had not seen his wife in more than two years. Two years and five months to be precise. He could probably estimate the time in hours, minutes even. For every second of that separation he had torn himself apart with self-recrimination and guilt. Now, he didn't even know where Hayley lived, what she was doing. He had hurt her by not being there when she'd needed him. But she hadn't given him a chance to make it up to her. With a ruthlessness he had not believed his sweet, gentle wife had possessed, she had left him and completely deleted him from her life.

As his cousin Alex and his wife Dell kissed to the sound of exuberant cheering, Cristos closed his eyes as he remembered the joy of kissing Hayley when the celebrant had told him he could claim his bride. They had been as happy as these two. Excited about the prospect of a lifetime together. Deliriously in love. Confident that all they'd needed was each other when the world had seemed against them.

'We were once just like them.' The words were no more than a broken murmur, as light and insubstantial as the breeze playing with the branches of the tree above him.

Cristos's eyes flew open in shock at the wistful tones of a once familiar voice. *Hayley.* From somewhere below his shoulder, where she'd used to fit so neatly, he seemed to breathe in the elusive hint of her scent. Crazed by regret, he must be conjuring up a ghost from his past.

He turned his head. His heart jolted so hard against his ribs he gasped. She stood there beside him, looking straight ahead towards the church, not up at him, as if she couldn't bear to meet his gaze. *His wife.*

He put out his hand to touch her, to make sure he was not hallucinating. Her cheek was soft and cool and very, very real. 'It's you, *koukla mou,*' he said, his voice hoarse. He had not used that term of endearment for years—it belonged to her and her only.

Immediately he regretted his words. Drew back his hand. He had loved her unconditionally but she had thrown that love back at him. Yes, he had made mistakes he deeply regretted. But she had not given him the chance to remedy them. She had hurt him. Humiliated him. Put him through hell as he'd searched Europe for her. But she hadn't wanted to be found.

'Don't call me that,' she said. 'I'm not your little doll or your gorgeous girl or whatever that word translates to. Not any more.'

'Of course you're not,' he said tersely.

Her gaze flickered away from him and she bit her lower lip with her front teeth as she always did when she was nervous. Or dreading something. *What was she doing here?*

He stared at her, still scarcely able to believe she was real. Hungry, in spite of himself, for every detail of her appearance. She was wrapped against the late morning February chill in slim trousers and an elegant pale blue coat he had once bought for her from a designer in Milan. The coat, belted around her narrow waist, was the same but he was shocked to see Hayley was not. The image of her he had for so long held in his mind shimmered around the edges and reformed into a different version of his wife.

Her beautiful blonde hair that had tumbled around her shoulders in lush waves was gone, shorn into an abbreviated pixie cut. *Like a boy* was his first dismayed thought. He had loved her long hair, loved running his hands through it, tugging it back to tilt her head up for his kiss. But a deeper inspection made him appreciate how intensely feminine the new style was, feathered around her face, clinging to the slender column of her neck. Her features seemed to come into sharper focus, her cheekbones appeared more sculpted, her chin more determined. Her youthful English rose prettiness that had so attracted him had, at twenty-seven, bloomed into an even more enticing beauty.

'Where the hell have you been?' he said. 'What are you doing here after all this time?'

She met his gaze. 'To see you. What else?'

Hope that she might be there to—at last—explain why she had abandoned their marriage roared to life only to be beaten back down by the cool indifference of her blue eyes, the tight set of her mouth. He wanted to demand that she explain herself. *She was still his legal wife.* But there was a barely restrained skittishness about her that made him hold back. He couldn't risk her running away from him again. *He wanted answers.*

She looked over to the gathering outside the church and then back to him. 'I didn't know your entire family would be here or I certainly wouldn't have come to this island,' she said.

There was something different about her voice. A trace of some kind of accent blurring the precise Englishness of her words. He was fluent in English and Italian, with passable French and Spanish, but he couldn't place it. *Where had she been?*

'This is a private function.'

'I would never have been on the guest list,' she said, a bitter undertone to her voice.

He was unable to refute the truth of her words. His family—in particular the grandmother who had raised him since he was fourteen—had disapproved of his marriage to Hayley and made no secret of it. For *Yia-yia* Penelope their union had been too rushed, too impulsive, too reminiscent of his own parents' hasty marriage that had brought the family so much grief.

'I want to know why you're here,' he said. 'The last time we met you told me you hated me. And then nothing.'

He didn't hate her, though there had been moments when he had wanted to. Since that day in the hospital in Milan when she had turned away from him, her face as pale as the hospital pillow, his emotions had gone from guilt for his neglect, to terror for her safety, through smouldering anger that she had thought so little of their marriage—*of him*—to wipe him without explanation from her life. Finally his anger had mellowed to a determined indifference.

Hayley made no reply. She placed great store on honesty. A shudder of foreboding made Cristos think her unexpected visit was not something he should be glad about.

'How did you get here?' Kosmimo was only accessible by boat. Or the helicopters of the wealthy guests who frequented the luxury retreat spa his hotelier cousin Alex had established on the island.

'I'd heard you were back in Nidri, staying with your grandparents.' His grandparents ran a tourist villa complex in the port town on the nearby island of Lefkada. 'Their maid told me you were here. I hired a man and his boat to bring me over.'

There'd been storms and the water was choppy. 'What man?' he said too quickly, too possessively. He wouldn't trust his wife to just anyone on these waters. Mentally he slammed a fist against his forehead. *She was no longer his concern.* Who knew what risks she'd taken in the last two years and five months without him to look out for her? More to the point, why should he care?

Her eyes narrowed at his tone. But she named a local boatman he knew well. 'Good choice,' he said.

Why had he doubted her ability to choose a safe boat ride? Hayley had always been practical, seeing a problem and finding a solution. Then she'd seen him as a problem and the solution as leaving him.

He looked over her shoulder, aware they had become the target of curious glances. Most of the people gathered here for the ceremony had never met Hayley. But he sensed their interest like a current buzzing through the congregation. Those in ignorance would very soon be made aware that this lovely blonde woman was Cristos's estranged wife. The one who had humiliated a Greek husband in a way a Greek husband should never be humiliated.

He shifted his body to shield her from curious gazes. That was all he'd ever wanted to do—protect her and look after her. Yet when she'd really needed him, he'd let her down so badly she had been unable to forgive him. Deep down, he had been unable to forgive himself.

'Why didn't you tell me you were coming?' he said, keeping his voice low.

'I wanted to see you face to face. But I wasn't sure you'd welcome me if I warned you.'

Banked up from years of frustration his words flooded out. 'Of course I'd want to see you. I need to know what happened. You left the hospital without telling me where you were going. I tried to find you. Your parents wouldn't tell me where you were. Or your friends. Your sister slammed the door in my face.'

She put her hand up to stop him. He noticed it wasn't quite steady. 'Stop. Not here. Not with an audience. What I have to say should be said in private. It's why I had to see you in person rather than—'

'Just say it,' he said through gritted teeth.

She played with the strap of her designer handbag—

another gift from him—twisting it until he thought it would snap. Then she looked up at him. 'I want a divorce.'

He glared at her. 'The sooner the better,' he said.

Hayley took a step back and looked up at her soon-to-be-ex-husband. *Why, oh, why had she come here?* She'd thought she could handle seeing Cristos again. In light of the love they'd once shared, surely it was the right thing to deliver the divorce papers in person rather than have them served on him by her lawyer?

But the moment she'd seen him standing under that tree in his dark coat staring moodily out to sea, she'd known it was a mistake. She'd been slammed by her impossible attraction to him with such force she'd had to plant her booted feet on the ground to keep herself steady. Dry-mouthed, heart pounding, she'd been unable to do anything but stare at him, stricken with hopeless longing.

He was now twenty-nine, and still the most beautiful man she'd ever seen. Perhaps *beautiful* wasn't the right word. But handsome, good-looking, striking, even *gorgeous* were not adjectives enough. Not for this man. Not for six feet two of broad-shouldered, narrow-hipped masculine perfection. Not for thick black hair, smooth olive skin that was a delight under a woman's stroking fingers, the surprise of pure green eyes.

Cristos could have modelled for the marble statues of the ancient Greek gods she had admired in Athens on their honeymoon. Instead just six months later, on a weekend break in London, he'd been scouted by an international model agency. As a macho Greek male, he'd scorned the idea. But they'd needed money badly and she'd talked him into at least trying it. He'd been booked for a prestigious job the first day he'd reluctantly signed the agency contract.

That was when she'd begun to lose him, Hayley reflected now, when he'd started to slip slowly away into a world that'd had no place for her. Pushing him into it was the stupidest thing she'd ever done. She had become the insignificant peahen to the glorious peacock of her magnificent husband. And he had allowed it to happen. He had left her alone to tend the nest while he strode with masculine insouciance the catwalks of the fashion capitals of Europe, shot advertising campaigns and commercials, all the while hobnobbing with the wealthy and well-connected. Every time she'd questioned him, he'd told her everything he did was for her and their financial security. For a while she'd believed him. Before she began to doubt him.

She gritted her teeth. The longing that surged through her wasn't for *this* Cristos. It was for the Cristos she'd fallen in love with as a student back in that pub in Durham when she'd been barely twenty-two. After her gap year, she was a year older than most of the people in her class and something about the group of older students had caught her attention. He'd been laughing with some fellow exchange students. The flash of his white teeth against his olive skin, the humour in those amazing green eyes had caught her attention then mesmerised her. He'd looked across to her and their gazes had connected. For a long moment there had been nothing—*no one*—else but him. The sounds of the pub had receded, the chatter and the clinking of glasses, until it had just been her and him, drinking in each other's eyes, their souls connecting. Or that was how it had seemed. Then his brow had furrowed in a quizzical frown. He'd put down his glass and left his friends behind to make his way to her side.

Even back then he'd been good at masking his feelings— she hadn't known for days he'd been as instantly smitten by her as she'd been by him. It was an attribute that had served him well in his unexpected new career. He'd easily been able to slip into the varied persona required of him as a successful male model. Smouldering and sophisticated in a tuxedo, or sporty and athletic on a yacht, he'd always looked the part on billboards all over Europe.

He'd got so good at donning those masks that towards the end she'd begun to wonder had she ever seen the true Cristos. But at the word 'divorce' his mask slipped and the raw anguish that momentarily darkened his eyes made her heart skip a beat. But it was gone so quickly she might have imagined it.

'Nothing about where you've been, what you've been doing—all you want to do is demand a divorce,' he said in a forced, neutral tone. But the tension in his jaw, the shadow in his eyes told her he wasn't as cool about it as he appeared.

She swallowed hard. 'It can't come as a surprise. We've been separated for two and a half years. That's more than enough grounds to dissolve our marriage.'

'So my lawyer told me when I instructed him to instigate proceedings two years after your desertion. The separation was proof the marriage had irretrievably broken down. That's all that's required.'

His words sounded so grim, so final. The excitement and passion of their early years together had disintegrated into disillusionment. Yet now, just looking at her husband made her remember exactly why she'd defied her family to marry him, given up her own dreams to let him follow his. But that was yesterday. She had to be strong. Good sex and fun weren't enough to build a lifetime on. She'd learned that on a heart-wrenching night in Milan two and a half years ago, alone in a hospital in a country where she didn't speak the language as she'd miscarried in pain and anguish, tears streaming down her face for all she had lost.

She cleared her throat. Although she'd practised the words over and over, they didn't come easily. 'I want to be free, to perhaps marry again one day.'

His mouth set in a tight line. 'Is there someone else?'

'He's just a friend at this stage.'

Steady, reliable Tim, as different from Cristos as it was possible for a man to be. There had not been one word of romance expressed between them but Hayley had sensed Tim wanted to grow the friendship into something more. She wanted security, stability, not the tumult her life with Cristos had been.

'Where did you meet this man?'

'In Sydney. But he's not—'

'You've been living in Australia?' He hissed a string of curse words in Greek. During their time together she'd worked to learn his language, but he'd refused to teach her the curses—such language was not befitting his wife. If he only knew it was nothing to what she heard in her job as a mechanical engineer—a woman in what was still essentially a man's world.

'I didn't think to look for you in Australia, of all places,' he said.

'That's what I thought,' she said. 'It was as far away from you as I believed I could get. I have an aunt there. My parents arranged it.'

He was silent for a long moment as he looked down at her, searching her face. 'Did I hurt you that badly?' His voice was low and hoarse.

She nodded, too choked to risk attempting to speak.

His words sounded as though they were being torn from him. 'So many times I've regretted the way I left you alone that day, that I wasn't there when you needed me. I—'

Hayley had tried to block that final scene with him from her memory; it was too painful to revisit. She put up her hand to stop him. 'I don't want to hear this,' she said.

His dark brows drew together. 'Like you didn't want to hear it then. You wouldn't let me explain or try to make it up to you. You were hurting but so was I and you kicked me to the kerb. Then left me and ran so far away I couldn't find you. After all we'd gone through together you did that. Now you show up out of the blue, crash my family's party and—'

'Please. I don't want to go there. It's over.' Her voice broke. 'I just want a divorce. That's the only reason I'm here.'

'You could have had divorce papers served on me from Australia. Notified me where you were so my lawyer could be in touch with yours. You shouldn't be here, Hayley.'

He turned from her, slanted his broad shoulders away so she once more could see the happy gathering outside the church doors.

'I hope I'm not intruding on a special family occasion,' she said a little stiffly. His family had hardly been what you would call welcoming to Cristos's young English bride the one and only time she had met them. His cousin Alex had been the exception.

'Alex and his Australian wife, Dell, are renewing their wedding vows. It's a special day for them, a gathering only for family and close friends.' His tone let her know she was now pointedly excluded from those categories.

'Your grandmother's maid told me. She said they'd only been married two years ago. I'm glad he found someone after the horror he went through.'

Alex's then fiancée had been killed in a hostage situation. It had made the news all around the world. 'We're all grateful to Dell,' Cristos said. The wife who had been accepted by the family, as opposed to Hayley, the unwelcome one.

She knew she didn't have the right to access his family news but she was curious. 'Why are they renewing their vows so soon? Isn't it usually older people who do that?'

'They had to get married in a hurry because their daughter Litza was on the way. Dell wanted to affirm their vows in a more relaxed manner.'

She looked towards the couple. 'Oh. That must be their

little girl with Alex.' The red-haired cherub was gurgling with laughter. 'And Dell has a baby in her arms who looks just like a tiny Alex.' Hayley forced her voice into neutral. She didn't trust it not to quiver when she talked about babies. Especially to Cristos.

Hayley actually knew quite a lot about Alex and Dell. She'd been dismayed when she'd got all the way to Sydney to find even there she couldn't escape Cristos's family. Alex had been Australian born and a hospitality tycoon. His relocating to Greece after his tragic loss and finding happiness with Dell was ongoing fodder for the press.

'Their son, Georgios. He was born just a year after Litza.'

Hayley couldn't meet his eyes. The tension between them must be palpable. Their baby would have been just a little older than the little girl being proudly held by Alex if she hadn't miscarried that terrible night. But she couldn't, *wouldn't* talk about that. Strained silence from Cristos told her he couldn't either.

The breeze had picked up. She shivered and huddled deeper into her coat—the beautiful, expensive coat Cristos had given her out of guilt for one of his lengthy absences. 'I've come from a hot Sydney summer. It's freezing here. Not at all how I imagined an idyllic Greek island. I mean, it's beautiful but so chilly. Why did they choose to renew their vows in winter?'

'Alex and Dell wanted to have the ceremony here in the chapel where they got married. The resort is fully booked out all through the warmer months. In summer they would not have had the privacy they wanted.'

She looked over to the group outside the chapel. 'I'm happy for them,' she said. 'I liked Alex when I met him and Dell looks lovely.'

'You weren't invited but he'll be glad to see you. And Dell must be dying to be introduced.'

Hayley took an abrupt step back. 'No! I've come to talk to you about the divorce and then go. The boat is waiting to take me back to Nidri.'

Cristos closed the gap between them with one long stride. 'You can't do that.'

'What do you mean?' He was too close. This close she was too aware of his warmth, his scent, his strength.

'I can't allow you to disrupt this special day.'

'That was not my intention,' she said. 'I just—'

He spoke over her, his tone low and urgent. 'Alex and Dell have been through more than you know. Allow them their day of celebrating their commitment to each other. Your abrupt departure would cause even more speculation than your arrival and put the focus on us instead of them. That wouldn't be fair. You've turned up here uninvited. But you are still legally my wife. Despite our separation, it would be expected that you would greet Alex and Dell and congratulate them. I'm asking you to do the right thing.'

Why did he have to put it like that—appealing to her innate sense of justice? 'I suppose I could say hello,' she said tentatively. Although it would take a monumental effort to congratulate the happy couple on their successful marriage while her own was in its death throes. 'It wouldn't take long to chat with them and then slip away to the boat.'

Cristos shook his head. 'That would cause even more disruption than if you left right now. There is to be a lunch at the resort. Stay here for that. Surely we can be civil to each other. But don't mention the divorce to anyone. It's none of their business. Let people think we are discussing reconciliation. Just until the party is over and you can leave with the other guests.'

She frowned. 'You mean pretend I'm still your wife?'

He shrugged. 'If you put it that way. Just for a few hours. Legally you *are* still my wife.'

'You mean I'd have to act loving and—?' Her breath started to come in tight gasps at the thought of it and she had to put her hand to her chest.

'Just civil would do, if you find the thought of pretending an affection you no longer feel so distressing,' he said. 'Just keep it dignified. You've caused me enough humiliation.'

'I don't know that I could face explanations and—'

'No explanations would be required. I have told my family nothing of what happened between us.'

And, no doubt, his relatives had assigned all the blame for the end of their union to her. Slowly, she shook her head, forced her breathing to return to something resembling normality. 'I'm sorry but I can't do it.' Such a charade would bring back old memories, old feelings she had fought so hard to put behind her.

He frowned his displeasure. 'Do it for my cousin's sake who liked you and stood up for you. Don't let us ruin this day for them.'

Us. How thrilled she'd been when they'd become a couple. How she'd loved to drop those magical words *we* and *us* into the conversation, preferably while flashing her engagement ring at the same time. Now Cristos used the word in such a different context it made her shudder. *Us* united in a charade of dishonesty. Although, she was forced to admit, it would be with the best of intentions and just for a few hours. She sighed out loud. He still knew which of her buttons to press. The last thing she'd ever want to do was ruin someone else's hard-won happiness. Everyone in Sydney knew the tragedy Alex had gone through.

She looked up at Cristos. At that handsome, handsome

face that had once been so beloved. 'I'll do it. Then after lunch I'm out of here. With the divorce papers signed.'

And she would say goodbye to her husband for the very last time.

CHAPTER TWO

CRISTOS FISTED HIS hands by his sides. He could lie to himself all he liked but his indifference towards his wife was just another mask. Seeing Hayley again had stripped it away, leaving raw the ache for her he had never been able to suppress.

Call it desire, need, obsession—when she had first smiled at him across that crowded pub in Durham it had lodged in his heart like an arrow from Eros, the ancient Greek god of love and desire. He had found it impossible to wrench it out—even when he had tried to hate her for the way she had left him.

What he had felt for her defied logic, reason, common sense. But it hadn't been enough to see them through the loss of their baby, a time that should have brought husband and wife closer together in a shared grief rather than driven them inexplicably apart. *What had gone wrong?* He needed answers. And he had to get them from Hayley before she took that boat back to Nidri.

Of course, it wasn't as simple as that. Hayley had barricades up around her that might be impenetrable. But Cristos was an optimist. To be a successful gambler you *had* to be an optimist. And he was a gambler. His was not the kind of reckless, addictive gambling that had driven his late father to embezzlement and fraud and stints in prison. Not to mention unending shame for his mother's family.

Cristos's gambling took the form of calculated business risks that had led him to invest in start-up internet businesses—most of which had succeeded beyond all expectations. At not yet thirty, he was a multimillionaire. These days the wide spread of his investment portfolio ensured his fortune was secure—and kept growing. Yet he kept the gambler aspect of him a secret from his family. And had never shared it with Hayley.

His father had died when he'd been thirteen, followed six months later by the death of his mother. His grandparents had brought him back to Nidri, aged fourteen, to live with them. He'd been embraced with love by his grandparents and extended family. But he'd soon become uncomfortably aware of how closely he was scrutinised.

He looked so like his father that his family were terrified he had inherited his nature as well as his good looks. It felt as if they were always waiting to pounce and stamp out any undesirable traits. As soon as he'd realised that, he'd become adept at masking his feelings, hiding his true risk-taking self. It was allowed to come out only when he played football where a winner-takes-all attitude was encouraged.

He had started investing in a small way in app developments by his fellow students at university but had kept both his successes and failures well hidden. Even though he saw himself as a canny businessman, he could never admit to his worried grandparents that he could be in any way like his father, the man they blamed for the death of his mother, their only daughter. The secrecy had become a habit, another mask he was beginning to weary of wearing.

But optimism was all he felt now as he looked down into Hayley's face—a face he had doubted he would ever see again. It was difficult to stop himself from glancing at her every few seconds just to reassure himself she was really there. The sheen of her hair, the blue of her eyes, the curve of her mouth. She was here with him, in the same country, by his side. They were headed for divorce. But he intended to make the most of the hours ahead to get answers to the questions that had plagued him. Then he could put her firmly in the past and move on without being haunted by guilt or bitterness.

That was a much better position than he could have dreamed he'd be in when he'd thought back to their wedding this morning.

'Alex is looking our way. Let's go say hi,' he said. It seemed natural to reach for her, to fold her much smaller hand in his for the first time in years. But she stiffened against him.

Did she hate him so much she couldn't bear the most simple of touches?

'You agreed to do this—we have to make it look believable,' he said in a gruff undertone intended only for her.

He could tell the effort it took for her to release the tension from her body. 'I guess so,' she said, expelling a sigh.

She left her hand in his as he led her towards the chapel but there was no answering pressure, no entwining of her fingers through his. Their linked hands were purely for appearances' sake. But it signalled they were together—for today at least. The fewer questions his family had about her sudden appearance, the better. They would take their cues from him. If he appeared unperturbed they would not question what Hayley was doing here.

His cousin and his wife had been posing for photos with their children but had now handed them over to their doting grandmothers. Cristos was glad. He would find it impossible to keep his mask in place if he had to watch Hayley react to the children, knowing how much she had wanted the baby they had lost that terrible night in Milan.

The night that was branded on his memory for ever, to be brought out and poked and prodded in an agony of self-recrimination for failing her. But there had also been fault on her part. He had wanted the baby, but she had not allowed him to share her grief—let alone acknowledge his.

He'd been in a business meeting—a meeting that had turned out to be pivotal to his rapid rise to riches. The deal he'd done that night had been a major step up to the fortune he had sought as security for his wife and the family they had wanted to raise together. He'd had his phone turned off. When he had switched it on it had been to find a series of messages from Hayley, escalating in urgency until the last one had said she was being taken by ambulance to hospital.

When he'd got there it had been too late. She had lost the baby. And he had very quickly realised he had lost his wife.

Now Alex and Dell stepped forward from their crowd of well-wishers to greet him and Hayley. He could tell Dell was bubbling over with curiosity about this unexpected visit from the wife she had never met but had heard so much about. He had to tamp down on his own curiosity at what his lovely wife had been up to since their split. Who was the man who had prompted her to seek a divorce? Jealousy, dark and invasive, roiled in his gut. It was an emotion relatively new to him. He had always felt certain of Hayley's fidelity. But he had spent the past two and a half years tormented by graphic imaginings of her in the arms of another man.

Alex gave Hayley a welcoming hug. But over Hayley's shorn blonde head he questioned Cristos with his eyes: *What's going on?* Alex had become as close as a brother. They shared secrets. Cristos knew the truth behind his cousin's hasty marriage and Alex and Dell knew the extent of Cristos's fortune. Alex would be as surprised as he was by his wife's sudden reappearance.

'Where have you been hiding?' Alex asked Hayley, valiantly tiptoeing around the truth. Alex knew all about Cristos's fruitless search for her.

'Sydney,' Hayley said after hesitating a moment too long.

Alex's dark brows rose.

'I was living there for—'

Auburn-haired Dell interrupted. 'Sydney is my home town!' she exclaimed. 'I'd love to hear what you got up to there. Not only that, of course—I've been longing to meet you. Unfortunately we now have to go share ourselves around the other guests. But I'll seat you near us for lunch so we can chat.'

Her ebullient welcome defused the awkwardness of Hayley's surprise visit and Cristos shot his cousin's wife a glance of gratitude. He'd made friends with Dell when she had been working for Alex on Kosmimo, before there had been any romance between her and his cousin. There had been no one more delighted when they'd got married and he'd been their best man. If Hayley and Dell hit it off it would help make the rest of the day go smoothly.

'I'll look forward to that,' Hayley said, returning Dell's smile—her smile was pointedly not directed at him. Dell hugged Hayley before she turned to move away.

That left just the two of them, standing apart from the other guests in the glorious but increasingly chilly grounds of the chapel. But Cristos didn't even notice the view of the white-capped sea or the profusion of dark clouds rolling in. His senses could only register the presence of his wife. Hayley might be hostile but she was *here*. Before she got back on that boat to Nidri he would insist he got answers.

But his spirits dipped as he noticed his seventy-seven-year-old grandmother heading their way. Hayley noticed too. He heard her dismay in a hiss of indrawn breath and she tensed as if to flee. 'I don't think I can handle a confrontation with your grandmother,' she said. 'That wasn't part of the deal.'

Cristos's protective instinct kicked in. He'd kept his anger about the ugly way Hayley had ended their marriage to himself. He would not tolerate criticism of her from anyone else. Not even his beloved grandmother, who had rather an impressive track record in that regard.

He put his arm around Hayley and drew her close. She did not object, realising, perhaps, that it would be easier if they gave the appearance of being a couple. 'Leave my grandmother to me,' he said.

Dell called Penelope the purveyor of information for the extended family—kind terminology to describe an unashamed gossip and self-appointed matchmaker. His *yia-yia* had worked to get Alex and Dell together despite seemingly impossible odds. But she was convinced Cristos had made completely the wrong match in Hayley. She'd made that very clear to Hayley the one time they'd met when he'd brought Hayley home to introduce her.

The old woman's journey towards them now was hindered by the other guests greeting her, but she would be with them in mere minutes. He could not allow old grievances to erupt that might make Hayley change her mind about staying for lunch. Not before he'd had time to thrash out the truth behind the reasons they had parted.

Hayley twisted within the protection of his arm to look up at him, her blue eyes clouded with concern. The wind lifted fine wisps of blonde hair that feathered around her face. He resisted the urge to smooth them into place. Such an intimate touch belonged to their past.

'Your grandmother hated me before. What will she think of me now?' she whispered.

'Hate?' He frowned. 'That's too strong a term. Penelope didn't approve of you—or me at the time, for that matter—but I'm sure she didn't hate you. We didn't ask their permission and married without inviting them to the wedding. That meant we broke all sorts of Greek family rules.'

Her mouth turned down. 'I didn't make it any better by telling her that my own parents weren't invited either. Your grandmother drew her own conclusions about that. Conclusions that didn't reflect well on me.'

'Remember your parents didn't approve of me either. That was another reason we didn't tell any family about the wedding until we were Mr and Mrs.'

Hayley didn't deny it. 'They thought I was too young to get married. Especially while I was still at uni. My father was so disappointed in me.'

There had been more to it than that. 'They might have thought better of it if you'd married someone they approved of. Your mother was disappointed I was from humble origins.' Her mother had had a particular sneer for him that had let him know she'd thought her daughter had married way beneath her.

'That you were a foreigner was reason enough for her disapproval.' Was that a glimmer of a smile of complicity from his estranged wife, as the memories danced across her face? 'She saw it as an act of defiance on my part. To get married at the register office and have lunch afterwards at the pub with our friends. What a crime that was in "Surrey mother" circles.'

He smiled in return. 'We got married exactly the way we wanted. Free from anyone's expectations but our own. I never regretted that, in spite of the dramas it caused with my family.'

'Me neither,' she said. 'No matter how it turned out in the end.' Her gaze met his for a long moment. Then the shutters came down and she turned her face away. Why would she want to indulge in reminiscence about their wedding when she'd come seeking a divorce?

'Penelope is heading our way,' she said.

He felt a shiver run through her. 'Cold?' he asked. As the wind rose, the temperature was beginning to drop.

'A little scared, to be honest. Your grandma is a formidable lady. She doesn't look any less hostile than when she interrogated me the first time we met when we came to Greece on our honeymoon.'

'Which is why we never came to the islands again.' His family's rejection of his wife had hurt Hayley so much he had decided to give his grandparents time to get used to the idea of his marriage before they met again. Then when the modelling career he had fallen into so reluctantly had taken off with such speed there hadn't been the chance to come back, to try and mend bridges. Or, indeed, time to work on the cracks that had been appearing in his marriage that he had seen as hairline and Hayley as canyon-like crevices.

He'd eventually returned home without a wife. And given no explanations for her absence other than she had left him. And that he didn't particularly care. He'd hidden his heartbreak behind that mask of indifference.

'Now I'm wishing I'd never come here,' Hayley said. 'How can I face her?'

'Does it matter?' he replied. 'You won't have to see my grandmother again after today. Or me. But for now, let's present a united front. To keep the peace for Dell and Alex's sake.'

'I'll try,' she said, slowly. 'They're really nice people.' To his relief, she stayed by his side.

Hayley braced herself. The last thing she wanted to do was cause a scene with Cristos's grandmother. But she wasn't twenty-two any more. Twenty-two and desperate to impress her new husband's family. Back then she might as well have festooned herself with signs begging them to like her. Now she had learned not to take rubbish from anyone, no matter their age. She had wanted approval and acceptance from Penelope, instead she had been crushed by rejection for no real reason that she could see.

Cristos's grandmother's shrewd black eyes flitted from Hayley to her grandson and back again. In spite of her resolve to stand up for herself, Hayley couldn't help but feel intimidated by the elderly Greek matriarch in full sail. She took a deep breath.

'It's always a surprise to see you, Hayley,' Penelope said in her charmingly accented English, with a smile that didn't reach those eyes. The surprise of their marriage had not been welcomed by Cristos's clan. Her surprise visit this time obviously wasn't either.

Before she could think of a suitable reply, Cristos spoke. 'A wonderful surprise, *Yia-yia*, that Hayley could join us for Alex and Dell's celebration.'

'Is that why you came here?' Penelope addressed her question to Hayley.

Hayley wasn't good at lying; she had to think about her reply. 'A loving marriage is an excellent thing to celebrate,' she said.

The old lady's eyes narrowed until they were mere slits in the wrinkles of her face. 'And your own marriage? Have you come back to be with your husband?'

'That's between Cristos and me,' Hayley said without hesitation.

'Hayley is right, *Yia-yia*.' Cristos's tone was kind—she knew how much he loved and respected his grandmother— but firm. His grip around Hayley's shoulder tightened and she automatically leaned in closer to him. Accepting his protection was something she had always done. Until she'd had to deal with the biggest crisis of her life without him.

Again Penelope addressed Hayley. 'You've put my grandson through hell, young lady. And if you—'

'There are always two sides to the story,' Hayley retorted. 'I—'

'Our seeing each other again really is our business,' said Cristos smoothly. 'While we appreciate your concern, you need to let us handle it in our own way.' He turned to Hayley. 'Isn't that right?'

Hayley nodded. 'It most certainly is.'

Penelope muttered something in Greek under her breath. Hayley had made an effort to learn Greek when she'd fallen in love with Cristos. She'd let it lapse with the end of their marriage; she didn't have the heart to speak Greek if it wasn't to her husband. But she knew enough to know that whatever Penelope had said wasn't polite. Hayley gritted her teeth. She did not want to get into an argument with Cristos's formidable grandmother. What would be the point? Their paths would not cross again after today. She looked up to him in mute appeal.

In response, Cristos looked deep into her eyes and smoothed the flyaway hair from her forehead with gentle fingers. Her breath caught at his touch, so familiar and yet so startlingly new, and she could not break her gaze from the deep green of his. 'I am so happy to have my wife back with me,' he murmured in that deep, rich, lightly accented voice that had always thrilled her.

Hayley knew he didn't mean that. It was a message for his grandmother—a subtle way of defusing the situation. But it felt anything but subtle to her as shivers of awareness rippled through her. Her body had not forgotten the pleasure his touch could bring.

It had been so long.

She lifted her face and closed her eyes to better savour the sensation as he made the act of smoothing her hair into a caress. She was so lost in the feeling she was totally unprepared when he kissed her.

Oh!

His mouth firm and warm on hers, the roughness of his chin, his scent, spicy and male. Her own lips soft and yielding under his. His hands sliding around her waist, pulling her closer. This felt so good. *Too good.* Her eyes flew open.

She didn't want this. Not this languorous warmth overtaking her. Not this feeling of being lost in his possession. Not this surge of awakening when she'd worked so hard to suppress her longing for him. She didn't want *him.* The marriage had been all on his terms—and in loving him so desperately she had lost herself.

She tried to pull away. 'We have to make this look believable,' he murmured against her mouth.

Why? She had agreed to play along with the charade of reconciliation so as not to disrupt his cousin's festivities. *Not* to kiss Cristos. She did not welcome the whoosh of long-banked-down embers igniting into flames. Because of a kiss. A simple—you could almost call it chaste—kiss.

'Don't kiss me again,' she murmured back against his mouth. His grandmother, watching intently, might take it for sweet talk. She stepped back with a shaky little laugh that sounded fake to her own ears but might fool the grandmother. The smile he gave her in return seemed equally fake, though ragged at the edges. And as soon as his grandmother headed away from them she shrugged herself free, making a play of smoothing down her coat.

'We should follow the others to lunch,' she said.

CHAPTER THREE

HAYLEY FOLLOWED CRISTOS into the dining area of the resort where some forty guests were gathering for an early lunch. In spite of all her resolve, she could not help but admire the splendour of the view of his back. His immaculately cut dark charcoal jacket—no doubt from the collection of his favourite Italian designer—worn with equally well tailored tapered trousers. The suit emphasised his broad shoulders and perfect behind, his long, leanly muscled legs. Cristos wore his clothes with effortless, masculine grace. No wonder he'd been such an instant hit as an international model.

Did he sense her gaze on him? He paused, turned back to her and reached out his hand. His eyes urged her to take it, for appearances' sake.

Her first instinct was to pull back from any further physical contact, even such a simple act as holding hands. It aroused too many memories of happier times. Times when she'd felt a surge of joy as Cristos's much larger hand had closed over hers. She had felt safe, protected and proud to let the world know that the extraordinarily handsome man by her side was hers. Then there were the memories of those skilful, loving hands on her body...

She shook her head to rid herself of unwanted thoughts. She especially didn't want to think about how she had reacted to his kiss back there in front of his grandmother. Those feelings should be firmly relegated to the past. She could not lose control of her life again. Since she had left him she had learned to be *herself* instead of the support act to her handsome, glamorous husband. She wanted it to stay that way.

But some kind of show of togetherness would be expected of a husband and wife having a civilised meeting and she didn't want to draw unwanted whispers from the people she knew were observing them. So she let her hand stay in his and made appropriate small talk about the resort as she walked by his side. It was just an act, she told herself, on his part as well as hers. He'd made steps towards divorce too. She could endure it for a few hours.

'You're not seeing the island at its best,' he said in a casual, conversational tone that anyone could overhear and think nothing of. She was grateful to him for that; she was aware that many ears in the room were tuned into their conversation hoping for a hint of what was going on between Cristos and the wife who had left him. Even if they could lip-read they wouldn't catch anything titillating. 'We're having an unusually cold winter,' he added.

The weather was always a useful standby but in this case it was a topic of genuine interest. The breeze that had outside played havoc with her hair had turned into something much stronger, buffeting the windows that looked out to the sea. The view was magnificent, the deep turquoise sea whipped up to whitecaps, grey clouds scudding across the sky.

'It must be breathtaking here in summer,' she said. 'But I can see the place has its own wild winter beauty too.'

'Kosmimo is special at any time of the year,' he said with an air of possession that surprised her. As far as she knew, his cousin Alex owned the island. But then his family were very close—perhaps what belonged to one belonged to the others. Who knew? She had an older sister but they weren't particularly close.

Hayley didn't have to fake how impressed she was by her surroundings. The resort building was white and elegant in its simplicity as it stepped down the side of the slope to the sea and the single jetty that served the private island. As she had approached it by boat earlier in the day she had admired the way the structure sat so perfectly in the landscape.

The interiors exceeded all expectations—strikingly stylish with pale marble floors, whitewashed woodwork, large shuttered windows and wide balconies facing the incredible view of the sea to the front and the forested hills to the back. It seemed serene, she thought, but with a subtle air of energy as well, fitting for a holistic resort where the guests came to rest and recharge. She was not surprised when Cristos told her the fit out had won design awards.

'Why is the resort called Pevezzo Athina?' she asked Cristos as he led her to their table.

'*Pevezzo* in the local dialect means safe haven. Athina is after our family-run *taverna* on the island of Prasinos not far from here. It's also the name of the restaurant my great-uncle, Alex's grandfather, started in Sydney.'

'So the name is a tradition,' she said. Once she had realised the connection to his family, she had not gone anywhere near that Sydney restaurant.

He nodded. 'Tradition is important to my family.'

When she had met him in Durham they had both been strangers away from home. His English had been near perfect, just slight differences in inflexion giving away that he was not a native speaker. They had been lovers and partners and husband and wife. The fact he was Greek and she was English hadn't mattered. It wasn't until they had visited Greece on their honeymoon that she had appreciated how Greek he was and how important his culture and traditions were to him.

'A safe haven.' She nodded slowly as she looked around her. 'I can see that. And the way the wind is starting to lash around the windows I want to feel safe.' She glanced down at her watch. 'Do you think it will be okay for you to take me back to Nidri in your boat after lunch?'

Cristos had suggested she cancel the return trip she had booked with the boatman and let him take her back along with other guests in his bigger boat. Looking through the windows at how angry the sea had turned, she thought it had been a wise decision for her to agree.

He followed her gaze and frowned. 'We checked all the weather forecasts for this day when we were planning the celebration, but they didn't predict this. Hopefully it will blow over. Most of the guests need to leave after lunch. I'll check the reports again.'

From the time she had met him until the time she had left him, Hayley had leaned on Cristos. It was something she was determined never to do again. But checking weather forecasts in Greek was something she was happy to leave to him.

She knew she was gawking as she looked around her. The place really was extraordinary and she wasn't used to such high-end luxury. She earned a reasonable salary as a mechanical engineer, but a resort like this would be way out of her reach, the stuff of dream vacations. Cristos had coerced her into staying for lunch—she was determined to lap up the luxury and enjoy it.

True to her word, Dell had seated her at the round table where she was already waiting with Alex. Hayley returned Dell's big smile. Dell was one of those people she had liked on sight. Under different circumstances she felt they would be friends.

'Kalos eerthes,' Dell said to her and Cristos. 'Welcome.' She introduced Hayley to the other guests at the table: cousins from Athens and two sets of parents, Dell's and

Alex's, who had flown from Australia. The family connections were all too much for Hayley to take in, though she recognised some of the names from long-ago conversations with Cristos.

She was seated next to Cristos as was her due as his legally wed wife. It was surreal to be treated again as a couple, to be swept back into something that was once so everyday. *Hayley and Cristos.* They'd once been an entity. How much did his cousin and his wife know of their history? Hayley certainly didn't intend to mention anything of their future. The divorce was hers and Cristos's business alone.

However, she suspected Dell and Alex might have guessed not all was what it seemed between her and Cristos, the way they steered the conversation strictly to neutral territory. Alex explained the history of the island, how it had long ago been owned by Cristos's and Alex's family, more recently by a Greek magnate, then the Russian billionaire who had sold it back to Alex. He and Dell had developed the resort, building around an existing unfinished building.

Then there was chit-chat about the food. The meal was certainly conversation worthy. *Mezze* platters with a selection of Greek appetisers to start, followed by lamb and chicken cooked with lemon and Greek herbs, accompanied by seasonal vegetable dishes made with artichokes, beets and spinach.

'Most of what we're eating is grown on the island,' Cristos explained. 'Even the olive oil and the honey. The cheeses come from the milk from their herd of goats, and eggs from the chickens kept here.'

Hayley was surprised at his depth of knowledge about the resort and the island. Perhaps he had been working here for his cousin. As far as she knew he had stopped the lucrative modelling. She wondered what he had been doing since to earn a living. Her lawyer wanted to find out but Hayley had instructed him that there was no need to investigate Cristos's finances. She didn't want to make any financial claim on him. A complete severing of ties was all that was required.

'It's fantastic to be practically self-sufficient for food,' she said. 'I saw water tanks and solar panels too.'

'The island is self-sufficient for power,' he said. 'I'm not surprised you noticed. You were always interested in alternative energy sources.'

'I'm working for a solar-panel development company in Sydney,' she said, then immediately regretted letting slip the information. Her life in Sydney was hers; her independence had been hard won. She didn't want to share the details of her new life with Cristos. When she went back she wanted to forget she had ever been married.

'Lots of sunshine in Australia, I guess,' was all he said. His eyes narrowed. She was grateful for the semi-public forum they found themselves in so he didn't press for details. Or perhaps he simply didn't care what she'd been doing with her life since she'd left him.

The placement of the chairs around the table was close—perhaps because they'd had to accommodate her as an extra guest. But it meant she was sitting very close to Cristos. Too close. Whatever she did—reach for condiments, lean aside to give access to the waiters—meant her shoulder brushed against his arm, his thigh nudged hers. She was as aware of the slightest contact as if there were a jolt of current connecting them. But it would appear too obvious to jump back from the contact.

She found the proximity disconcerting. Cristos seemed to take it in his stride. In front of a table of people he knew well, he played the role of husband with aplomb, always taking pains to include her in the conversation. Perhaps more so because he must be aware the other guests were dying to know the truth about the sudden reappearance of his English wife.

But this whole fake reunion thing was messing with her head. Particularly disconcerting had been her reaction to his kiss back at the chapel. She couldn't stop thinking about it. How could she have reacted like that when she was so determined to put him in her past?

The physical attraction between them when they'd met had been instant and magnetic. In the first blissful months of their marriage they had not been able to get enough of each other. Even when things had started to sour as he'd gone from business student to the hot man of the moment, any argument had ended up in bed. But physical attraction was not enough. Great sex was not enough.

She'd been so naïve when she'd met him. Maybe she'd been not just old-fashioned but misguided to insist on staying a virgin until marriage. Then she might not have rushed into marriage. That overwhelming hunger for him had blinded her to other issues that had in the end unravelled. Like trust. And honesty.

Right now she had to be honest with herself—she needed to fight that physical attraction so she could free herself from him and move on. Sitting so close to him at the table for lunch, she was preternaturally aware of him— every nuance in his expression, every shift in his body. He had once been her world.

It wasn't just his extraordinary good looks that were so compelling. It was also his effortless personal charisma. Switching between Greek and English, he had the entire table laughing at his story about a fishing expedition gone wrong. Yet when he turned to her, to translate a Greek phrase, his green eyes bright with laughter, it was as if she were the only person in the room who was of any importance to him. Once she had believed that to be true— before she'd had to share him with the rest of the world.

She forced a smile in response. He would know she was faking it but she hoped the others wouldn't. This was Dell and Alex's day and not to be marred by any antagonism between her and Cristos.

After the main course had been served, the guests on either side of both her and Cristos excused themselves from the table; those opposite were engrossed in conversation. Cristos picked up her left hand. 'You still wear your wedding and engagement rings,' he said in a low voice meant only for her.

'Just to transport them safely back to you,' she said. 'They're safer on my finger than in my handbag. I'll give them back to you when we say goodbye.'

His face tightened, all traces of his earlier good humour extinguished. He released her hand. 'There is no need for that. The rings are yours.'

'What use are they to me?' she said. 'I'll never wear them again. And I don't want to be reminded of our marriage. I want to put all that behind me.' She had been in the nebulous state of being separated for too long. Not a wife, yet not single either.

He swore in Greek under his breath. Hurt? Pain? Anger? It certainly didn't sound like relief. She had agreed with Cristos not to disrupt the wedding renewal celebration. Now that she'd got to know Dell and Alex a little better she was glad she had stayed. But at what cost to her? And perhaps also to Cristos? She should never have come here.

'Did you wear your rings in Australia?' he asked abruptly.

She glanced down at the simple sapphire and diamond cluster set in white gold, the matching plain band. The stones in the engagement ring were tiny. When they'd got engaged Cristos couldn't afford anything more than a ring from a chain of high-street jewellers. But she'd thought it was beautiful and Cristos had declared the stone was nowhere nearly as beautiful as the colour of her eyes. Later, when the money from his new career had started to flow, he'd wanted to buy her a more expensive ring but she'd refused. She'd cherished that ring. It had symbolised everything good about their love. If he wouldn't take it back she would give it away.

'No. I didn't wear my rings in Sydney. And I didn't go by my married name either. I used my maiden name, Hayley Clements. It was easier than explaining a Greek surname when I so obviously didn't look Greek.'

Cristos slammed his right hand, where he wore his simple gold wedding band in the Greek tradition, on the table. 'I have never taken mine off,' he said.

Hayley swallowed the sudden lump in her throat. 'You took it off many times for your modelling shoots.'

'I was playing a role when I was working. Most often that role was not of a married man. I could not be seen to be wearing a wedding ring.'

'I understood that. Of course I did. But then you started to leave it off all the time.'

'You know why,' he said, tight-lipped. He shifted in his seat. This wedding-ring thing had become an issue in their short marriage. One that had festered with her in their time apart.

'Because it was seen as a disadvantage to your career to be married. A wife was a hindrance. *"It would be better for your fans—both female and male—if you were seen to be single."* Don't you remember your agent saying that?' She hadn't meant to blurt that out. She'd been determined not to speak of their mutual past. No recriminations. No blame. Just a clean cut.

He frowned. 'Of course I remember. We discussed it at the time—over and over. Then we agreed to take my agent's advice. We needed the money too much to argue with him.'

She looked down at the table. Smoothed a barely visible crease in the white tablecloth. When she'd got engaged to Cristos her parents had cut off her allowance, stopped the rent on her accommodation. They'd both been students. To get extra money, he'd tutored kids studying Greek, she'd taught dancing. Neither pursuit had been lucrative. They'd struggled.

'The idea was that we would still be together but not acknowledged as husband and wife,' she said. That still stung—though it had made sense at the time and she'd gone into it with eyes well and truly open. 'A girlfriend was acceptable. She was dispensable. That gave your fans hope that one day in their fantasies they might win you. The presence of a real-life wife ruined the fantasy.'

'That's how it was supposed to work,' he said. 'We both agreed I would take my wedding band off when I was in public. Then put it back on in private when I came home to you.'

Hayley couldn't keep the sadness from her voice as she looked back up at him. 'Until there were more and more times when you didn't come home. When you were on shoots all over Europe. Then exotic, far-flung places like Morocco and Africa.'

'Those jobs were the most lucrative,' he said, his jaw set. 'And the conditions weren't as glamorous as they looked. You didn't complain about the income they generated. I only did it for the money.'

Perhaps. But she would see the results of those shoots plastered all over billboards and in glossy magazines. More often than not they would feature Cristos, his body toned and buffed to perfection, wearing nothing more than swim-briefs or even underpants, with a gorgeous female model with next to nothing on draped all over him. She doubted even the most secure of wives wouldn't help but feel threatened. And a wife who had to keep her presence hidden, who didn't live up to the glamorous standards set by his new world, had found it difficult to deal with.

'You know I asked could you come with me,' he said. 'Repeatedly. It just wasn't done.'

The conversation was heading into territory Hayley had no wish to revisit. She picked up the little marble dish containing organic salt crystals from her place setting then put it down again. 'I know you tried to include me. And I appreciated it.'

On one stomach-churning occasion she had overheard his agent's reply when Cristos had asked could his beautiful wife perhaps join his agency as a model too. The agent had replied very quickly that it wasn't a good idea. *'She's pretty enough. But she's too short and too wide in the hips.'*

His words had been so brutally dismissive. Even the word *pretty* had sounded like an insult. Was it then that she'd begun to believe that her husband's new world would not have room for her?

Cristos realised there were several ways Hayley looked different from when they'd been husband and wife. The short hair for one. But it was in her eyes he saw a shadow of sadness that wrenched at him.

'You're thinking about that comment my agent made, aren't you?'

Back then he had been furious at the insult to his wife and had wanted to walk out. He had cursed. He had fisted his hands by his sides to stop himself from punching the agent out.

But Hayley had swallowed the insult, had placated him and talked him into staying—for the sake of the money modelling had brought them. 'It's such an opportunity for us. How many people our age get that chance?' she'd said. Her strategy had been to put everything they saved into the bank to give them a better start than many young couples starting off life together. He'd preferred a riskier, higher-yielding investment option—but he hadn't told her that. Not then. Not ever.

Now she waved his comment away with a flick of her wrist. 'I can laugh at that awful guy now,' she said. Cristos doubted that was true. 'I got used to people like him treating others like commodities, where the length of a woman's legs or the shape of a man's nose made them marketable or not.'

'Yeah. It could be brutal,' he said. In Cristos's eyes, Hayley had been the most beautiful woman in the world. His agent had seen her differently. If a woman wasn't fit for purpose then she had no use. Or a man. That was an inescapable reality of the business. And one he'd ultimately walked away from. He'd only endured it for her sake. When they'd discovered she was pregnant he had worked even longer hours for financial security for his wife and child.

It wasn't a business Cristos had signed up for intentionally. Six months after they'd married, when he had finished his master's degree in business and Hayley still had a term to go to finish her degree in engineering, they'd taken the train down to London for a mini-break.

Cristos's patience for shopping was limited. While Hayley had looked through every dress on the rack in a boutique in Covent Garden, Cristos had leaned against a wall outside and waited for her. Hands shoved deep into the pockets of his black jacket, he'd been happy to watch the world go by. London and the people from all around the world who flocked to it had fascinated him.

When the very fashionably dressed middle-aged man had approached him and asked him had he ever considered being a model, he'd brushed him off. Less politely the second time. Cristos had never lacked female attention, and often male attention too. He hadn't wanted to insult the guy but he'd made it clear in no uncertain terms that whatever pick-up line the older man chose to use it would not work on him. He was a happily married man.

Cristos had taken the man's card just to get him off his back. It had indeed been from a talent agency but anyone could print off a business card and make it say whatever they wanted. He'd put it in his pocket and forgotten about it.

Later at lunch in an Italian restaurant off Leicester Square he'd remembered and pulled the card out of his pocket to show Hayley. Her eyes had widened. 'If that guy was genuine, this is one of the biggest model agencies in the world. I think you should follow it up.'

'Me? A model?' he'd scoffed. He'd thought himself way too macho to even consider it. In his world, modelling wasn't a serious man's profession. 'No way. Never.'

'You're more than good-looking enough,' Hayley had said, her eyes narrowed thoughtfully. 'Ask them what kind of money you could make.'

The model scout had, in fact, been genuine. And the potential earnings Cristos had been quoted had been enough for him and Hayley to turn to each other and grin. When the agent had moved away to a filing cabinet to get a contract, they'd given each other a high five behind his back. 'This might be fun,' she'd said, laughing.

Turned out Cristos had had just the look big-brand clients wanted. In a sea of underfed, androgynous male models he'd stood out with his muscular build and intense masculinity. He'd been booked solid straight away. Had been hailed almost immediately as the new David Gandy.

But commuting from Durham in the north of England had become problematic. He'd moved to a small flat in Camberwell in South East London and seen Hayley as often as they had been able to manage between her studies and his modelling commitments. It hadn't worked. They hadn't been able to bear to spend so much time apart. He had missed her with an intensity that had made it difficult to concentrate on his work. She'd deferred her final term and moved to London to be with him. Stints in Paris and Milan had followed. And Hayley had never got the chance to go back to university.

'Are you still modelling?' Hayley asked.

He shook his head. 'After you left, I honoured existing contracts then retired.'

'And came home to Greece?' She paused. 'You don't have to answer that question. What you do now is none of my business.'

He wanted to say that of course his life was her business. Legally she was still his wife. But that would involve coming clean about his taking risks with their savings—even though it had paid off more than handsomely. He hadn't felt able to tell her then. Nor to mention that one of his collaborators had been female. For such a sweet, petite woman Hayley could be very feisty and he hadn't wanted to face her justifiable wrath. By the time he'd hit the jackpot with that first online shopping comparison app, she'd been gone from his life.

Now it would all come out in the property settlement. No doubt her lawyers had burrowed into his business and discovered his net worth down to the last cent. This divorce wouldn't come cheap. Perhaps that was why she'd come here—time for her to collect financially from their brief marriage. Whatever she was legally due, she would get. But no more. He would not fund her life with a new man.

She was playing her part well but he noticed her getting edgy about leaving—this time for ever. She tried to be discreet about checking her watch but he noticed. Dessert would be served soon. When that was over, he would have no choice but to take her off the island in his boat. He had to manoeuvre some private time with her. Otherwise he might never get answers to his question.

'Hayley, I want to—'

But he got no further.

'Cristos. I need to talk to you.' Alex's voice was low and urgent. Startled, Cristos looked up to find his cousin standing behind him. He'd been so intent on his conversation with Hayley he hadn't noticed that Alex had left the table.

His grandfather Stavros was also there. Both wore grave expressions. 'There's a weather alert,' said Alex. 'A severe storm approaching. Big seas. No boats can leave the island.'

There was a gasp from Hayley beside him. 'You mean we're stuck here? But I need to—'

Cristos sensed the panic in her words. Stuck on the island meant stuck with *him*. The man she had come here to divorce.

Alex completely misunderstood Hayley's panic. 'Don't worry, Hayley. We'll be safe here,' he reassured her. 'There's room for all the guests to stay overnight. The storm will most likely blow over by the morning. I'll put you and Cristos in the penthouse. It's the best room in the house and only fitting for you to celebrate your reunion.'

'The penthouse?' she said, barely able to get the words out. 'Isn't that reserved for you and Dell?'

Alex dismissed her objection with a wave of his hand. 'We have our own house on the island.'

He looked pleased with himself for giving them the penthouse and the privacy he seemed to assume they needed to rekindle their relationship.

Hayley's face had drained of all colour.

Cristos fought to supress a grin of exultation at this unexpected new hand he'd been dealt.

He would be spending more time with his wife.

CHAPTER FOUR

HAYLEY COULD NOT, *would* not, share a room with Cristos. 'No way. Never. Not in a million years,' she hissed at him after Alex had left them. She stood braced with her back to the table. 'I can't stay here. Isn't there another way to get off this island?'

'No,' he said.

Panic strangled her lungs so her breath came short, set her heart pounding. Why, why, why had she done the right thing by Cristos's cousin and ended up like this? She should be back on Nidri and on the way back to Sydney. Everything had seemed so simple as she'd geared herself up for it on the flight from London where she'd met with her lawyer—deliver the divorce documents, have polite exchange with love of her youth, move on to new life and forget he had ever happened. She hadn't counted on that intense flare of the old attraction. Now *this*.

She managed a deep breath to calm herself. 'That can't be true. I saw a helipad behind the main building.'

'Wealthy guests use it in summer. There's no helicopter here now and even if there was it wouldn't be safe to fly. It's hazardous conditions for boats and aircraft. There is no way off or on the island.' His tone left no room for uncertainty.

Hayley's eyes narrowed. 'Did you plan this?' she said,

keeping her voice low. 'Did you know when you coerced me into staying for the lunch that this would happen? That I'd be stuck here unable to get away?'

Cristos stared at her. 'Why would you say that? Choppy seas were predicted but not a storm of this magnitude. My family have been sailing these seas for ever, *koukla*, we know—'

'Don't call me *koukla*,' she interjected.

'Force of habit,' he said.

He rolled his eyes, which rather than making her indignant made her, in her semi-hysterical state, want to smile. She clamped her lips together to fight it. That was the trouble with Cristos. He could charm you even when you didn't want to be charmed. She could not let herself be ensnared by that charm again.

Cristos continued. 'From the reports we saw this morning I was totally confident I would be taking guests off the island this afternoon. Even the weather forecasters have been caught out by this storm. The weather has been so unpredictable. This is the coldest winter for many years.'

Her eyes narrowed. 'Are you sure you didn't suspect this storm might happen earlier, when it would still have been safe for me to leave? That you kept me here knowing this might happen?'

'I swear not.' He frowned. 'When did I ever force you into doing something you didn't want to do?'

She looked up at him and was struck by the sincerity in his eyes. Those remarkable eyes that she had seen sparked by love and desire and righteous anger but never force. He had wheedled her and teased her and kissed her into agreeing with him but he had never forced her to do anything against her will.

'Never,' she said. She had willingly let herself be carried along by the force of his personality because nothing had been more important to her than being with him.

'I don't fly out of the airport at Preveza until tomorrow so staying here tonight won't be a total disaster. That being so, I still don't want to share a room with you. I have to have a room by myself.'

'Not possible,' he said. 'As it is, people will have to double up in rooms. It's a privilege for us to be given the penthouse just to ourselves.'

She closed her eyes. This must be some kind of nightmare. But when she opened her eyes he was still there. All six feet two of handsome soon-to-be-ex-husband she so desperately didn't want to be near. *Trapped.* 'I could share a room with someone else.'

His dark brows rose in an infuriating manner. 'Really? Who?'

She cast a quick glance towards the other tables. She didn't know another soul well enough to share a room with them. Certainly not Grandma Penelope.

She made a sweep of her arm around the airy white room. 'I could sleep down here somewhere.'

'And freeze? The temperature will plummet overnight.'

'Maybe you could—'

'Forget it. I'm not sleeping down here either. Not only is it too cold it would have everyone talking about us. We're still married. People don't know it's not for much longer. It's expected we would share a room.'

He stepped closer. Put both hands on her shoulders. To anyone watching it would seem like an affectionate gesture. He spoke in a low, urgent undertone. 'Please don't kick up a fuss. The other guests are in the same situation. This is not what Alex and Dell need. It could ruin their day completely if everyone started complaining that they needed a single room.'

'But all the other guests wanted to be on the island. I'm here by default. I really can't be here with—'

'With me. You've made that clear,' he said. 'You don't need to be frightened of me, Hayley.'

'Frightened?' Her chin rose. 'Of course I'm not.'

Didn't he realise? She wasn't frightened of *him*. She was frightened of herself. The more time she spent with him, the more she feared her attraction to him. The more she risked leaving this island with her heart torn and aching over what could no longer be with the man she had married with such high hopes.

'It's inconvenient, I know. But like everyone else here you have to accept it.' He shrugged broad shoulders. 'Why not think of it as an adventure? When we…'

'When we what?' She had a horrible feeling he was laughing at her. That he liked seeing her put on the spot. Payback for the way she'd left him.

'When we were first together we would have thought being forced to stay the night in a luxury hotel for free would have been an adventure.'

Of course, it would have. They would have ordered room service, would never have got out of bed. They would have made love in the bathtub… *Stop.* That was yesterday. A different life. A different relationship. A different Cristos.

'Yes,' she said, knowing everything she was thinking must be showing in her eyes and seeing the same thoughts reflected in his. Their gaze held for a long time until she looked away.

A spasm of that old longing shuddered through her. In that lay danger. She remembered those long lonely nights when he was away from her, where her imagination had tortured her with thoughts of what he could be doing with the beautiful female models who worked with him. Then the night she had lost the baby when she'd needed him so desperately and he hadn't responded to her calls. The more she'd loved him, the more she'd ached for him every minute they'd been apart. Then the worse she'd felt when all those dreams and hopes they'd held in trust had shattered.

'I remember those times only too well,' she said. 'Which is why I'm seriously considering taking the risk of catching pneumonia and sleeping down here tonight.'

He sighed. The *you are testing my patience* sigh she also remembered. 'No need for that. The penthouse has a king-sized bed and a sofa. I'll take the sofa,' he said.

Even having him in the same room would be distraction enough. There would be no chance of sleep. But it seemed she had no choice. 'Okay,' she said reluctantly. 'If we can just stay out of each other's way it might be all right. After all, it's only for one night.'

Behind Cristos's mask of relaxed indifference simmered a heady elation. *One night.* He had one night with Hayley where she would, indeed, be trapped with him. Not trapped in any malevolent sense. Rather she would be forced into his company in the close proximity of a private hotel room.

Alone with Hayley for the first time in two and a half years. And despite her determination to divorce, he had twice glimpsed a hint of something very like desire in her eyes. Maybe he had wanted to see her answering desire so badly he had imagined it, maybe he hadn't. But a gambler got used to reading body language—and he had known her as intimately as only a loving husband could.

There was that simple kiss staged for his grandmother's benefit. Just a brief kiss. Yet it had ignited an old hunger in him. He had convinced himself it was extinguished, that it had gone to ashes. But the embers had been there, had burst into flames at the touch of her lips. By the way she'd reacted, it seemed she had felt it too.

He had wanted her from the get-go—and she'd felt the same. She'd been an innocent when they'd first met, de-termined, in spite of the sensual hunger he'd aroused in her with his kisses, to preserve her virginity until her wedding night. She'd had her reasons and he had respected her choice, admired it even. In his traditional culture a virgin wife was prized, although he certainly hadn't expected her to be chaste. Once they were married he'd been surprised and delighted at her passion and enthusiasm for lovemaking. No matter what else might have gone wrong in their relationship, they had been utterly in tune in bed.

Now he would be once more sharing a bedroom with her. But he had meant it when he'd said he'd sleep on the sofa. A fling with his soon-to-be-ex-wife wasn't on the cards. Even if she were willing, which seemed highly unlikely. Not when she backed away from even holding hands with him.

He would grab this chance to ask questions. No doubt she had questions of her own. They needed to talk. Something, he had come to realise in the soul-searching time they'd been apart, he should have done more of when they were together. Instead of silencing her concerns about the turn their life together had taken with kisses, he should have listened to her.

While legally Hayley was still his wife, he knew he had lost her nearly two and a half years ago. This night together was a gift and he had to be careful not to squander it. He had to get answers to his questions. Why had she pushed him away from her that night when she'd lost the baby instead of grieving together? Why had she run so far away? What had she been doing in Australia? Who was this other guy and did he pose a threat?

Was there any hope of a second chance with the woman he had never stopped wanting?

But right now she had questions of her own. Practical questions as befitted his down-to-earth, organised wife. Soon-to-be-ex-wife unless things between them changed dramatically, he had to remind himself.

Hayley tapped her booted foot with such annoyance he had to suppress a smile. That short haircut made her look like a cranky pixie. 'How can this work? My suitcase is in a hotel in Nidri. I don't have a change of clothes. Scarcely any cosmetics. All I have is a toothbrush and paste from the plane in my handbag.'

'You don't need cosmetics,' he said. 'You're beautiful without them.' He didn't mean that to sound cheesy. The compliment had come automatically.

She flushed high on her cheekbones. 'So you always said.'

'But you never believed me.'

'It was difficult when you worked with those gorgeous models.'

'Some of whom were so plain without make-up you wouldn't give them a second look.'

'But the camera loved them, you said.'

'Whereas you look lovely with or without make-up,' he said. 'A natural beauty.'

'Pretty, remember, not beautiful,' she said with a down-turned twist to her mouth. 'Not that I care about the difference.'

He added another curse to the number he had already hurled at his then agent for the thoughtless comment that had so wounded Hayley. Seemed that wound still hadn't healed.

'There is nothing wrong with pretty,' he said. 'In fact it's very, very right. You're looking good, Hayley. Life in Sydney must suit you.'

'I like it,' she said dismissively. No answers there, then. 'But talking about Sydney is not solving my problem now.'

'The resort store will stock everything you need.'

'Like pyjamas?'

Since when had she started wearing pyjamas? There'd been no need for pyjamas in their marriage.

'There are some very smart pyjamas there.' Dell had stocked the small store with the upscale resort-branded products wealthy customers did not hesitate to spend on. 'Dell has probably already thought to open the store. You won't be the only one who might need to stock up. Whatever you need I'll pay for, of course.'

Hayley drew herself up to her full diminutive height. 'That won't be necessary. I have some euros and my credit card with me.'

He shook his head. 'It's my fault you're stranded here. I insist on paying for whatever you need.'

Her chin lifted in the stubborn way he remembered only too well. 'In that case I won't get pyjamas. I'll go without.' She must have caught a gleam in his eyes at the thought of Hayley in bed with nothing covering her but the sheets because she faltered to a halt. 'I insist on paying my own way. Some Greek pyjamas might be a nice souvenir to take home with me to Sydney.'

He shrugged. 'Have it your way,' he said, pleased that he could fluster her. He'd arrange with Dell for any payment on Hayley's card to be reversed so she wouldn't be out of pocket.

'What about you? You weren't expecting to stay the night either, were you?'

'You know I never wear pyjamas.' He watched, amused, as her blush deepened.

'Uh…yes. I remember.' She seemed to take a sudden interest in the marbling of the floor beneath them.

He let her off the hook. 'But in this case I will also ensure I wear something to bed. I keep some clothes in the office here.'

She looked up at him again. 'Do you spend much time here? You seem to take a great interest in the resort.'

He should tell her he was a co-owner, having invested in the resort at the start. But that would involve telling her so much more and now wasn't an appropriate time. No doubt her lawyer would discover what he owned. 'I work along-side Alex,' he said. 'It's somewhat of a family business.'

'As is your tradition.'

'That's right,' he said.

'I…well, I wondered. I have no idea what you've been doing in the years since I last saw you.'

Tonight, he would clearly not be the only one asking questions. He needed to think how he would answer her questions without revealing how much he had left unsaid during their marriage. His habit of masking his true self to the woman he'd loved had backfired. He had told himself he was working towards their future. But he couldn't deny that he had hidden from her the truth of what he was—a gambler and a risk taker, his father's son. No amount of subsequent safe investments that had secured his fortune could change that.

He had feared if she had known what he really was, she would have spurned him. From the start he'd known her middle-class parents had looked down on him. How could he have admitted that his father had been in prison—not once but multiple times? That would only have reinforced their opinion of him as an unsuitable spouse for their daughter. And perhaps made Hayley start to believe it.

'He's NQOC, dear,' he had overheard her mother say about him to Hayley the only time she had taken her new boyfriend home to her family's house in a gated estate in posh Surrey.

Cristos hadn't told Hayley what he'd heard, hadn't asked her what her mother had meant. But back in Durham he'd asked an English friend what it had meant. 'Not Quite Our Class,' his friend had explained, puzzled that anyone would use such an outdated and snobbish expression.

Cristos had been both horrified and furious that Hayley's mother had used such a term about *him*. He was proud of his hardworking and honest grandparents, his relatives who owned fishing boats and *tavernas*, no matter what 'class' Hayley's mother might assign them to.

But then there was the reality of his jailbird father. His grandparents could quite likely have given his *baba* the same snooty label. They had despised him and seen their daughter's husband as the biggest mistake of his mother's life. When Cristos had gone into their care, they had instilled in him that his father was someone to be ashamed of—so ashamed they would have liked to deny his existence.

Cristos had told Hayley his father had died but not the circumstances of his death. The odds against them as a young couple facing opposition to their marriage had been high enough without throwing that into the game. That and the underlying fear he had inherited his father's bad traits—although the years since had proved him to be a hard-working businessman.

There would be so much at stake tonight. Much as he might want to, he would not try and seduce Hayley into that king-sized bed in the penthouse. Because, before anything else, he had to win her trust. Without that he had no hope of discovering the truth and making reparation for their past.

As Alex went from table to table with the news about the storm, a babble of chatter erupted in the room.

'I don't think I'm the only one not happy about being stuck on the island,' Hayley said with a wry smile.

'It seems that way, doesn't it?' he said. 'Do you mind if I go and give Alex a hand?'

'Please do,' she said.

'Will you be all right by yourself?'

'Of course. I can see Dell's parents heading back towards the table. I'll have someone to talk to.'

'I'll get back to you as soon as I can.'

'Don't worry about me,' she said. 'I'm a big girl used to looking after myself now.'

And I don't need you were her unspoken words that came through to him loud and clear and as sharp as a shard of ice stabbing his heart.

She still had the power to hurt him.

CHAPTER FIVE

HAYLEY KNEW ONLY too well the look of another woman who desired her husband. One of the perils of being married to a man as handsome and charismatic as Cristos was that other women wanted him too. And were sometimes blatant about letting their interest be known.

After lunch, the guests had gathered in the resort's meditation room, a large, airy space overlooking the water. It was there she saw the open, hungry yearning on the face of a dark-haired, attractive Greek woman who stood opposite her, shoulder to shoulder with Cristos's grandmother.

Hayley had to look away, swallowing against a sudden surge of nausea. She'd thought she'd got immune to the kick-in-the-stomach feeling that kind of undisguised look caused her. Seemed not. Maybe she never would. It shouldn't matter now that she and Cristos were on the brink of divorce. Yet her heart still felt scorched.

In the first blissful months of their relationship, other women's reactions to her husband's extraordinary good looks had never bothered her. Secure in his love, she had laughed and said how lucky she was Cristos had chosen her. 'You'd better believe it, *koukla*,' he'd used to say.

But as his career had unexpectedly skyrocketed, so had the level of female interest. A mini-movie-type commercial for a luxury men's cologne had gone viral—shared all over the internet—delighting the advertiser and making a star out of Cristos. Neither she nor Cristos had anticipated the attention it would bring him. To give her husband his due, he had never encouraged his admirers. But Hayley hadn't realised that, by agreeing to be a secret wife, she would have to endure seeing other women openly lust after her husband.

And here she was facing it again. She had left Cristos nearly two and a half years ago. Her choice. She could not reasonably expect that he'd been on his own all that time. But the thought of him with someone else was still unbearable. Who was this woman? And why was Cristos so insistent on them presenting as a married couple if his girlfriend was around?

Hayley closed her eyes and wished she were anywhere else but the island of Kosmimo. She could do without this added angst. All she wanted was to be free of the soul-destroying insecurities that had come part and parcel with her marriage. And then to move on.

The meditation room was minimally furnished in shades of white to allow people to meditate or practise mindfulness without distraction. Silence was usually a requirement. It was anything but that now with the buzz of people concerned about the disruption to their travel plans. Alex and Dell's families from Australia had planned to stay on anyway so weren't complaining. But some of the guests were from Athens, others the surrounding islands. It was Saturday and they were concerned about getting back to work on Monday. Hayley hoped she'd be allowed to leave on the first boat in the morning to make her connections to first Athens, then Dubai, for her flight to Sydney.

Cristos took to the floor with Alex to explain how their enforced stay at Pevezzo Athina would be handled in terms of accommodation and meals. Dell stood by to hand out keys to the rooms they had allocated their unexpected overnight guests. Dell's children were in the care of their two sets of grandparents from Australia who seemed to compete with each other to be the most doting.

If only... What might it be like to be here with her own child toddling around with his or her little cousins? Part of a big, welcoming family? Hayley pushed the thought right to the shadowed back of her mind where painful memories had been relegated. Instead of being a beloved wife and mother she stood on the sidelines of Cristos's family, never welcomed into it, and now straining to break the legal bonds to it.

The dark-haired woman couldn't tear her gaze from Cristos's face as he effortlessly commanded the attention of everyone in the room. At one stage, Penelope leaned up to whisper something in the younger woman's ear, and then looked pointedly towards Hayley. What was that about? Hayley flushed. But she held the old woman's gaze and nodded in acknowledgment of the exchange. She refused to be cowed.

But when Cristos returned to Hayley's side, she didn't say anything about the woman or his grandmother's obvious attachment to her. Truth be told, she didn't really know what to say. No longer did she have the right to question him. And, perhaps, she wanted to spare herself his answers.

'That seemed to go well,' she said instead. 'Poor Dell and Alex having their day end like this. What rotten luck.'

'Or they could look at it that the party goes on for so much longer than intended,' Cristos said with a grin. 'The resort is well stocked with food and drink and all these people are their friends.'

'That's one way of looking at it,' she said, unable to resist an answering smile. But she was aware of the dark-haired woman's eyes drilling into her now and it made her self-conscious. She had to say something. She moved closer to Cristos, kept her voice low so her words were only for him. 'That woman standing next to your grandmother, the gorgeous dark-haired one. Is she…are you…?' Her throat closed around the words.

Cristos looked deep into her face, not taking his eyes from hers for even a second to look across to the woman. To anyone looking it would seem as if they were exchanging intimate talk. 'You mean Arianna? The answer is no and no.'

Hayley swallowed against an inexplicable relief. 'She's giving you "the look",' she said. She didn't need to explain any further. In those early days, when him being a successful male model was still fun, they'd laughed together about how predatory some of the women had been. Not to mention the men.

'She's being encouraged by my grandmother to do so,' he said with a low groan.

'While Penelope believes we're still married? I should be grossly offended by that.'

'I'm not defending my *yia-yia's* behaviour. But you were away a long time.' His mouth said one thing, his eyes so much more. Anger. Betrayal. Loss.

She gritted her teeth. Answered only his words. 'I know that. It's just disconcerting to have your grandmother encouraging my successor while I'm still here.'

His dark brows rose. 'Your successor? Arianna was here before I ever met you. I chose you over her long ago. In fact there was no choice to make. Her grandparents are friends with my grandparents. Penelope considers herself a *promnestria*, a matchmaker.'

'In our case she tried to be a match-breaker.'

'Maybe so,' he said. 'She had Arianna earmarked for me from when we were babies.'

'Oh.' Hayley was angry at herself for the hurt that crept into her voice. 'I can see why. She's beautiful. And sexy.'

Still Cristos didn't look over to Arianna. His eyes were only for her. He cupped her chin in his hand so she was forced not to evade his gaze. 'I dated her once when we were sixteen. It was a mistake. I wasn't interested in her then and I'm certainly not now. How could I be when you are here, *kou*—?' He stopped himself from completing the word.

He seemed determined to make this as difficult as he could for her, using his pet name for her, invoking the past. She did not want to remember such a deeply unhappy part of her life or to endure recriminations or blame. He had said he wanted the same thing she did—divorce. She screwed up her face in appeal. 'Cristos, please—'

He turned his head away so she could no longer see the unspoken message in his eyes. When he looked back to her his gaze showed only unconcerned good humour. 'Yes. I know you are only here to divorce me. But that doesn't stop me from thinking you're more beautiful than any other woman I know.'

He dropped a light kiss on her mouth. For Arianna's benefit? His grandmother's? Or to remind her of just what a kiss from him could do to her? If it was the latter, he succeeded as a thrill of delight tingled through her body. His kisses had delighted her from the very first time on the night they'd met.

She stepped back. Crossed her arms across her chest. 'Thank you,' she said, knowing it would be ungracious not to accept the compliment. And to block the traitorous racing of her heart. It was frightening how her body still reacted to his touch.

She couldn't face his gaze again. Who knew what she might see in those eyes this time? Instead she looked across through the floor-to-ceiling glass doors that led out onto a marble balcony. They were obviously designed to frame a view of sparkling sun-kissed aquamarine waters and blue skies. Ominous dark clouds were banking up out to sea, obliterating the sky, their shadows darkening the choppy sea below to a sullen grey. A sudden gust of wind made the glass shudder.

Cristos followed her gaze. 'You can see why we couldn't take a boat out in that. The storm is gathering strength. It's going to be fierce when it hits.'

'What are you doing to secure the building?' she asked.

'Alex and I will get some of the guys to go outside and make sure—'

'I'll come too,' she said.

'Perhaps you can help Dell inside,' he said, relegating her to the 'women's work' of the traditional Greek family.

She squared up to him. 'You might not know that I finished my degree in mechanical engineering at the University of New South Wales in Sydney. I'm working as an engineer and considered very competent. You must remember me telling you I worked as a teenager with my father on all the home maintenance. I probably know more about what to do than you or Alex.'

Cristos looked down at her with a mixture of admiration and reluctant defeat. 'You're probably right,' he said.

'Not that I'm taking anything away from your Greek male authority,' she said, teasing him the way she used to. Then realised she shouldn't say anything that could be construed as flirtatious.

'Of course not,' he said. 'I learned early on not to underestimate you.'

Then later on you took me for granted, she thought, but didn't say.

She glanced down at her expensive biscuit-coloured trousers and fine ivory cashmere sweater—both from her life with him after his meteoric success when designer clothes came easy. 'I'll go to the resort store and buy some jeans and a sweatshirt, see if Dell can loan me a weather-proof jacket.'

'If that's what you want to do.'

She felt trapped. Trapped on the island, trapped with him, held hostage by old emotions and hurts. She needed to do something. Not just stand around wringing her hands over her plight or using her enforced time as an excuse to party. She needed to roll up her sleeves and work. Doing something useful might take her mind off her body's re-action to his touch. Then there was the blatant interest of another woman in the man she had once thought she would grow old with. Too much of the past was coming back to haunt her and taunt her.

'I'll get a team together and meet you at the utility area,' Cristos said.

'Right,' she said.

He handed her a key card. 'It's to our room.'

Our room.

That was another disconcerting event she hoped a good dose of solid physical work—like shoring up windows and checking electrical connections—might take her mind off. The prospect of sharing a bedroom with the man who was still legally her husband.

Hayley's laughter pealed out from the direction of the pool house. High on a ladder, Cristos paused in his task of se-curing the upper-storey window shutters. He hadn't heard that joyous sound for too many years and he stilled when he realised how much he had missed it.

He turned and his eyes widened at the improbable sight of his wife—he couldn't think of her as anything other—working together with his grandfather. They were moving the outdoor furniture from around the swimming pool to where it would be safe in the case of high winds.

It wasn't a matter of Hayley assisting Stavros—young

Englishwoman deferring to Greek patriarch. Rather his petite wife and his aged and somewhat stout grandfather were well matched in terms of strength and made a surprisingly effective team. They'd already cleared the gardens of any equipment that had been left lying around.

He was further surprised by the sound of his grandfather's gruff laughter. Stavros was a man of few words; he always said his wife, Penelope, had words enough for both of them. Since the death of his only daughter, he was also a man of little laughter.

What had Hayley said to provoke that rusty laughter from the man who had disapproved of his grandson's marriage to an English stranger every bit as vehemently as his wife had done? Cristos decided not to question it, but to enjoy it.

The cold wind whipping his face raw, he watched Hayley and Stavros for a long moment. He imagined an alternate universe in which he and Hayley were still married, living perhaps in London, and visiting the family in Greece for Alex and Dell's vow-renewal ceremony. In this happy world, Hayley was a much-loved member of his extended family, Penelope extending to her the same warmth and welcome as she did to Dell. While he and Hayley worked outside to secure the resort against the coming storm, their child—he'd hoped for a boy but would have loved whatever baby they'd been gifted—was safely inside playing with Litza, her little cousin. At night he and Hayley would sink happily into bed, drowsing off to sleep in each other's arms after making love knowing they had tomorrow and all the tomorrows after it together.

That was where he had to put the brakes on his daydream. He stared at the window he was meant to be securing. In the reflection he saw his face looking tight and haggard, hardly the image of Europe's one-time top male

model—the role he had come to hate. It had lost him everything he had valued. His wife. His unborn child. His future.

Hayley had never acknowledged his anguish and grief
at the loss of the baby he had wanted so much. In fact she
had pushed him away from her. Perhaps her own grief had
been so intense she hadn't been able to deal with his. He
didn't know. She hadn't given him the chance to comfort
her—or she him.

He looked down again at Hayley and his grandfather,
chatting companionably as, in the looming evening, they
walked towards the pool house where both sets of visiting Australian parents, Alex's and Dell's, were staying.
He couldn't hear what they were actually saying from this
distance but their voices carried enough for him to realise
Hayley was trying to speak Greek with Stavros and he
was correcting her usage. Not in a disparaging way but
in a helpful way, obviously pleased that she had tried to
learn their language. Perhaps her mistakes had prompted
the laughter.

A wave of overwhelming sadness swept over him, sending his determined optimism tumbling over and over as
it struggled not to drown. Somehow he and Hayley had
detoured from the path their marriage should have taken.
He was not at all certain it was possible after all this time
apart to right past wrongs and consider the possibility of
getting it back on track. He doubted they could even sal-
vage a friendship. Perhaps this gambler should accept it
was time for him to throw in his cards.

For nearly two and a half years when people had asked
him why his wife had left him he had shrugged and said, as
if it didn't bother him, 'I don't know.' *He still didn't know.*

Then both his wife and his grandfather, sensing perhaps
the intensity of his gaze on them, turned and saw him. In
perfect synchronicity, they waved to him. With the hand

that was not gripping the ladder, he waved to them in return, forcing a smile he hoped they could see.

At their answering smiles, the gloom receded. He had tonight with Hayley. Just him and her, with nowhere for her to run. He was determined to make the most of it. If there was ever to be a chance for them to understand what had gone wrong, this was it.

CHAPTER SIX

OUTSIDE, EVERYTHING AROUND Hayley had gone very still and the island seemed quiet with expectation. Nobody had asked her to look at the solar panels but she'd wanted to check them anyway. Air like icy needles stung her face and she shivered. The sky darkened with an ominous yellow tinge and she hastened to make it safely back inside the resort.

As she pulled off the work gloves Stavros had found for her and shrugged out of Dell's too-big jacket, Hayley looked around for Cristos. She'd lost track of him; last seen he'd been working alongside Alex fixing a loose shutter. She wrapped her arms around herself. It felt odd not to have him by her side. There was no role for her in this place without him.

What was she doing here?

The storm hit with its full fury just minutes later, in a frenzy of crashing thunder and lightning that forked through the sky. Violent winds whipped around the building. Rain lashed against the windows with the sound of pebbles being hurled against the glass. The building shuddered and shook with each assault from the skies.

The guests had all been allocated their rooms, but many now gathered again in the far from quiet meditation room. Hayley joined them; it was more comforting to be among

people even though she was still the object of either curious glances or tentative smiles. She suspected, as far as
support for Cristos's errant wife went, they might have
divided into Team Penelope and Team Dell.

Alex reassured everyone in the room that the resort
was well built and sturdy and they were all perfectly safe.
But children among the guests screamed with each crash
of thunder until their parents made a game of it that had
the kids competing who could jump the highest when the
thunder erupted.

Dell's toddler Litza joined in with the bigger kids, attempting to jump but not getting very high and then chor-
tling with sweet baby peals of laughter. She was adorable
but Hayley found it unbearable to watch her. Most of the
time she didn't allow herself to wonder what her baby—
girl or boy—would be like now if her pregnancy had
proceeded. She had forced herself to bury such painful
thoughts. But Litza, her baby words alternating between
English and Greek as her child would likely have done,
was too much of a reminder of what she'd lost, what might
have been.

She turned her back on the kids and stood watching the
sky, keeping a safe distance away from the glass doors in
the meditation room. She would be out of here tomorrow
and this would seem in retrospect like a bad dream.

Every so often lightning would illuminate the darkness,
reflecting in the roiling sea below. She sensed Cristos come
up behind her. After all this time, she still recognised his
footfall, his scent, his presence, *him*.

'Here you are,' he said, as a husband seeking his wife
might say. He took his place beside her, close enough that
his arm brushed against her, showing—consciously or
not—to anyone watching them that they were a couple.
He didn't say anything else, rather joined her watching

the pyrotechnics display in the sky for a surprisingly companionable moment.

'They say the negative ions released into the atmosphere by an electrical storm can make you feel wonderful,' she said, without turning to him. 'I wish I could go outside and breathe them in but I know it wouldn't be safe with all that lightning about.'

'Why is that? The ions, I mean.'

She slanted her shoulder towards him; in profile he looked pensive and heartbreakingly handsome. Was he really interested in ions or just asking so they would appear deep in husband-and-wife conversation?

'Apparently they cause some kind of biochemical reaction that releases feel-good hormones in the body.' She didn't mention that she'd read the effect of the negative ions included heightened sensual awareness—back when they were together it would have been the first thing she'd told him. *A kiss from Cristos was more powerful than any negative ions.*

He smiled. 'Maybe I can tell that to the disgruntled people who are complaining about missing transport connections.'

'You mean suggest they step outside and take a deep breath? They might not thank you if they're struck by lightning.'

She giggled at the thought of it, and was warmed by Cristos's quiet laughter in return. In another life she might have asked him which of the guests he would like to shove outside on the balcony during a storm. But not here, not now when the room was full of his family and their friends and she was the outsider.

At that moment there was an almighty crack and sheet lightning illuminated the sky and the sea below as if a set of stadium lights had been suddenly switched on. Hayley couldn't help but start in reaction. From behind her came a chorus of squeals from the kids.

Cristos put his hand on her shoulder. She leaned into him without thinking, then pulled away when she realised what she had done. 'Are you frightened?' he asked.

Hayley shook her head. 'When I was tiny I was terrified of storms. It would be a race for who would hide under the bed first—me or my dog. But my father reassured me in much the same way the parents here are doing. "It's just nature's fireworks," he'd say.'

'That's a good way of putting it,' Cristos said. 'I hadn't thought of your banker father as being that lyrical.'

'He has his moments. He was—is—a good father but totally henpecked by my mother. The times when I was out working with him in his shed or building a wall in the garden—things she thought were totally unfeminine— were when we were closest.'

Lightning flashed again. 'Nature's fireworks,' said Cristos. 'I like that description.'

'Magnificent in its own way, isn't it? There are worse things to be frightened of.'

Like loneliness. Despair. Isolation. The feeling of being in an endless dark tunnel with no light ahead to guide her. Feelings she hadn't been able to share with him towards the end of the marriage. Why would she now?

'I guess so,' he said. There was a ragged edge to his voice. Had he suffered when she'd left him? She hadn't thought he would care. Even before her miscarriage she'd begun to believe he wanted out of the marriage. His unexplained long absences, with the nebulous excuse of 'business', on top of the shoots away with the glamorous female models, had had her doubting his commitment. When he hadn't been there for her the day she'd lost the baby, when he had once again said he'd been in a meeting to earn more money for her and the baby without specifying where he had been, her belief in him had been struck a mortal blow.

No. She wouldn't ask how he'd felt when she'd left. She'd always been there to encourage and support him. Until she'd felt so unsupported herself she'd had to go. She'd spent the time since their split building her strength and independence. That independence had been hard won. It had taken her all this time to feel she was ready to face him.

'What was your father like when you were little?' she asked. 'You never talked about him.' She knew he'd been orphaned when he was fourteen but he'd talked more as if Stavros and Penelope had been his parents.

His hand tensed on her shoulder. 'He was away a lot. My mother and I always seemed to be waiting for him to come home.'

His hand slid from her shoulder and for a moment she missed its warmth and strength. 'What about happy father and son memories from when you were little?'

He hesitated. Frowned as if it was a real effort to dredge up the memories. As if he wasn't used to revisiting his childhood. 'I remember him teaching me to fish. When I was about five, I think. Not in the sea. We moved around a lot. In a river with a hand-held line. He was very patient.' He fell silent and Hayley was about to move the conversation on when he spoke. His words were slow and thoughtful as if he was lost in his reminiscence. 'He taught me English. His English was excellent. Heaven knows where he learned it from. I remember him telling me English was the best second language to have. I didn't appreciate it at the time, of course.'

'And you ended up getting a postgraduate degree from one of the top universities in England. Your dad would have been very proud of you.'

He nodded slowly, as if it were a new thought. 'I guess he would.'

Her watch beeped. Silently she cursed it. She wanted to talk more to Cristos about his childhood. But she had made a promise. 'I should go. I volunteered to help Dell in the dining room.'

'Do you need to? You've already done so much work outside,' he said. 'You must be exhausted.'

She remembered how solicitous Cristos had been in the early weeks of her pregnancy. The pregnancy hadn't been planned. But he wouldn't let her refer to it as 'an accident'. Their baby would never feel anything other than wanted and loved, he'd declared. Then he'd used impending fatherhood as an excuse to spend more time away from her. He'd said he had to earn as much as possible for his family, that no child of his would ever lack for anything. Looking back, she wondered why she hadn't believed him.

'I like Dell. I feel sorry for her that she's having to run around after everyone when I'm sure she and Alex had more romantic plans for the evening. The catering staff are stuck here like we are and already run off their feet after the celebration lunch. I'm happy to help.'

'Dell will appreciate it. And remember—you're family.'

'Not really,' she said, aghast.

'As far as everyone here is concerned you are my wife. That makes you family,' he said, stepping closer so no one could overhear, taking up the personal space a husband might expect as his right.

She took a step back, trying not to make it look obvious how shaken she felt by his closeness. 'Family or not, I did promise to help. You know me, I like to keep busy.' She knew she was speaking too fast.

'Yes,' he said. 'I remember.'

Did he still know her? Was she even the same person? She'd never really known him. Not that it had stopped her loving him unconditionally. Looking back, she realised Cristos was very good at being who he thought people wanted him to be. Had seemed to show different facets of himself at different times. What had he kept from her?

By the time Hayley had helped out in the dining room and got back up to the penthouse suite she was exhausted but wide awake. How could she be anything else when she knew Cristos would soon be joining her?

She quickly showered and changed into the new silk pyjamas she'd bought from the resort store. They were tailored man-style, beautifully cut, white and piped around the collar, cuffs and hems in ice blue. She topped them with the plush white velour bath robe she'd found in the closet. There was a matching one in a larger size for Cristos. Couple's robes hanging in a closet for two.

It was very much a couple's room. An enormous king-sized bed dominated, topped with so many pillows it would take her ages just to clear the bed for sleeping. She would never be able to remember how to rearrange them when she made the bed. In the bathroom there were his-and-hers basins, a shower designed for two and a huge free-standing tub.

The spacious suite was all white-veined marble luxury, with pale rugs underfoot and splashes of colour on the walls from the original artworks that seemed to be of the surrounding islands. The balcony doors were closed and shuttered against the storm, but she could imagine it had a spectacular view. The room shrieked 'honeymoon suite', which made it even more of a concern to have to share it with Cristos.

She was so on edge at the thought of him joining her in a honeymoon suite she couldn't settle. In all her plans for the delivery of their divorce documents, she hadn't counted on this.

She paced the marble floor. Fiddled with the television controls with no luck, just a static screen. Examined the contents of the refrigerator—no alcohol, only health drinks. Finally, she lay down on the top of the bed and started to read a novel on her tablet. Useless. She realised she had read the same paragraph three times without absorbing a word. When she heard a bold, loud knock on the door she jumped.

'It's me,' came the deep, masculine voice. *Him.* The door opened. She realised she was clutching the edge of her tablet so tightly she was in danger of cracking it.

The moment he entered the spacious room it seemed smaller. He was so tall and broad-shouldered he seemed to dominate it, to use up more airspace than one man should. Hayley jumped up. She didn't want the fact she was lying on a bed to be misconstrued.

He took a step closer to her, all six feet two of him, in black jeans and a dark charcoal shirt rolled up at the sleeves, his hair a touch dishevelled, the shadow of the day's beard growth darkening his jaw. Without her heeled boots, just the hotel slippers, he towered over her. She felt at a disadvantage in just pyjamas and a robe. She stepped backwards so the edge of the bed pressed against the backs of her legs.

'You're here,' he said. It was the first time they'd been truly alone since she'd arrived on the island.

'Yes.' She looked around her, anywhere but at him. 'I don't know why Alex and Dell gave us such a lovey-dovey room.'

'You know why,' he said shortly. 'They like you and are hoping we'll reconcile.'

'Surely we can ditch the charade now?'

'Absolutely. No need to play games with just the two of us here,' he said. 'In fact, while we're forced into each other's company, it's time for some truths. Starting with why the hell you ran out on me.' His eyes bored into her. At once the practised civility displayed for the wedding renewal guests was dropped. She could sense the anger vibrating from him, extinguishing the traces of their earlier shared intimacy. 'You discharged yourself from hospital without telling me and disappeared. One minute we're married, the next you're gone.'

'You left me alone, terrified, in pain. You switched off your phone. You weren't working that day. I didn't know where you were.'

'I was in a business meeting. My agent kept calling me and hassling me about some stupid contract detail. I turned the phone off to get him off my back. As soon as I switched it back on I got your messages. I was devastated that I'd missed your calls. You know I got to the hospital as fast as I could. You shouldn't have been on your own and I'll never forgive myself for not being there.'

'All the time I was thinking he'll call me. He'll check in to see how I am. But you never did. I had to go through it all on my own. I felt abandoned.'

'When I got there it was too late.'

'Yes.' She still remembered her agony of despair when the doctor had told her. With no husband by her side.

'If I'd got you to the hospital earlier, could they have saved the baby?'

She couldn't look at him. 'I don't know. Maybe. I don't think so.'

'What caused the miscarriage? You were thirteen weeks—we thought you were safe. I never got to ask you, never found out.'

'They didn't know. The doctors said miscarriage is common in first pregnancies. There was no cause they could identify.' They'd told her to give herself a few months to get over it then try again. But she wasn't going to share that with him.

'I was distraught that we'd lost the baby. Terrified you were so unwell, that I might lose you too. I wanted to comfort you. We should have comforted each other.'

'I wasn't just unwell. I was angry with you. Not just about the phone call. Other things. It all built up.' The days both before and after the miscarriage were a blur; she didn't clearly remember the details. Only her grief and pain.

'What other things? What could have been so bad we couldn't have worked through them? In the beginning we had to fight to be together. We were happy. Then at a time when we should have been there for each other, shared our grief, you ran away. Put yourself right back into the power of your parents, who guarded you from me like rabid watchdogs then spirited you away to Australia. I was your *husband*. Didn't that mean anything? Help me understand why I lost my wife.'

She put up her hand. Had to force her voice to be steady. 'Cristos. Stop right there. I don't want to talk about it. That was the worst time of my life. I took so long to get over it. Reliving it all is too painful.'

He paused. 'I get that. I'm sorry. More sorry than you could know that I wasn't there for you. We won't talk about it if that's what you wish. But can you please fill me in on what you've done in the time we've been apart? You'll be out of here tomorrow. This is our last chance. I know nothing about your life.'

'I guess I owe you that.' She swallowed against a suddenly dry throat. 'I need to get a glass of water first.'

She walked past him, intent on staying a good distance away. So intent she stumbled over the too-big hotel slippers. He caught her arm to steady her.

'No need to be nervous,' he said. 'I'm not going to try to seduce you.' His deep voice, the way his green eyes looked at her as though he could see right through her pyjamas, belied his words. *Why not?* The thought sprung from some wayward corner of her heart.

'I... I didn't think you were going to. That isn't part of the deal,' she said, unable to control the tremor in her voice.

Would it be so bad to have one last fling with him?

It wasn't as if they hadn't made love every night they'd been together of their married life—and often in the day as well. *No!* How did she stop her body from remembering the intense pleasure they had found in each other?

He indicated the white linen sofa that was arranged, with two matching armchairs, around a coffee table carrying an artfully fanned selection of holistic health magazines. 'I told you I'd sleep over there.'

'Thank you,' she said, not sure why she was thanking him. He'd put her in this position. If he hadn't insisted she stay for lunch she would be resting comfortably in her hotel room in Nidri right now, probably checking in online for her flight to Sydney via Dubai.

Or would she?

How well would she have slept just a short boat ride away from Cristos, wondering what he was doing?

'Nice pyjamas,' he said. Was it a subtle reminder that they had always slept naked entwined in each other's arms? On their wedding night, the night she had lost her virginity, she'd worn a slinky silk nightgown. But he'd peeled it off her and told her there was no need for that—he would keep her warm. And he had. She felt herself flush at the memory of how thrilling it had been and headed to the bar area to get a glass of the filtered water in the fridge. She automatically filled two glasses as she always had during their marriage.

He flung himself down on the sofa that was to be his bed. She placed the glasses on either side of the coffee table, kicked off her slippers and sat down in the chair opposite, drawing her knees up tight. 'What do you want to talk about?' she asked.

'Anything and everything. Finishing your degree,' he said. 'How did that happen?'

'As you know, I was close to finishing when I left Durham. But the way we moved around it seemed impossible. Mine weren't the kind of subjects you could study in an online podcast from a hotel room in Paris.'

He frowned. 'I didn't mean for it to happen that way. I always felt bad about it.'

'I'm not blaming you. It was a decision we made together.'

For her, there hadn't been a choice between staying behind by herself in Durham while her new husband lived in London or Paris or Milan. Back then, every minute without him had been a minute not lived. He had felt the same. 'We couldn't have done it any other way. But I was never going to be happy without a career of my own.'

'Granted,' he said.

'I got credit for my studies at Durham and was admitted to the degree at the University of New South Wales. I fell on my feet.'

'And found a job.'

'While I was at uni I did an internship with a solar energy company. They asked me to get in touch when I graduated. So I did.'

Cristos picked up his glass of water and put it down again without drinking any. 'All this time you were living a completely different life, one I can't even imagine,' he said slowly. 'What about the guy back there?'

'He's a friend,' she said.

'A friend with benefits?' he said tersely.

'No! We haven't even dated.' Now it was her turn to pick up her glass, take a sip of water to moisten a suddenly dry mouth. 'But he's nice. And who knows what might happen after I'm divorced?' She looked down at the glass.

'There must have been other men.'

'No,' she said. 'I wasn't interested.'

'I find that difficult to believe,' he said.

Now she looked up to meet his gaze full on. There was no point in talking in circles. 'I was in a very bad way after losing the baby. Dating was the last thing on my mind.'

His eyes narrowed. 'Are you telling me…?'

'There hasn't been anyone since you. There wasn't anyone before you. There's only been you, Cristos. Legally I'm still married to you. I couldn't sleep with another man while I was still your wife. It wouldn't have been right.' And she hadn't wanted it—hadn't wanted another man touching her. It had been too soon, she had rationalised.

Cristos made an inarticulate sound deep in his throat. 'I thought… I imagined…' He choked out the words.

She realised she hadn't actually given a thought to Tim since she'd set eyes on Cristos again. Tim, who would be waiting at the airport in Sydney to meet her like the good friend that he was. The kind man who had tried to kiss her and she had pushed him away.

Because he wasn't Cristos.

'What about you?' she said. 'Freed from that inconvenient wife. What about that gorgeous American model who was always hanging about? Ginny. I felt sure you and her—' She put up her hand. 'Don't answer that. I don't want to know. I really couldn't bear to hear about you with someone else. Even…even when I don't want you for myself.'

In turn he held up his right hand, his fingers splayed to display his wide gold wedding band. 'I didn't take this off. I still considered myself married to you. That meant being faithful to my wife. Like I always was when we were together. There haven't been other women for me. From the moment I met you in the pub in Durham, there was only ever you.'

Hayley wasn't often lost for words but she struggled to breathe, let alone speak. Silence hung between them for a long moment. 'That can't be true,' she managed to choke out.

'Believe it,' he said.

'Not Ginny? I felt sure—' Never had she felt shorter or more wide-hipped than in the presence of tall, rangy Ginny.

'I talked business with Ginny. Nothing else.'

'That last morning, she called the apartment wanting to speak to you.'

'About nothing but a deal I was discussing with her,' he said dismissively. It had sounded more than that to Hayley but she hadn't exactly been in a good frame of mind. Besides, this was hardly the time to argue it.

'No Ginny, no one else? But you're such a sexy man. And all those women wanting you. Even here today.'

'I'm certainly not celibate for lack of offers. Perhaps I've been a fool. Staying faithful to a wife who didn't want me. *Who ran away.*' He turned his wedding band around and around his finger.

She hadn't expected this. Not in a million years had she expected this. Believing he had been unfaithful was one of the reasons she had hardened her heart towards him. Feeling ill, cramping, in pain, unable to reach her husband to help her, she had imagined him with another woman, with Ginny's lithe limbs wrapped around him.

His green eyes infinitely sad, Cristos started to slide off his wedding ring.

Hayley's mind was reeling. Her intake of breath was so swift it came out as a gasp. 'No!' she said. 'Not now.'

She reached over to stay his hand. 'Time enough for that tomorrow. You take off your ring. I take off mine. Then we say goodbye.'

CHAPTER SEVEN

FOR MORE THAN two years Cristos had been torturing himself with thoughts of Hayley with another man.

But she had stayed true to him.

He could scarcely believe it. He wondered at her reasons. But he didn't doubt her. To his knowledge, Hayley had never lied to him. He rode a great surge of exultation that rushed through his heart.

He was still her only lover.

Surely that meant something. He pushed his wedding ring firmly back into place. Perhaps, if he played his cards right, there could be a chance it would stay there. Because he still wanted her.

It took all the self-control he could muster not to sweep her into his arms and kiss her—properly this time. Not some polite charade of a kiss for the benefit of observers. A hungry, passionate kiss that was a prelude to possessing her, to reminding her why no other man would ever make her body sing the way he could.

Instead he relied on his gambler's instincts and waited to see what she might say next.

Being in a hotel room alone together gave a false sense of intimacy. But the coffee table was a barrier between them. Hayley leaned against the back of her chair, as if to emphasise the distance, perhaps to give him the impression she was relaxed. But her shoulders hunched defensively and she nervously twisted the ends of the hotel robe's tie without seeming to realise she was doing so.

She seemed swamped by the robe—a generic size designed for a woman less petite. It gave little hint of her slim, shapely body. The thick fabric wrapped over her breasts up to her neck, fell down past her knees. Her hair framed her face in tiny, damp tendrils—that short, short hair he was still getting used to. With her face free of make-up she looked very young. He had only two years on her but he felt infinitely older.

Finally, she stopped fiddling with the tie of her robe. She looked up at him, her blue eyes clouded. 'How did we get here, Cristos?' She had always called him by his Greek name, had never shortened and anglicised it to Chris or lengthened it to Christopher as some of his English friends had done.

He knew she didn't mean here in Greece, here on this island. 'I don't have an answer for you. But here we are. In the same room. Speaking to each other. Trying to make sense of our past.'

She jumped up from her chair, paced its length and back again. She rested her forehead in the heels of her hands, her fingers clutching her hair, then dropped them to look up at him. Her hair was tousled, her eyes red rimmed. 'I'm confused.'

Cristos kept a poker face as he got up to stand near her. 'Confused in what way?' He had to tread cautiously, as if through a field of landmines.

She flung out her hands. 'This isn't how it was meant to be. You. Me. Getting trapped here with you. Pretending we're still together. I intended to give you the divorce documents and then be gone. To put our marriage behind us. But then you threw a curve ball—that you haven't been with another woman. I'm reeling from your revelation.

You see, I thought there must have been another woman in Milan, if not Ginny someone else. Maybe more than one.'

He frowned. 'Because I'm a man? That my gender makes me predisposed to cheat? Despite our marriage vows? You insult me. I loved you, Hayley. There was no other woman. I didn't want anyone else.'

'I so want to believe you. But it's difficult for me to believe there weren't women flinging themselves at you, Mr Sexiest Man in Europe.' He had hated that name—bestowed on him by one of the international gossip magazines.

'Of course there were,' he said. 'Thousands of them. More than one man could possibly handle.'

That forced a reluctant hint of a smile. 'Really.'

'What did you call yourself earlier? An "inconvenient wife"? I never saw you as that. I didn't want anyone but you. Even after you ran away. But you didn't want to be found.' He hadn't thought of searching for her somewhere as far-flung as Australia.

'No, I didn't.' Her face drooped; lines of weariness bracketed her mouth.

He chose his next words carefully. 'So, I didn't date.'

'But you're such a sexy man.'

'I'm also a man of self-control. Once we are divorced it will, of course, be different. I won't want to stay alone.'

Her mouth thinned. 'Of course.'

'Though how I'll choose from among those thousands of women, I'm not sure. I might have to run auditions.'

Hayley stifled a little whimper that tore at his heart. 'That isn't funny,' she said.

He took a step closer, so close he could breathe in her warm, freshly showered scent—lemon and thyme from the hotel's artisan soap and shampoo overlaid the essential sweet scent of his wife. 'I'm sorry. That was a joke in bad taste. The truth is once we split for good, I will find someone else.'

He wanted her to deny the divorce. To say that after seeing him again she didn't want to go through with it after all. But she didn't. And the flame of his optimism flickered and dimmed.

'I... I suppose so.' But her uncertainty made him wonder about the guy in Sydney. How serious she was about him. Was there really another player in the game?

'That is, if you are still determined to go ahead with the divorce.'

She tilted her chin upward and met his eyes defiantly, but then betrayed herself by biting down on her lower lip. 'Yes. I am. That's why I came here. You want it too.'

'We could always change our minds,' he said. He gripped the tops of her arms and looked down into her face, urging her to give him the answer he wanted. She stilled under his touch; if she'd attempted to move away he would have let her go. But she didn't.

For a long moment she looked back up at him, her blue eyes clouded with uncertainty. *He had to kiss her.* To taste her sweet mouth, to try to communicate with touch what words could not. He drew her close, felt the warmth of her body through the cool silk of her pyjamas, her slender curves. He smoothed a thumb along her jaw, learning the feel of her soft skin again, traced the outline of her lips. She shuddered a little and he stopped. Then he dipped his head, brushed his lips gently against hers. Nothing too demanding. Nothing too passionate. He wanted her so desperately with the pent-up longing of years but he didn't want to scare her off.

She stayed rigid, as if bracing herself against her own response. Her breathing quickened but still she stayed still. *She wasn't ready.* Reluctantly he drew away. He wouldn't let her sense his disappointment.

Then suddenly *she* was kissing *him*. She pulled his head down to hers, pressed her mouth urgently against his, whimpered her need. He drew her to him again and kissed her back. Her tongue slipped into his mouth, he met it with his and they danced the familiar dance as if there hadn't been years since their last real kiss. He slid his hands down her back, pulled her closer. His optimism flamed back into life as if she had thrown accelerant on his hopes.

Then Hayley abruptly pulled away. Her face flushed, eyes dilated, her mouth swollen. She looked down to the floor. 'No. We can't do this.' She drew in her breath in a sob. Finally, after what seemed an age but was probably only seconds, she looked up, her expression determined. 'I'm sorry, Cristos. That wasn't fair of me.'

'Not fair? In what way?' he choked out. *Fair* wasn't the way to describe the dynamics of that kiss. He struggled to get his breath back on an even keel.

'I thought I'd talked myself out of my attraction to you,' she said. 'But it's still there. I still want you.'

And that was something to worry about?

'I've never stopped wanting you.' He felt fired by an urgency to reassure her. But she put up one small, pale hand to stop him. He knew that look of old—a 'but' was certain to follow.

'But that isn't enough. There has to be more than great sex to make a marriage, to make a family.'

He had to stamp on a cynical laugh. Hayley spoke as if 'great sex' were something casually acquired—almost to be disparaged. She'd been untouched when she'd come to him. Did she really have no idea of how rare that perfect sexual connection they'd shared from the start was between a man and a woman? She'd had no other man to compare—but surely she'd be aware of how special it was?

He frowned. 'I don't know where you're coming from. Yes, we had great sex. But we had so much more than that. We had each other's backs. We were life partners.'

His marriage to Hayley had given him everything that had been missing from his life—love, security, his own place in the world as her husband and, he'd hoped, the father of their child.

She drew her mouth in a tight line. '*Had* being the operative word. Past tense. We started off brilliantly. But then things changed.'

'Of course they did. We moved to different countries. I switched career. We grew up.'

She made an impatient gesture as if waving away his words. 'I didn't mean that. I meant we started off equals. Both sitting on the same perch making the decisions that affected us both. Talking things over if we disagreed. Making compromises.'

'That's right, we did,' he said, puzzled as to why she would bring that up.

'Then it seemed all the compromises were one way. Made by me.'

Behind the sweetness was a toughness in her stance, the way she stood with legs braced, a simmering aggression— as if a fluffy kitten had grown spikes like a porcupine. He frowned. 'The way I remember it, we both made compromises.'

She shook her head. 'I remember it differently. The first thing to go was my career. Big compromise. There wasn't much I could do without completing my degree. Maybe in London I could have got a halfway decent job. Even in Paris I spoke enough French to get work waitressing. Thank heaven for that gap year I spent working as an *au pair* in the south of France. But I didn't speak a word of Italian. By the time we got to Milan I was pretty much a housewife. Just Mrs Theofanis. Housewife to a husband who was never there. Who kept me in ignorance about where he was, what he was doing. Not to mention the fact that you actually had a wife was a deep, dark secret.'

He spread out his hands like an open book. 'You knew where I was when I was on assignments.'

'What about when you were "doing business"? I didn't know where you were or who you were with. I felt I was pushed down rung by rung off that perch beside you until I found myself scrabbling on the ground below.' There was a note of anger, of bitterness he had never heard before. Or perhaps he had never listened.

Cristos closed his eyes. 'I had no idea you felt that way.'

That was when he realised the first mistake he'd made. Choosing not to tell her the risks he was taking. Hiding from her the fact he'd knocked back lucrative modelling jobs so he could work on his own investments. Not when security had seemed so very important to her. 'Everything I did was for you, for us.'

Hayley played again with the tie on her dressing gown, twisting it tightly around her fingers like a tourniquet. 'I wish I could believe that. Seemed to me the marriage became all about you.'

He cursed under his breath. Not at her. At himself. 'You know I never wanted you to be a "secret wife".'

Her voice softened. 'I know. But it went on for too long. I began to feel invisible to you as well as to your fans.' She dropped her eyes down to where her bare toes were making a small circle in the rug. 'From invisible I began to feel inadequate.'

'Koukla.' He went to reach for her but she twisted away to evade his touch.

'If you think you can kiss me into submission, forget it,' she said. 'That won't work any more.'

'I didn't want to kiss you. No. I've always wanted to kiss you. I wanted to apologise. To say how sorry I am that you felt that way and that I didn't know.'

The modelling. That disruptive lifestyle. The pressures on him—and on her. It all came down to that. Again he cursed. How many times had he wished he had never showed Hayley the model scout's business card? Yet he'd been able to piggyback on the good money he'd earned to make a fortune.

'I understood that,' she said. 'You blame the modelling career for what went wrong between us. In some part, I agree.'

'That's when things changed between us.' He spoke the words leadenly.

'Not in the beginning. It was amusing then, a novelty. The parties were fun too, places we'd never been, people we would never have met. A lifestyle neither of us could ever have imagined. But the more popular you got, the more I got left behind.' She turned so he could only see her in profile. 'I got to hate your job. But I never wanted to tell you that. You loved it and it was so very well paid.'

Cristos abruptly turned from her, then swung back. '*You* got to hate it? Not half as much as I hated it.'

Her eyes widened in disbelief. 'What do you mean? I thought you loved being the man of the moment? A star.'

'I loved the money being a model brought us. The opportunities it gave us. In the beginning, some of the jobs were a buzz. But much of it I found demeaning. Not to mention just plain boring. I was a commodity. The director and photographer discuss you as if you're not present. On a shoot they push and pull you into place as if you're some kind of store mannequin, not a person. If I didn't know my nose cast the wrong kind of shadow before, I sure knew it after. And to my traditional family to be a model means a man must be gay—'

'Do you remember my parents asked me if you were gay when I told them what you were doing?' she asked. 'And how I laughed at the idea of it.'

'Constant slurs on my masculinity got more difficult to laugh off.'

'I didn't realise,' she said.

'You can imagine what my grandparents thought. Having their grandson splashed over billboards in his underpants was not, in their opinion, a worthy job for a Greek man with my education. If my *yia-yia* could have got a can of black paint and got up on a ladder to mask me out of those adverts she would have. Of course I heard all this after I came home—their disappointment in me spelled out in excruciating detail.'

'I'm so sorry to hear that. But forgive me for smiling at the thought of your grandmother with her bucket of paint, scrambling up the buildings in Times Square in New York with her paintbrush.'

'She would have been very busy. The posters were everywhere.'

'You looked darn good on those billboards,' she said. 'Mr Sexiest Man in Europe all right. At the time, your agent told me sales of those underpants rocketed all around the world.'

'The underwear people weren't happy when I refused an encore performance. They couldn't believe I would walk away from such a lucrative contract.'

'So why did you walk away?'

'Without you there, what was the point? I was fed up with some of the temperamental people I was forced to work with. The pressure to stay in peak form. Living in Italy and not able to eat what I wanted. All those hours at the gym keeping in shape. No wonder so many of the models—male and female—had eating disorders.'

'Those hours at the gym weren't a bad thing.'

He was aware of her not so covert inspection of his body, fitter and stronger even than when she'd last seen him. He liked to keep active. At first he'd pounded through the gym out of anger and despair and frustration. Forcing his body into submission to banish thoughts of Hayley. Back here on the islands, he'd found again the things he'd loved like swimming and running, hitting the gym for enjoyment rather than punishment. He had to counteract with physical activity the long hours he spent at a desk managing his wide-ranging investments.

'Modelling was a means to an end,' he said. 'I never saw it as a career. Rather a way to get some money together before we started our real lives.'

'I thought that was your real life. And that there was no place in that life for me.'

How could he have allowed her to think that? So maybe he had been dazzled by the so-called glamour of it all to start. He'd been so young, fresh out of uni. And there had been good times. But nothing could have made up for going home to the empty apartment. When he'd cleared it, he'd found tucked away in the back of a drawer a little knitted yellow hat Hayley must have bought in anticipation of the baby. For a long time he had stood with it held to his face. Only when he'd gone to put it away had he found he had wet it with tears he hadn't known he had shed.

He cleared his throat. 'You couldn't have been more wrong. I did it for you. For our future. Once you were out of the picture there was no incentive to keep on pushing myself in a role I'd grown to loathe.'

And by then he'd found a more lucrative way to make money, one that satisfied him intellectually and fed his gambler's soul. He couldn't deny the rush when a gamble paid off—but unlike his father he had weighed up risks with an acute business brain. The apps had kicked it off. Then he'd gone on to invest in property, industry, even a successful West End musical.

'I was surprised when I heard that you came back to your childhood home. I thought you might have gone to Athens. Got a job there.'

'I was in no frame of mind to do that. Not when all my

efforts were directed into finding my wife. I hunted for you, Hayley. But met a dead end everywhere I looked.'

'When did you give up?' she asked in a very small voice.

'When your mother decided to take one of my regular but usually unanswered calls and informed me that you were perfectly healthy, perfectly happy and did not want to see me ever again. After two years I talked to my lawyer about divorce.'

'I'm sorry. About my mother, I mean. She was overly protective. I'm also sorry you didn't get to use your business degree.'

He gave a short bark of laughter. 'Don't be sorry about that. I'm my own boss. I like it that way.'

Her forehead pleated into a frown. 'Is ferrying people on your boat enough? You're a very smart man, Cristos.'

He should tell her now how wealthy he was. But then he would have to tell her about the secrets buried in his past, the risks he had taken, his fears, the insecurities he had never wanted to admit to her. 'The boat is a hobby. Relaxation. If I can help people out with a ride between islands that's good too. But I don't earn my living as a boatman.'

'How you earn your living isn't actually any of my business now. But you got used to a certain standard of living with what you earned. I'd hate to see you go backwards.'

'My investments make me a more than good enough living. That's what the business meetings in Milan were about. I'd made some good contacts. I was looking to the future.'

Their future.

Hayley was more relieved than she could have imagined to hear that Cristos was doing okay. They'd had such a struggle at the start. The modelling career had seemed like a godsend.

But she was astounded to discover how much he'd hated

it. Why hadn't she known that? Had she really listened when he'd come home exhausted and complaining about some tyrannical fashion director? She'd wanted so much to be a support to him, as her mother had never been to her father, yet it seemed she had failed. Even before her pregnancy had brought on its problems and changed everything.

'What about you?' he said.

'Sydney is an expensive city to live in. But I'm sharing an apartment with a very nice girl and doing okay. I really like my job. People only know me there as Hayley Clements. Not as the appendage of a dominant male.'

His face contorted with what looked like real concern, pain and a good dose of anguish. But, Cristos being Cristos, he only looked more handsome. Dark and brooding suited him. Dark and brooding had brought him a lot of work. Although she'd loved him most when he was laughing, those fabulous white teeth against his warm olive skin, his green eyes sparkling with good humour.

'I'm gutted you thought you were in any way lesser,' he said now. 'I blame myself entirely.' A bleak shadow darkened his eyes. 'If I could turn back the clock I would. Especially to the night we lost our baby.'

Hayley tensed. 'I told you I didn't want to talk any more about that.'

To talk further about her miscarriage meant having to reveal more of her life afterwards. The deep, dark depression that had overwhelmed her. That had worried her parents so much they had admitted her to a clinic. The long struggle back from those black depths.

'I'm sorry,' he said.

'I'm sorry too,' she said. 'Looking back, I didn't realise the pressures on you. My only excuse is that I was young, inexperienced and maybe not ready to be a wife.'

'I wasn't much older. Maybe neither of us was ready. Maybe we—'

'Should have got to know each other better before we—'

'Dived into that shark pool of the modelling world.'

'It was a shark pool, wasn't it? Seething with vicious creatures, jaws open and snapping with razor-sharp teeth. Your agent, some of those bookers, even the clients. They were predators.'

'And we were naïve, fresh prey,' he said.

'Now, a few years on, I wouldn't put up with being made a secret wife hiding in your shadow. Not for a moment.'

'I wouldn't have allowed it. I didn't want to allow it then. I should have trusted my instincts.'

Hayley's instincts were begging to be heard right now. Go to him. Put your arms around him. Hold him close. *Don't let him go again.*

But her instincts had seen her give up her life for him. Her intellect told her to hang on to her independence.

She yawned. A genuine yawn. But she exaggerated it. 'Bed time,' she said, then immediately regretted her choice of words. 'I mean…well, I don't mean—'

'Bed time for you. Sofa time for me. I get it.'

She clutched her robe closer to her. 'Uh. Okay. Do you need to use the bathroom?'

'No. You go,' he said.

When she came back into the room, he had changed out of his jeans and shirt, and was wearing his boxers and a white T-shirt. He'd pulled a sheet, blanket and a pillow from the closet and was throwing them across the sofa.

Her mouth went dry at the sight of him in so little clothing. He was cut, every muscle honed. In even better shape than when she'd last seen him like this. For some of his jobs he'd had to wax away all his body hair. She'd never liked it. Now he had just the right amount of dark hair on his chest, his legs, that she had found so exciting.

How could one man be so perfect?

'I…well, I'll say goodnight.'

He looked up. 'Goodnight, Hayley.'

For a long moment their gazes met. 'Does this seem seriously weird to you?' she said.

'Yeah. It does. This morning I had no idea I'd ever see you again. Now we're sharing a room. But I'm glad you're here. Happy we could talk.'

'Me too.' *He had not been with another woman.*

He lay down on the sofa, pulled the blanket over him and rolled away from her. He pummelled his pillow into place—as he had always done. Only that had been after they'd made love and she'd snuggled beside him and used his chest as her pillow. Now all she could see was his broad shoulders and the back of his dark head. 'You can turn the lights off from the switches by the bed,' he said.

She made her way over to the big, empty bed. Slid into the cool sheets. Resisted the urge to pummel her pillow because that was what he'd done. Reached over to fumble for the light switch. Then lay on her back and stared at the ceiling. Sleep would never come.

But it must have.

She awoke with a start. Didn't know where she was for a moment. Saw by the light from the bedside clock it was past midnight.

The bed seemed very big and empty. She'd barely made a bump in the bed linen. Outside the wind had dropped completely and it seemed utterly quiet and perfectly still. So still, it felt scary. As her eyes adjusted to the gloom she could see Cristos, illuminated by the faint light from the clock and the glow from the standby light on the television, as he lay on the sofa just steps away from her bed.

She could hear the rustling of the sheet as he turned. Then turned again. His breathing was too loud for him to be asleep. He bashed the pillow with his fist and crashed back onto the sofa as if he were diving into a belly flop. Definitely awake.

Hayley sat up, resting on her elbows so she could better see him. One long, muscular leg was hanging off the sofa from under the covers. His arm trailed the floor. He turned again but it was obvious the sofa was much too small for him to be comfortable. Or rather he was too big. She was so much smaller than him. She would fit better. The sofa should be hers.

She swung her legs to the floor. Made her way over to him. 'Cristos,' she whispered. He pretended to be asleep and didn't reply. 'I know you're awake,' she said in her normal voice.

'I'm trying to sleep,' he mumbled.

'You're never going to get to sleep on that sofa,' she said. 'It's too small. You take the bed. Let me take the sofa.'

'I'm fine,' he protested.

'You're not.' She pulled the sheet off him. Gasped. His T-shirt had ridden up to show his hard chest, his perfect six-pack. 'Give me the sofa.'

He snatched back the sheet. 'No.'

She sighed. 'This is ridiculous. Neither of us is going to get any sleep.'

He dropped his guard momentarily as he lifted his head to face her. She took her chance and grabbed both sheet and blanket from him. 'You'll freeze without them.'

'A gentleman takes the sofa,' he said.

'I don't know in what guidebook to chivalry that's written,' she said.

'You wouldn't know—girls don't read them,' he said. 'Besides, my copy is written in Greek. Ancient Greek. In Cyrillic script.'

She smiled and rolled her eyes, even though he couldn't see her. 'So we'll share the bed.'

'Not a good idea,' he said.

'It's the size of a tennis court,' she said. 'You stay your side and I'll stay mine. We could put a barricade of pil-

lows down the middle if you'd like. Now get up, please. I
can't sleep knowing how uncomfortable you must be on
that sofa. You've got a big day ahead of you tomorrow ferrying people over to Nidri.'

'You always were a bossy little thing,' he said with a
mock groan.

Not bossy enough, she thought. Knowing what she now
knew about their time in Milan she might have done things
differently. If she'd asserted herself more she might not
have grown so insecure about her husband. Might not have
constantly compared herself to the beautiful women he
worked with and found herself lacking.

'Come on,' she said. 'I need my sleep too.'

He rolled off the sofa. Stretched. Her heart stopped at
the splendour of him. Could she really sleep in the same
bed as him and not want to jump his bones? Ill-advised as
that might be? He staggered towards the bed, pretending,
she thought, to be drowsier than he was.

She'd always slept on his left. Nearer to his heart, he'd
said as he'd pulled her close. Now they fell into the marriage-
allotted sides of the bed without question. Only he was as
far to the edge as possible on his side and she the same on
hers. He turned his back to her. She did the same. Was he
thinking the same jumping-the-bones thing she was?

'That's much more comfortable for you,' she said.
'Goodnight.'

'G'night,' he said, in a voice that already sounded half
asleep. But she knew he was feigning sleep and she was
glad. It made the awkward situation so much easier. Maybe
she should wait until he fell asleep and then creep over to
the sofa.

Stay where she was and she would probably lie there
rigidly unable to sleep, conscious of his presence in her
bed for the first time in two and a half years. But it happened the opposite way. Just knowing she wasn't alone

in the bed, that Cristos was there, made her relax and she was asleep before she'd even had a chance to worry about not being able to fall asleep.

The next time she woke, it was very early morning, a hint of grey pre-dawn light creeping through the shutters. For a moment she didn't know where she was. A warm, male *familiar* body was spooned against her back, his arm flung around her waist, his hand resting on her hip. *Cristos.*

She stilled. Breathed in his scent, felt the warm whisper of his breath on her skin, the subtle scratch of his beard. Cristos was right. It hadn't just been about sex with them. After they'd had sex they would lie like this to go to sleep. It had also been about comfort, reassurance, *love.*

Why had they let it go?

It was dangerous to stay here like this. It would be too easy to turn in his arms, to wake him with kisses, to slide off his clothes—and hers. To open her body to him—and risk opening her heart. What if he were to plant tiny kisses on the sensitive nape of her neck? What if his hand slipped upwards to cup her breast? In the past they had indulged in a morning delight whenever they'd had a chance. But it couldn't happen. She should edge away from him and hit that sofa. But she would allow herself just one more minute with him. And another. Until she couldn't bear to leave his embrace and drowsiness overwhelmed her.

CHAPTER EIGHT

HAYLEY WOKE TO a cold morning light flooding through the open doors of the balcony. And a cold morning breeze wafting towards the bed that made her shiver and tug the duvet over her shoulders.

The glass doors to the balcony had been flung open. Cristos stood framed by the doorway, looking out to sea with his back to her and his arms outstretched, as if making a homage to the morning. He wore just his T-shirt and boxers. Broad shoulders tapered to a narrow waist and the best butt she had ever seen on a man. Not that she had ever actually seen another man's butt clad in just underwear—knit cotton boxers that emphasised hard male buttocks and muscular thighs—to compare but she could not believe any other man could compete. It was a fine view to wake up to.

She reached out a hand to the rumpled sheets beside her. The high-thread-count linen was still warm. He must not be long out of bed—her side of the bed.

She had slept the night with her soon-to-be-ex-husband.

How warm and comforting it had been with him spooned against her. Yet she was glad it had not led to more. Today she would be flying more than fifteen thousand kilometres back to her life in Sydney.

Cristos would like Sydney.

Perhaps he could come visit. Perhaps—

'You're awake.' Cristos turned to face her. 'Come see.'

The doors to the balcony had been shuttered the night before. Yes, she would like to see the view. She checked to see if her pyjama top had slid open in the night then slipped into her robe and the too-big slippers before heading to join him.

It was the first time she had seen Cristos in the morning for a long, long time. Her heart flipped over inside her at the sight of his handsome, once so beloved face.

His black hair was all ruffled and standing up in peaks. She had to shove her hands in her dressing-gown pockets to stop herself from reaching up to smooth it into place. His beard had grown overnight to shadow his jaw, a look she had always found incredibly sexy. She ached to stroke the roughness that contrasted with his smooth olive skin elsewhere, but kept her hands fisted firmly in her pockets. His extraordinary green eyes, framed with thick black lashes, still looked sleepy, half lidded and sensual.

This was *her* Cristos. Not the Cristos she'd had to share with his fans. The man no one else saw, though they'd strived to give a taste of intimate, early-morning bedroom Cristos in countless photographic shoots and commercials. The captured images had come nowhere near the heart-rendingly beautiful reality of the man.

For a moment, she thought he was going to lean down and kiss her and she was unsure how she would react.

Kiss him back and drag him over to the bed?

But the moment passed. Cristos stood aside to give her access to the balcony. Icy air needled her face. She soon saw the reason why. 'Snow,' she breathed. 'It's beautiful. Not what I ever expected to see on a Greek island.'

'It's not usual here,' he said. 'I told you, this is the coldest winter I can remember.'

Heavy snow had fallen overnight and flakes still drifted slowly down. The balcony and its railings were frosted with it. She leaned forward to see as much as she could without venturing out onto the balcony in flimsy slippers and risking frostbite.

Ahead of her was the sea, below the curve of the beach, and to each side forested hillsides that sloped down to the water. Everywhere but the water itself was covered in white. The trees. The beach. The boats moored at the resort dock. It was magical. A fairy-tale landscape. 'You could make snowmen on the beach,' she said, reaching up to catch snowflakes in her hands.

'No doubt the kids will be doing just that very soon,' he said.

She pivoted to face him. 'But we'll all be leaving this morning.'

'I doubt that,' he said, leaning back against the door-frame.

'What do you mean?'

'Look at the sea,' he said, indicating the white-foamed, choppy waters. Blue sky was struggling through gaps in the clouds but the sea still looked wild and forbidding.

She shivered. 'But you said we could leave today.'

'Weather permitting was always the proviso.'

'And you're telling me the weather is saying "no way".'

'I'm afraid so. Even if we could get off the island, the roads will be closed, as will the causeway that links Lefkada to the mainland. They might have lost power in Nidri.'

'You mean I'm still stuck here? For how long?'

'Indefinitely, I suggest,' he said. Was that a grin hovering around his mouth?

'How will I get to the airport?' she said, knowing how ridiculous the question sounded as soon as it left her mouth. 'The airport will most likely be closed too, won't it?'

'Most likely,' he said.

Her voice rose with the panic that gripped her. 'I'm meant to fly to Dubai this afternoon.'

'I wouldn't count on that,' he said.

'Damn! One night I could manage but this. Trapped here indefinitely. It's unbearable.'

'You're welcome to stay here as long as you want.' The grin burst into full, disarming life. 'Not that you have any choice.'

She stared at him. 'You're glad about this.'

'Guilty as charged. Fate has dealt me an unexpected good hand. More time together.' His eyes narrowed. 'Maybe a second chance with you.'

A second chance.

Her heart gave a betraying little leap at his words. But she shook her head. 'It's way too late to consider that.'

He pounced. 'So you have considered it?'

Kissing him. Lying in that honeymoon bed with him so close. The thought had crossed her mind, in a 'what if?' kind of way. 'No. That's crazy talk,' she said. 'We're strangers to each other now.'

He frowned. 'Do you really think so? That there's nothing left of the people we used to be?'

'I've changed since we were together. I'm sure you have too. We hurt each other in the past. One conversation isn't enough to heal those old hurts.'

'We can have more conversations.' His gaze was intent.

Her heart skipped a beat with panic. 'Please don't put pressure on me.'

For a long moment he looked down at her. She felt her body stirring at his closeness. The only man who had ever made her feel like this. But she had to protect herself. Her life now was ordered and stable, not the wild swings life had been with Cristos. And that stability had been hard won.

'No pressure,' he said finally. 'I'm just asking you to give our marriage a second chance.'

'And I'm telling you I can't do that. It's been less than twenty-four hours.'

'I still want you. You can't blame me for trying.' Maybe she would have been insulted if he hadn't. As she'd told him before, she was confused about her reactions to him.

'We could try to get to know each other again while I'm trapped here on the island,' she said.

'Why do I feel I've been handed the booby prize?' he said. 'But I'll play it your way.'

'Thank you,' she said with relief and a curious sense of anticipation. 'So, what will happen at the resort now? This room. Will we stay in here?'

'I'm sure Dell and Alex will expect people to remain in their allocated rooms. You stay here. But I'm going to bunk down with my grandparents in their room.'

She stared at him. 'Why? There's plenty of room here. I'll take the sofa tonight.'

His face tensed. 'I cannot sleep another night in the same room as you, and certainly not in the same bed, without making love to you. It's too much to ask of a man. Self-control can only go so far.'

'It was difficult for me too,' she said.

'Don't tell me that,' he groaned. 'It makes it worse.'

She couldn't look at him, scared of what she might see, how she might react. 'What will people think about us in separate rooms?'

'Who will know?'

'Your grandparents might have an idea if you're planning to be in their room. What will you tell them?'

'That you couldn't put up with my snoring and kicked me out.'

'But you don't snore.'

'I hope not. But that's beside the point. If you can think of a better excuse, tell me. I don't want to tell them the truth.'

She smiled. 'I doubt Penelope would want the X-rated reason.' He rolled his eyes in the way she had always found endearing. 'What about the others?' she said. 'Do we keep up the pretence?'

'It would be easier than making awkward explanations at this stage.'

'I think so too,' she said. They were on such friendlier terms it didn't seem such a sham.

He glanced at his watch. 'The place is probably in an uproar with interrupted travel plans. I'll get dressed, head down to the office and look at the weather reports on the internet. There's WiFi in this room. Better check your phone for airline information on your flights.'

'I'll do that,' she said, turning to head back into the room.

He caught her by the arm to stop her. Turned her to face him. She looked up into that handsome face she had once loved so much. His eyes seemed to do an inventory of her features, as if memorising them. 'I want to know you better, Hayley,' he said in that deep voice. His slight accent became more pronounced, as it had used to in times of deep emotion.

She caught her breath. 'Me too. I mean, know you better.'

Within minutes he had gone, leaving Hayley alone and realising the room felt very empty indeed without him.

For nearly two and a half years Cristos had been haunted by his last sight of Hayley, pale and drawn in that hospital bed. He'd let her down and he'd paid the price.

She had changed. It wasn't just the hair. It was the demeanour too. He liked that she was tougher, stronger, particularly as he wasn't around to look after her any more.

He'd always wanted to look after her and protect her. On their wedding day he'd made an extra, private vow. He would never treat his wife the way his father had treated his mother.

His father hadn't looked after his mother the way she'd deserved. He'd left her and himself as a child to fend for themselves while he was incarcerated. Then done nothing to mend his ways to avoid another prison sentence. Thankfully his grandparents had always welcomed his mother back to Nidri. But the welcome had not been without conditions—his mother had to be always grateful, never rock the boat and have a feasible story to explain why her husband was away on business for so long. Then, acting against all the family's advice, she had always gone back to him, taking Cristos with her, until the time had come that he'd had to stay with his grandparents in term time to ensure some continuity of his education.

He saw, now, that he took after his mother as much as his father. She had been a one-man woman, never giving up on the husband she'd loved and married against all advice. He was the same with Hayley. He'd wanted only her from the time he'd met her. No other woman had interested him. He'd persisted in his search for her long after he should have given up on her. He didn't intend to give up now.

CHAPTER NINE

IT WOULD BE so easy to fall in love with Cristos again, Hayley thought. *Too easy.* Memories of how caring he could be wrapped around her with the same enveloping warmth as his body had provided, spooning hers last night. He had been everything she'd wanted before things between them had gone so wrong.

After the miscarriage and her spiral into depression, she'd been forced to protect herself by putting a lid on her good memories of her husband. But the seal was beginning to loosen.

Here on Kosmimo, she'd begun to recognise glimpses of the old Cristos—the man she'd vowed to love 'until death do us part'.

Not that those words had been spoken in the ceremony that had united them in law as man and wife. They'd murmured them to each other later, in the privacy of the big four-poster bed in a bed and breakfast near Durham where they'd spent their wedding night. Her new husband had wanted to make her first time special. He hadn't thought that likely in her cramped room in the student house in the Viaduct.

Cristos had been tender, patient and passionate. The pleasure he had brought her to had been so intense she had fallen apart in tears afterwards. She had sobbed, not because it had hurt—though it had a little—but in wonder and appreciation of the perfectly splendid man she had married. After that, each time they'd made love had been more memorable than the last as they'd grown to know each other's wants and needs.

He'd been surprised when she'd first told him she was a virgin and wanted to stay so until she got married. At twenty-two, she'd been a rarity. Gradually he'd got the story of why she'd taken such a stance. Her mother had fallen pregnant to her father at age nineteen. She'd 'had' to get married at an age when settling down had been the last thing on her fun-loving mind.

'Fun-loving' was hardly the term to describe the mother Hayley knew. Her mum had spent the rest of her life resenting her forced marriage and the man she'd experimented with but hadn't been in love with. That pregnancy had resulted in Hayley's older sister, Laura, who had shouldered the burden of being the reason for her mother's unhappiness and her father's long-suffering misery. Hayley had decided she would not have sex until she was married to a man where an unexpected pregnancy would be welcomed. Because, with the best will in the world, contraceptives could fail, as they had for her and Cristos.

Now she paused on the threshold of the breakfast area, arrested by the sight of him sitting alone, dark head bowed over a laptop, a coffee cup shoved to one side. She had no doubt it was a self-imposed exile from the rest of the guests enjoying breakfast. Cristos would only be by himself from choice. Yet he seemed so alone.

Her heart turned over at the sight. After she'd left she'd been so intent on hating him she hadn't given much thought to how he'd been handling the split. Yet he'd never given up on her. She hadn't realised the efforts he'd put into finding her—thanks to the protective barrier put around her by her parents. For a long time she'd thought he'd abandoned her.

When her parents had finally admitted they had shielded her from him, she'd established a life on her own. Had been, she realised, too scared to see Cristos again until she'd got herself completely together.

She had a sudden impulse to creep up behind him, wrap her arms around him and plant a kiss on the back of his neck as she'd often done. Then he would have pulled her into his lap, laughing and covering her face with kisses.

Instead she slid into the chair next to him. 'As you advised, I got through to the airline. My flight from Preveza is cancelled. Even if I could get to Lefkada, road transport to Athens wouldn't be a possibility. Apparently there's heavy snow all over the country and transport is in chaos.'

He closed his laptop. 'Then I guess you have to stop worrying and enjoy your bonus stay on Kosmimo.'

'I intend to,' she said. 'I texted my boss. Being stranded on a Greek island isn't a bad excuse for being late back to work. I feel like I've been let off school for a snow day.'

She leaned closer so only Cristos could hear. Felt her heart trip faster at the familiar scent of his skin. 'I'm sorry, Cristos. I know this isn't your fault that I'm stuck here. I've been most ungracious. Thank you for putting up with me.' On impulse, she kissed him on the cheek, closing her eyes for a brief second at the bliss of her lips on his smooth skin.

His eyes widened and she realised it was the first physical contact between them she had initiated. She pulled back to put more space between them.

'You're very easy to put up with,' he said with a slow lazy smile.

'Can I get you some breakfast?' she asked. 'Cake?'

When they'd visited Athens on their honeymoon she'd been amazed to find cake as a breakfast staple alongside the usual breakfast offerings at their hotel. Cakes like those she'd expect at morning or afternoon tea.

'None of that kind of cake at Pevezzo Athina. Remember, this is a holistic retreat style of resort. Here the cake is gluten free, dairy free and sugar free.'

Hayley wrinkled up her nose in dismay at the thought. He laughed. 'It's surprisingly good. You'll also find Greek yogurt, feta cheese, boiled eggs and fruit as well as some traditional Greek rusks that I think you might like. There's also a bar with lots of different teas.'

'And coffee, of course,' she said. Cristos had always loved his coffee, dark and thick.

'Only the best,' he said. 'I'm on my second. I've already eaten breakfast.'

Hayley glanced over at the buffet table. 'Alex and Dell have done very well to rustle up that kind of breakfast, considering the resort is closed and they weren't expecting all their guests to stay on.'

'They live on the island in the house Alex built on the next bay. No doubt they stocked up with the Australian visitors in mind. I don't know how long supplies will last if we're here for more than a few days though.'

'Surely the bad weather can't last that long. The reports I looked up said it was a freak snowfall.'

'Who knows?' he said with an eloquent shrug of his shoulders. 'I hope for all our sakes it clears up. Everyone here is being positive about it but that won't last long.'

'Like you said, I intend to make the most of it. With that in mind, I'd better go get some breakfast while the food lasts,' she said, only half in jest.

As she got up from her chair the overhead lights flickered, went dark, then came on again. There was a collective, accompanying gasp from everyone in the room.

Cristos cursed. 'Losing power is just what we don't need.'

Hayley's engineer brain went into action. The company she worked for dealt mostly with large-scale, industrial solar-power plants but they also worked on smaller-scale projects like this one. 'There might be snow covering the solar panels. And a slide of heavy, wet snow can break connections. What kind of battery storage do they have here?'

'Enough for a few days, I assume,' he said.

'Diesel generator backup?' she asked, her mind racing.

'Yes,' he said. 'Though they've never had to use it.'

She thought for a moment. 'I've volunteered to help clear up after breakfast. I think I could be of more help with restoring the power. I'll go and see what I can do.'

Cristos picked up his laptop. 'I'll come with you.'

Cristos was lost in admiration of Hayley's knowledge and practical skills when it came to working with the island's power system. Fortunately, although there was a solid cover of snow, the wind had dropped so the low wind-chill factor made it possible for her to work outside.

She teamed up with one of the Athens cousins who was an electrician. Between them, Hayley and the cousin did their best to make sure the resort wasn't going to lose electricity. They fixed the faulty connection that had caused the power hiccup and got the generator ready to kick into action if required. There wasn't much for him and Alex to do except provide muscle where required.

It was a novelty for Cristos to take orders from his wife as she enlisted help to clear the snow from the panels. With a bunch of Greek men taking direction from a petite, blonde woman doing skilled manual work there was much good-natured banter. Cristos was surprised to see how well she took it, how happy and relaxed she seemed, giving as good as she got. He realised he knew nothing about her work in Australia, the life she had built up as an apparently single woman with no ring on her finger and no husband's name attached to hers.

And yet there had been no other man in her bed.

When it was done, he offered Hayley a hand to help her down the ladder, was surprised when she accepted. She'd been so keen to assert her independence.

'Thanks,' she said as she jumped the final step back onto the ground. This was the only time he'd been alone with her all morning.

'Careful, it's slippery there.' He put his arm around her to steady her. A helpful, impersonal touch, as even his grandfather might offer.

'Yes, we've churned up the snow and it's freezing into ice.'

She was wearing sturdy work boots provided by, surprisingly, his grandmother. Her work gloves had come from his grandfather. Stavros had helped wherever he could. Penelope had stood for a while observing the process before she'd disappeared back inside. Cristos detected a grudging admiration for Hayley from his *yia-yia*. His grandmother was a great believer in honest hard work— another of the reasons she'd loathed his father.

Once Hayley gained her balance she shrugged off his arm and rubbed both gloved hands together. 'A job well done,' she said with a sigh of satisfaction. 'We shouldn't have to worry about lighting or heating or access to the internet now. But we should try and keep the panels free of any further snowfalls.'

Her face was flushed high on her cheekbones, which accentuated the blue of her eyes and her naturally pink lips. It wasn't just cold, he realised, but exhilaration.

'You enjoyed that, didn't you?' he said.

'I did. I was glad to be able to help. It was interesting too, to see how things are done here with solar. There are some slight differences.'

'I can speak on behalf of everyone here when I say how grateful we are for your help.'

Hayley wore a bulky too-big jacket in an unflattering

shade of brown and an even uglier fleece hat she'd found somewhere, her hair was dark with damp and clinging to her face, and her nose glowed red with cold. She looked beautiful.

'I thrive on hard work, Cristos. Always have.'

And he hadn't seen that. Or he'd seen it and glossed over it. He'd been so determined to give her the life his father had never given his mother that he had failed to see Hayley's needs—needs so very different from those of his mother from another generation and culture. He'd thought he knew what his wife needed—and hadn't listened to her when she'd told him what she wanted.

'It wasn't enough, was it?' he asked her now. 'The apartment in fashionable Brera in old Milan, the designer clothes we got at a discount, the parties.'

'I wasn't cut out to be a housewife, Cristos. Not at that age. Probably not at any age. The apartment was so tiny it took no time to clean. Brera was funky and fun but even shopping gets boring. Sitting at a café nibbling on *biscotti* and drinking the best *cappuccino* in the world paled after a while. If I didn't bury myself in a book, the Italian guys were annoyingly persistent in trying to pick me up. Remember, I didn't wear my wedding ring in public. I tried to learn the language but missed classes when you were back from a shoot so I could be with you. My friends had all finished uni and were working. The life of a kept woman wasn't really for me.'

'You tried to tell me all that—'

'But maybe not loudly enough. I didn't want to sound ungrateful. I mean… *Milano*. People would kill to live in such an exciting city.'

'But you were there too often on your own. I see that now.'

'Yes,' she said. The one word told him more than she might have imagined.

'And you thought I was with other women.'

'Sometimes. You're such a handsome man, I could see the hunger for you in their eyes.' Her voice trailed away.

'But not in my eyes,' he said. 'That was only for you.'

He'd had to handle unwanted attention from when he was a young teenager. Living in a tourist area meant women looking for a fling with a local. Someone to boast about after they'd gone home—like a sexual trophy. He'd even had older women suggesting they could initiate him. It had disgusted him. He'd only been interested in girls his own age. Good looks could be a burden, which was why he had been willing to try and earn money by exploiting them commercially—for him and Hayley. 'Do you believe me now that there was never any other woman?'

'Yes, I do,' she said firmly. 'Back then I doubted you because I was insecure. You were sometimes away for weeks at time. A man used to regular sex.'

'With his *wife*. I was trying to do the best I could for you, for *us*.' He couldn't keep the note of anguish from his voice, cursed himself for it. One thing that had been drilled into him was that a man never showed weakness. He couldn't let the mask slip.

'And I wanted to let you shine,' she said. 'I never wanted to squash my husband the way my mother did to my dad. Whatever you felt you needed to do, I was behind you. But while you shone, I… I grew duller and duller. Until I was so tarnished I felt you didn't see me any more.'

How could his beloved Hayley ever have got to feel that way? How had he taken his eye so off the ball? 'Never,' he said. 'You were never, *ever* dull in my eyes.' He looked down into her face. 'You have to believe that. You were smart, beautiful—still are—and all I wanted to do was give you a good life.'

'You came home with stories of shoots in Venice and

I struggled to find something interesting to say about my day. I needed to work, to have a life outside that apartment.'

'We should have moved back to London.' He cursed. 'Why didn't I know you were feeling like that?'

'Why didn't I tell you? I look back and see I also was at fault when back then I thought it was only you in the wrong.'

He shook his head. 'You're being way too reasonable. Way too English. You shouldn't have had to tell me. I should have realised. And then when you got pregnant I—'

A switch seemed to turn off behind her eyes and she put up her hand in the thick glove. 'You know I don't want to talk about that. Especially not here, not now.' She looked over his shoulder and he turned.

Dell was headed their way with steaming mugs of coffee and his favourite cheese pie, *tiropita*. His cousin's wife, a food blogger, had become quite the Greek food aficionado since she'd married Alex.

'Hayley, you're a wonder woman,' Dell said. 'I can't believe you know how all that stuff works and how to fix it.'

Hayley shrugged but she looked pleased. 'It's my job,' she said. 'And I'm glad to be of help.'

'Seriously, we would have been in big trouble if we'd lost power. I really don't know how to thank you.'

Hayley, flushed with pleased embarrassment, looked up to Cristos for help with the answer.

'My wife is a wonder woman all right,' he said. He put his arm around Hayley to draw her close, though he could scarcely feel where her waist was through the jacket. 'And she's family, of course she wants to help.'

Dell smiled and Cristos could tell she was delighted that he and his estranged wife were getting on so well. He hoped he would never have to tell her the truth. Dreaded the thought of Hayley becoming part of family history as Cristos's English ex-wife.

Dell indicated the coffee and pie she held on a tray. 'I've brought nourishment, but you should come inside.'

Hayley shook her head. 'I'd love a snack but I don't want to go inside. It's cold out here but so beautiful. Like a fairyland.' The clouds were clearing and a pale sun glinted off the snow reflecting like tiny crystals. They had woken up to a completely different, snow-shrouded landscape.

'I'll stay here with you,' he said, holding the tray for Dell. 'I've never seen the island under snow either.'

'None of us have,' said Dell. 'But it's too darn cold for my Aussie blood.'

Hayley took a piece of the pie—crisp filo pastry enclosing a savoury cheese filling—and a mug of coffee. 'Thanks Dell, it was worth getting up on that roof just to taste this.'

'Don't thank me,' said Dell. 'Thank Penelope. She baked the *tiropita* and she suggested I bring it out to you.' She smiled at Cristos. 'And you too, of course, Cristos. She said it's been your favourite since you were a little boy.'

Hayley's eyebrows rose. 'Did I hear that right? Penelope sent me out some pie?' She glanced up at Cristos.

'Looks like you're making a good impression,' he said. 'Who knew getting your hands dirty on a diesel generator would get you into *Yia-yia's* good books.'

He laughed, but inside he felt bleak. Maybe if Hayley had felt welcome in his family she might not have run so far away from him. But perhaps that had had more to do with her parents' dislike of him. Whatever had happened, he'd always had a feeling her mother had stage-managed it.

'What was that you said about making a snowman on the beach?' he asked Hayley. 'When you've finished your pie, I'll take you down there.'

'I'd like that,' she said. 'I might even challenge you to a snowball fight.' Cristos tried not to think of tussling with Hayley in the snow, pinning her down, claiming a kiss because he won. Or conceding defeat and letting her have her way with him.

'Before you do,' said Dell, 'I'd like to run an idea by you. The troops are getting restless, not knowing when they're going to get off the island. Alex and I thought we might have a party tonight. What do you think?'

'I think it's a very good idea,' Cristos said.

'Me too,' said Hayley.

'It's Valentine's Day tomorrow,' said Dell. 'What do you think of a Valentine's theme? You two lovebirds should approve.'

Cristos sensed Hayley still and watched the colour drain from her face. How could Dell be so insensitive? But how could he blame her? He and Hayley had obviously put on too good an act of being reconciled.

He shrugged. 'Valentine's? Sure. Why not?'

'What about you, Hayley? You seem a bit stunned by the idea,' said Dell.

Cristos could see Hayley's struggle to compose herself. 'I was just wondering what people would wear. I've only got the trousers and sweater I wore yesterday and these jeans.'

'That's not a problem,' said Dell. 'I can loan you something. I'm a size bigger than you now but I've got smaller clothes I haven't been able to fit into since Georgios was born. The other guests are in the same boat clothes-wise but no one will really care. They all wore something nice for our vow-renewal ceremony—they can wear that again.'

'Okay,' said Hayley. 'I'll take you up on that offer. Thank you.'

She didn't meet his gaze. The word *lovebirds* hung between them as if it were really a bird, fluttering its wings for attention.

'It doesn't matter what people wear,' he said. 'It will keep people's minds off their plight and we'll all have fun.'

'What can I do to help?' asked Hayley.

'Nothing,' said Dell. 'You've done more than enough. All you have to do is enjoy yourself. Isn't that right, Cristos?'

Dell glanced back over her shoulder to give him a knowing look before she headed back into the resort with her tray.

CHAPTER TEN

HAYLEY DREADED THE Valentine-themed party. Not because she didn't think it was a good idea. As Dell had said, the guests were indeed getting fed up with their enforced vacations and wanting to get back to their homes. Tempers were fraying and annoyance being expressed, even with the awareness that the delay was no one's fault but Mother Nature's. Down on the beach that afternoon some of the snowballs had been thrown by the older kids with rather too much vigour and there'd been more than the odd tantrum from the toddlers. A party might help everyone relax.

No, that was not what bothered her about the party. The reason she was tying herself up in anxious knots was that she and Cristos were obviously expected to act like 'lovebirds'.

Getting to know Cristos again wasn't in any way straightforward. Being in such proximity to him was slowly scratching at the scars of old memories from their shared past. And then there were the scars beneath the scars. The painful process was forcing her to really look at her relationship with her husband and the circumstances that had ended it. And some of it puzzled her.

Then there was the shadow that the past threw on the present. She'd thought she was happy in Sydney. But seeing Cristos again was messing with her head—as well as sending all sorts of confusing messages to her body. Her job was fulfilling, she'd made new friends, she lived in a charming older-style apartment on the north shore near Sydney Harbour. What was missing was a man. *Her* man.

Could any man ever match up to Cristos?

Rather than bundling the past into a big box to shove somewhere in the recesses of her mind, with the divorce being the ribbon neatly tying it all up, she was beginning to rethink her time with Cristos.

Could she have got him wrong back then?

Trouble was, if she were Hayley and he were Cristos, Dell and Alex's guests having just met for the first time yesterday—she'd be madly attracted to him and excited at the possibility of falling for him.

As it was, she and Cristos were still wearing their wedding rings and she was more mixed up than ever. Would the evening involve more fake embraces and fake kisses? Each time she remembered how happy she'd been with him, she wanted those kisses to be real.

Cristos had not been back to 'their' room since he'd left that morning and it felt very empty without him. She closed her eyes to try to recapture his presence, his scent, but there was only the lemon and thyme tang of the resort shampoo she had just used in the shower. She looked over to that big, empty bed. Forced herself not to walk over to it. *Not* a good idea to go lie down on 'his' side, put her head on his pillow and try and breathe in his essence. Though she couldn't promise she wouldn't do that after the party when she climbed between those cold solitary sheets.

She wondered what his grandparents would make of Cristos bunking down on their sofa. Penelope would probably be delighted. And yet... Penelope was turning out to be not quite the witch Hayley had thought her. As evidenced by the gorgeous shoes Cristos's grandmother had loaned her for the evening.

She was going to the party in borrowed finery. Dell had rummaged through her wardrobe to find her a stylish dress in just the right size, elegant with a nod to retro. The fitted bodice with a scoop neck enhanced her curves and revealed a glimpse of cleavage; the tight, three-quarter-length sleeves were perfect for the cold weather, and the skirt was cut in a slim line with a split at the back. It made her wiggle when she walked.

'Perfect for Valentine's,' Dell had enthused. 'It really suits you.'

Trouble was, the dress was pink. And Hayley never wore pink. She'd always wanted to be taken seriously in her career in a man's world. Petite, blonde and dressed in pink just didn't cut it.

But to refuse Dell's kind offer would have been exceedingly impolite. 'Thank you, Dell,' she'd said as she'd hugged her new friend. 'It's a lovely dress.' Besides, it wasn't a bright candy pink, it was more a soft dusky rose. And looked way better on than she would have imagined. Maybe she should rethink pink.

But she only had knee-length daytime boots with her. And Dell's shoes were too big to borrow. That was where Penelope, who had the same size feet as Hayley, had come to the rescue. She'd insisted Hayley borrow a pair of smart, pewter-coloured stilettos subtly adorned with anthracite-like beads across the pointed toes. 'I brought an extra pair with me for the ceremony,' Penelope had explained. They'd fitted perfectly and looked fabulous with the dress.

She'd just slipped into the shoes ready to go downstairs. She pointed her foot in front of her to better admire them. These were not old lady shoes. Hayley had lived in Milan long enough to recognise them as Italian designer. She had thanked Penelope with genuine delight.

But she'd fussed around with the dress and shoes long enough. Her hair and make-up were fine too. Luckily she'd had some basic make-up packed in her handbag—for a final touch up after the boat ride before she'd faced Cristos yesterday for the first time in so long.

Now it was time to head down to the party. If she was late, she would only draw attention to herself and she had no desire to be conspicuous. It was bad enough knowing she'd be entering a room where everyone knew each other and where they all were, in one way or the other, curious about her.

She picked up the small purse Dell had loaned her and click-clacked in the stilettos across the marble floor to the door. As she did so there was a knock on the door. Cristos.

'Are you decent?' he called as she slid open the security lock.

'If your definition of "decent" includes a pink frock, then I'm decent enough.' This was a game they'd used to play. The favoured answer had been: *No, I'm indecently naked and what are you going to do about it?* Hardly appropriate on this occasion. But how much fun their inappropriate, private times had been.

Hayley had to brace herself against the wall against a paralysing wave of sadness for all they'd lost. The fun— that was what had gone first. The love had dissipated more slowly.

Her heart kicked up a beat as she opened the door. Wearing black jeans and a black linen shirt, with his black hair and his jaw already shadowed, Cristos's dark-lashed eyes blazed green, the only colour in a gloriously dark image. He'd starred in a magazine campaign once where the page was printed in black and white, the exception being his extraordinary eyes. Here was the commercial come to life and she swooned over it.

She stared at him, unable to move, unable to say anything, overcome again by that yearning she was powerless to control. Never could she want another man the way she wanted him, had always wanted him.

It's just sex, it's just sex, she chanted to herself in time to the frantic thudding of her heart.

Did he guess?

He didn't say anything, just looked at her in return, that green gaze taking in her appearance from her hair—which she suspected he didn't like cut so short—right down to the tip of his grandmother's shoes. He used to look at her like that just before he was about to kiss her.

Her breath quickened and her lips parted as if of their own volition. *Yes!* But he stepped back and the moment was broken. She found her voice, forced it to stay steady. 'Did you come to check on me?'

'It would be expected that I escort my wife into the party,' he said.

'Of course,' she said.

'I've never seen you wear pink,' he said. 'It suits you, your skin, your eyes.' His voice broke, perhaps from the same effort she was making to ignore the sexual hum between them. 'You look beautiful. You have never been invisible to me. It's unbearable that you should ever have thought that true. Unbearable you should think it now.'

'I... I...' She didn't know what to say to him.

For a long moment, his gaze connected with hers and she could not look away. He reached out his hand to trace a line with his thumb from her cheekbone to the edge of her mouth. A wave of awareness swept over her, and she trembled beneath his touch.

He used to work such magic with his fingers.

'Th...thank you,' she managed to choke out.

He pushed his fingers through her hair and she closed her eyes for a moment at the bliss of it. 'Why did you cut it?'

'For a change,' she said.

Because he had loved it and she'd wanted in some way to spite him.

'When I got to Australia I wanted a new start, a new me. Also it gets very hot and humid in the summer in Sydney. It's more comfortable this short.'

'I like it,' he said.

'You do? I thought you would loathe it.'

'It was a shock, I admit. But it's cute and—'

'You know I don't like being called "cute",' she said with mock reprimand.

'If you'd let me finish, I was going to say it was cute and elegant at the same time. It suits you. So does the pink dress.'

'It's a nice dress, isn't it? Although it's not really my colour.'

'Maybe it should be. As I said, you look beautiful.'

'I'm glad you think so.'

He looked down. 'Are those my grandmother's shoes you're wearing? Surely not?'

'She loaned them to me.'

'Really? She has quite the shoe collection. A friend of hers owns an upscale shoe store and she gets them at a discount. I can't believe she loaned them to you. That's quite an honour.'

'I know. First the cheese pie and now Italian shoes. I'm wondering what's going on when I know she hates me.'

'She never really knew you.'

'You mean she never gave me a chance.'

'Maybe you've surprised her.' He shrugged. 'Whatever the reason, it was a long time ago. Right now I think my *yia-yia* is very impressed with you. I don't know, though, that she could actually come out and say it. Perhaps this is her way of letting you know that maybe she thinks we're not such a bad match after all.'

Her mouth twisted. 'Ironic, isn't it? Now that we're no longer a couple.'

Cristos put up his hand to stop her. 'Hayley, can we put aside all that for tonight? Let's forget our issues, forget why you're really here. Let's just enjoy this party. Have fun. You used to like parties and Alex and Dell throw a good one. Besides, the weather might lift in the morning and you'll be gone and we won't see each other again.'

It was what she wanted—or at least what she'd thought she'd wanted—but she felt as though his words had turned into frosty shards, like the icicles that hung from the windows, to pierce her heart.

'You mean we should celebrate the end of our marriage?'

His brow furrowed. 'I don't see it as something to celebrate. But since yesterday everything has been turned upside down and I don't know what's normal or not. If you like, you can call it our own private divorce party while the others are celebrating Valentine's.'

'That's awful. No. We can celebrate Valentine's too and remember—'

'How we were once happy, we once loved each other and we should celebrate the happy years while we mourn the end of them?'

'Okay. Yes. Good idea.' She thought it was a terrible idea. She wanted to cry rather than act as if she were having a ball.

'C'mon. I'm going to a party with a girl who looks delectable in a pink dress and my grandmother's shoes.'

'And I'm going with The Sexiest Man in Europe—'

He groaned. 'Can you please not call me that?'

'Who…who used to be my best friend.' Her voice trailed away.

He was silent for a long moment. 'And who will be your friend for one more night,' he said, his voice husky.

She forced a smile; if she didn't she would break down into sobs. 'Right. Let's get on with it, shall we?'

'It's party time.' He cleared his throat and she could see it was an effort for him to keep up the jolly pretence.

Why had they hurt each other so much?

'Is there anything you need from the room before we go?' she asked.

'No,' he said. 'I'll stay on my grandparents' sofa tonight.'

'You'd better remember to pretend to snore if you're going to go with the I-kicked-you-out-of-our-room story.'

'I'll do that,' he said, making a snoring noise that made her smile. Her smile turned into a smirk and he immediately picked up on it. 'What's that for?'

'If my own grandparents are anything to go by, it will be the old people doing the snoring. Hope you've got some earplugs.'

He rolled his eyes. 'Can we not even think about that?' He took her arm. 'Let's go or we'll be late. Are you ready?'

'I think so,' she said, drawing out the words, narrowing her eyes.

He gave a mock patient sigh she recognised of old. 'You're not going to turn back as soon as we get to the elevator because you suddenly remembered you need to go to the bathroom? Or want to fill your water bottle?'

She raised her eyebrows. 'Would I do that?'

'You know you would. Why do you think I came to get you five minutes earlier than I needed to? Just like I always did.'

Hayley laughed but her heart felt as if it were bleeding. Those private little rituals of a long-time couple. She'd forgotten how comfortable she had felt with them. She had always checked to see if he'd shaved properly; he'd often miss a little patch of those dark bristles on the underside of his chin. If she reached up to look now, to trail her fingers over his skin, she'd probably break down. Or maybe he'd managed so long without her he didn't need her to check for him.

The advantage of no one knowing her in Australia was they took her at face value. The disadvantage was that no one really knew her. But then no one had ever known her better than Cristos. Or so she'd thought.

'I'm not taking a water bottle to a party. But come to think of it, I do need to touch up my lipstick.'

He made a big exaggerated groan. 'Be quick, will you?' Just as he'd always said.

'Kidding,' she said. 'I just wanted to make you bite. Like you always did.'

He laughed. Then took her by surprise with a swift, hard kiss on her mouth. 'Now you do need to fix your lipstick but I'm not going to let you. C'mon, let's go party.'

For the last time.

CHAPTER ELEVEN

CRISTOS WANTED TO rip off the masks he felt obligated to wear and enjoy without pretence the company of his wife while he still had her by his side. But he was caught between two masks that were becoming increasingly suffocating.

To his family and friends, he presented a united front with the woman who had left him and had put him through the humiliating experience of not being able to find her. The masquerade of playing reconciling husband and wife had been his idea, intended only for the duration of Alex and Dell's celebrations. He had not anticipated the charade extending the way it had because of the extreme weather. The more Cristos and Hayley acted as husband and wife, the more his family and friends believed in it—and the more they welcomed her as part of the family. It would be awkward when she left.

The second, increasingly uncomfortable mask was the one he wore when he was alone with Hayley. He could not reveal to anyone—least of all to her—that she still had immense power to wound him and how spending so much time with her was a constant stab to his heart.

She was different but still the Hayley he had signed up to for a lifetime of commitment. He'd agreed to a civilised, getting-to-know-each-other-again way to spend her enforced time on the island. In truth, what he wanted to do was find out what the hell had gone wrong, fix it and have her back where she belonged. With him. As his wife.

But she'd made it clear she didn't want that. Didn't want him to pressure her. He couldn't very well grab her and drag her back to his cave.

As soon as he walked into the party with his beautiful girl in her pink dress on his arm, Cristos felt the change in attitude towards Hayley from the gathered family and friends. There were more warm smiles and less curious glances. As Hayley had said, it was ironic that just as they were headed for divorce, his English wife was being embraced by her Greek in-laws.

Several people approached them with the express purpose of thanking Hayley for her work on ensuring the electricity supply to the resort. Hayley, in her usual modest way, demurred, explaining it was her job to know such things but thanking them with warmth.

He was so proud of her.

And yet that pride was mingled with pain that she'd had to leave him to achieve her own career. He had not nurtured her or encouraged independence while leaving her on her own. If he had his way, things would now be very different—he worked mainly from home and the face-to-face meetings he had were brief. But her heart was barricaded against him.

Hayley looked around her. 'Dell has done a fabulous job decorating the room. How did she conjure all this up?'

His cousin and his wife had rearranged the guest living room and dining area to allow an area for dancing. Big pink and red paper hearts and bunches of red and white balloons festooned the walls. The wealthy, sophisticated guests who usually frequented Prevezzo Athina would probably be horrified at its transformation into a Greek family party venue. What did Hayley call this kind of gathering? A knees-up. But the stranded guests were hooting their approval.

Valentine's Day had never been a big thing for Cristos. He'd celebrated it because Hayley had got a kick out of it. But to him Valentine's was for single people looking for love, not for couples who celebrated their love every day. Now all the references to romance just reminded him at every turn of what he'd lost. But she was here and, as he had reminded himself many times already, that was a much better situation than the two years and five months he'd spent without her.

'Dell has kids,' he said. 'She probably has all that craft stuff stashed at home. And remember Alex was the night-club king of Sydney. He knows a thing or two about hosting a party.'

'They've done a great job, especially considering the circumstances.'

He agreed. To have got all this together at such short notice was impressive. There was a barman serving pink and red romance-themed cocktails with names like Love Bite and Kiss on the Lips, as well as champagne. A young DJ with a hipster beard, who was the boyfriend of someone's niece, was in charge of the music. Heart-shaped hors d'oeuvres were circulating on trays to a roomful of guests determined to have a good time.

Including Cristos.

He was just about to suggest to Hayley that they dance when his grandmother came over to greet them. She was not, he was relieved to see, accompanied by the ever-present Arianna. He was not in the slightest bit interested in hooking up with his childhood friend. He'd thought it was incredibly bad form of Arianna to ogle him in the presence of his wife, with the implicit approval of his grandmother, and he'd done his best to avoid her.

But tonight Penelope's attention had switched to Hayley. She stood back at arm's length and critically surveyed his wife's outfit, finally giving it the thumbs up. 'Very nice,' she said.

'I'm grateful to Dell for the dress. But it's the shoes that make it, don't you think?' said Hayley. Bravo to his wife, who had no cause to like Penelope, for playing along with her game.

'I think so too,' said Penelope, preening at the compliment to her taste.

Hayley pointed her foot out in front of her. 'These shoes make me feel like Cinderella.' With his *yia-yia* as the fairy godmother? Cristos supposed stranger things had happened.

'You must have them,' Penelope said immediately. 'To keep, I mean.'

'Really?' said Hayley with genuine surprise. 'But I couldn't—'

His grandmother threw out her hands in a dismissive gesture. 'I have bunions that make these narrow shoes uncomfortable. I've only worn them once. They are yours now.'

'Are you sure?' Hayley asked. 'They're designer shoes and—'

Cristos nudged her. 'Thank you, *Yia-yia*. It's very kind of you,' he said. He nudged Hayley again.

Hayley leaned across and kissed Penelope on each cheek. '*Efcharisto poli*—thank you very much *Pentherl* Penelope.'

Penelope laughed. 'You called me your mother-in-law when I am your grandmother-in-law.'

Hayley flushed. 'I stand corrected.'

'It's no matter,' Penelope said. Her eyes clouded. 'I have been mother to Cristos since he was fourteen years old so you can think of me as your mother-in-law. I would like that. Or you can call me *Yia-yia*.'

After Penelope left them Cristos rolled his eyes. 'I think the unthinkable has happened. The matchmaker has reversed her decision—it will never be official, of course, but you've won her over, Hayley.'

'How?'

'By being your own sweet self. By pitching in and helping whenever you had the opportunity. Finally, she has respected my choice of bride.'

'Which isn't really valid any more, is it?' she whispered. 'She'll hate me more than ever when I leave.'

'I doubt that. Besides, you won't be here to worry about it.'

'But you will,' she said.

Worrying about his grandmother's reaction would be the least of his problems when he had to say goodbye for the last time to the wife he still wanted. But he didn't let his mask slip and let her know how he really felt.

It wasn't just Cristos's grandmother who welcomed her, the whole family embraced her and Hayley was surprised how good it felt. Thank heaven she'd made an effort to learn Greek when she'd first met Cristos. Her language skills were rudimentary at best but people seemed delighted she'd made the effort. Then proceeded to chat in what was usually excellent English.

The only exception was a brief and rather unpleasant encounter with the woman who had been staring so lustfully at Cristos the day before when they were told about the storm. Thankfully Dell had seen what was happening and come over to rescue her.

Hayley told Dell about Penelope's gift of the shoes. 'That was nice of her. I'm so pleased you're getting on well with Penelope. She's a real friend to me, was wonderful from the word go. Wait until you and Cristos start a family—you'll never have to worry about a babysitter.'

Hayley tried to smile but she knew it came out as a poor imitation. She couldn't bear to think about babies and Cristos in the same thought. Dell misinterpreted her expression. 'Sorry. Silly of me. Of course you won't be living here. I guess you'll live in Cristos's apartment in Athens? Or maybe London?'

'We…er…haven't really got that far yet.'

'Of course, he could move to Sydney to be with you. I hope not. I mean, not that I don't love Sydney. It's home. But it's too far away from us here. I hope you stay in Europe. You know I love Cristos to pieces—as a cousin, of course—and I think you and I are friends already.'

'Of course, we are,' said Hayley. She'd liked Dell immediately.

'Keep that in mind, won't you?' said Dell. 'About us being friends, I mean.' She hugged her and Hayley hugged her back with genuine feeling.

'I most certainly will,' she said. 'And thanks again for the dress.'

'You're welcome,' said Dell. 'Please keep it. Now I've seen how great you look in it, I probably won't wear it again.' She patted her hips. 'By the time I shift this baby weight the dress will be out of fashion. Besides, I can't be outdone by Penelope, much as I love her.'

'You're too generous,' Hayley said, touched almost to tears. 'I love the dress. Thank you.' This particular shade of pink was growing on her.

'Think of your friend Dell when you wear it and I'll be happy.'

Hayley hugged her again. 'I see Alex beckoning you,' she said, looking over Dell's shoulder.

'He wants to dance. Alex was such a party boy before we met. I had to have dance lessons to keep up with him.'

Dell headed off to her husband. He swung her up in his arms and Dell laughed. Their love and joy in each other shone from them. When did that joy start to fade from her love for Cristos?

What would it take to fan it back to life?

The music switched to a Latin beat and within minutes Dell and Alex were dancing the salsa, dipping and twirling and undulating to the infectious beat. Hayley's feet started to tap and her body to sway.

'They look good, but are they as good as we were?' Cristos's voice came from behind her.

'I very much doubt it,' she said. 'We were the best.'

At Durham, she'd dragged him along to salsa-dancing classes not long after they'd met. He'd turned out to have amazing rhythm and style and had been very soon by far the best male dancer in the class.

Now he handed her a cocktail, a very pink cocktail speared with a red cherry on a toothpick. 'The mixologist behind the bar—'

'The *what*?'

'That's what he called himself. He offered me a Lady in Red. I asked him to make me a Lady in Pink, just for you.'

'How gallant.' She sipped at the frothy pink confection. 'Very nice, and packs quite a punch. What are you drinking?' She eyed his red cocktail.

'A pomegranate martini, using pomegranates grown on the island.'

'Very Greek,' she said. 'It looks good.' In the old days, she would have leaned forward without hesitation for a sip to taste.

'He told me to come back for a Kiss on the Lips.' Hayley raised her eyebrows. 'For you,' he hastily explained. 'The drink would be for you.'

She laughed. 'I dare not ask what comes next in that sequence. Perhaps a Screaming Orga—'

Now, why had she said that?

He grinned. 'This is a family party. He did mention he had some Hanky-Panky on offer.'

Hayley spluttered on her drink. 'We might leave it at that,' she said, laughing. 'Please don't abandon me for too long when you get me my Kiss on the Lips. Dell had to rescue me from your friend Arianna.'

He frowned. 'She's really not a friend of mine. Our grandmothers were friends and as kids we got thrown together, whether I liked it or not.'

'She actually isn't very nice, you know.'

He groaned. 'Tell me something I don't know. Even as a kid she had a hard edge to her. Hence the one ill-advised date.'

'You must have given her hope of some kind. She asked me had I left you because you were gay or did you leave me because I wasn't woman enough for you.'

Now it was Cristos's turn to splutter into his drink. He cursed in Greek. 'What did you say? I would have—'

'I can't remember the exact words but I think she got the message that it was none of her business.'

'Where is she now?'

'Diagonal corner, glaring at us. I think she's had quite a bit to drink.'

'She can't speak to you like that,' he said grimly. 'I'm going to—'

Hayley had always loved it when Cristos went all super-protective on her. But a confrontation with his unwanted admirer, who also happened to be a family friend, might not be the best idea. Something needed to be done to defuse the situation.

She put down her cocktail. 'Maybe a kiss on the lips might be a good idea right now.'

'But you haven't finished your—'

She looked up at him. 'I meant a real kiss on the lips,

not the cocktail. You know, to show her that it was for neither of those reasons we split.'

Cristos stared at her for a long moment, disbelief in his
eyes, then a slow smile spread across his face. 'With the
greatest of pleasure,' he said.

She'd spoken more in jest but suddenly Hayley wanted
Cristos to kiss her for real. No pretence. No hidden agenda.
Just Cristos kissing her as he had so many times before.
She wound her arms around his neck, tilted her head back
in invitation. 'C'mon, kiss on the lips.'

His lips brushed hers gently at first, then with more
pressure, his mouth firm and warm. She kissed him back
with an enthusiasm that wasn't in the slightest bit staged.
'More,' she murmured against his mouth. 'We're lovebirds, remember.'

He needed no further urging and he claimed her mouth
in a full-on passionate kiss, the tip of his tongue teasing
hers. His kiss felt familiar, yet thrillingly new and she relaxed into the pleasure of it.

The public kiss, staged for the benefit of a mean-spirited
woman who showed no respect for a man's wedding band,
should have been enough but Hayley's body urged more.
She wanted tongues and teeth and moans and sighs and
that delicious shiver of want rippling through her body that
a kiss from Cristos could always evoke. She wanted more
than his kiss; she ached for the pleasure of his touch on
her body, his hands running down the sides of her breasts.
She wanted—

But they were at a family party on full display in front
of his grandparents, cousins, friends and a number of kids.
They couldn't continue this for longer than would consti-
tute appropriate under such circumstances—even for a
married couple.

But it was long enough and passionate enough to bring

all the old feelings rushing back. And she kissed him back wholeheartedly and without reserve.

Finally he murmured against her mouth. 'That should do the trick.' But by then she scarcely remembered the original purpose of the kiss. She just wanted more. Perhaps it was the Lady in Pink loosening her inhibitions. Perhaps it was the build-up of tension between her and Cristos since she'd first sighted him on the clifftop outside the chapel. The unacknowledged desire that had never gone away. She strained against him, breast to chest, thigh to thigh, but even through the fog of want and unanswered questions common sense prevailed.

'Yes,' she said breathlessly, pulling away from him. She looked around him to where she'd last seen the woman who had given her a most unpleasant few moments. 'She's turned her back on us and is walking away.'

'I think that's the last trouble you'll get from her,' he said.

'As long as she doesn't trouble you after…after I go.'

He put his fingers on her lips to stop her. 'Didn't I ask you not to talk about that? Tonight, it's just us partying and enjoying ourselves.'

'Sure,' she murmured. He obviously hadn't been as affected by the kiss as she had, although she noticed he was having to control his breathing. What could she do to let him know she wanted more, wanted *him*?

He took her hand, tugged her towards him. 'Come and dance with me. Ever since I saw Alex and Dell burning up the floor I've had a strangely competitive urge to show them what we can do. Are you with me?'

She took a deep breath to try and gather her thoughts, still her racing heart. 'Oh, yes. May the best couple win. And may that couple be us.'

'That's my girl,' he said.

They stood facing each other, waiting for the beat to

start. Hayley felt a ripple of nerves. They'd danced so many times together in the past—would it be the same?

He swung her into the salsa. Immediately they found their rhythm. Salsa was fast, energetic, sensual with lots of hip swaying and turning, improvised lifts and shoulder shimmies. Their dance teacher had told them it had roots in Latin dancing like mambo and cha-cha but was also influenced by Afro-Caribbean rhythms. Hayley had done ballet and jazz for years and enjoyed them but it wasn't until she'd joined the dance club at uni that she'd got into salsa and loved it. But she'd never had a partner like Cristos. He was a superb dancer and she knew she was good too. Together they'd been sensational.

He'd started classes with her at Durham before they were married. Latin dance was sensual and passionate; dancing with him had been like extended foreplay, fully clothed. But she'd been determined to wait to make love until after they were husband and wife. She had wanted him so desperately, and he her, that she sometimes wondered if they'd got married young simply so they could have sex. But she dismissed the thought. How could she separate the lust and love and sheer enjoyment of a man's company? It had always been more than lust between them.

Back then they'd been perfectly matched as dancing partners. Now they slipped right into the steps as though it had been days rather than years since they'd danced together. She'd prefer a dress that wasn't as tight, and dancing shoes, but the tighter skirt gave more sway to her hips and she managed just fine. Cristos all in black was sensational; she found herself gasping at how sexy he was when he danced, how utterly beautiful. They were so in tune when they danced. As they had been in bed.

What would it be like to make love with her husband again?

They danced alongside Dell and Alex. 'Are you chal-

lenging us to a dance-off?' Alex called to his cousin. 'If
so, bring it on.'

The two men threw their partners into ever more complex moves. Soon the other dancers had melted away from
the dance floor as the two couples danced. Alex and Dell
were good, very good. But Hayley thought Cristos was
the superior male dancer and she was a trained dancer
so that gave them an advantage. The observers cheering
them on from the sidelines seemed to give them louder
cheers but Alex and Dell were beloved and it was, after
all, their party.

The dance-off was ultimately declared a draw, which
was the only possible result. 'Although we really were
the better dancers,' her competitive husband whispered
in her ear.

Hayley could barely answer him. Dancing with Cristos
had the same effect on her it always had. She felt flushed,
exhilarated, breathless and more turned on than she would
admit to from being held against his hard, strong body,
pulsing her hips against his, feigning looks of passion that
were anything but feigned. Excited because she realised
his looks weren't feigned either.

But then she was whirled across to partner Alex while
Cristos danced with Dell for a final salsa. The music
switched to something more sedate and she found herself dancing in turn with the architect cousin from Athens, Alex's doctor father from Sydney, and finally her
grandfather-in-law, Stavros, who tested her on the Greek
he had taught her while they'd been packing away the outdoor furniture before the storm. She found she enjoyed
the big Greek family celebration more than she would
ever have imagined.

There was a short break for refreshments when the DJ
switched to traditional Greek music. 'Are the men going
to dance?' she asked Cristos, now back by her side.

He nodded. 'The men in our family enjoy *horos*. The traditional dances of these islands are always part of our celebrations.'

'And the women? Do they dance too?'

'Of course. But not tonight.'

'Will you wear traditional costume?'

'At other parties, yes. But this is an impromptu party. No one would have come prepared.'

'Shame. I would have liked to see you in it.'

When the men started dancing to the infectious music, Hayley couldn't keep her eyes off Cristos. His natural rhythm and grace made even the simplest of steps look accomplished.

Dell was beside her, her eyes on her beloved Alex. 'They say some of these traditional dances started way back when as an innocuous way to flirt with women,' she said.

'I can see that,' Hayley replied, mesmerised by the sight of her husband as he dipped and swayed and turned in step with the other men in the traditional dances, laughing, happy, relaxed. She'd been kidding herself the whole time she'd been in Australia that she could forget him. And it had been a battle with herself to channel her thoughts towards divorce since the moment she'd first seen him again at the chapel. It wasn't that she was falling in love with him all over again.

She had never stopped loving him.

Finally the dancing ended and the guests started to dissipate and head to their rooms. Hayley stood about, uncertain of what to do next. Cristos had stated in no uncertain terms that he would not be sharing a room with her tonight. Yet they needed to keep up a pretence of unity.

Cristos was talking with an older man she had scarcely spoken to. She walked up to her husband, planted a kiss on his cheek and said she was going up to their room and she'd see him when he came up. It was a typical husband-and-wife exchange, words only meant to maintain the illusion of their marriage, and she thought she handled it well. But it took a real effort to keep her voice steady and light when she really wanted to beg him to come to her bed.

When she got there, she moped around the empty room. Her footsteps echoed on the marble floor, emphasising her aloneness. It was quiet outside and still. No new snow had fallen since dinner time. There was a chance this might be her last night on the island. She felt immeasurably sad at the thought of the divorce papers still packed away in her handbag.

She showered and changed into her pyjamas. They were very nice pyjamas and had cost an extraordinary number of euros. But she wouldn't take them back with her to Sydney. Wearing them would only evoke unwanted memories of her time on Kosmimo.

Thankfully her life in Sydney was so different it held no memories of Cristos. She would be able to put this episode behind her as if it were some kind of dream. Scratch that. Not dream. Nightmare. Because she had a niggling feeling that this night—the party, the kiss, the dancing—had been the last chance to put things right with Cristos.

She was brushing her teeth when she heard the knock on her door. At this time of night she thought she must have imagined it. But it came again.

Without thinking twice, she opened the door. There was no stranger danger here. But that was no stranger standing there. *Sheepish* wasn't ever a word she would have applied to her six-foot-two dark-haired Greek god of a husband. But that was the word that immediately sprung to mind.

'Cristos. Aren't you meant to be with your grandparents?'

He shrugged. And behind the sheepishness she could see a hint of devilment in his green eyes. 'They kicked me out. No sofa for this bad grandson tonight. Stavros told me to get upstairs and fix whatever I did wrong to my lovely wife.'

CHAPTER TWELVE

COULD SHE HAVE a one-night stand with her hot husband? With hungry eyes, Hayley drank in the sight of Cristos as he stood at the threshold of her room, his broad shoulders and powerful body framed by the doorway. She wanted him so much she felt giddy.

He looked vaguely dishevelled in the sexiest possible way, his jaw darkly shadowed, his eyes hooded, his mouth in a half-smile. The fact he looked uncertain of his reception made him seem even more appealing. Desire for him rippled through her.

The only man she had ever wanted.

She wanted to grab him and haul him to the bed. Or to the sofa or the rug or even up against the wall. They'd made deliriously exciting love in all those places.

Just one more time with him.

'Come in,' she said, her voice tight with pent-up longing. *Now.*

Her husband stepped across the threshold. She kicked the door shut behind him. 'But you're not sleeping on this sofa either,' she said.

His dark eyebrows rose. But she didn't give him an opportunity to question her. Instead she wound her arms around his neck and looked up at him with what she hoped he would recognise as blatant invitation. 'You're in the bed with me. And not with a row of pillows or any other barrier between us.' She suffered a momentary loss of bravado. 'Er…that is, if you want to be with me.'

His eyes narrowed in the way she had always found unbearably sexy. 'I never stopped wanting you, *koukla*.' His voice was deep and husky and she thrilled to his words.

He dipped his head and kissed her. In her bare feet she had to stretch up on tiptoe to meet his mouth with hers. She surrendered with a sigh to the bliss of his tongue stroking the seam of her lips, of her tongue welcoming his. *At last a proper kiss.* Not the fake, for-show kind that had been so deeply disturbing and unsatisfying. The kind of kiss with Cristos she remembered, so familiar yet so new and different.

How she had missed him.

So many kisses given and received over several years of marriage. There was the sweet, triumphant kiss of commitment on their wedding day; the quick friendly kiss to let her know he was home; the comforting kiss when something had gone wrong and a kiss was just the thing to help; and then the kiss like this one. A kiss of hunger unleashed, of rapidly rising passion, a no-going-back kiss that was the prelude to the kind of lovemaking that would have her almost fainting with pleasure—both the taking of it and the giving of it.

She clung to him, weak with excitement and arousal as her tongue answered his, as she pressed her body close to his, breasts to solid male chest, hips to the hardness of his thighs. Her murmurs of pleasure were answered by more pressure, more urgency, his groan of impatience. His hands slid down her shoulders to tear open her pyjama top, the buttons bouncing on the marble floor. At last he cupped her breasts, stroking and playing with her nipples, already erect and aching for his touch.

It felt so good.

She slid her hands down his back to tug his shirt free from his trousers, slid them up to caress his back, smooth skin over rippling muscles.

At last.

She didn't have to haul him to the bed. He picked her up as if she weighed nothing and carried her there, breaking the kiss only for as long as it took to place her down then join her. He slid the silky pyjama top over her shoulders and down her arms until it lay next to her and her breasts were bared. She raised her hips to help him tug her pyjama pants down and toss them on the floor.

'I liked my lady in pink,' he murmured, his eyes narrowed and intent as he stroked the length of her body, first with his eyes then with his large, warm hands. 'But I so prefer my lady in nothing.'

'Two can play at that,' she said, laughing, as she fumbled with the buttons of his shirt, quickly rid him of his clothes. Then there was no more talk, just a slow burn of moans and sighs as they explored each other and made up for lost time.

Cristos had fallen into the deep sleep of a sexually satisfied, contented man. Contented because he had made love with the wife who had been missing from his life for so long, but whom he had never stopped wanting. Satisfied because they had lost count of the times they had brought each other to the ultimate peaks of pleasure.

The early-morning light filtering through the shutters woke him. For that split second between sleep and awareness he wasn't sure where he was. Then he remembered and a great surge of exultation had him wide awake. *Hayley.* This was not one of the many dreams of her that had haunted him for so long. She was real.

His wife lay beside him, her head nestled against his shoulder, one arm flung across his chest, one leg entwined with his. Her cheeks were flushed, her mouth swollen to a pout from his kisses. In places her tender skin was reddened with beard rash. He felt not a jot of regret. He had been tender with her but they had kissed and made love with mutual enthusiasm. His beard had left its mark on her and not just on her face—he had kissed her all over. He was glad he had marked her. *She was his.*

Her fine, short hair was tousled and he gently smoothed it back into place with his hand. He breathed in the intoxicating scent of her, of *them*. Risked dropping a gentle kiss on her temple.

She stirred. Cristos held his breath. He wanted to prolong this quiet moment of union. Just he and Hayley together as they should be, husband and wife. Because he knew it couldn't last. Making love hadn't solved their problems. Might even have caused more.

He didn't want this to be the end of it for him and Hayley. A night together for old times' sake and then they both moved on. If she went back to Sydney—perhaps tomorrow, maybe even as soon as today—he wanted to go with her. He never wanted to let her go.

However, if there were to be any chance of moving forward together, they had to revisit the past. And he did not imagine it would be anything other than a painful journey. For each of them. But he had to know the truth about why she had left him and made it impossible for him to find her. In turn, he had to strip himself of the masks he had variously worn and present his real face to her. To right the wrongs he had done her.

After that, he hoped they could find their way back to each other. He imagined a renewal-of-vows ceremony like the one Alex and Dell had just taken part in. Perhaps a service where the church blessed their union as his traditional grandparents had so wished.

Or not.

Cristos didn't want to think about the *or not* option. He did not want to give up on Hayley. He wanted to right the wrongs of the past and have his wife back by his side. This time for the rest of their lives. The thought of growing old with her made him smile—she would be a cute, feisty old lady—and he longed for it to happen so desperately he found himself praying for the first time in many years.

His leg was starting to go numb from the pressure— light though it was—of her leg over his when finally Hayley stirred. Her eyes fluttered open, looked uncertain for a moment then widened when she realised where she was. The first expression was happiness, joy even, and as she reached out for his hand they shone a brighter shade of blue. But the joy was quickly suffused with panic and she started to edge away from him. He held her hand firm.

'Before you try to scoot away from me and go back to being ice princess Hayley, you need to tell just why you left me nearly two and a half years ago.'

She bit down on her lower lip. 'You know, I've told you—'

'Not all of it. There are gaps in your story, *koukla*. Gaps I've puzzled over how to fill for too long.'

He pulled her close to him, loving the slide of her nakedness against his. His arm secured her close to him.

'You know all you need to know.'

Her voice quivered and he knew she wasn't telling him the truth. *Why?* He thought he'd gone through every possible scenario in his mind but had never reached a viable conclusion.

'No, I don't know,' he said. 'Those last weeks, those last days, you need to fill me in. There are also things I have not told you about me that you might want to hear.'

He felt her stiffen beside him. 'Such as?'

'Things about myself I felt…ashamed to tell you.'

'What do you mean?' She twisted so she lay on her side

and her eyes met his. 'I've often felt that I don't really know you. That perhaps I never really knew you at all.'

Those blue eyes saw through him, realised the masks were there. She was, perhaps, the only person who had ever sensed there was someone different underneath.

'I always thought I knew you,' he said, not intending tit-for-tat, just telling it the way he saw it. 'It was a shock to realise I didn't. I had not imagined the Hayley I loved could be so callous.'

She gasped. 'That's very harsh.'

'That's how it felt. Complete indifference on your part to my feelings, to our marriage. Not to mention I was worried sick about you. I had questions about why you left but could never find answers—because I couldn't find you. Of course, me being away that night and leaving you alone was unforgivable. You know I will never forgive myself.'

He didn't expect her to contradict him. She nodded mutely in acknowledgment and again his anger at himself burned through him. But he would have been there afterwards for her—if he'd been given the chance.

'Losing our baby was tragic,' he said. 'With you thirteen weeks pregnant, us becoming parents was beginning to feel real. Something I really wanted. I mourned the loss too, although I never got the chance to cry with you. But other couples survive a miscarriage and go on to try again. I know you blame me for not being there—and I was at fault, more at fault than you guessed—'

Her eyes narrowed. 'So there was something—'

He gently laid his finger over her mouth. 'Let me speak, *koukla*. You never gave me the chance to speak with you about that night that tore our marriage apart. Then you ran away from me. Can you imagine how worried I was? How frantic to find you?' How like a piece of dirt on her shoe his mother had made him feel when he had arrived on their doorstep in Surrey looking for his wife.

Hayley turned away so he couldn't see her face and her voice was muffled by the pillow. She might have said she was sorry but he couldn't be sure. He put his hand on her bare shoulder, warm and soft. He never wanted to lose her again. But something poisonous had happened that night and it had festered. There could be no hope for a genuine reconciliation unless it was lanced.

Hayley turned to face him again. All colour had drained from her face. 'I only realised in these last days what it must have been like for you. I had convinced myself I hated you. My family—my parents and my sister—never told me how hard you'd tried to find me. It hurt that you'd let me go so easily.'

'I assure you I did everything in my power to find you. I had lost my world. Not just the child I wanted so much, but you. The wife I adored.'

'Why did my parents—?'

'I think we know the answer to that,' he said. There had been a distinct note of triumph in her mother's voice at their last encounter. But he had not given up.

'I didn't know. But at first I wouldn't have cared if you were hurting. In truth, I wanted you to hurt. After a while I convinced myself you were off with another woman. Probably Ginny. Living happily ever after with a tall, long-legged model.'

To hear such bitter words spoken, not with venom but with sadness, was devastating to him. 'I can't believe you thought that,' he said. 'That you ever thought I wanted anyone but you. From the moment I saw you in that pub in Durham there was only ever you.'

He turned her so that she was forced to face him. She sat up, blushed, clutched the sheets to cover her nudity. She *blushed*. After all the ways he'd made love to her and she to him over the last hours, and she blushed. He found it delightful.

'I have to go to the bathroom,' she said.

For one hideous moment he thought she would go into the bathroom and not come back. She would somehow escape and find her way out of the resort and onto a waiting boat and he would never see her again. He gritted his teeth to restore sanity to his thoughts. There was no trap-door in the bathroom, no secret network of tunnels under the building. It was just his imagination running crazy, as it had when he'd feared something was wrong with her.

Until first her sister and then her mother had told him Hayley was alive and well but just didn't want to see him. He had thought he'd heard her mother mutter, *Can't you get that into your thick Greek head?* But perhaps that had been an echo of his own thoughts. Many times he had be-rated himself for continuing the search for a woman who didn't want him.

Now he watched as she made a dash for the bathroom. Her back view was as beautiful as her front, slender with a narrow waist and curving hips too wide to make her a model but just right for a sensuous woman who was everything he'd ever wanted. He loved the new way her hair feathered to the nape of her neck, soft and fine. He had enjoyed kissing her there.

She came back with a white hotel towel wrapped around her from her chest to her thighs. He was sad as he could never have enough of admiring her body. But perhaps it was for the best as he would only want to make love to her again and there were things that had to be said. He pulled the sheet over himself and sat up straight.

'We need to talk,' he said. He'd always found that an ominous set of words when someone said it to him. But in this case it was true. He was no closer to understand-ing what had gone wrong.

She carried two glasses of water and handed him one without speaking. They'd always joked that making love was thirsty work. He wanted that ease between them back. He wanted the laughter. Most of all he wanted the love. He had never stopped loving her. He had to give his everything to this last-ditch effort to mend things between them.

Hayley sat on the edge of the bed next to him, modestly tugging the towel into place. He felt at a disadvantage reclining against the pillows and sat up so they could face each other as equals.

'Why were you so concerned about Ginny?' he said. He wished he'd never met the woman—although he wouldn't have made so much money so quickly without her.

'We seemed to bump into her more than could be put down to coincidence within the circles we moved in. I could see she wanted you, and she was the kind of woman who dismissed me with indifference. As if I were beneath her tall, skinny attention. Even though she believed I was your girlfriend, if not your wife.'

'I didn't know that,' he said.

'Why would you?' she said. 'What was she to you?'

'I was doing business with her.'

Hayley took a sharp intake of breath. 'So, I wasn't wrong that there was something going on between you two.'

He put up his hand. 'Strictly business.'

He hadn't realised until he was well into the deal how predatory Ginny was. How at one stage she'd intimated that *he* was part of the bargain. He had quickly disillusioned her about that—he loved his girlfriend, he'd told her, choking on the lie 'girlfriend' when he'd proudly wanted to proclaim Hayley as his wife.

'What kind of business?'

'She and her brother are both very smart people. They were developing a shopping comparison app. I invested in it. It was a brilliant concept, just right for the time.'

She frowned. 'You didn't tell me.'

'I didn't want to concern you.'

'That's rubbish. Surely any business deal you were doing was my concern. We were married. And I thought we shared everything.'

This was it. The make it or break it. The kicker that might cause her to walk right out of the room and his life. No need for escape routes through the bathroom. 'I didn't want you to know I was a gambler. And I had put a considerable chunk of our savings at risk.'

He couldn't meet her eyes, dreading what he might see there.

CHAPTER THIRTEEN

HAYLEY STARED AT CRISTOS, unable to comprehend what she was hearing. 'What do you mean?' Her husband, now her lover again, was suddenly a stranger to her. Even though he lay naked in her bed. Cristos a gambler?

What else had he been hiding from her?

She swallowed hard against her disbelief and disappointment. 'What was it? Horses? Casino? Online gaming?'

He shook his head. 'Not that kind of gambling. I told you about my trading stocks and shares at university, backing the small apps my fellow students were developing. Once I started to earn big money with modelling, I upped the stakes and took that a step further. Investing a lot more money in untried businesses where I saw potential. With a lot more risk.'

Hayley frowned. 'I'm not sure what you're getting at. Are you talking something dishonest?' Fear grabbed at her with icy claws. Cristos a criminal? She couldn't bear the thought. 'Something illegal?'

He shook his head. 'I'm talking one hundred per cent legitimate investment. But not of the blue-chip kind— think the total opposite of blue-chip investment. Where the risks are so much higher.' There was an edge of excitement to his voice.

'You sound as though you enjoyed it.'

'I did. I do. When the odds are stacked against you, when it's a bigger leap of faith than you thought yourself capable of, when there's a very real risk you could lose everything on something as intangible as an idea to be thrown out into cyberspace—there's something heart-stopping about it. That's the kind of gambling I risked our savings on.'

The feeling that she had never known this man intensified. 'How? I would have known. We had a joint bank account.'

'Confession time,' he said, his green eyes sober. She steeled herself for his answer. 'I still had my own account. I diverted some of my earnings into it. You never saw them. That was my seed money.'

'But you were earning so much.' More money than two young people could have dreamed of at that time.

'More than you knew.'

She clutched at her heart. 'I can't believe you did that. Why didn't you tell me?'

'Two reasons. The first was that I was ashamed to be a gambler. I was doing it for our future. But I didn't want to look diminished in your eyes. Be someone less than you thought me.'

'Less? Why would you think that? My father is a banker. He used to say that the money market was just one big gambling den. Trading on currency, trading on futures, on the price of commodities. Not the kind of desperate gambling that's an addiction, an illness, that ruins people's lives. That wasn't you, was it, Cristos?'

She held her breath for his answer. He gave it to her immediately. 'No. That wasn't me. The risks I take are informed by business savvy and market awareness as well as gut instinct. I didn't do that Master's degree for nothing.'

She let out her breath on a sigh of relief.

'But it was my father.'

'*What?*' Was there to be one unexpected blow after another?

'He was the kind of gambler that you described. But he wasn't a clever gambler. He lost more than he ever won.'

'Gambling—the sure way to get nothing for something,' she said slowly. 'I don't know where that saying comes from but it seems apt.'

'You're right,' he said. 'But with my kind of gambling I've ended up way ahead.'

'But not your father.' Why hadn't he told her this before? What other secrets were there for him to spill?

'He was also a petty criminal, a grifter. Fraud. Embezzlement. Out and out theft.' Cristos spoke in a matter-of-fact way and she knew it was because he found this 'confession' so difficult. 'That's why he worked to improve his English—it made it easier to target tourists. Ripping off naïve visitors to the Greek islands was his specialty. He was handsome and charming and people believed his schemes and fabrications.'

'Cristos, I'm so sorry.' She reached out her hand to clasp his. 'When did you find out?'

'I think I always knew,' he said. His grip tightened on her hand. 'Was always aware there was something not right about our family. That my *baba* was someone I couldn't boast about like other kids did about their dads.'

Compassion for him swelled in her heart. She imagined him as an adorable little boy, feeling different and alone. 'That must have been tough for you.'

'It was much worse for my mother.'

'I can imagine. How did your mother get involved with him?' His family seemed so traditional, so straight. Now she realised in the time she'd been here no one had ever mentioned Cristos's parents. It was as if they'd been wiped from the family history.

'He was working as a barman in Nidri when he met my

mother. He conned her into falling in love with him. By the time she realised what he was, she was pregnant. She married him anyway. Soon after, they had to leave town before the bar owner discovered he'd been cheated of his profits.' He paused and her heart clenched at the anguish on his face. 'We were always having to leave town.'

'You said he was away a lot of the time. I assumed you meant on business.'

'He was in prison,' he said bluntly.

His answer was not totally unexpected, but no less shocking all the same. 'Oh, Cristos. I'm so sorry. How awful for you. And for your mother.'

'Yeah. It was.'

She could see how difficult it was for him to divulge these long-held secrets, revisit unpleasant memories.

'What did your poor mother do?'

'She would try to get work near the prison so she could visit him whenever she could. She was a nurse. Or we would go to live with my grandparents while he was doing his time. My education was interrupted. As I got older, I lived with my grandparents even when he was out so I could have some consistency at school.'

She searched his face, saw all the pent-up pain she had never before recognised. 'Cristos, why didn't you share this with me before?'

He couldn't meet her gaze. 'I was brought up to be ashamed of my father. Not to ever talk about him. To believe that my lovely mother was foolish for loving him. My mother adored him. She always went back to him no matter what. Even though she must have known his promises to change were worthless.' He sighed and Hayley wondered if he was aware of the depth of anguish he revealed. 'Another reason my family hated him is because they think she died of a broken heart after he died. His fault, of course. The diagnosis was a fast-acting cancer but to my grandparents it was because their only daughter couldn't live without her feckless husband.'

'Tragic. And horrible for you to be left without parents.' Was it surprising Penelope was so protective of her grandson? No wonder she'd been averse to hasty marriages with strangers.

Cristos took her other hand so he held both clasped in his. 'Here's the thing. The truth I struggled with as a kid—I loved him too. I couldn't help but love him although I wasn't allowed to admit it. Now I'm admitting it to you. Finally.'

'That's very sad. He was your father...you were a little kid.' In spite of all her mother's idiosyncrasies—including a blatant dislike of Cristos—Hayley loved her mother. Her father too.

'*Baba* was charming and fun and carried you along with him with his grand ideas—like a big kid himself, I suppose. I wanted to believe in him. Of course, he always disappointed me in the end. He disappointed everyone.'

Hayley thought of how Cristos had struggled to recall any simple father-son moments. No wonder, with a dad in and out of prison for much of his childhood.

'That's such a sad story, Cristos. But you could have told me. I wish you had.'

He raised his head in challenge. 'Would you have married me if you'd known my father was a jailbird?'

'Without question,' she said immediately. 'However, if you'd been the jailbird I might have thought twice.' Even so. From what Cristos had said, his father was very handsome and very charming. Like father, like son. Would she have been any more capable of resisting him than his mother had been unable to resist his father?

'I plead totally innocent on that one,' he said, raising his hand as if swearing an oath. 'My grandparents kept such a close eye on me, terrified I would turn out like my father. Any boyhood naughtiness was firmly jumped on, I assure you.'

Sitting in the bed, with a shaft of morning sun highlighting his bare shoulders, with his hair all messed and his stubble halfway to a beard, Cristos looked every inch The Sexiest Man in Europe. 'You probably look like him, don't you?'

'Yes. And I am a gambler. I tried to deny that instinct but I couldn't.'

'Though you channel it in a very different way. You also have a highly developed business sense that it seems your father lacked.'

'And an education, which he also lacked. He was determined that I would do well at school. He wanted more for me than he ever had.'

Hayley nodded thoughtfully. 'So he loved you back.'

There was a long pause before Cristos answered. 'I guess he did. So did my mother—she didn't want to leave me, she fought that cancer. And my grandparents care so much. I was lucky.'

She loved him too.

Her heart swelled with a rush of love for him.

She had never stopped loving him.

She wanted to tell him no one loved him more than she did, never had, never would. That while he wanted to protect her, she had always wanted to care for him. But this wasn't the time. If she told him she loved him she would want to kiss him. She would want to cover that handsome, beloved face with kisses, kiss all over his Greek god, perfect body. She knew what that would lead to. There would be no more talk. And they still needed to talk. *She had secrets to share too.*

'So, no one other than me knows about what you call "gambling" and what I would call "astute, high-risk investment strategy"?' She made quote marks with her fingers.

He smiled, white teeth against olive skin; dark, sexy stubble; raven-black hair, and those seductive green eyes. Her heart turned a somersault. Intense desire mixed with intense love—a potent mix.

He was still her husband.

The way she felt right now those divorce papers would never be signed. But she had to be practical. Continue the conversation. See where it led them. They might never get another chance.

'That terminology would be debatable if my grandparents, who feared my turning out like my criminal father, ever found out how I earn my living these days. Playing the stock market, trading, investing in cyber products, is too intangible for them. I got in the habit of never mentioning it.'

'That's why you never thought to mention it to me.'

'That's right.'

'Even though you were doing a deal involving a good deal of our money with a woman who made no secret about wanting you.'

He shook his head. 'She might have wanted me. Be in no doubt that I didn't want her. I made it very clear to her that I wasn't interested, that I loved you.'

'How did she take that?' Hayley still felt nauseous at the thought of the gorgeous-looking woman and her supercilious ways. But also somehow relieved to know she hadn't been imagining Ginny's interest in snagging her husband. She'd had enough other reasons at the time to question her sanity.

'Ginny threatened to pull out of the deal. It was…unpleasant to say the least. I was battling it out with her on the day you lost the baby. It's why I missed your calls. I switched off the phone so I could concentrate on salvaging the deal.'

'You were with her that day? So she wasn't lying.'

He frowned. 'What do you mean?'

'That morning, after you'd left, Ginny called our apartment. To tell you that you'd left your jacket at her hotel room the day before. She spoke to me as if I were the maid but she knew it was me and I got the message she intended. Why was your jacket in her room?'

Cristos cursed. 'I was at a business meeting in the hotel suite she shared with her brother, who'd flown in from San Francisco. I was never alone with her there. I made damn sure of that. My jacket? It was still there when I went back the next day. I was on the point of walking out when thankfully her brother saw sense and the deal went through.'

'To think I tortured myself over her. If you'd just told me—'

'I didn't want to stress you or upset you. Remember, there was a second reason I kept you in the dark.'

She frowned. 'A second reason?' Why did that sound so ominous?

Cristos chose his words carefully. He dreaded hurting his beautiful, vulnerable wife. 'This is difficult,' he said.

'I don't know what you mean by difficult. But I'm sure I can take it,' she said, obviously puzzled.

'I didn't think you could take it back then. You were too...fragile.'

She frowned. 'What do you mean?'

'You changed after you got pregnant,' he said. 'Really changed. I didn't have any experience of pregnant women. I knew about morning sickness, expected it.' But not that his sweet wife would suddenly turn irrational and aggressive and accusatory in one breath, a sobbing heap in the next.

'I didn't have morning sickness, apart from some initial queasiness.'

'No. But you got very moody.' He knew he had to be

extremely careful with his choice of words. 'I never knew what version of Hayley I'd find when I got home.'

She got up abruptly from the bed, took a few steps away from him and then turned back. 'Grumpy, suspicious, paranoid or just plain mean. Is that what you're talking about?'

He jumped up from the bed, wrapped the sheet toga-style around him. They had to be on an equal footing for this kind of conversation. 'I wouldn't put it quite like that,' he said cautiously. But she was right.

Her mouth twisted. 'You're being kind. I was up and down and all over the place. Some days when you weren't coming home I'd cry all day. Other days I stayed in bed unable to get up. I didn't really know what to expect about being pregnant. I thought all that must be normal.'

'*Koukla*, that doesn't sound right. What did your doctor say?' He should have been at the doctor's appointments with her, not away working in another city.

'The lovely *dottoressa* said I was in perfect physical health and all was progressing as it should. She spoke good English but I didn't feel I could tell her about how I was feeling. I figured it was part and parcel of being pregnant. Turns out it wasn't.'

Alarm shot through him. 'What do you mean?'

'That's the gap in the story you wondered about. Now it's my turn to share secrets. I was suffering from depression.'

'You were depressed?' He drew her into his arms, hugged her close. 'Why didn't I know?' He had let her down in so many ways.

She pulled back so she was still in the circle of his arms but could look up at him. Her face was drawn and the blue of her eyes as dull as the sea on a cloudy day. 'I don't want to go over old ground but you weren't there a lot.'

Because he'd become obsessed with accumulating wealth for her and the baby. To be the good Greek provider his father hadn't been. He'd played his cards completely wrong.

'Did the depression have anything to do with the miscarriage?' He didn't really know what were the right questions to ask. He went with asking the ones where he genuinely wanted to hear the answers.

'They don't know. Pre-natal depression is not that common apparently.'

'Pre-natal depression? If you didn't tell the doctor how you were feeling, how do you know that was the diagnosis?'

Her smile was shaky around the edges. 'I'll have to explain backwards.'

'I'm listening,' he said. And not letting her go.

'The day of the miscarriage I woke up feeling terrible, nauseous when I hadn't been feeling nauseous. I had a headache but I didn't want to take any medication. I started a row with you when you asked me what was wrong. You wanted to stay but I insisted you go. Then felt aggrieved you hadn't insisted on staying. I couldn't settle. The phone call from Ginny set me into a spin. Then in the afternoon the cramping started. I was petrified. That's when I called you the first time and kept on calling you. When you didn't answer, I called my mum. When there was blood, I called the ambulance.'

Cristos closed his eyes against the rush of guilt and regret. 'The next time I saw you was in the hospital. You'd lost the baby. I was devastated. Worried sick about you. You looked as white as the hospital sheets. You turned your head on the pillow and closed your eyes. Then mumbled something. I leaned closer. Only to hear you tell me you hated me and to go away.' He'd felt as if he'd been kicked in the gut by a gang of thugs wearing steel-capped boots.

'That was the depression speaking, even then,' she said in a voice so low it was practically a whisper.

'Then you sat up and shouted for me to leave you alone. I was escorted from the room by two burly wardsmen and not allowed back.' His humiliation and anger was still raw.

'I don't remember,' she said. 'My memories of around that time are very hazy.'

'I was your husband so I had some rights. Eventually I was told you'd been taken in for a procedure. I wouldn't be allowed to see you until the morning—that is, if you gave me your permission.'

'I'm sorry, Cristos.' He hugged her close and she buried her head against his shoulder. 'What did you do?' Her voice was muffled.

'I found a waiting room but got kicked out of it so I went back to the apartment. I didn't sleep. I got back to the ward in the morning to be told you'd been transferred to a private hospital. And you didn't want me to know where.'

'I can only say I'm sorry again,' she said.

'I was frantic with worry about you. But I spoke Italian and understood they believed I was an abusive husband. That perhaps my abuse had something to do with you losing the baby. I half expected to get arrested.'

She groaned. 'That was my parents. They'd flown to Milan after my first phone call. They listened to my delirious garble and thought the worst.'

'Then they spirited you out of the country and I didn't see you again until you turned up here. You can see what I mean about gaps.'

She stood very still in his arms. 'I meant it when I said I don't remember much of that time. I fell into a deep depression, which can, apparently, happen after a miscarriage. But as the weeks went by I didn't pull out of it as the hormones settled. My parents were so worried about me they booked me into a clinic where I was diagnosed and treated. Post-natal depression is relatively common.

Not so post-miscarriage depression and pre-natal depression dating right back to the beginning of my pregnancy.'

'Why wasn't I told about this? I should have been there to help you.'

'I'd been told you hadn't tried to see me. I didn't think I was going to get better. And I blamed you.' Her voice caught at the edges.

'But you did get better.'

'Thankfully, with the right treatment and medication. But it took a long time. I was still on the medication when I went to Australia.'

Cristos gritted his teeth. 'And still the husband wasn't told.'

'You know the story of what I did there. How I became the person I wanted to be. Maybe I needed to grow up. Maybe I'd be a better wife now.'

Hope flared. 'What do you mean, "be a better wife"?'

'I was speaking hypothetically,' she said hastily.

'You came here to divorce me,' he said. 'Have you changed your mind?'

She twisted back out of his arms. 'Yes. No. I'm not sure of anything after last night.'

'Could we make our marriage work again?'

She raised her beautiful blue eyes to him and he could see they were still clouded by uncertainty. 'We learned so much about each other this morning. Then there was last night—it meant a lot, Cristos.'

He pulled her back to him, held her so close he could feel her heat through their informal attire of towel and toga. 'It meant a lot to me too, *koukla*.' She might still have doubts but he didn't. 'And I'm sure I want us to be together again.'

'But there's still a lot more to learn. We've barely scratched the surface. I'm frightened we might make the same mistakes.'

'You yourself said we were different people. Surely we've learned from our mistakes. You are my wife and I don't want to let you go again. We've got time today to find out everything you need to give our marriage a second chance.'

He was about to set out a plan of action that would include more time in that big bed, followed by some serious discussion about what a shared future could involve. Then his mobile phone rang. Alex.

He listened to his cousin. 'I'll be down,' he said and terminated the call.

'What's happened?' asked Hayley.

Cristos strode over to the balcony doors and flung first the shutters open and then the doors. Sunlight streamed in from a blue sky clear but for a few drifting white clouds. Snow on the tree canopies sparkled with reflected sunbeams. Beyond was a millpond-calm sea in shades of aquamarine and turquoise. A perfect crisp winter's day on Kosmimo.

Cristos cursed under his breath. He would so much have preferred to see choppy, stormy water that would keep Hayley on the island.

He stepped aside. 'You can see for yourself. The storm has blown itself out. No fresh snow has fallen.'

Hayley joined him at the doors to the balcony. 'Does that mean—?'

'There's no reason boats can't leave the island.' His voice was gruff with disappointment.

'And the roads to the airport are open?'

He could lie and say no. But she would find out the truth soon enough. 'I'm sure they're clearing them as we speak.'

'That doesn't necessarily mean I have to leave the island, does it? Not when we've still got so much more to say to each other. Can I stay another day? I don't have to be back at work just yet.'

He swung around to face her, not even attempting to conceal his urgency. He couldn't lose her again. 'Stay, Hayley. Not just for today. Or tomorrow. Stay with me for ever.'

CHAPTER FOURTEEN

HAYLEY LOOKED UP at Cristos, wrapped in a sheet and looking more like a Greek god than ever. 'For ever? Surely it's too soon to talk about for ever. We've only had two days back together.' She wanted him. She loved him. But she needed more time to be certain that she wanted to commit again to a marriage that had ended in so much pain she'd had to flee to the other side of the world.

'Two days? I had more than two years missing you, aching for you. It would kill me if you flew back to Australia. You are the only woman I have ever wanted. Stay here with me as my wife. Make your life with me again, *koukla*.' His eyes narrowed with the sensual, hungry look that made her want to melt back into his arms and forget everything but him. 'This time for ever.'

He drew her to him for a quick kiss that lingered in its deliciousness. He ran his finger down her cheek and traced her lips, swollen with the countless kisses she had enjoyed during a long night of loving. Loving as she knew no other man could ever give her.

He was six feet two of dark-haired, green-eyed temptation enticing her into forgetting everything she'd learned about what she needed while they'd been apart. 'But I have a job in Australia. A good life.' A hard-won life of security and certainty, a private life of answering to no one but herself.

A lonely life with no Cristos to warm her bed and her heart.

'You can have a better life with me,' he said dismissively. 'A new job in Europe.' She'd forgotten how arrogant he could be. How certain he was about the decisions he made. But then he bowed his head. 'I can't lose you again, Hayley.' Along with that arrogance was a hint of uncertainty, of vulnerability, that tugged at her heart. It was one of the reasons she had fallen so deeply in love with him back when they'd been students.

'I don't want to lose you again either.' She was suddenly very sure of that. She had never wanted any man but him. But she had to weigh up the costs of—again—giving up her life for him.

With all the soul searching this morning, she found herself digging deeper into her own motivations. Was this what she'd secretly wanted all along—from the time she'd packed her bag back in Sydney? She hadn't needed to deliver the divorce documents in person—in fact she'd been advised against it. Deep down had she hoped, by her coming to Greece, she and Cristos would rediscover what they'd lost?

That they would fall in love again?

'We've wasted so much time already,' he said. 'Why waste any more spent apart?' His hands rested possessively on her shoulders. 'We were happy at the start. We can be happy again. I guarantee it. Say yes, *Kyria* Theofanis, like you said yes when I asked you to marry me the first time.'

It had been so long since she'd been called *Mrs.* Yes, she wanted to be his wife again. She couldn't risk losing him a second time.

She took a deep breath. Excitement rippled through her.

Time to commit. To reclaim the man she loved as her husband. 'Cristos, I want—'

His phone sounded again, its shrill tone intruding on the quiet and privacy of the honeymoon suite. He uttered one of those interesting Greek swear words. 'Alex again. I don't have to answer it to know he wants me downstairs. It must be pandemonium with everyone wanting to get home.'

She frowned. 'Why does he need you? I know he's your cousin and your friend. But surely there are others who can help him.' Wasn't being here with her more important?

'Because I'm co-owner of the resort. I'm as much responsible for whatever is happening as he is.'

Hayley struggled to get enough air to fill her lungs. This was a multimillion-euro property. 'Since when?'

'I invested in Pevezzo Athina early, when it was just a dream in Alex's hotelier heart. It's an investment that's paid off handsomely already.'

'Why didn't you tell me?'

More secrets.

'We hadn't had the opportunity to have the money conversation yet.'

'What do you mean? You said you were comfortable. But you must be more than comfortable to be able to afford a place like this.'

'You could say that. Dell likes to call me the secret millionaire. Multimillionaire is a more apt description. As my wife, you won't have to worry about money ever again, *koukla.*'

She stepped back to release his hands from her shoulders. 'Were you testing me? Keeping your millions out of the equation in case they swayed my decision to reconcile with you?'

He frowned. 'Of course not. Why would you think that? My fortune is not something I boast about but I wasn't trying to hide anything from you. I was lucky to be in at the beginning of exciting new developments—shopping apps and transport-sharing apps, pretty-much-anything-sharing apps. The internet couldn't get enough of them back then. I sold my initial investments at the top of the market.'

His phone rang again. Then again. And again. He scowled. 'I have to get down there. Just to see what's so urgent. Don't go anywhere, Hayley. Stay here. Please. I'll be back.'

She was too shocked to say anything other than yes. She watched as he hastily dressed in the clothes she had wrestled off him last night and tossed on the floor.

More secrets and lies.

She'd thought he'd spilled all his truths the night before. She had nothing more to lay on the table. But not her husband.

Her multimillionaire husband.

What else hadn't he told her?

'Kiss me, Hayley. I know the bank balance comes as a shock. But not a bad kind of shock, right? Remember how skint we were when we were first together?'

'It just takes some getting used to.'

'Everything I've done was for you, *koukla*. And without you, I'm worth nothing. Not a cent, penny or *lepton*.'

She rose up on tiptoe to kiss him on his mouth. Even that swift touch made her shudder with pleasure. His eyes darkened and he returned the kiss, hard and possessive. 'I'll call you on that kiss when I get back,' he said, his voice deep and husky and laden with promise.

He slammed the door shut behind him. Hayley heard his footsteps disappear down the marble corridor towards the stairs. In a daze, she looked around the room. The rumpled sheets. Her silk pyjamas discarded on the floor. His glass of water on the table beside the bed. An empty bottle of health drink from the fridge. He'd joked he needed to restore his stamina after their third—or was it their fourth?—bout of lovemaking. She'd insisted on sharing it because she'd needed the stamina too. His scent—their mingled scents—hung in the air. The room already had the familiar scent of the rooms they'd shared during their married life. It echoed with his absence.

She was back in that tiny apartment in Milan. Cristos off at work doing his thing, her left on her own, kept out of the picture. Pushed firmly right back down on the lowest rungs of the decision-making perch. Once again she felt like that little brown peahen pecking away at her life in the shadow of her glamorous peacock husband. Nothing had changed. *He* hadn't changed.

But she had. Back with Cristos, it would be too easy to lose herself again. Now she was used to a different life. A life she'd fought hard for, where she sat proudly on the top perch when it came to determining how she lived it. Had Cristos grown too rich and powerful to ever want to share it with her? Too used to having his own way? She couldn't go back there. And the longer she stayed with him, the more difficult it would be to leave.

There would be a boat going back to Nidri this morning. She needed to get down to the dock so she could be among the first to leave the island.

It would take her five minutes to pack everything she had into her handbag. She would take only what she'd come with. Even Dell's pink dress and the beautiful shoes from Penelope she would leave behind. She wanted nothing that would remind her of her time on Kosmimo.

As Cristos had predicted, it was chaos downstairs with everyone who wanted to get off the island determined to be in the first boat. He'd got immediately caught up in it, especially as he was not only a co-owner of the resort, but also captain of a boat with the capacity to carry a good number of passengers.

He wished he'd brought Hayley down with him to help. After all, she would have a stake in the resort too. Not to mention a calm, efficient manner. Then the truth of what he'd done hit him with the impact of a sledgehammer. He totally ignored a friend of Alex's who was demanding to be first on board. Why the hell had he left Hayley back up in that room by herself? As he'd done back in Milan. He cursed himself under his breath for his stupidity. Only it couldn't have been under his breath as the guy he was dealing with took offence and kicked up a stink about his rudeness.

He didn't care. The only thing to concern him was what an idiot he'd been. Hayley hadn't even said yes to his new proposal and he'd slid right back into the behaviour that had driven her from him. He understood now that it wasn't just the day she'd lost the baby that he'd let her down. It was also the build-up to that day, as he had so relentlessly pursued a policy for the future without consulting her. What had she said about being booted off the perch?

He had to get back up to that room. Apologise. Grovel. And explain how different things would be if she took him back. How they would go back to the equal partnership that had started their marriage. When they'd been happy.

But she wasn't in the room. Her jeans, her sweatshirt and the pink dress were neatly folded on the bed. Everything she'd acquired on the island, in fact, was still in the room. Her blue coat and her smart boots were gone from the closet. Of course she could have gone outside to wave goodbye to the guests departing the island. But the echoing emptiness of the room didn't suggest that. He took the marble stairs two at a time.

He checked the common areas downstairs. No Hayley. There were still a good number of people milling about. Including Arianna, who immediately approached him. 'Are you looking for your wife?' asked Arianna.

'Yes,' he said shortly, not trusting himself to say more to the spiteful woman who had been so rude to Hayley.

'I saw her heading down to the dock with the others leaving on the boat to Nidri. She was all dressed up to go. Sorry it didn't work out with you two.' She didn't sound sorry at all.

Cristos brushed past her without a further word, not caring if she thought him ill-mannered. He didn't want this woman on Kosmimo or anywhere near him. If Penelope wanted him to fix things with Hayley, she could get Arianna out of their hair. Not that he needed his grandparent's urging to fix things with his wife. He'd made that decision all on his own. And then totally stuffed up the execution of it.

He ran down the steps that led to the bay, heedless of the puddles of melting snow. Immediately he saw Hayley, not waiting on the dock with the others, but sitting a good distance away to the side on a rustic bench Alex had placed there because it was such a pleasant place to sit in summer. It seemed a lonely place to be in winter.

The Ionian Sea stretched out ahead of her, the wooded hills of the island behind. She looked small and vulnerable in the landscape, and very alone. Cristos fisted his hands beside him. He could tell by the slump of her shoulders and her stillness that she was hurting.

His fault.

She shouldn't be sitting there alone and melancholy. They had wasted too many years apart. She should be with him, cherished and loved and making a new life together. But it seemed he still had some work ahead of him to convince her of that.

He didn't immediately alert her to his presence, just took the moments before she would sense he was there to observe her.

She was wearing the blue coat he'd bought her back in

Italy from a favourite designer he'd walked for at Milan Fashion Week. He'd thought it would be perfect for his lovely wife. But Hayley hadn't been as excited about the expensive gift as he'd thought. She had only just had her pregnancy confirmed and hadn't been showing at all but she might already have been suffering from depression.

Was she depressed now? With her head bowed she certainly looked it. But what did he know about depression? Only that it meant more than just feeling down sometimes, that it was an illness. No matter, he would love and cherish her all the more.

She needed him.

He cleared the distance to the bench. She must have heard him but she didn't turn around. 'May I sit next to you, Lady in Blue?' he asked, not taking anything for granted.

She nodded wordlessly, shuffled along to make room for him. She was wearing not just the coat, but also the trousers, sweater and boots she'd worn the day she'd arrived on the island. Her travelling outfit. Her hands were clasped together on her lap. He noticed she was only wearing one of her fine leather gloves on her right hand. Her rings were still on her bare left hand, he noted with relief.

'You're only wearing one glove,' he said. 'Isn't your other hand cold?'

'One of the goats ate the other one when I was helping Penelope put them away before the storm.' She gave a watery smile.

Her answer was so not what he'd expected that he laughed. '*Koukla*, you always surprise me.' He wanted to reach out and take her cold little hand and warm it between his. But her body language screamed, *Don't touch!*

'What are you doing here?' he asked.

'Thinking about my next step.'

'All by yourself? I'd hoped your next step would be taken with me,' he said.

'So did I.' She heaved a great sigh. When she turned to face him he saw her eyes were red-rimmed. He felt gutted that he had upset her.

'You haven't changed,' she said. 'If I went back to you it would be more of the same. You ruling the roost, me clucking along below with never a compromise from you.'

'That's not true. I have changed, even if I didn't show it this morning by leaving you in the hotel room. But how much more honest could I have been with you last night and this morning? I shared things with you that I've never told anyone.'

'I appreciate that. But would you ever make a life decision that was about what I wanted? I want to be with you, Cristos, make no mistake about that. But it means giving up my life again. You want me to throw away everything I've achieved in Sydney, my career, my prospects, to stay here with you. I'd be as miserable as I was in Milan.'

'It doesn't have to be that way,' he said. 'We could work out a way to be together that suits us both.'

Her chin tilted upward; her eyes challenged him. 'What if you came with me to Australia?'

'That's a great idea. I've always wanted to visit Sydney, see where Alex and Dell came from, the restaurant my great-uncle started. I could easily live there with you.'

'Really? What about your work?'

'I can run my business anywhere there's WiFi and an international airport. I just want to be with you, living as husband and wife. I honestly don't care wherever that might be in the world.'

Now he did take her bare hand. It was icy cold and he rubbed it between his own much larger hands. 'We only started to talk about this a few hours ago. As you said, we've still got a way to go.'

She caught his hand and closed hers over his. 'I'm sorry I doubted you. I hope you're not having second thoughts about me.'

'Never. Not since the day we pledged to spend our lives together.'

She turned her face for his kiss. It was short and very sweet, a kiss of comfort and confirmation. He could carry on kissing her all morning but there was more that needed to be said.

'There's something else I want to tell you,' he said. 'One more thing my family keeps hidden because of the shame.'

She raised her brows. 'About your father?'

'My father died in prison.'

'Cristos, no. I'm so sorry. Did he…end his own life?'

'Nothing like that,' he said. 'He died in prison on the day he was due to be released. In a fight, protecting a younger inmate in a notoriously overcrowded and under-staffed hell-hole.'

She gasped and her grip on his hands tightened. 'So it was an honourable death.'

'Yes. He died with honour, although that was no consolation to us. My mother and I were waiting outside for him to come through those prison gates. I was holding a balloon saying "welcome home Dad". We waited for hours but he never came. When eventually we were told what had happened, that's when I—a thirteen-year-old boy—saw the moment my mother's heart broke. Not for all the wrongs he did to us and to others. Not for when he had stolen money from her purse to place a bet on a "sure thing". Or purloined my pocket money. But when she realised she would never see him again—the man she adored.'

'And you?' Her voice broke.

'That's when I vowed that no woman I ever loved would go through what my mother went through. My wife would be honoured and cherished and want for nothing. That was my only motivation in our marriage—to look after you. I made mistakes and I'm sorry for them. But everything I did, the modelling, the investments, the risk taking was for us. To secure our future. And the future of our children. More than anything I want our futures to be spent together.'

'Oh, Cristos, I don't know what to say.' Tears glistened on her lashes.

He cupped her chin in one hand, gently wiped away the tears with his other. 'That's what Greek men do. We protect our women. We look after our families. It's in our blood. Don't say anything, except that you'll stay.'

She blinked away the remaining tears. 'Before I do, there's one more thing. Not a secret, a worry. You mentioned children.'

He nodded. 'You know I want a family with you.'

'Me too,' she said. 'I long to have your baby. But I'm petrified of getting pregnant again. The depression was so frightening. Both during the pregnancy and afterwards.'

'You're quite over the depression now?'

'Yes, thank heaven.'

'What do the doctors say? Is it likely to happen again with another pregnancy?'

'They can't predict how my hormones will react. The depression might strike, it might not.'

'That's simple, then. We won't have children. It's not worth it if you—'

She put up her hand to stop him. 'No. I'm prepared to take the risk. But not if it would be like last time. I can't be left on my own to cope with it.' Her mouth twisted. 'Or not cope as I did then.'

He put his hands on her shoulders to reassure her. 'It would be very different next time. I work from home. I would always be there for you when you needed me.'

'Thank you,' she said. 'I mean, it might not happen but if it did, if I—'

'Whatever does or does not happen, I would be there for you. We're a partnership.'

He put his arm around her shoulder and they both sat looking out to sea. Silence hung between them. Slowly he became aware of the sounds of the small waves swishing on the beach, the wind rustling through the trees, chatter and laughter from the direction of the dock. He was aware of the sound of his own breathing, his heart thudding against his chest.

'Why did you really come down here?' he said. 'Just to think or were you planning to take the boat to Nidri?'

'Yes,' she said. Again he felt that kick to the gut so he felt like doubling over with the pain.

'I felt like nothing had changed. After all we'd gone through, I'd be signing up for the same relationship that had ended in so much pain and regret,' she said, her voice unsteady. 'I thought my only option was to go through with the divorce. My plan was to leave the divorce papers in the room for you to find after I'd gone with a note asking you to sign and return them to the lawyer.'

'I didn't see any divorce papers there. Did you hide them somewhere or—?'

'I didn't leave them. And I didn't ask for a place on the boat. I realised running away wasn't going to solve anything—like it didn't last time. It would have been a stupid, childish thing to do. And this time I didn't have a depressive illness to blame my behaviour on. Difficult as I might find it, I had to do the grown-up thing and confront you. Talk about what we both expected from a reconciliation. See if we could make it work.' She looked away. 'Sorry, long speech.'

'A speech I'm glad I heard. Glad you stuck around to

deliver it. Although I would have followed you, you know. All the way to Sydney. I had no intention of letting you go again.'

'I'm glad I didn't make you chase me all that way.' But the curve of her smile told him she was delighted that he would have done so. 'I'll look forward to us travelling back together and starting our new life.'

'Do you have any more questions? Have I explained myself well enough?'

'Very satisfactory answers. No more questions.' Her voice hitched. 'Because the main reason I didn't leave was that I simply couldn't bear to be away from you. Two mornings of waking up next to you made me know I wanted to be there with you for the rest of our lives.' She sniffed.

Cristos wished he could do the chivalrous thing men did in movies and offer her a big snowy white linen handkerchief. But the best he had to offer was an oil-soaked cloth from the boat, which he doubted would be appreciated so he left it in his pocket.

She lifted her face to his. 'Because I love you, Cristos. I never stopped loving you. I think I came to this island in the first place subconsciously hoping I might find you still loved me too.'

'And you found I had never stopped loving you, not for a minute. I love you, Hayley. There has only ever been you. The years apart were torture for me. When I saw you at the church on Saturday I thought you'd come back to me. My spirits soared. When you talked divorce you drove me to my lowest point. I can only thank the forces of nature that conjured up a storm to keep you here until you changed your mind.'

'Being with you is what changed my mind, not the weather,' she said. 'My wonderful, wonderful man.'

A burst of cheering erupted from the people on the

dock. Startled, Cristos looked up to see the boat they'd booked to pick up the guests was heading toward the dock.

'Do you know why they're so excited about going back?' Hayley asked.

'Because they're sick of being trapped on the island?'

'Because it's Valentine's Day. I'd forgotten.'

'Of course, it's February the fourteenth,' he said. 'Valentine's Day is a big deal in Greece. The whole Cupid's arrow thing started here. Only it belonged to Eros, the god of love in ancient Greek mythology. The ancient Romans called him Cupid. Greeks do like to get loved up on Valentine's Day.' He felt that arrow still in his heart, only now it would stay lodged there for the rest of his life. He would never, ever let Hayley go again.

'So it's a good day for a reconciliation?' she said.

'It's an excellent day for a reconciliation. Because in Greece Valentine's Day is not just about romantic love, it's also about forgiveness. Will you forgive me, Hayley? Because without forgiveness, without letting go of the past, we won't be able to go forward.'

'Of course I forgive you. If you can forgive me for hiding from you. I didn't realise how much I hurt you. And I guess I have to forgive myself for that.'

'Clean slate, then?' he said.

She nodded. 'I just want to be your wife again. No pretence. No secrets. I want you to be my husband again. Looking after me, but letting me look after you too.'

'We can celebrate February the fourteenth each year as the anniversary of our new marriage.'

'You mean we get to celebrate two anniversaries each year?'

'Why not? Both days are special. And you get two lots of presents.'

'What could there possibly be to complain about that?' she said, laughing. 'I love you, husband.'

'I love you, wife.'

He helped her up from the bench with an arm around her. 'C'mon, *koukla*. Let's go start our new life together.'

EPILOGUE

Fifteen months later

HAYLEY STOOD OUTSIDE the little white chapel perched on the edge of a white limestone cliff on Kosmimo. The sea ahead of her was the most glorious turquoise imaginable, a lone sailboat tacking across the horizon. There wasn't a cloud in the deep blue sky and the late spring sun glistened on the water and warmed her skin through her long white lace dress. The air was fresh with the tang of salt and the scent of the herbs that grew wild on the island.

She and Cristos had just had their photo taken and were waiting for the photographer to organise the next one. Hayley turned to Cristos. 'This is how I always imagined a Greek island to be.'

'It's good to be home,' he said with a deep sigh of satisfaction.

He lifted their four-month-old son, Damianos—named after Cristos's father in the Greek tradition—to show him the view. 'This is your heritage, *ogios mou*, my son—paradise.' Their beautiful baby boy chuckled, which seemed the appropriate joyful response.

She and Cristos had left Sydney behind them to come back to Europe, to be closer to their families. They were living in his apartment in Athens, but Hayley thought they would probably settle somewhere in London. She had worked right up to a month before the baby was born but wasn't thinking of finding another engineering role until Damianos was at least a year old.

Thankfully, her pregnancy had gone smoothly without a hint of depression except the brief burst of the hormonally induced 'baby blues' that had hit her a few days after the birth and had just as quickly disappeared.

Cristos had been lovingly supportive all the way through and had been with her at the birth. They had both cried as he'd first held his son in his arms, and vowed to be a good father. The baby had black hair and blue eyes and promised to be every bit as handsome as the daddy who adored him.

The last time she'd stood here was in the winter chill and she'd been an outsider. This time the visit to the chapel was for her and Cristos to renew their vows, have their marriage blessed and for the christening of their son.

At last their respective families were getting the celebration they felt they had been cheated of by their hasty register office wedding. Hayley was dressed as a bride in a simple white dress of heavy lace with sweet-scented freesias and apple blossom twisted through her hair. Around her neck was a pendant of a single large tear-shaped sapphire surrounded by diamonds and set in platinum. She had refused to replace her original humble sapphire engagement ring that she cherished for something more elaborate befitting her multimillionaire status. The necklace had been Cristos's gift instead.

The ceremony had gone without a hitch. Little Damianos had howled at being anointed with oil and immersed in water by the priest but had quickly recovered with cuddles from his female relatives, who fought to be the one to comfort him.

He had even been well behaved through all the photos

but, like his father, was beginning to grizzle. The photographer had better be quick with the final group photo before their precious baby erupted into hungry howls.

'How many more photos, Lady in White?' Cristos grumbled. 'This is beginning to feel like work for me. Pose, smile, pose, smile. It's taking me right back to my modelling days.'

'Just this one final family shot,' she said. 'It will be worth it.'

At last they were all assembled. She and Cristos stood at the centre with Damianos—who her mother insisted on calling Damian 'as, after all, he is half English'—in his father's arms. They were flanked by the baby's godparents, Dell and Alex, with their two children; his doting Greek great-grandparents; his equally doting grandparents and aunt from England; and his great-aunt from Australia, who'd been so supportive of Hayley during her pregnancy and Damianos's birth. Her family. She couldn't imagine being happier—especially with the husband she loved more and more each day by her side.

She smiled once more for the camera—she had unlimited smiles today, fuelled by the intense joy bubbling through her. The day brought back memories of her wedding in Durham, of her first visit to this island bearing documents for a divorce she'd never really wanted, but most of all of the perfectly wonderful times with her husband once they'd put the unhappy times behind them.

Her tiny son continued to give his best gummy smiles to the camera. But abruptly he'd had enough. His little face screwed up and he wailed, a surprisingly loud sound for one so small.

'He's hungry. Hand him over to me,' Hayley said to Cristos. She took the precious bundle into her arms. Her exquisite dress had been designed by a dressmaker friend of Penelope's to suit a nursing mother. Now she and Cristos took their baby to a private spot at the back of the chapel so she could discreetly feed him.

She sat with her baby making sweet little snuffling sounds and her husband's protective arm around her. Cristos kissed her, a brief gentle kiss. 'I have never felt happier, *koukla*,' he said.

'Me neither,' she said. 'This is the happiest day of my life. But then I thought yesterday was the happiest, and the day before that. And I know tomorrow will be even happier as it will be one more day with you.'

He kissed her again. 'Do you realise this now makes three anniversaries for us to celebrate each year?'

'All the better to bind our little family together,' she said.

'Doesn't the love we have for each other, for our son, do that?'

'You're absolutely right,' she said, looking up into his eyes and thinking again how incredibly blessed she was to be married to this man.

* * * * *

AN ENGAGEMENT FOR TWO

MARIE FERRARELLA

To
Charlie.
Bet You Never Thought
When You Sauntered
Into My Second Period
English Class That
First Day
That Half a Century Later,
We'd Still Be Together,
Did You?

Prologue

"Hi, Mom."

Maizie Sommers stopped short as she entered the ground-floor office of the real estate business she had lovingly nurtured and guided into a thriving enterprise over the last decade and a half. She was just returning from helping a young couple find the home of their dreams, something that always gave her an immense amount of pleasure.

The very last person she expected to see in her office, sitting in front of her desk, was her daughter, Nikki. Nikki, a pediatric physician and her only child, was responsible for Maizie initially dipping her toe into the—at that point—very unfamiliar waters of matchmaking.

She and her lifelong best friends, Cecilia Parnell and Theresa Manetti, had done so well finding a match for Nikki that they were encouraged to continue in their endeavors and find perfect matches for Cilia's daughter and Theresa's children.

When that worked out, they decided to continue matchmaking as an occasional hobby.

The hobby caught fire, and while all three women went on to maintain the separate businesses they had built over the years, matchmaking became very near and dear to their hearts—as was their determination to remain quietly behind the scenes. They were in it for the satisfaction, not the recognition—and certainly not the money since there was never any charge.

Maizie and her friends were quite proud of the fact that the couples they had brought together over the years never knew they were being skillfully guided to come together.

But that certainly wasn't the first thought that entered Maizie's mind when she saw her daughter sitting there.

"Is something wrong with Lucas or one of the children?" Maizie asked, giving her daughter a quick kiss hello.

Concerned, she dropped into the chair behind her desk, scrutinizing her daughter's face and looking for some sort of indication as to what had brought Nikki here in the middle of the day.

"What makes you think there's something wrong with one of them?" Nikki asked.

"Well, let me see. You're a highly regarded pediatrician whose hours are only slightly shorter than God's. You're a wife and the mother of three very energetic young children. That alone uses up every moment of your day and night, and I haven't seen you since Ellie and Addie's party," Maizie reminded her, mentioning the twins' fourth birthday last month. "My guess is that only an emergency of some sort would bring you here to see me in the middle of the day."

Nikki sat up a little straighter in the chair, although she was unconsciously knotting her fingers together. "Well, you're wrong."

Maizie continued to watch her daughter's hands. "Good."

"It's not an emergency," Nikki emphasized.

"Happy to hear that." Although, Maizie thought, something was definitely wrong. Those were not the hands of a carefree, untroubled person.

"Not exactly," Nikki amended.

"Ah." Now they were getting to it, Maizie thought. "And what is it, exactly?" she asked her daughter.

Just then her phone rang.

Nikki looked at the landline on her mother's desk. "You want to get that?" she asked.

"No," Maizie answered. She didn't want her daughter using the call as an excuse to suddenly change her mind and leave. "That's why God created answering machines."

Nikki appeared guilty. "I feel bad, taking up your time like this." She looked at the phone. The call had obviously gone to voice mail. "You worked really hard to get here."

"One delayed call isn't going to torpedo my business, Nikki. Besides, Susanna, my assistant, is due back from lunch soon. She can call whoever it is back. You are, and always have been, my first priority," Maizie insisted. "I've expanded that to include Lucas and the children, but you are still in first place. Now, what's this all about? And why are you about to twist off your fingers?" She nodded at her daughter's hands.

Stilling her hands, Nikki sighed. "I don't quite know how to say this, Mom."

"One word at a time is usually the way to do it," Maizie encouraged. "At this point in my life I've heard just about everything," she added, "so just spit it out, my love."

"I know—" Nikki began and then she paused, at a loss how to continue.

"You know what, dear?" Maizie asked, waiting.

Nikki took a breath, then blurted it out. "That you arranged to bring Lucas and me together."

Maizie smiled. She was surprised that it had taken Nikki so long to come to this conclusion. "I see. Well, those were just the circumstances that arranged themselves, dear."

"That you took advantage of," Nikki said, knowing the way her mother operated.

Maizie tried to understand what her daughter was getting at. "You're not telling me that, after all these years of marital bliss, you're going to get upset with me for meddling in your life, are you?"

Untangling her fingers, Nikki gripped the chair's armrests to keep her hands apart. "No, I'm not."

"Well, I'm glad we cleared that up." Maizie smiled at her. "Anything else?"

Nikki still hadn't gotten to the reason she was here. "Yes, um…"

"Go ahead, dear," Maizie urged patiently.

"I need you to meddle again, Mom."

"You're looking for another husband?" Maizie asked wryly.

Nikki's eyes widened. For a moment, she didn't realize that her mother was kidding. "No!"

"Good, because I really do like Lucas." Still smiling, Maizie became serious. "Talk to me, Nikki," she encouraged. "It never used to be this hard for us to talk. What's on your mind?"

Nikki decided to choose a roundabout approach instead of being direct. "Do you remember my friend Michelle McKenna?"

"Mikki? Of course I remember her. Lovely girl. Not the best parents," Maizie recalled, "but a lovely girl. She was over at the house a lot when you were younger and you two went to medical school together," she said to prove that she really did remember the girl. "What about her?"

"I want you to do for her what you did for me," Nikki said.

Ah, now it was all beginning to make sense, Maizie thought. "Does she know you're asking me to...matchmake?" Maizie asked tactfully.

"Oh, no, no, and I don't want her to know," Nikki said with feeling. "She'd never agree to it."

Maizie was well acquainted with that sort of reaction. "Why would you want me to do it, then?"

"Because she's a wonderful person, Mom," Nikki cried. "And she deserves to be happy. But I'm worried she's going to wind up alone. She's so afraid of making her mother's mistakes, she won't even think about going out with anyone."

Maizie looked at her daughter thoughtfully. She was well aware of the other young woman's situation. Mikki's parents had fought constantly and then went through a vicious divorce when she was a preteen. Her mother went on to marry—and divorce—three more times. She had no idea how many times Mikki's father had gone that route. The man had dropped out of sight, from what she gathered.

What she did know was that all this had taken a heavy toll on the young woman. She'd had Mikki stay over for sleepovers as often as she could to spare her daughter's friend from witnessing the acrimony manifested by her parents.

"Will you do it, Mom? Will you work your magic for Mikki?" Nikki asked her.

Maizie was more than happy to help. "Yes, of course I will. On one condition, though," she added, eyeing her daughter.

"What?" Nikki asked.

"You tell me how you found out that I had a hand in bringing you and Lucas together."

Nikki laughed, relieved. "You mean other than the fact that I'm brilliant, like my mother?"

Maizie smiled. "Yes, other than that."

"Jewel figured it out and told me," Nikki answered. Jewel was Cilia's daughter and she, like Theresa's two offspring, was Nikki's friend.

"I see." She nodded, accepting the explanation at face value. "All right then, I'm going to need some current information about Mikki—it's been a while since I've seen her," Maizie told her daughter. And then she smiled. "Don't worry, this'll be painless, and Mikki will never know that you came to me—unless you want her to know," she qualified.

"Heaven forbid," Nikki cried. Then, in a more subdued voice, she asked, "Will you let me know who you pick out?"

Maizie smiled mysteriously. She knew it would be for the best if her daughter remained in the dark until the proper meeting was arranged and pulled off.

"Oh, darling, a magician never reveals her secrets," Maizie told her daughter with a wink.

Chapter One

"There's someone to see you, Mrs. Manetti."

Melinda Jacobsen's announcement as she peered into Theresa's back office was accompanied by a giggle best suited to the teenager she'd been eight years ago when she had first come to work for Theresa's catering company in an apprentice capacity.

Theresa jotted down a last-minute thought about a menu she was creating in her notebook and then looked up.

"Bring her in, Melinda," Theresa told the young woman whom she'd eventually placed in charge of baked goods.

Hearing Melinda giggle again, Theresa wondered what had come over her. Melinda was usually very level-headed.

"It's a *he*." This time the giggle came before the words, further arousing Theresa's curiosity.

In less than ten seconds, her curiosity was laid to rest. Jeff Sabatino stepped around Melinda and entered the small, crowded office where she took her calls and created the menus that made her catering business such a prosperous success.

As if reading her mind, the young woman reluctantly left the room before Theresa could ask her to leave.

The tall, broad-shouldered man with thick, slightly unruly dark hair smiled at his former boss. "Hello, Mrs. Manetti. I hope you don't mind my stopping by without calling first."

Jeff had gotten his start with Theresa's catering business before branching out and opening his own restaurant a handful of years ago. Theresa had been one of his first customers and was proud of his success. She had always thought of him as a protégé.

"Of course I don't mind. And Jeff, you own your own restaurant, and I saw that you've been getting some really stunning reviews lately. I think you can call me Theresa now," she told him warmly. Theresa gestured toward the two chairs that were facing her desk, the ones where clients usually sat when they came to engage her services. "Please, sit."

"That's all right," Jeff told her. "I'm not staying long."

"Looking to buy me out?" Theresa asked with a trace of amusement. She knew that wasn't the case, but Jeff appeared way too serious for this to be strictly a social call. "Or are you here because you need help—because your restaurant is doing so well, you find that you just can't keep up with the demand?"

"Neither," Jeff answered, "although I'll never forget the debt I owe you. I would have been nothing more than a short-order cook if it hadn't been for what you taught me."

Theresa thought back to when he'd first walked into her establishment, a very handsome, very nervous young man with a great deal of promise. The memory warmed her heart and made her smile.

"Ah, but you had the *potential* to do so much more than that, and you wanted to learn. Desire is something I can't teach, Jeff. Everything else, I can." She assessed him more closely as she stood. She saw worry in his light green eyes. "This isn't a social call, is it, Jeff?"

"Not exactly," Jeff confessed.

Theresa made her way behind him to the door of her office and closed it. She had a feeling her former protégé would prefer privacy.

Turning around to face him, she said, "I'm listening."

Now that he was here, Jeff wasn't sure how to start. He wasn't in the habit of asking for favors, especially not from the woman he credited with giving him not only his start, but also the push to open his own restaurant—not to mention that she had also lent him the money to get started.

He'd paid off the latter, but in his heart, he would forever be in Theresa Manetti's debt. Which made coming here, hat in hand, rather awkward for him.

But this wasn't for him, Jeff reminded himself. It was for his mother. Thinking of that now, he pushed on. "I remember that you once said one of your close friends has a daughter who's a doctor."

"I might have mentioned it," Theresa recalled. "And if I did, I was talking about Maizie. Her daughter, Nikki, is a doctor." A slight note of confusion entered her voice. "But Nikki's a pediatrician and I don't imagine that you're looking for a baby doctor—are you?" she asked suddenly, looking at him in surprise.

It had been a while since she'd been in contact with Jeff, and although she would have liked to think he would have gotten in touch to tell her if he was getting married, she really had no guarantee of that. After all, he was a very busy young man these days.

"No," Jeff quickly answered. "But your friend's daughter does interact with other doctors, doesn't she?" he asked. "At the hospital, I mean."

She wasn't accustomed to seeing Jeff this unsure of himself, not since he'd first come to work for her. She tried to set him at ease.

"Nikki's a very friendly young woman, so yes, I'm sure she does. What's this all about, Jeff? Are you ill?" she asked, displaying a deeply ingrained mother's sense of concern.

He suddenly realized how he had to be coming across. "Oh, no, not me—"

"Your wife, then?" she asked, watching his face to see if she'd guessed correctly.

"No, no wife. No time," Jeff added, then told her, "You know I'd never get married without inviting you, Mrs. Man—Theresa," he corrected before she could. "You're like a second mother to me." He sighed. "Which brings me to my first mother."

"Your mother's ill?" Theresa asked, recalling how supportive the woman had been of her son when he'd first opened his restaurant, Dinner for Two. "What's wrong, Jeff?"

"That's why I need the name of a good doctor— preferably one with a really good bedside manner about him—or her," he added quickly. "Actually, I think my mother would prefer a her," he told Theresa. "As for me, I'd just prefer a good doctor."

"When was the last time your mother saw a doctor?" Theresa asked, curious.

He really didn't have to stop to think. He knew. His mother avoided doctors as if they carried the plague in their pocket. "When she gave birth to my sister. Tina's twenty-nine now," he added.

That was really hard to believe. "You're kidding," Theresa said.

"No, I'm not," he said honestly. "My mother doesn't trust doctors. A doctor misdiagnosed my father's condition until it was too late to save him." It had happened twenty-five years ago. At the age of ten, he'd suddenly been the man of the family. "He died."

"I'm very sorry to hear that," Theresa said with genuine sympathy. "But that doesn't mean all doctors are like that."

He blew out a breath, feeling very weary all of a sudden. "I know that, but my mother, well, it's hard to win an argument with her. However, she's getting weaker and I just might be able to bully her into it—if I can find a competent, sympathetic doctor to take my mother to."

"Which is where I come in," Theresa concluded.

Jeff nodded. "Could you put me in contact with your friend's daughter? Or have your friend's daughter recommend someone to you? I don't care how it's done," he told her, feeling just a little desperate, as if he was fighting the clock.

He had no idea just how serious his mother's condition was, but she'd been in pain recently. A lot of pain. "I just need it done. I'll take my mother to see this doctor on your say-so. My mom's only sixty-five, Theresa, and she has a lot of life left—as long as I can get her to see reason and get treatment for whatever it is that's making her feel so weak and ill."

Theresa smiled at him. She found his concern for his mother touching.

"You're a good son, Jeff," she told him affectionately.

Jeff shrugged away the compliment. He appreciated what Theresa was saying, but he really needed the name of that doctor. "She's a good mother. I'd like her to live long enough to see her grandkids."

Theresa's ears perked up. "So there is something I should know about?"

Jeff laughed softly. "My sister, Tina, has got two kids and my brother's wife is two months away from giving birth to their first baby."

Since he'd opened the door, Theresa saw no reason not to slip in and satisfy her curiosity. "What about you, Jeff? Would you like to have children?"

It wasn't something he thought about often. "First I'd have to find a wife who would be willing to put up with my crazy hours—"

Theresa's antennae went up a little higher. "But if you did?" she pressed.

"Then yes, I guess I'd like to have kids," he allowed. "But right now, I just want to find someone who can get my mom well."

Theresa nodded. "I'm on it," she told the young man she thought of as a son. "Consider it already taken care of, Jeff," she added with a smile.

He paused to kiss her cheek before leaving. "You're the best," he told her.

"At what I do, yes," Theresa replied softly. She doubted that her former protégé heard as he hurried from her office.

* * *

"You'll never guess who came to see me today," Maizie Sommers told her two best friends as they all gathered around the card table in her family room for their weekly game of poker.

"Considering all the traffic that your office sees, my guess would be just about anybody," Cilia Parnell quipped.

"Try harder," Maizie coaxed, displaying her customary patience. "Who's the one person you'd never think would come to see me? I'll give you a hint—it's about our matchmaking hobby," she told her friends, her eyes shifting from Theresa to Cilia and then back again as she waited for one of them to make a guess.

"Well, that narrows it down to half the immediate world," Cilia quipped. And then she took a closer look at her friend. "You look like the cat that ate the proverbial canary. I suggest you tell us or we'll be sitting here guessing all evening—and getting it wrong."

"Besides, I have to ask you something—and I have news," Theresa announced excitedly, "so get on with it, Maizie. You know I hate it when you just leave off the ending like that."

Maizie shook her head, surrendering. "Oh, all right. You two do take the fun out of this, you know that, don't you?" she said, feigning disappointment.

"The person's name?" Cilia prodded her friend, waiting.

She thought she'd at least get them to play along once or twice. However, since they didn't, Maizie told them, "Nikki."

Theresa looked slightly confused. "Your daughter, Nikki?"

"I've only got one daughter," Maizie pointed out, thinking it was needless to add her name in like that. "Yes. Nikki."

"She came to you about *matchmaking*?" Cilia asked, astonished.

"Yes," Maizie replied patiently.

It didn't make any sense to Theresa. "Well, your granddaughters are too young, so Nikki didn't come about them—" And then something else occurred to her. "How does she know that you're into matchmaking?"

To the best of Theresa's knowledge, none of their children knew anything about this side venture she and her two best friends were engaged in, despite the fact that they'd secretly arranged all four of their children's marriages.

"Apparently, Jewel told her," Maizie said, shifting her gaze toward Cilia.

Very little ruffled Cilia, but this clearly astonished her.

"*My* Jewel?" Cilia asked incredulously. This was the first she'd heard even a hint of this. Certainly Jewel had never said anything to her.

Maizie nodded. "*Your* Jewel," she confirmed. "But the really astonishing thing about this is that Nikki wants me to 'work my magic,' as she put it, to arrange a match for her friend Mikki. The two of them were roommates all through college and then they graduated medical school together—"

"Wait, so this Mikki you're talking about, she's a doctor?" Theresa asked, wanting to be absolutely sure she was getting the story straight before she allowed her imagination to run off with her.

"That's what usually happens when you graduate medical school," Maizie replied, her voice somewhat strained.

A doctor.

That was all Theresa needed to hear. She clapped her hands together in a sudden, uncharacteristically overwhelming burst of joy.

"Perfect!"

Maizie glared at her friend oddly, wondering what had come over her. "I think so, too. But why did you just say that?"

To explain, Theresa felt she had to backtrack a little. "Do you two remember Jeff Sabatino? That very handsome boy who used to work for me and then went on to open up his own restaurant right here in Bedford?" She looked at Maizie and Cilia, searching for any signs of recognition.

"Oh, that's right. Dinner for Two," Maizie recalled. "I went there when it first opened. Wonderful food. You taught him well," she told Theresa with a warm smile. And then she paused. "But why are you bringing him up?"

"Well, initially I wanted to ask if Nikki could recommend a good doctor for his mother. Seems Mrs. Sabatino refuses to go see one, and Jeff thinks she's in failing health," Theresa answered. "He asked me to ask you to ask Nikki—"

Cilia held up her hand, stopping her friend from continuing. "Cut to the bottom line, Theresa. None of us are as young as we used to be."

Maizie gave her friend a look. "Some of us are younger than others, Cilia—but yes, Theresa, what is the bottom line?"

Theresa told them Jeff's request. "Can you have Nikki recommend a good doctor—preferably female—with a good bedside manner?"

Maizie hadn't come this far in life without the aid of well-honed intuition. "There's more, isn't there?"

Theresa loved it when things just all seemed to come together. They all did.

"Well, Jeff is extremely good-looking. He's got chiseled features and liquid green eyes a woman could get lost in," she told her friends. "I'm speaking as a grandmother, by the way," she added in case her friends had any doubts about her interest in the young man, "and there's no girlfriend in the picture. He said something to the effect that he'd like to have kids, but he's too busy right now making a go of his restaurant—and taking care of his mother."

Maizie needed no more. Her eyes lit up. "We could get two birds with one stone."

"Exactly what I was just thinking when you started talking about Nikki's friend," Theresa said. And then a bubble-bursting thought suddenly occurred to her. "This friend, she's not a specialist, is she?"

"From what I remember, Mikki is an internist who specializes in cardiology," Maizie answered.

She smiled broadly at the two other women sitting at the card table. A single hand hadn't been dealt yet, and quite possibly, one wouldn't be, at least not tonight, Maizie thought. Tonight was for making plans and laying groundwork.

This was going to be good.

Maizie smiled broadly at her friends. "Ladies, I believe—in the words of Sir Arthur Conan Doyle's most famous character, Sherlock Holmes—that the game is afoot."

"I think the quote ran a little differently than that," Cilia corrected.

Theresa waved her hand at the possible contradiction. "The exact wording doesn't matter, Cilia. What does matter is that we just might have ourselves another match in the offing."

"Details," Maizie said aloud what they were all thinking. "Let's review details." She turned toward Theresa. "You tell us about your former protégé and then I'll tell you about my daughter's friend so that there are no surprises—other than pleasant ones, of course," she added.

Theresa rubbed her hands together and smiled broadly at the two other women at the table. "I *knew* today was going to be a good day."

"Put your cards away, Maizie," Cilia said, noticing that the deck was still out. "Looks like we've got work to do."

Chapter Two

"Oh, come *on*, Michelle. Come to the party with me. You work too hard, darling. Don't be afraid of having a little fun."

Mikki McKenna suppressed a deep sigh.

Served her right for answering her cell phone without looking at caller ID. But she'd just pulled into her parking spot in front of the medical building, and because of the hour, she had naturally assumed that it was someone in her office or the hospital calling.

Either that, or it was one of a handful of patients she'd entrusted with her private line in case of an emergency.

She hadn't expected her mother to call. That came under the heading of an entirely different sort of emergency. Something just short of the apocalypse.

It had been several months since she'd heard from

her mother. Thinking back, Mikki vaguely remembered that it had been right between her mother shedding Tim Wilson, husband number four, and going off on a cruise to some faraway island paradise, the name of which presently escaped her. Her mother *always* went off on a cruise after every divorce. Cruises were her mother's primary hunting grounds for potential new husbands. She kept going on different cruises until she found someone to her satisfaction.

"I'm not afraid of having fun, Mother," Mikki began, attempting to get her mother to see *her* side for a change even though, in her heart, it was a hopeless endeavor.

Veronica McKenna Sheridan Tolliver Wilson—her mother thought that having so many names made her seem like British royalty—immediately interjected, "Well, then come! This promises to be a really wonderful party, Michelle. Anderson throws absolutely the very best parties," she said with enthusiasm.

Anderson. So that was the new candidate's name. She wondered if the man had any idea what he was in for.

"I'm sure that he does, Mother," Mikki said, humoring her. "But—"

Veronica was quick to shut her daughter down. She'd had years of practice.

"Michelle, please, you need to have a little fun before you suddenly find that you're too old to enjoy yourself. Honestly, I don't know how I wound up raising such a stick in the mud," Veronica lamented dramatically.

Possibly because you didn't raise me at all, Mother, Mikki thought.

Between her parents' arguments and the almost-frenzied partying they both indulged in, singularly and together, she'd hardly ever seen her parents when they were still married.

She remembered being periodically dropped off to stay with various relatives as a child. As she got older, there were sleepovers at friends' homes instead, especially her best friend, Nicole. Envious of the family unity she witnessed, Mikki had made sure she was the perfect houseguest, going the extra mile by cleaning up after herself as well as her friend and even preparing breakfast whenever possible.

It was her way of ensuring that she would be invited back.

By the time she was twelve, her parents had divorced, and they'd professed to want shared custody of her—which meant, in reality, that neither parent really wanted to be saddled with her upbringing. Each kept sending her to the other. Money was substituted for love. The only interest from either one of her parents came by way of the actual interest her trust fund accrued.

If it hadn't been for her great-aunt Bethany, Mikki would have felt that she had no family at all. It was Great-Aunt Bethany who took an interest in her education and suggested that she consider attending medical school.

The latter had grown out of her having nursed an injured bird back to health after it had flown into the sliding glass patio door.

"You have a good heart and good instincts, Michelle. It would be a shame to let that go to waste," Great-Aunt Bethany had told her that summer, literally dropping a number of medical school pamphlets in her lap.

And that had been the beginning of Mikki's career in medicine. Her desire to help others, to make a difference, took root that summer. Very simply, it was the reason she had decided to become a doctor.

There had also been a small part of her—because for the most part, she had given up hoping to make any meaningful connection with her mother—that *did* hope her mother would be proud of her choice.

She supposed she should have known better.

"Well, if that's what you want, I suppose you should go for it," Veronica had said when she told her mother of her plans to go to medical school. "But personally, I can't see why you'd want to go poking around people's insides or whatever it is that you'll be doing. It's all so very icky, darling." Mikki could still picture the look of revulsion on her mother's face. "And you really don't have to do that, you know. You don't need to earn a living."

She let her mother go on trying to talk her out of her choice until Veronica lost interest in the subject.

Her mother was always losing interest in subjects, this included the various men that she had married. It was always "the next one" who promised to be better. Until he wasn't.

Watching her mother over the years, Mikki had become sure of one thing. That was *not* the kind of life she wanted.

"I'm only going to be in town for another day or two," her mother was saying now. "I don't know why you don't want to take the opportunity to come out of your shell and see me."

"Because I won't be seeing you," Mikki pointed out patiently. "Not personally, at least. You'll be partying with an entire ballroom full of people." Her mother was never happier than when she was the center of everyone's attention. And if she wasn't the center of attention, she did something to make that happen.

"And what do you want me to do, Michelle? Would you like me to sit by the fireplace like some old woman, mourning over things that didn't happen?" Veronica asked testily.

"No, Mother," Mikki replied. Because it was getting warm in her car, she put her key in the ignition and cracked open a window. She knew she could just as easily step outside, but she didn't want anyone overhearing her conversation with her mother. "I want you to do whatever makes you happy. Just like I want to do whatever makes *me* happy."

"But—"

She could hear her mother's frustration vibrating in the single word. But she'd learned not to allow her mother to play her.

"Sorry, Mother. That's my other line. I've got to go," Mikki told her, terminating the call.

Mikki held the cell phone against her for a moment and sighed. For once, there was no other incoming call, but she couldn't think of another way to get her mother to stop going on about the party at the Ambassador Hotel that she wanted her to attend. She had absolutely no use for those kind of vapid parties. Mingling with a roomful of strangers wearing overpriced clothes seemed like a colossal waste of precious time to her.

She supposed that the invitation could be her mother's way of trying to connect with her after all this time, but she really doubted it. Most likely, her mother was just trying to assuage her guilty conscience, although that in itself was rather unusual. Guilt and Veronica Mc-

Kenna Sheridan Tolliver Wilson did not coexist on the same plane.

Best guess was that Anderson Pierce, Veronica's boy toy of the month, had probably expressed an interest in meeting her daughter. Mikki wouldn't have agreed to go even if she *wasn't* busy, which she was.

All the time.

She had a thriving internal medicine practice associated with Bedford Memorial and, if that wasn't enough, she also volunteered on Saturdays at the free clinic.

She would sleep, she often said, when she was dead.

That would also be when she'd party, Mikki thought with a smile. When she was dead.

Her cell phone began to ring again. This time, she looked at caller ID before answering. The number on the screen was not familiar, but the name above it was.

She couldn't remember the last time she had spoken to Maizie Sommers.

"Mrs. Sommers?" she asked uncertainly, still not sure this was the woman she was thinking of.

The second the woman spoke, all doubt vanished. No one could pack as much warmth into a simple sentence as her best friend's mother could.

"Mikki, how wonderful to hear your voice again. How are you?"

"I'm well, thank you—"

"And busy, I hear," Maizie said, reading between the lines. "Nikki tells me that you're extremely busy these days."

"Well, yes, I am," Mikki admitted, but she didn't want to just brush the woman off because of that. She had some very affectionate memories associated with her best friend's mother. She'd lost count the number of times she had slept over Nikki's house—or the number of times she had wished that Nikki's mother was *her* mother, as well. "But never too busy for you, Mrs. Sommers. What can I do for you?" she asked, certain that the woman had to be calling about something. It wasn't like her to just call up for no reason.

"That's very sweet of you, Mikki," Maizie responded. "As a matter of fact, I did call you for a reason—"

Mikki was quick to tell the woman some necessary information. "I'm not in my office right now, but I know that my schedule is full for the next few days. However, I can see you either before office hours or after office hours, whichever would be more convenient for you, Mrs. Sommers."

She heard Nikki's mother chuckle softly. "You haven't changed a bit. You were always such a very thoughtful young woman. This isn't about me, dear. It's about—a friend," Maizie said, finally settling on a satisfactory wording for her request. "The poor dear hasn't been well lately."

Maizie paused for a moment to recall exactly what Theresa had told her. "She's been experiencing sharp pains in her abdomen and a general feeling of being unwell—"

"And what does her doctor say about her symptoms?" Mikki asked. She didn't like stepping on another doctor's toes unless she thought that there might be malpractice at the bottom of the case.

"That's just it, dear. She doesn't have a doctor. Absolutely refuses to go see one," Maizie added for good measure.

In this day and age, that didn't make much sense to her. "Why?" Mikki asked.

"It's a very sad story, really," Maizie said. "Her husband was misdiagnosed many years ago, and the poor man died as a result."

"And so now she doesn't trust doctors," Mikki concluded.

"No, not since that day," Maizie confirmed. "She's adamant about it."

"I can see why she might feel that way, Mrs. Sommers. But I can't exactly examine her against her will," Mikki pointed out.

Maizie started talking a little faster as she tried to change Mikki's mind about the matter. The way she saw it, there was a lot at stake here, more than just Jeff's mother's health.

"Her son is very worried about her," she stressed, continuing to set the stage. "If I can get him to bring her in to your office, can you give her a thorough examination?" Maizie asked. "You always had such a wonderful, calming manner about you."

Mikki laughed quietly. "I never examined you, Mrs. Sommers."

"I meant in general," Maizie said. "You know, I always thought you were the perfect friend for Nikki."

That brought back memories. "I always thought it was the other way around, really."

Mikki thought for a moment. Her cell was beeping, letting her know that this time there *was* another call coming in. However, she didn't want to put Maizie on hold or risk disconnecting. She wanted to finalize things before ending the call.

She thought for a second, then asked, "Could either you or your friend's son bring this lady to my office at eight tomorrow morning?"

"Eight?" Maizie repeated.

"I know it's early," Mikki allowed sympathetically. She was an early riser, but she knew a lot of people weren't. "But it's the only vacant time I have until the following day—"

"No, that's fine, really," Maizie assured her. "I was just making sure I heard you correctly." She knew Jeff's restaurant didn't open until eleven so, technically, he was free at that time in the morning. And from what Theresa had told her about the young man, even if he wasn't free, he would still make the appointment. "I'll have to call and make sure that he can bring her," she said, just so Mikki wouldn't suspect anything. "Is it all right if I call you back?"

"Of course it's all right," Mikki responded. "By the way, my office is in the medical building across the street from Bedford Memorial."

"I know," Maizie replied. "Just like Nikki's."

"Right." Mikki realized that of course Nikki's mother would be aware of that. Only her own mother had no idea where she practiced and what hospital she was associated with, Mikki thought ruefully. "Except that Nikki's office on the fifth floor. I'm on the third. Suite 310."

Maizie had already done her homework, but to keep from arousing Mikki's suspicions, she repeated, "Suite 310. Got it," Maizie said. "I really appreciate this, Mikki. Or should I say Dr. McKenna?"

"For you I'll always be Mikki," Mikki told the older woman.

"Yes," Maizie said warmly, "you will." And with all her heart, she sincerely hoped that this match, like the others so far, would work out. Very few young women deserved to be happy as much as Mikki did. "I can't tell you how much I appreciate this, Mikki."

"There's no need to thank me, Mrs. Sommers," Mikki told her with genuine sincerity. "I'm a doctor. This is what I do."

"You mean fit patients in at the last minute and come in to see them at hours that are way too early?" Maizie asked, amused. That wasn't a doctor, Maizie thought. That was a saint.

"Perfect description of my life," Mikki told her friend's mother with a laugh.

Memories from bygone days when her daughter and Mikki were just starting out on their journey came flooding back to Maizie. She found herself growing nostalgic.

"We really need to get together at your earliest convenience, dear."

"You're not feeling well, either?" Mikki asked, concerned.

"Oh, no, I'm fine," Maizie said quickly, not wanting her to get the wrong idea. "I just meant that I would love seeing you again. It's been a while, you know."

"Yes," Mikki agreed. "It has." And unlike her conversation with her mother a short while ago, Mikki found herself really wanting to get together with the woman on the other end of the call.

"Please call me the first moment you find time in that busy life of yours," Maizie encouraged.

"I'll be sure to do that. In the meantime, see if your friend can come in tomorrow morning. If he can't, call me back and I'll see what other arrangements I can make."

"I will," Maizie promised. "You were always one of the good ones, Mikki," she added.

"Funny, that was always what I thought about you, too," Mikki said before terminating the call.

The next second, her cell phone beeped again. "Dr. McKenna," she answered.

"I know who you are, dear." She closed her eyes. It was her mother again. "Have you had time to come to your senses about attending the party yet?"

"My senses are fine, Mother. And the answer is still no. Now, if you'll excuse me, I have a patient to see," she added quickly. "So goodbye again, Mother. Have fun at your party."

With that, she ended a call from her mother for a second time and hurried off to her office in order to officially begin her day.

Chapter Three

"I know you mean well, Jeffrey, but I don't want to go to see any doctor," Sophia Sabatino protested early the next morning.

The petite woman with salt-and-pepper hair was clearly in distress as she did her best to get her son to change his mind about "dragging" her off to some unknown doctor's office.

Like his two siblings, Jeff loved his mother dearly, and he usually gave in to the diminutive martinet, but not this time. He had made up his mind. This was too important. His mother needed to see a doctor, and he was taking her to see one before it was too late.

"Sorry, Mom," he told her. "I'm overriding you on this one."

She looked at him in exasperation. "You're taking

advantage of the fact that I'm too weak to put up a good fight," Sophia complained.

"Mom," he said patiently, "try to understand. It's *because* you're feeling so weak that I'm taking you to the doctor." Handing his mother her purse, he tried to get her ready to go with him.

Sophia defiantly dropped her purse to the floor. "I'm not going to see some quack and taking off all my clothes," she declared. Lifting her small chin, she crossed her arms before her chest.

"This isn't a quack—" Jeff began. This time, as he picked up the purse, he decided it was useless to return it to his mother. She'd only drop it again, so he slung the straps over his own shoulder.

"They're all quacks," Sophia informed him. "Your father, God rest his soul, thought all doctors walked on water, and look where it got him," she pointed out. "Dead," she declared when Jeff didn't answer her.

With determination, Jeff took hold of his five-foot-one mother's elbow and guided her out the front door. His goal was to get her to his car, which was parked in the driveway, as close to the front door as possible.

"They're not all like that, Mother," he said patiently. Bringing her to the passenger side, he held the door open for her. When she remained standing where she was, he very gently "helped" usher her into the seat. She remained sitting there like a statue, so he wound up having to strap her in before closing the passenger door.

Rounding the front of his car, he got in on the driver's side as quickly as possible. Weak as she appeared to be, he wouldn't put it past his mother to bolt from the car.

As he buckled up, then started the engine, his mother

picked up the conversation as if there had been no long pause.

"Of course they're all like that," she insisted. "It's all right, Jeffrey. Don't trouble yourself about me. I've had a long, full life. I'm ready to go meet your father."

"Well, you're just going to have to postpone that meeting, Mom," he told her firmly. "Tina, Robert and I aren't ready for you to lie down and die just yet."

"That is not your decision to make, Jeffrey," Sophia sniffed.

"It's not yours, either," he countered. "Lying down and dying isn't your style, Mom. You've still got years of nagging left to do."

Sophia opened her mouth to protest his disrespectful attitude, but instead of words, she uttered a surprised gasp as a hot wave of pain washed right over her.

Torn between thinking his mother was resorting to even more theatrics and believing that she really *was* in acute pain, Jeff drove faster.

"Hang on, Mom," he told her in the most calming voice he could summon. "It's going to be all right. My old boss's best friend's daughter recommended this doctor," he said, hoping that would give his mother some confidence.

Sophia's breathing was labored, but she still managed to ask sarcastically, "Couldn't find one on Doctors Are Us?"

It was more of a gasp than a question, and Jeff had to listen intently to make out what she was saying. He didn't want her dismissing the doctor he was bringing her to before she even met her. "Mom, I'm serious. *This* is serious—"

"I know." Pressing her hand against her abdomen,

Sophia closed her eyes. "Which is why I just want to be left alone to die in peace, not have some wet-behind-the-ears would-be doctor try to earn back his entire medical school tuition by treating me and pretending he knows what he'd doing."

"Mom—" Jeff's voice grew sterner despite his concern about her condition "—you're beginning to make no sense." His mother grabbed his arm. Her long, thin fingers felt surprisingly strong as she clutched at him. "Mom?" Concerned, he spared her a glance as he made a right at the corner. The hospital and the adjacent medical building were just up ahead.

Jeff didn't have to look closely to see the perspiration not just on his mother's brow, but on the rest of her face, as well. She had to be reacting to the pain she was experiencing, because it wasn't that warm a morning.

He'd waited way too long to strong-arm his mother. He just hoped it wasn't too late.

"Hang in there, Mom, we're almost there." He did his best to sound encouraging.

Clutching the armrest on her right and her son's arm on her left, Sophia waited for the pain either to pass or totally consume her. Her breathing was growing more labored.

"Do you think your father'll recognize me? It's been a long time and I'm not the young woman I was when we lost him," she said hoarsely in between panting.

"He won't have to recognize you, because you're not dying, Mom."

Parking in the closest spot available, which because of the hour was right up in front of the medical building, Jeff got out and quickly hurried over to the passenger side. Opening the door, he slowly eased his mother out and to her feet.

She looked rather unstable.

"Do you want me to carry you?" he offered.

"No." Sophia pushed his hands away. "I'm going to walk into this charlatan's office on my own two feet," she announced with far more bravado than she was actually feeling.

He knew it was an act, but for once he encouraged it. "That's my girl."

She looked at him accusingly. "If you really cared about me, you would have let me stay home and—" Her eyes widened as a sudden new onslaught of pain seized her, causing her to clutch at her abdomen. "Oh, Jeff, it hurts. It really, really hurts," she cried, all but sagging to her knees.

Jeff was torn between putting his mother back in the car and driving over to the hospital's emergency entrance and taking her upstairs to see the doctor who was waiting for her. The doctor who Theresa Manetti had assured him would be able to calm his mother down and find out what was wrong with her.

Jeff quickly weighed the options. He knew his mother. She'd balk at the emergency room, but he had managed to half talk her into seeing this doctor.

He went with door number two.

"What...what...are you doing?" Sophia gasped as he closed his arms around her. "I'm too heavy...for... you," she protested.

Jeff had lifted his mother up into his arms and proceeded to carry her into the medical building. "I've carried bags of rice heavier than you," he informed her, heading over to the elevator bank.

Because it was so early, there was an elevator car standing on the ground floor with its doors wide-open. It was empty.

He walked right in.

"Can you press three, Mom?" he asked, taking nothing for granted.

He could see more perspiration forming on her brow. She had to be in pain, he thought.

"This…is…a waste of…time," Sophia told him, trying hard not to gasp between each word. With visible effort as well as a show of reluctance, she weakly raised her hand and pressed the number three.

The doors barely closed before they opened again on the third floor.

Getting out, Jeff glanced at the signs on the wall, saw the arrow, then went right. Reading the numbers, he looked for suite 310.

Arriving in front of the door, he tried to angle the door latch with his elbow to push it down. When it didn't give, he tried again.

When the latch still didn't move, he used his elbow to bang on the door, hoping there was someone inside who would hear him and let them in.

Mikki had arrived at her office even earlier than she normally did. She'd let herself in through the back door because Angela, her receptionist, and the two nurses who worked for her, Virginia and Molly, weren't due in until regular hours, which officially began at nine.

Just because she was doing a favor for Maizie Sommers didn't mean that her staff had to be inconvenienced and come in earlier than usual, as well, Mikki thought. They worked hard enough as it was.

Mikki had just slipped on her white lab coat over a simple gray pencil skirt and blue-gray blouse when she heard a loud thud against the front office door.

Actually three thuds, she amended. Someone with a very heavy hand was either knocking on the door or trying to break it down.

Since she didn't keep a weapon in the office, she slipped her cell phone into her lab coat pocket after first pressing nine and one. All she had to do was press one more digit and the police would be on their way, she thought confidently. Bedford had next to no crime to speak of, and the well-trained police force, from what she'd heard, were eager to exercise their muscles.

Hopefully they wouldn't have to, she thought as she carefully approached her front office door.

"Who's there?" she called out.

"Dr. McKenna?" a deep male voice asked. "I'm Jeff Sabatino. I've brought my mother in to see you."

Relieved, Mikki quickly unlocked the main door—she hadn't had a chance to entirely open up the office yet.

She was about to say as much when she saw that the man she was speaking to was carrying an older woman in his arms.

"What happened?" Mikki asked, immediately opening the door wider and stepping aside to allow him to walk in.

"My mother started complaining of this stabbing pain on our way over here, and then when she got out of the car, her legs suddenly seemed to give way and she collapsed."

"I didn't collapse," Sophia protested indignantly. "I had a twinge of weakness. But I'm all right now," his mother declared with determination. "My son exaggerates things. I just want to go home and get into bed." She said the latter as if she was issuing an order to her son.

"Soon, Mrs. Sabatino," Mikki promised. "But I'd like to examine you first, if you don't mind."

"I do mind," Sophia retorted stubbornly.

"She's very grateful," Jeff corrected. His mother still in his arms, he looked around the general area. "Do you have an exam room?" he asked, then mentally upbraided himself. He hadn't meant to ask her that, he'd meant to ask where her exam room *was*.

Mikki smiled. "Actually, I do. I find they come in very handy in my line of work. Right this way," she told Jeff, leading him to the back of the office.

There were three exam rooms located in the back, one right next to the other. She opened the door to the first room and gestured for him to bring his mother into it.

"If you just have her lie down on the exam table," Mikki instructed, "I can get started."

Jeff did as she asked, placing his mother gently on the paper-covered examination table. Mikki couldn't help noticing that he had a very sensitive manner about him. It seemed almost in direct contradiction to the masculinity the tall, dark-haired man exuded.

"I've got her insurance cards and her driver's license," Jeff said, reaching for his mother's purse in order to produce the items.

But Mikki shook her head. "Don't worry about that right now. My receptionist isn't in yet. She handles all that. Right now, I'm more interested in why your mother had to be carried in—other than the fact that she didn't want to come to see me. Mrs. Sommers told me that you don't have any confidence in doctors," Mikki said, turning to her patient.

"I don't trust them," Sophia all but growled, keeping her hand firmly pressed against her lower right abdomen and grimacing.

"Mom!" Jeff admonished. He knew his mother had a take-charge attitude and she had no problem with making her opinion known, but he'd never seen her acting rude before, and it surprised him. It also wasn't any way to behave toward a woman who had gone out of her way to come in early and see her before office hours.

Mikki raised her hand, silently asking him to hold his peace for a moment. She was interested in her patient's response.

"Why not?" she asked the woman.

"Because a doctor killed my husband," Sophia cried with a hitch in her voice.

"Killed him or didn't save him in time?" Mikki asked diplomatically.

"What does it matter?" Sophia snapped. "He's gone. My Antonio's gone," the woman lamented.

"It matters," Mikki said gently. She began to slowly move her fingers along the perimeter of what seemed to be the painful region. "But right now, what matters more is what's going on with you. What are you feeling, Mrs. Sabatino?"

"Like someone's cutting up my insides with a burning-hot band saw." Her statement was punctuated with another audible cry of pain as she clutched at her abdomen again, almost pulling herself into the fetal position.

"I'm going to press a little more on your abdomen, Mrs. Sabatino. I want you to tell me if it hurts," Mikki requested.

"It hurts, it hurts," Sophia cried immediately.

"Mom, she hasn't touched you yet," Jeff pointed out, then turned toward the woman examining his mother. "I'm really sorry, Doctor," he began.

Mikki shook her head, wanting to put him at ease. "Don't be. Your mother's pain is very real," she told him. "She's obviously hurting without my touching her." As she spoke, Mikki subtly placed her hand first near his mother and then very gently on the area where she thought the pain originated.

She was right.

"Argh!" Sophia cried, her eyes narrowing as she angrily looked at the doctor. "You're *hurting* me!"

"I'm sorry," Mikki apologized. "I just want to be sure what's going on. How long have you had this pain?"

Sophia shrugged carelessly, avoiding her son's eyes as she mumbled, "A few weeks, I guess."

"Mom!" He'd only become aware of the problem in the last couple of days. "A few weeks? Why didn't you call me?"

Still avoiding his eyes, Sophia sighed. "I didn't want to bother you. You have that restaurant and everything. You're always so busy," she said just before her expression changed as she noticeably braced herself for another wave of pain.

Instead of reaching for a thermometer, Mikki opted to test her theory the old-fashioned way. She lightly placed her fingertips against the woman's forehead, finding it quite warm.

"Okay," Mikki murmured to herself. "I think that proves it."

"What is it?" Jeff asked, looking at the doctor quizzically. "Can you tell what's wrong with my mother?"

Mikki didn't want to be premature, but she had a very strong suspicion about what was going on. "Well, I think that we'd better get your mother into the hospital," she began.

"No, no hospital!" Sophia interrupted.

"Mom, let the doctor talk," Jeff told her, trying to get his mother to calm down long enough to hear the diagnosis.

"I don't care what she's going to say, I'm not going to die in a hospital," Sophia declared.

"No," Mikki responded with confidence. "You're not. But in order for you *not* to die, we need to get you there in time."

"In time for what?" Sophia demanded. "To cut me up into pieces?"

"No, just one piece," Mikki answered quite seriously.

"What is it, Doctor?" Jeff asked. His mother was clutching his hand and he wanted to do his best to calm her, but right now, he wasn't feeling all that calm himself. "What's with my mother?"

"I need to run some tests," Mikki prefaced.

"I got all that. I understand. Just tell me what you *suspect* is wrong," Jeff said.

"Well," Mikki began, "with any luck—"

"Luck? You call feeling like someone set your insides on fire lucky?" Sophia cried indignantly. "Take me home, Jeff!"

"Let her talk, Mom," Jeff ordered, surprising his mother with his abrupt tone. He turned toward Mikki. "Doctor?"

"Best guess," Mikki said, enunciating every word

as she looked at the all but terrified woman on her examination table, "is that it looks as if your mother has appendicitis."

Chapter Four

The pain had momentarily abated, and Sophia sniffed. "Some doctor. She doesn't know what she's talking about," she told her son.

Jeff prided himself on his patience. He had a nearly infinite amount, both at work and when it came to dealing with his mother when she was being difficult. But his ample supply was just about used up this particular morning.

A warning note entered his voice. "Mother—"

Ignoring him, Sophia said, "I had my appendix removed when I was six," just before she suddenly doubled up in pain again.

"Are you sure?" Mikki questioned. "Forgive me," she quickly interjected, "but according to what you just said, you *were* six, and maybe you're not remembering things quite clearly."

"Of course I'm sure," Sophia bit off, annoyed that this slip of a girl was doubting her. "My mother told me that's what happened." About to continue, she suddenly grew very pale as she grabbed her son's hand. "I can't take this anymore, Jeffrey. Put me out of my misery."

Interceding, Mikki laid a gentling hand on the woman's arm to get her attention. "I fully intend to, Mrs. Sabatino, but not the way you mean." Mikki looked at Jeff. "I have to get her to the hospital and run some tests," she explained. "I still think it's appendicitis, but if it is something else, the CT scan and abdominal ultrasound should show us what we're up against."

Jeff looked at her, puzzled. "How can it be appendicitis if hers was removed?"

"She could be mistaken," Mikki pointed out. "At six, it's easy to misunderstand what's happening. Checking to make sure the appendix was removed is a simple process."

Sophia's laugh was harsh. "She just wants to get me into the hospital and do all those expensive tests on me."

He was aware that the doctor was doing him a favor, seeing his mother so quickly. She certainly didn't deserve to be treated this way. "I'm sorry about this," he apologized to Mikki.

Mikki's smile wasn't strained. Instead, it was understanding.

"It's okay, really," she told him. "I'm not offended. Your mother's afraid. Who wouldn't be?" she asked, giving Sophia an encouraging look. Sophia appeared to be totally oblivious to it. "Let me just leave a note for my receptionist and I'll ride over to the hospital with you and your mother," Mikki told him, picking up a pad and pen.

Jeff realized what a huge imposition this had to be for the doctor, especially since his mother wasn't even one of her regular patients. He could see why Dr. McKenna had been recommended to him. She seemed to have an infinite amount of patience.

"I really appreciate this, Dr. McKenna," he told her, then lowered his voice before adding, "My mother can be very difficult."

Mikki thought it prudent not to comment on that as she quickly wrote a note to her receptionist. He could say anything he wanted to about Sophia, but after all, the woman *was* his mother. If she agreed with his assessment, in all likelihood he would become defensive and that would make further communication difficult.

Being vague about her new patient's disposition was the best way to go.

"Let's just try to get her better," Mikki responded. "I'm going to call ahead so that we can get her into the radiology lab for those scans quickly."

With that, Mikki turned away in order to make her call.

The pain abated again for a moment. Concerned that she was disrupting his life, Sophia looked up at her son. "Just leave me here, Jeffrey. You have to get to work," she reminded him.

"Not for a few hours yet," Jeff corrected, "and anyway, I have people to cover for me. Let's just focus on finally getting to the bottom of this pain you've been having."

A ragged sigh escaped Sophia's lips. "Everyone dies, Jeffrey."

His mother could never be accused of being happy-go-lucky, Jeff thought. Or an optimist. "But not today," he told her firmly.

Sophia began to protest just as the woman she viewed as far too young to be a doctor, much less one who was exceptionally skillful, rejoined them.

"Everything's set," Mikki announced. "Let's get your mother over to the hospital. We'll use your car."

He didn't ask her why, but once they arrived in the hospital parking lot, the answer quickly became apparent. The doctor pointed out a space marked Physician Parking Only and told him to park there.

"My car's a small two-door," she explained, "and I wanted your mother to be comfortable." Quickly getting out of his vehicle, she told Jeff, "Wait here. I'm going in to get a gurney for your mother."

The moment the doctor walked in through the electronic doors labeled ER Entrance, Sophia grabbed her son's arm again. "I don't know about this, Jeffrey."

"Well, I do, Mom. We're here and we're getting to the bottom of all this. You almost cut off my circulation the last time you grabbed my hand."

"I won't squeeze your hand again, I promise," Sophia told him.

"That's not the point, Mom," Jeff said. "You're in a great deal of pain, and we need to find out why before your condition gets any worse."

"It's just indigestion," Sophia cried, trying not to writhe in pain. She was desperate to have him take her back home. She hadn't been inside a hospital since she'd lost her husband, and just being outside one brought back terrible memories.

"Enough excuses, Mom. You're having these tests and that's that," he told her firmly just as Mikki returned with a nurse and an orderly in tow. The latter two were pushing a gurney between them.

"Your chariot's here, Mrs. Sabatino," Mikki announced, smiling as she and the two hospital staff members approached Sophia.

Sheer panic entered Sophia's eyes when she looked up at her son. "Jeffrey?"

He forced himself to ignore his mother's pleading tone. "You're going in for those tests, Mom, and I'm going to be right there with you," he promised.

"Well, maybe during the ultrasound, but not during the CT scan," Mikki told him. Seeing the panicked expression on his mother's face, she added, "But I can come into the room with you."

That did little to comfort Sophia. "But I don't know you," she protested.

"Well, we'll use the time to get to know each other," Mikki told her.

Sophia murmured something under her breath that neither the doctor nor Jeff could make out. Jeff expected to see Mikki become annoyed. After all, she was bending over backward for his mother, who was being far from her usual genial self.

But the doctor only smiled, saying something encouraging to her in response.

Theresa had been right, Jeff thought as he accompanied his mother and her new doctor into the emergency room. Dr. McKenna was an absolute treasure. She was going out of her way to humor his mother and she hadn't lost her temper once. Most people did when his mother behaved this way. It wasn't often, but it was grating when it happened. He dearly loved the woman, but he wasn't blind to her faults.

Once inside the emergency room, his mother was taken to a curtained-off bed in order to prepare her for the CT scan, ultrasound and several other necessary tests. Jeff waited outside the curtained area as one of the nurses went in to help his mother change into a hospital gown.

"I'll take good care of her," Mikki said, coming up behind him.

Surprised—he'd assumed that the doctor had left for the time being—Jeff turned around to look at the petite dark blonde.

"What about your other patients?" he asked. He remembered that Theresa had told him the doctor had a full schedule today. That was why she'd asked him to bring his mother in so early.

"I take good care of them, too," Mikki answered with a smile.

He had no doubt that she did. There was something exceptionally competent about the woman. "I hope they're not all like my mother."

She laughed, and he liked the way her blue eyes crinkled.

"Oh, you'd be surprised," she told him. "A great many of my patients require a lot of hand-holding and reassuring."

"How do you do it?" he marveled.

"One hand at a time" was her answer.

Just then the nurse stepped out from between the curtained-off section. "She's all ready," the nurse told Mikki.

The latter nodded in response. "Then let's get the show on the road."

"Before you get started, Doctor," Jeff said, stopping her for a moment, "I just want to say thank you."

Her smile was warm and genuine. "No problem," Mikki said.

"But there will be," he replied with a sigh.

Mikki merely laughed in response.

The tests went far more quickly than he'd thought they would. He and his mother had arrived at the hospital at eight thirty. By ten fifteen the doctor had returned to tell him that she had all the results and she'd been able to diagnose his mother's condition.

When she paused for a moment, he immediately asked, "Is it appendicitis?"

"In a way," Mikki replied.

Anxiety sent a cold shiver down his spine. "There's more?"

"Yes." She chose her words carefully in order to explain the situation to him and not cause any undue confusion. "Fortunately for her, your mother's appendix apparently wasn't removed when she was six."

That didn't sound right at all to him, Jeff thought. Did the doctor have a macabre sense of humor? "What do you mean, fortunately?"

"Well, if your mother's appendix hadn't been there," she told him, "then we might not have ever known about the existence of the tumor until it was too late to do anything about it."

"Tumor?" he asked. It was all beginning to sound frighteningly surreal to him. "There's a tumor?"

She nodded. "It appears to be benign, but we won't know until we do a biopsy on it." She went on to paint a picture for him. "If the appendix hadn't been there, the tumor might have continued growing until it just burst on its own. The appendix got in its way, and the tumor was pressing on it. That's what caused your mother all that pain. We're going to be removing all of it, the tumor and her appendix."

He struggled to come to grips with the idea—and its possible implication. "Will this affect her in any way?" he asked.

"You mean the operation? Yes. Once it's over, the pain'll be gone," she told him. And then she smiled. "Your mother will be up on her feet and back to her old self in six weeks—or less."

That sounded almost as impossible as his mother having a tumor. "Really?" he questioned.

"Really," she assured him. "The whole thing sounds worse than it is, trust me."

He found himself doing just that. Which raised another question. "Who's going to be doing the surgery?" Jeff asked.

"Well, unless you have someone in mind who you want me to contact," Mikki began, waiting. When he didn't say anything, she went on to say, "It'll be me."

"Oh, I want you," Jeff told her with feeling. Then realizing how that had to sound, he tried to correct the impression. "I mean—"

Mikki laughed, and he caught himself thinking that the sound was almost endearing.

"I know what you mean, Mr. Sabatino, and I appreciate the vote of trust," she told him. Mikki glanced at her watch. "This is going to take a couple of hours once we get her ready and wheel her into the OR. After that, she'll be in recovery for another hour. From there, she'll be taken up to her room.

"If she responds like everyone else, your mother will be in and out of consciousness for the rest of the day, so I suggest that if you want to go to work, you do so without any guilt. Your mother's not going to be fully awake until sometime tomorrow morning, if not later."

"Is my mother still conscious now?" Jeff asked.

Mikki nodded. "We haven't given her anything to sedate her yet. So if you want to say a few encouraging words to her before we put her under, now would be the time to do it. They're getting the OR ready for her."

He heard something else in the woman's voice besides a recitation of the chain of events. "Then it *is* urgent," he asked her.

She didn't want to frighten him unnecessarily, but she didn't want to be evasive, either. Mikki offered him a smile. "Let's just say—without being melodramatic—that you brought your mother in just in time."

He was both relieved and stunned by the news. "Does she know?"

"I believe in keeping my patients informed, but not in scaring them," she replied. "Now, if you'll excuse me, I have to call my office to tell them I won't be in for a while—and then I have some less than fashionable blue scrubs to put on." She turned to go, but paused for a moment. She sensed that the tall, handsome man standing in the corridor needed a little reassuring. "She's going to be fine, Mr. Sabatino."

"Jeff," he corrected as he took in a steadying breath, thinking of the bullet they'd just been dodged. "Call me Jeff."

Mikki nodded. "Okay. Are you planning on staying here until your mother's in recovery—Jeff?"

He knew he wouldn't be able to focus if he went any-where right now. "Yes, I am."

"Then I'll send someone out to let you know how it's going," Mikki promised.

"That's very kind of you," he told her.

"Practical," she corrected. "Otherwise, your imagi-nation might just run away with you and then I might have another patient on my hands."

The moment the doctor left, Jeff went in to see his mother.

"Jeffrey, she's operating on me," Sophia lamented the second she saw him.

"I know that, Mom," he said kindly.

She looked somewhat surprised—and perhaps even upset. "And you're all right with this?"

"I wouldn't have it any other way, Mom," Jeff told her.

Sophia fixed the drooping shoulder of her hospital gown and drew herself up. "I think we need a second opinion."

"This from the woman who didn't want any opinion," Jeff remarked. He took her hand in his. Hers was icy to the touch. "Mom, you're just stalling. You know that a second opinion is most likely going to be the same as the one you just received."

"Maybe not," she cried.

It had never occurred to him until just now how much his mother looked like a little girl. A frightened little girl.

Closing his hand over hers, he assured her, "It's going to be fine, Mom. When you wake up, the pain'll be gone."

"Ha! You've obviously never had an operation," his mother said.

Jeff inclined his head, giving his mother her due. "Okay, let me rephrase that. The pain that brought you here will be gone."

Sophia snorted dismissively. "Trading in one pain for another doesn't exactly put me ahead of the game, you know."

"It does if the first pain can eventually kill you," he pointed out. The nurse entered just then, saving him. "They're going to get you ready for surgery now, Mom." He saw the clear panic in her gray eyes. "I'm going to be right here, waiting for you. I'll see you when this is all over," he promised.

"You hope," Sophia said.

"I know," he corrected. "Now, behave yourself," he told her, giving her hand a squeeze.

"Sir, we have to begin," the nurse gently prodded.

Releasing his mother's hand, he stepped back, about to leave.

"Tell Tina and Robert I love them," his mother suddenly said.

"You'll tell them yourself after this is over," he told her patiently.

"And if this doesn't turn out well, tell them that I forgave you," she called after him.

Jeff suppressed a sigh. "I'll tell them, Mom."

Chapter Five

Jeff felt antsy enough to want to set up camp right outside the operating room doors.

Since that wasn't really possible without having someone from security come to remove him, he settled on the nearby lounge.

Initially.

He really had intended on waiting there until his mother's operation was over. But despite his calm outward demeanor, when it came to being concerned about someone in his family, Jeff's patience tended to wither.

As a compromise, he settled for pacing in the lounge—and then up and down the corridor—slowly, doing his best to kill time and to get the antsy feeling under control.

For as long as Jeff could remember, his mother had been the family rock, the one everyone else turned to when they needed support. She wasn't supposed to be the one who needed support, but well, here they were.

Damn, but he hoped he'd done the right thing, bringing her to this doctor. He had a great deal of faith in Theresa Manetti, and in a roundabout fashion, Theresa had recommended this doctor.

But the doctor who had inadvertently misdiagnosed his father's condition had been recommended by a friend of his father's, and that had certainly turned out badly.

What if, well-meaning though she seemed, this doctor wound up botching the surgery she was about to perform on his mother?

He just couldn't seem to shake the sinking feeling that was snaking its way through him, undermining his confidence.

When his cell phone began to vibrate, he all but yanked it out of his pocket, fearing the worst. All he needed now was an emergency at work. He felt that he'd left the restaurant in capable hands, but there was always a chance that something unforeseeable would happen.

Jeff debated not answering his phone, just turning the cell off and slipping it back into his pocket. But the next moment, he acknowledged that was being cowardly. It wasn't the way he handled things or shouldered responsibilities.

Making himself look at the cell phone screen, he recognized the caller ID. Relieved and somewhat puzzled, he accepted the call.

"Theresa?" he asked.

"Hello, Jeff," he heard his former boss say. "I hope you don't mind my calling you."

"No, of course not." He just thought it rather odd—Theresa wasn't in the habit of calling him to chat. "Is there anything I can do for you?" he asked.

"No," she answered. Maybe it was his imagination, but Theresa sounded rather uncomfortable. "Actually, I'm just calling to see how everything went with your mother's appointment with that doctor I told you about."

Jeff glanced over toward the OR doors. He'd seen several hospital staff members go in after his mother had been wheeled into the operating room, but there'd been no one going in or out for the last forty minutes. He told himself that was a good sign, but the truth was, he didn't know.

"Well, I'm at the hospital," he answered rather guardedly. "My mother's being operated on right now."

He heard Theresa stifle a gasp. "My goodness. Jeff, do you want me to come down there to wait with you?" she asked.

The offer heartened him. Again, he couldn't help thinking that Theresa Manetti was certainly like another mother to him.

"No, that's okay. There's no need for you to come. It shouldn't be that much longer." Unless he thought of it in seconds, because time was passing as if it was being dragged by an arthritic turtle with a pronounced limp.

"You're sure?" Theresa didn't sound convinced.

"I'm sure," he told her with as much conviction as he could muster under the circumstances.

"What kind of an operation is it?" Theresa asked.

"It's kind of involved," he admitted. At the moment, he really didn't want to get into it, or explain the details. "But the doctor seems confident that my mother's going to be all right." He sighed, looking back at the OR doors again. And then he shared what had been weighing on his mind. "The doctor said we got her here just in time."

"That's all your doing, dear," Theresa assured him. "If I remember correctly, you once told me that your mother can be a very stubborn woman."

"Well, yes, she is," Jeff admitted, although right now he didn't want to say anything that sounded the least bit negative about his mother.

He felt somewhat disloyal for having voiced that opinion. After all, he knew that she was only trying her best. It hadn't been easy for her, raising three kids as a single mother.

Theresa laughed softly. Then, as if reading his mind, she assured him, "All the best mothers are stubborn. Nothing wrong with that. Let me know how it goes, dear. Please call me if there's anything I can do."

"I will," he promised, "And thanks for calling."

"My pleasure, dear. Remember, call me," Theresa repeated just before she ended the call.

Sighing, Jeff tucked the cell phone back into his pocket.

There were a dozen things he needed to see to and a whole host of arrangements he had promised other people that he'd get to at his restaurant. He had a more than able crew at Dinner for Two, but it was up to him to keep everything running smoothly.

However, it felt as if everything had ground to a halt the moment he watched his mother being wheeled into the operating room. He really wasn't up to focusing his attention on anything else.

Parents were supposed to live forever. At least the good ones were, he thought as the corners of his mouth quirked in a smile. But his father had died all those years ago, and now his mother might be in danger of joining him.

No, damn it, he wasn't going to think like that. He'd gotten her here in time and Dr. McKenna seemed like she was very capable, so he was just going to stop entertaining these negative thoughts, stop feeling as if he was on the cusp of becoming an orphan and concentrate on the fact that his mother was going to make it through this operation and get well.

Jeff slipped his hand into his pocket and curled it around his phone. Contact with the phone made him debate calling his brother and sister to tell them what was going on. They were a close family, and he knew they wouldn't take kindly to being kept in the dark.

But what good would it do to make them worry? Robert was at a business meeting in Los Angeles today, and Tina had small kids. She couldn't rush over to the hospital with them, and finding a sitter would take a while. By the time either one of his siblings could get here, their mother would be out of surgery and most likely out of recovery, as well.

He'd rather be the bearer of good news than to be the one to lay worry on their doorsteps.

Out of the corner of his eye, Jeff saw one of the operating room doors open, and he was instantly alert. He held his breath as a nurse wearing scrubs and a surgical mask approached him.

"Are you Mr. Sabatino?" the nurse asked, peering up at him.

If he were any tenser, Jeff thought he'd probably snap in half. Automatically, he braced himself for bad news. "Yes, I am."

"Dr. McKenna sent me out to tell you that everything

is going according to schedule and that your mother is doing well. The operation's going to take about another hour, and the doctor suggested that you might want to get some coffee from the cafeteria downstairs. She said to tell you that the coffee from the vending machines up here'll kill you." The woman's eyes crinkled above her mask as she smiled.

Jeff almost laughed out loud at the comment. Tension began to drain out of him.

"Tell the doctor thank you," he said, "but I'll take my chances. I'm staying right here until she's finished operating on my mother."

The nurse nodded, giving no indication that his answer surprised her.

"I'll let her know." Her eyes crinkled slightly again above the surgical mask and she turned to walk back into the operating room.

He felt like a marathon runner who had just passed the halfway point.

He knew he should sit down, that marching up and down the length of the corridor was annoying to anyone who might be looking out of the doors located along the path he was taking, but he was just too restless to remain still for more than a couple of minutes at a time.

Finally, after what felt like forever plus twenty minutes, as he turned on his heel to retrace his steps past the OR doors for what seemed like the thousandth time, he saw them opening. This time, it was the doctor who came out.

Technically, because of the surgical mask, it could have been anyone in those blue scrubs, but he knew it was Dr. McKenna.

No one else had clear-water eyes quite that shade of blue.

Jeff cut the distance between them in less time than it took to think about it.

"Is the operation over?" he asked, suddenly afraid to ask the real question that had been preying on his mind for the last two hours.

"Yes," Mikki replied as she removed her mask. "And your mother, I'm happy to say, came through it with flying colors."

"Was it a tumor?" he asked, bracing himself for the worst while praying for the best.

"Yes, it was," Mikki replied. "But the preliminary biopsy said it was benign."

"Not malignant?" he asked, wanting to be very, very sure.

Mikki smiled. "Not malignant."

The dam gates opened and Jeff felt relief flooding through him. Overjoyed, he wasn't completely aware of what he did next. Wasn't aware of throwing his arms around the woman who had come bearing good news until he suddenly realized he was doing it.

He felt her blue-clad body against his as he spun her around in a circle.

The very next second, common sense made a belated appearance, and he quickly set her down again.

"I'm sorry, I didn't mean to—"

What he meant to tell Mikki was that he hadn't meant to get so personal, or so exuberant because he was afraid he'd insulted her.

Mikki absolved him of any guilt before he could get the words out.

"That's all right. That spin was probably the most

fun I've had in a month," she told him with a laugh. Gaining her bearings, Mikki went on to say, "As I told you earlier, your mother's going to be in recovery for an hour, then they'll take her up to her room. You're free to go visit her then, but she's probably going to be asleep for most of that time."

He remembered her telling him that before and nodded. But he was more interested in something else she'd said.

"When I asked you about the tumor, you mentioned the word *preliminary*," he began, wanting to have everything spelled out for him. It was important that he didn't misunderstand or get his facts mixed up.

By the expression on her face, he could tell that the doctor knew what he was thinking. "We always like to double-check results to make sure we haven't missed anything, but right now, it's all looking very good, Mr. Sabatino."

"Jeff," he reminded her.

"Right. Jeff," she repeated with a smile, just happy that she was able to give the man good news.

For now he had just one more question. "And was my mother mistaken about her appendix having been removed years ago? I mean, it didn't grow back or anything, right?" he asked. "Just curious," he added, not wanting her to think that he was in any way doubting this woman who, in his opinion, had done the impossible and gotten his mother into the operating room.

"No, it didn't grow back, and yes, your mother was mistaken about it being removed when she was a little girl. As I said to you before we took her into the OR, your mother's very lucky that she hadn't had her appendix removed the way she thought she did. Having her appendix there was what saved her life."

But Jeff shook his head. "*You* saved her life," he corrected.

She was definitely not going to argue with him. The operation had been a complicated one, and she was tired. Tired with a full day still ahead of her.

"Let's compromise and call it a team effort," she told him. "Now, I've got a whole office full of patients waiting for me," she said, already backing away. "But I will be back to look in on your mother tonight. And, of course, she'll have nurses monitoring her progress all day.

"If you have the time now," she said, raising her voice so that it would carry as she continued backing away, "stop by inpatient registration and give them your mother's insurance cards and her personal information. They get very nervous if that's not entered into the system for someone staying in one of the hospital's single-care units."

He had brought all the necessary papers with him. They were in his wallet.

"I'll do that," he told her. Then looking around, he asked, "Um, which way—"

"Inpatient registration is to your left," Mikki called out. Then, seeing him start to go the wrong way, she prompted, "Your *other* left."

He gave her a quick salute as he changed directions.

There was a lot of background noise, but he still managed to hear her laugh. The sound connected with something within him and buoyed him up.

Jeff hurried off to comply with the doctor's request.

After everything Dr. McKenna had just done, he wasn't about to drop the ball and neglect to register his mother.

He knew that they couldn't very well evict her—did patients get evicted from hospital rooms? he wondered. But he had no doubt that there was probably someone who was in charge of all this who might take it upon themselves to admonish Dr. McKenna about her unregistered patient.

After everything that she had just done, he wanted the doctor canonized, not given grief for an oversight, especially if it was *his* oversight.

And after he got his mother all squared away and properly registered, Jeff told himself, he was finally going to call Tina and Robert to let them know that their mother was in the hospital and that she had gotten through her operation with flying colors.

He intended to emphasize that she was doing just fine thanks to a very able, very kindhearted surgeon who also happened to be extremely sexy.

Maybe he'd keep that last part to himself, Jeff amended. At least for the time being.

Chapter Six

"Wow, you look as if you were rode hard and put away wet," Virginia Masson, Mikki's head nurse, commented the moment she saw her walking in through the rear entrance to the medical office.

"Words every woman longs to hear," Mikki said with a sigh.

The moment she'd finished the operation, she'd raced back into the locker room and changed out of her scrubs into what she'd worn when she came in this morning. She hadn't even bothered look in the mirror before hurrying back to the medical building—on foot because she'd made the trip to the hospital in Jeff's car.

Mikki ran her fingers through her hair in lieu of using a brush and looked in the general direction of the waiting room. "How many are out there?" she asked.

"Enough to put a chill in your heart if you were Marie Antoinette," Virginia answered.

In other words, a crowd scene, Mikki thought. "My, you are colorful today. Fill me in on why after I see a few of these patients."

"They all waited for you, you know. Angela did her best to try to get them to reschedule, but they wanted to wait it out." Virginia shook her head. "Must be wonderful to have so many adoring fans," the dark-haired nurse teased.

"They just appreciate a good doctor," Molly Campbell, her other nurse said, coming out of the last exam room to join them.

Mikki flashed the second nurse a smile as she shrugged into her lab coat. "You—I think I'll keep," she quipped. "Her—I'm not so sure about," she added, nodding toward Virginia. "Okay, who's in exam room one?" she asked, mentally rolling up her sleeves to plunge into her day.

"Emily Rodriguez. She's waiting to hear the results of the lab tests she had done last week." As Virginia spoke, she produced several sheets of paper the lab had sent over and placed them in the file Mikki had just picked up from the reception desk.

A quick study, Mikki scanned all three sheets before she reached exam room one. She looked over her shoulder at the remaining files on the desk.

"Maybe I should have gone home," she murmured to herself.

Centering, she summoned a wide smile, opened the door to the exam room and walked in. "Afternoon, Emily. Sorry to keep you waiting so long—"

It was nonstop from there. Mikki saw one patient

after another, pausing only to take an occasional sip of coffee, which went from hot to lukewarm to cold. She hardly noticed. All she cared about was that it was black. As such it served as her fuel and kept her going.

By three forty-five, she had made a sufficient dent in her patient load. Going nonstop, she'd almost managed to catch up.

Tired, Virginia leaned against the wall as another patient received her paperwork from Angela and left the office. The woman looked at Mikki, not bothering to hide her admiration.

"Damn, lady, you have to let me know what brand of vitamins you're on, because they just can't be anything normal people have access to," Virginia commented.

"It's called fear of letting anyone down," Mikki told her.

Overhearing her, Molly laughed. "Like you ever could," the young redhead responded.

Mikki nodded toward the waiting room. "How's it going out there?" she asked.

Virginia looked down at the sign-in sheet. "Eight more patients and then I believe freedom is yours," she said, peering out into the waiting room to double-check. And then she looked again. "Oh, wait, I think we have a walk-in."

Mikki closed her eyes. "I don't know if I'm up to this." Her day had felt like an endless parade of patients. "Angela, see if Dr. Graves is available to take the overflow."

"No," Virginia told her, forestalling any such inquiry. "I think you're going to want to take this one yourself."

Mikki was about to tell her head nurse that the woman was crediting her with being superhuman. But just as she opened her mouth to protest, she caught a glimpse of the person who had just entered the waiting room—a deliveryman holding a large crystal vase filled with what looked like at least two dozen long-stemmed pink roses.

Virginia looked at her in utter stunned surprise and cried, "You're seeing someone and you didn't tell us?"

It took a second for the words to sink in. Another to realize that both nurses *and* the receptionist were staring at her. Virginia appeared a little envious, while Molly seemed almost hurt.

"No, I'm not seeing anyone," Mikki responded. "There must be some mistake." Leaning over the reception desk to peer into the waiting room, she told the deliveryman, "You have the wrong suite."

The young man looked at the clipboard tucked under his arm, then at the card attached to the arrangement. The name on the envelope was facing him. He raised very pale eyebrows to look at her. "You Dr. McKenna?"

"Yes, but—"

"Then I've got the right suite. I need one of you to sign for this," he said, setting the vase down on the reception desk and holding out his clipboard.

Both nurses were now flanking Mikki. "If I sign for them, do I get to keep the flowers?" Virginia asked her.

Molly, a veteran of fifteen years of married life, made a dismissive noise. "I'd probably have to die before Walter would send me flowers that looked like that," she commented. "Hell, I'd probably have to die before he sent me a single daisy."

"They certainly are beautiful," one of Mikki's remaining patients said from the waiting room.

Well, there was no denying that, Mikki silently admitted.

Quickly signing her name on the line the delivery-man pointed out, she returned the clipboard to him. Pausing only to take the small envelope that had come with the flowers and pocketing it, she turned toward her receptionist and said, "Please send in the next patient, Angela."

Virginia looked at her, totally mystified. "Don't you want to know who the flowers are from?" she asked Mikki as she went into exam room three to prepare it for the next patient.

"They're probably from some broker who's trying to sell me a retirement plan," Mikki guessed. "This is just a sales ploy, and things like this pop up all the time. I'll look at the card later."

There was no one in her life who would be inclined to send her flowers, much less do it. And there certainly was no occasion, large or small, coming up in the near future that necessitated any sort of celebration. She was convinced that it had to be some mix-up at the florist, and she'd see about straightening it out after she saw her last four patients of the day.

And once she did that, she still had to get back to the hospital, Mikki reminded herself. She wanted to look in on Mrs. Sabatino before she called it a day. Mikki was fairly confident that the woman would still be asleep—and would remain that way through the night—but that didn't change the fact that she wanted to check on her just to see how her impromptu patient was doing.

"Okay, you did it. Mr. Meyers was your last patient of the day," Virginia announced three hours later.

Crossing the reception area, the head nurse locked the office door, then turned around to waylay her friend and employer before Mikki had a chance to slip away.

"*Now* will you look at that card and see who sent you those flowers?" she asked.

Mikki suppressed a laugh, not wanting to hurt the nurse's feelings. "I think you're more excited about those flowers than I am," she told Virginia.

Frowning, Virginia shook her head. "That's another thing. You're *not* excited about them. What's wrong with you?" She waved her hand in the general direction of the vase with its profusion of pink roses. "These are gorgeous, not to mention expensive. If someone had gone to all this trouble for me, *I'd* certainly be excited." She looked at Mikki closely. "*Do* you know who sent them?" she asked.

"No," Mikki admitted. And then she let the woman in on a little secret. "And as long as I don't know, I can pretend that they *are* for me. Once I look at the card and see that the florist did make some kind of a mistake, then I'll know that they're not for me."

Virginia read between the lines. "Then you *would* like to get flowers," she concluded, happy to discover that Mikki was as normal as any other woman.

"I'm not a robot, Virginia. Of *course* I'd like to get flowers. But I'm pretty confident that these aren't for me, so—"

Uttering a sigh of exasperation, Virginia reached into Mikki's lab coat pocket and, with the expertise of a pickpocket, pulled out the card.

She was taller than Mikki and held the envelope out of the doctor's range while she extracted the card from the envelope.

"Give that to me, Virginia," Mikki ordered.

But it was too late. Virginia had managed to read the card. She looked at Mikki, curiosity etched on her brow. "Who's Jeff Sabatino?"

The name immediately caught Angela's attention. "Isn't that the name of the woman you operated on this morning?" she asked.

Mikki had called her receptionist from the hospital just before she began the operation. She gave her the woman's name and asked her to make an entry in the ongoing schedule that she kept on her computer.

Pulling the lanky nurse's arm down to secure the card from her, Mikki scanned it herself—twice to make sure she hadn't made a mistake.

"'Thank you for everything. Jeff Sabatino.'" The last time Mikki read the card out loud.

"Yes," she said slowly, remembering to answer Angela's question. Saying nothing further, Mikki tucked the card back into her pocket. And then she looked at the roses as if seeing them with fresh eyes. Despite her resolve to appear nonchalant and unfazed, she felt a smile slip over her lips.

The flowers really *were* absolutely beautiful, Mikki thought.

The next moment she realized that three sets of eyes were unabashedly watching her as the three women all grinned.

Mikki turned to her employees. They seemed to have questions sizzling on their tongues, all but bursting to come out. That was when she realized that what had been written in the card might have sounded a little ambiguous, causing her staff to start thinking all sorts of things.

That was all she needed.

"Not a word," Mikki warned. Shedding her lab coat, she left it slung over the back of Angela's chair and picked up her purse where she'd left it in the desk drawer. "I'm going to the hospital to see how my patient is doing. After you lock up, you can all go home," she told them. It was an order, not a suggestion. "You've put in a longer day than usual," she said, letting herself out into the hallway.

"You, too, apparently," Virginia called after her.

Mikki didn't have to turn around to know that the woman was grinning.

She took her car this time, parking it in the spot reserved for her.

Getting out, Mikki quickly hurried into the hospital and then up to the sixth floor, where most of her patients usually went after surgery.

She tried not to think about the flowers or the card that came with it.

Or the man who had sent them.

Consequently, she couldn't think of anything else, not just because the roses were so beautiful, but because no one had ever sent her roses before. She'd had grateful patients before as well as grateful family members, but none of them had ever sent her flowers.

The truth was, Mikki wasn't really sure how to react, or what she was supposed to say. She knew she had to acknowledge receiving the flowers. But there was this unusually warm feeling rattling around inside her that she wasn't exactly sure what to do about.

This isn't about you. It's about your patient, remember? Think about your patient. That's why you're here.

Check in on her, then check out. Her son is probably long gone, back to his home or his restaurant.

The thought that the man worked in a restaurant reminded her that she had been running on empty all day.

You haven't eaten since this morning, Mikki. Get something to eat. You need fuel.

As soon as she finished with Mrs. Sabatino, she promised herself.

Mikki paused at the nurses' station when she got to the sixth floor. It was her habit to always check in with the head nurse first.

"How's Mrs. Sabatino doing?" she asked the nurse who was watching the monitors.

The nurse, an older woman who had been on the job for close to twenty-five years, seemed a little preoccupied and didn't respond at first. However, when Mikki asked about Mrs. Sabatino again, the nurse suddenly jumped, as if she was being caught falling down on the job. She flushed.

"What? Oh, Mrs. Sabatino is fine. Doing fine," the nurse corrected herself. Glancing at notations on the computer that had been left by the last nurse, she said, "She's been asleep this entire time."

"But you have been monitoring her vitals, right?" Mikki asked. "And checking her temperature every hour?"

The nurse nodded. "Every chance I got."

Mikki thought that was rather an odd way to word the response, but it was getting late and it was obviously the end of this nurse's shift. The woman's eyes appeared to be drooping. Maybe the woman was just overly tired, she reasoned.

No more than me, Mikki thought.

She was just going to look in on Mrs. Sabatino herself and then, since the nurse had nothing to report, she was going to go home and collapse, Mikki promised herself. She was hungry, but there was nothing in her refrigerator that could pass for edible food and she was far too tired to stop to pick up something on the way home.

She'd get something tomorrow on her way in, Mikki promised herself as she went down the hall. Missing a couple of meals wasn't going to kill her.

The door to room 616, Sophia Sabatino's room, wasn't closed. There wasn't anything unusual about that. Mikki knew that it was easier for nurses to go in and out this way without waking up the patient.

Slipping quietly inside the room, she could hear gentle snoring. Just as she'd expected, Mrs. Sabatino was asleep.

That was good, she thought. The longer the woman slept, the longer her body would have to heal and recover from the trauma of surgery.

Moving in closer, she checked the monitors beside the woman's bed, all of which were hooked up to her patient, including an IV drip.

Turning to leave, Mikki didn't see him until he moved. Jeff Sabatino was sitting in a chair all the way over in the corner like a silent sentry, taking everything in.

Mikki dragged air into her lungs as she consciously stifled a gasp. Doing her best to collect herself, she said, "I didn't realize that you were still here."

Jeff smiled at her, rising. "I didn't mean to scare you," he apologized. "You said you were going to look in on her. So I thought it was only fair, since you were going out of your way like this for my mother, that I'd stay here and wait for you."

"That really wasn't necessary," she told him, aware that he had to be exhausted. He probably wasn't accustomed to running on empty the way she was. "If I had anything to tell you regarding your mother's condition or her operation, I'd call you."

Jeff nodded. "I know that, but I just thought that my being here was more personal—since you were going the extra mile the way you did this morning," he reminded her. "Besides, in my present state of preoccupation, if I went into work, I might wind up poisoning one of my patrons."

"I guess that wouldn't exactly be a selling feature for your restaurant." Without realizing it, she caught herself laughing.

Jeff nodded. "See? You agree. Everybody's better off with me here." An ironic smile curved his lips. "This is my first day off in five years."

Another workaholic, like her, Mikki thought. She glanced over toward her patient, who was sleeping soundly. "Well, then I'm glad it ended well," she told him.

"Yeah, me too," he replied with genuine sincerity.

Jeff was looking at her, rather than his mother, as he said it.

Chapter Seven

Jeff nodded toward his mother. "Do you really think she's going to sleep through the night?" he asked Mikki.

"I'd count on it," Mikki told him. "Feel free to make the most of what's left of your first day off in five years," she encouraged, smiling.

He looked back at his mother. "I feel like I'm too drained to do anything but go to bed and sleep myself," he confessed.

Mikki laughed. "I hear that," she agreed. She felt exactly the same way. It had been a tough day for both of them.

Just then, her stomach rumbled loudly, embarrassing her.

It was impossible to ignore, so she owned up to it. "Sorry," Mikki murmured, flushing. "It likes to complain."

"Have you had dinner yet?" he asked her.

"Dinner?" Mikki echoed with a laugh. "I haven't had lunch yet."

When she went nonstop the way she had today, eating was not only pushed to the back burner, it didn't really register with her at all. Not until she realized just how hungry she really was.

"Hey, my restaurant's not too far from here," he told Mikki. "The least I can do is feed you." Jeff felt responsible for her hunger, cornering her the way he had early this morning, and he wanted to make amends.

But Mikki shook her head. "Thank you, but I like to be conscious when I'm eating so I can enjoy the food, and right now, I'm *really* tired," she emphasized. "I need to get myself home before I wind up falling asleep behind the wheel."

What she said raised another concern for him. "If you're that tired, I could drive you home," he offered. Then, thinking that she might feel he was coming on too strong, Jeff amended his offer. "Or I could pay for a cab to take you home. I don't want anything happening to you on my conscience."

Mikki waved away his offer as well as his guilt. "There's really no need, thank you. And just so you know," she added with a smile, "I've been taking care of myself for a very long time. I can get home from here in my sleep—but I promise I'll stay awake for the trip," she added, amused. "Now go enjoy the rest of your day off, Mr. Sabatino."

"I'm trying to," he answered, looking at her pointedly.

But because he didn't want to make the doctor nervous, he made no further offer, allowing Mikki to leave first.

She'd just reached the room's threshold when she remembered. Pausing to look over her shoulder at Jeff, she said, "By the way, thank you for the roses. They're beautiful, but you really didn't have to go out of your way like that."

Oh, good, he thought, she'd gotten them. He was beginning to think they hadn't been delivered when she hadn't said anything.

"Neither did you," he countered.

She knew that arguing the point with him was only going to be a waste of time, so instead Mikki inclined her head and murmured, "Touché," just before she left the room.

Mikki could feel herself smiling during the short trip to her house.

Because she wanted to be able to get to the hospital as quickly as possible whenever she was needed, Mikki had deliberately purchased a house in a development close to Bedford Memorial.

Consequently, she really could drive home in her sleep the way she'd joked, although she had never attempted to put that to any sort of a test—and never would.

Twelve minutes after she had left Sophia Sabatino's room—and the woman's handsome son standing in it— she was crossing the threshold to her tastefully decorated, modest little two-story house.

That was when she remembered that she had left the vase with its plump pink roses back in her office. The roses would have looked nice on her coffee table. But then, she told herself, seeing them gave her something to look forward to when she went in tomorrow morning.

Not that she didn't look forward to seeing her patients, she quickly amended as she made her way up the stairs to her bedroom. She really did like interacting with the people who sought her out, hoping that she could fix what was wrong with them.

That was the wording her very first patient had used when the woman had come to see her. The woman had asked her to "fix what's wrong with me." Mikki recalled the phrase often and fondly.

As a doctor, she liked to think of herself in that capacity, as a person who fixed people. That was her real purpose in life.

She might have been oversimplifying it—or maybe even elevating it—but she knew that at least for now, that was how Jeff Sabatino viewed what she'd done. She'd fixed his mother.

Reaching her bedroom, Mikki stepped out of her shoes, quickly shed her clothes and threw on a short, well-worn nightgown.

Before going to bed, she usually undertook a nightly ritual which involved brushing her hair and her teeth and moisturizing everything that she didn't want to become wrinkled over time. But tonight, she really did feel too exhausted to lift a brush or patiently slather cream on various parts of her body.

She got as far as sitting down on her bed, contemplating just what she could actually do before she totally ran out of steam. That was when she realized that her eyes had shut and she'd slumped over onto the bed. With effort, she tried to give herself a pep talk to sit up and at least get into bed properly.

But all she managed to do was to pull her pillow farther under her head.

She didn't remember anything else.

Not until she felt her watch rhythmically pulsing against her wrist.

Never one for trinkets and toys, much less jewelry, Mikki had indulged herself in getting a watch that could be linked up with her smartphone. That way she'd never miss a call because she was unsuccessfully hunting for her phone, something she had a habit of misplacing more often than she cared to admit.

Because she hated being late for anything, Mikki had her watch set to go off in the morning, waking her well in time to get ready for work.

Blinking now, she focused in on her watch. As her brain cleared, she noticed that she had slept straight through the night, something that was highly unusual for her.

"I guess I really was tired," Mikki murmured to herself as she got up and hurried into the bathroom to take one of her six-minute showers.

It was something she'd perfected during her internship after graduating medical school. She didn't feel human until she had her morning shower, but time was so precious, she'd endeavored to take shorter and shorter showers until she'd learned how to do everything she needed to, including washing her hair, in six minutes flat.

Mikki could get dressed even faster, putting on only a smattering of makeup before going downstairs.

Reaching the kitchen, she remembered that she had yet to go to the supermarket to replenish her empty pantry or her refrigerator. Currently, there wasn't anything in either one that could be used in preparing the simplest of meals.

Mikki sighed.

Ordinarily she didn't frequent fast-food places or drive-throughs, but necessity was what caused a great many things to happen. At the very least, she needed coffee, and if she was stopping for that, she might as well get it from a place that offered something that could pass for breakfast on the run for those who were starving. And she was.

As Mikki got behind the wheel of her car, she thought of the offer Jeff Sabatino had made to her last night. Too bad the man's restaurant didn't open early for walk-ins, she silently lamented. She might have taken him up on his offer this morning. However, she'd heard that his was strictly an establishment that required reservations, so its not being open early was a moot point.

For the most part, she wasn't a reservations type of person. She was more of a spur-of-the-moment type, because she never knew when she'd actually have a moment to spare for anything beyond just seeing her patients.

So, resigned, Mikki forced herself to pull up to the first fast-breakfast place she passed on her way to Bedford Memorial. It was either that or putting up with hunger pangs.

Rather than idling in the drive-through line, spewing exhaust fumes as she waited to pay for a meal she really wasn't looking forward to consuming, Mikki parked her car as close to the front entrance as she could, then hurried into the establishment.

The line inside to order was far shorter than what was snaking its way around the building outside. Placing her order, she took the empty paper container that the sleepy-eyed teenager behind the counter handed her and went to get her coffee.

She'd just finished filling the container and securing the lid when she heard the teenager call out her number.

Efficiency always made her smile, and she smiled at the barely-out-of-high-school teen who handed her the bagged breakfast she'd ordered.

Mikki glanced at her watch as she went out through the establishment's swinging doors. It had taken less than five minutes from the time she'd ordered to the time her meal was ready. Pretty good. She hoped she could say the same thing about the meal itself.

Beggars can't be choosers, Mikki reminded herself, starting up her car again. And while she hadn't begged for the meal but paid for it, she felt that the saying still applied in this case.

At least the aroma that began to fill her vehicle was promising.

Pulling into her reserved spot at the hospital, Mikki was tempted to take a few minutes to eat her breakfast before going up to see Mrs. Sabatino.

But she had long ago schooled herself to put responsibility ahead of any personal gratification, and that included having a meal. So breakfast would have to wait until she looked in on Mrs. Sabatino.

Barring some sort of unforeseen emergency, her visit wouldn't take long, Mikki promised herself.

Crossing her fingers, Mikki got on the elevator and pressed six.

As always, she stopped at the nurses' station first.

"How's my patient?" she asked the woman seated at the desk. When the older woman eyed her blankly,

Mikki gave the woman the particulars. "Sophia Sabatino, room 616. She was operated on yesterday morning."

"Oh, right, that one," the nurse said as if a light had suddenly gone on in her head. She checked notations on the computer before saying, "She woke up a few times during the night, according to the chart entries. Sara said she kept asking if she was dead."

As Mikki recalled, Sara was the night-shift nurse for this part of the floor.

When the nurse paused, Mikki nodded. "That's the one. Are Mrs. Sabatino's vitals steady?"

The nurse laughed. She didn't even have to check the numbers before she spoke. "Hell, we should all have vitals like that one. Except for her operation, from all indications that woman's as healthy as a horse."

"Sounds good," Mikki commented.

Although she was always prepared for them, she didn't really care for surprises. She preferred seeing nice, steady numbers that neither rose nor fell.

Thanking the nurse, Mikki made her way to her patient's room.

Because she had a feeling that the woman preferred ceremony, Mikki knocked lightly on the door frame before walking into Sophia Sabatino's room.

"How are you feeling today, Mrs. Sabatino?" Mikki asked the woman, trying to sound as cheerful as possible despite the frown she saw on the woman's lips.

Sophia groaned dramatically before answering. "Like I died."

Mikki had a feeling that she could easily be sucked into a whirlpool if she attempted to reason the woman out of the dramatic assessment.

Instead, she said, "Well, I'm happy to say that you didn't." She gave the woman a bright, heartening smile. "And we'd like to keep you that way."

"I was right, wasn't I?" Sophia challenged, her surprisingly dark eyebrows drawing together over the bridge of her nose.

"Right about what?" Mikki asked.

"That I don't have an appendix," Sophia answered a little impatiently.

"Not anymore, you don't," Mikki replied, choosing her words tactfully. She didn't want to get into any sort of a debate as to why Sophia's mother might have lied to a six-year-old about having her appendix removed. "I removed it during your surgery."

"So it *was* appendicitis?" Sophia asked, her face scrunching up in confusion and disbelief.

"Not exactly," she said, realizing that the woman had probably forgotten what she'd explained to her just prior to the surgery. "You had a sizable tumor that was pressing against your appendix. The tumor had actually wrapped itself around your appendix and one of your ovaries. We had to take that out, as well."

"My ovary?" To Mikki's surprise, the woman chuckled to herself. "Well, I certainly haven't had any need for that for a long time," Sophia confided. And then she looked up at her surgeon. "And that's it?" she asked, amazed. "That's all you found?"

"Most people would say that was quite enough," Mikki assured her. "It everything continues going the way it has, you should be feeling better very soon."

"I'm feeling better now," Sophia told her, contradicting the doctor's assessment.

Mikki smiled. "That's probably because you're still on pain medication."

Sophia looked at her, horrified. "You mean I'm getting drugs?"

"It's standard procedure, Mrs. Sabatino." She could almost see the wheels in the woman's head turning, and it wasn't hard to guess what she was thinking. "Don't worry, you won't get hooked on them. You're being given just enough for your weight and height to take the edge off your pain, nothing more."

"Well, I certainly hope not," Sophia said primly, smoothing out the covers on either side of her.

"Give the doctor a break, Mom. The woman undoubtedly saved your life."

Sophia's entire countenance changed as she looked over toward the doorway and saw her son walking in. She seemed to light up.

Her warm smile lasted for a moment, then faded a little as she looked behind him. She pretended to sniff. "Where are the others?"

"They'll be here, Mom," Jeff said patiently, obviously accustomed to his mother's abrupt shifts. "Their hours aren't as flexible as mine are." And then, his smile widening, he glanced toward the doctor. "Good morning, Dr. McKenna. I thought I'd find you here." Recalling their conversation from last night, he asked, "Have you had anything to eat yet?"

"No, not yet," she admitted. She saw that he was about to say something, most likely about her unintentional starvation diet, and she quickly added, "But soon. Soon," she repeated for emphasis. "I'm going to have breakfast as soon as I finish making my rounds and leave the hospital," she said pointedly, looking at her patient.

Chapter Eight

"Well, my offer still stands," Jeff told her the next moment. "Any time you'd like to drop by my restaurant to take me up on that dinner—or lunch—just give me a call and I'll make sure there's a table reserved for you."

"He really does cook well," Sophia chimed in, her voice still a little reedy. The woman's eyes crinkled at the corners as she smiled at Mikki. "I taught him everything I know," she added with more than a little pride.

Jeff smiled, humoring his mother. He refrained from contradicting her, because the truth of it was, his mother *had* taught him everything she knew. The problem was, his mother's culinary abilities could be judged to be utterly unremarkable and very basic at best.

Sophia Sabatino had taught him how to find his way around a kitchen because, as a widowed mother, on occasion she'd had to leave him in charge. More than a few times she'd been forced to work late or to cover for someone at the social services office. It had been left up to Jeff to feed his siblings something that went beyond junk food.

As with everything else he undertook in his life, Jeff went the extra mile. He didn't just make sure his siblings did their homework, he quizzed them to make sure the lessons they read sank in.

And he didn't just throw together whatever he found in the refrigerator and call it dinner—he would painstakingly hunt for recipes that would turn what he had to work with into something enjoyable to eat. He started out by following recipes he found on the backs of boxes of rice and spaghetti, then very soon he began to augment them, creating recipes of his own.

It wasn't long before he'd started making dinners for his mother. From there, he became a short-order cook at a local restaurant in order to earn some extra spending money. Working for Theresa's catering company had been a natural step for him to take. There he'd learned a great deal, which eventually led to him opening up his own place.

"You must be very proud of him," Mikki told Jeff's mother.

Looking at her now, Mikki was willing to bet that Sophia was prouder of her son than her mother ever was of her. She couldn't remember a single instance when Veronica had displayed anything that even resembled pride. Her mother hadn't attended her medical school graduation because it would have meant rescheduling a cruise with husband number three.

Sophia beamed as she looked in her son's direction. "I am at that," she said.

Mikki noted that her patient's countenance toward her had changed since yesterday. The initial belligerence tinged with antagonism Sophia had displayed had completely disappeared, as had the suspicion in her eyes when Sophia regarded her.

"So—" Mrs. Sabatino did her best to sit up "—when can I go home?"

Mikki had pulled up entries the night nurse had logged. "Soon," she answered after scanning them quickly.

"Today?" Sophia pressed eagerly, obviously no longer feeling the need to act reserved or be on her guard.

Mikki smiled at the older woman even though she was forced to shake her head.

"Not that soon, I'm afraid. But soon," she reiterated. Making a final notation on the chart, Mikki looked at her watch. Why weren't there more hours in a day and more minutes in an hour? "And now I have fifteen minutes to get to the office before my first patient starts complaining that I'm late."

Jeff had remained on the sidelines, watching this woman who seemed to him to be a perfect combination of grace and effortless competence. It struck him that the doctor was the closest thing to flawless he had ever encountered. Now that the danger was over, he found himself intrigued.

"What about breakfast?" he asked. How did she manage to run on pure energy the way she did if she didn't eat, he wondered.

"Oh, it's in the car," Mikki answered, suddenly remembering that it was still waiting for her. "I'll eat while I'm driving over to the medical building."

Because of the business he was in, he met a lot of

people who lived to eat. Apparently, his mother's surgeon was one of those people who ate to live—when she remembered to eat.

"That can't be good for your digestion," Jeff commented.

He was right, but Mikki didn't have time to get into any sort of a debate about that.

"Better than not eating at all," she countered with a smile. Turning toward her patient, she said, "I'll see you tonight, Mrs. Sabatino." Then, nodding at Jeff as she hurried out, she said, "Goodbye."

His mother made a clucking noise he'd become all too familiar with throughout his childhood. "If that young woman's not careful, she's going to wind up in her own hospital."

"That's just what I was thinking, Mom," Jeff agreed. Turning toward her, he gave his mother his full attention. "So, how are you feeling?" he asked. Then, his eyes meeting hers, he emphasized, "Really?"

"Achy, tired and these stitches are beginning to hurt," his mother answered. "But I feel a lot better than I did yesterday morning and the days before that," she confessed.

There was no way to adequately describe the relief he felt. Smiling warmly, he said, "See? Sometimes it pays to listen to your son."

"Don't let it go to your head," Sophia warned, then reminded him, "Even a broken clock has the right time twice a day."

He laughed. "Ah, there's the mother I know and love. Welcome back, Mom," he said, bending over to kiss her forehead. Now that he was no longer worried about his mother's health, things could get back to normal again.

"I've got to get to the restaurant today. There's a retirement party coming in at four."

"Go, go, I'll be all right," Sophia told him, wiggling her fingers in his direction in lieu of waving him off.

"Robert and Tina are coming by to see you today," he reminded his mother in case she'd forgotten. Ready to leave, he asked, "Can I bring you back anything?"

"You're coming back?" Sophia asked, pretending to be surprised. She wasn't fooling him. He knew that his mother clearly expected him to return to the hospital.

But he played along, knowing his mother liked reinforcement. "Of course I'm coming back, but it'll be around seven. Sam said he'd cover for me tonight, and he's capable enough," he told her before she could ask, mentioning his assistant manager. He really had to go, so he cut the exchange short. "What can I bring you?"

Sophia answered without any hesitation. "Grandchildren."

It was a familiar topic. Hearing her touch upon it heartened him, because that meant that she really *was* on the path to making a full recovery. These last few days, when he'd spoken to her on the phone, she hadn't said a word about future grandchildren.

"Tina and Robert have that department covered," Jeff told her.

"Those are *their* kids. I'm taking about your kids," Sophia emphasized.

Jeff paused to press another kiss to her forehead. "Welcome back, Mom. Gotta go."

"You can't run from this forever," she reminded her oldest child.

"I'm not running, Mom. I'm just taking care of business—just like you taught me to," he added for good measure.

He heard his mother sigh dramatically just as he reached the doorway. The woman should have been an actress, not a social worker. His mother truly had missed her calling, he thought fondly.

"See you tonight," he told his mother right before he left.

His mother meant well, he thought, taking the elevator to the ground floor. Undoubtedly, there was some handbook that urged all mothers to attempt to indoctrinate their offspring with a desire to produce short versions of their own kind. And he understood that, he really did.

He had nothing against kids, Jeff thought as he left the hospital. He actually liked kids, and he was crazy about his niece and nephew. They were at an age where they were messy, sticky and noisy, but he still regarded them all with a great deal of affection. But to produce a kid of his own would require a female participant. Someone he'd presumably date before anything of a more serious nature happened between them.

However, in the last couple of years, the restaurant had consumed all of his time. This thing with his mother had been an aberration. He normally didn't have this kind of time to spare. Since this had turned out to be a life-or-death scenario, he'd had to *find* the time. There was no other choice. He'd taken charge because neither his brother or his sister could get their mother to do anything she didn't want to, and the situation had been dire.

Life or death or *dire* were not words that came up in reference to dating someone, so the whole concept of dating *anyone* fell by the wayside. And if he wasn't dating someone, there was no way he could make his mother's heartfelt wish come true and present her with a grandchild.

Not unless he won one in a lottery.

Still, Jeff caught himself thinking as he drove to Dinner for Two, if he *were* inclined to date someone, he'd like whoever fate eventually sent to cross his path to look like that sexy blonde surgeon who had saved his mother's life.

Jeff had no doubt that Dr. Mikki McKenna was already taken. An intelligent, highly professional woman who looked as if the term *knockout* had been coined with her in mind *had* to be in a relationship. Granted, he hadn't noticed a ring on her left hand, but that didn't mean anything. She probably didn't wear a ring because rings could get caught on any number of things, and as a doctor, she couldn't risk something like that happening.

Pulling into his parking space, he blocked out all further thoughts of the doctor, his mother and the grandchildren he hadn't given her.

It was time to focus on work.

Happily, there were no crises for him to handle.

The retirement party went off without a hitch, as did the regular service. Mercifully, everything went smoothly.

So smoothly that he caught himself thinking about his mother's doctor on several occasions during the course of the day.

He found himself wondering if she was going to be there tonight. He intended to swing by the hospital to see his mother just as he had promised. That led him back to thinking about Mikki. He tried to remember just when she had turned up at the hospital last night to check on his mother.

What are you, twelve? Trying to get a glimpse of the hot girl at school? Jeff admonished himself. His thoughts should be centered on his mother and his restaurant, not on what time Dr. McKenna would be making her rounds at the hospital.

Still, if he had any questions about his mother's condition, it wouldn't be a bad thing to run into the doctor, now would it?

You're rationalizing and you know it. What's come over you? he silently demanded, annoyed with the way he was behaving.

As the day wore into evening, he decided that he wasn't doing any good here. That being the case, he might as well leave.

"Hey, Sam," he called out to his assistant manager, "I'm heading out."

Across the kitchen, Jeff's assistant manager nodded. "About time," he quipped. "Say hello to your mom for me. Tell her we're all rooting for her and wish her a speedy recovery. How long is she going to have to be in the hospital, anyway?"

That was still up in the air. He hoped to have an answer when he saw the doctor tonight. "My guess is at least another day."

Sam nodded, taking the information in. "Maybe Ginny and I will go see her tomorrow. We'll bring Wendy," he added, referring to his two-year-old daughter.

Great, Jeff thought. That would only encourage his mother to ramp up her crusade for more grandchildren.

Still, he appreciated the man's thoughtfulness. So out loud he said, "That'll be great. Kids always cheer my mother up."

"Then we'll definitely bring her," Sam promised, calling after his boss.

When he arrived at his mother's room, Jeff found her talking to the nurse on duty. Her doctor, however, was nowhere to be seen. He wondered if he'd missed her.

"Hi, Mom. Brought you your favorite," he said, placing the bag from his restaurant on her serving table. Rather than say anything, or look pleased by the offering, his mother just lay there. Because she hadn't made any response, Jeff just kept talking. "Chicken parmesan."

His mother appeared even more dismayed. "I can't have anything solid until tomorrow night," she finally lamented.

"Okay." He was nothing if not flexible. "I'll bring you a fresh serving tomorrow night."

"You don't have to get rid of it," Sophia told him, suddenly brightening right before his eyes. "Maybe Dr. McKenna would like to take it home with her for dinner."

That was when he realized that the doctor had walked in right behind him. Turning around, he flashed a smile at the blue-eyed, diminutive doctor. "Hi."

Mikki nodded in acknowledgment. Noting that she had obviously walked in on something, Mikki framed her question carefully, just in case the thing her patient was saying that she could take home was her son. "Take *what* home with me?"

Jeff was quick to come to her rescue. "My mother's

talking about the chicken parmesan that I brought her tonight."

Oh, dinner. Relief washed over her, quickly followed by her thinking that she couldn't get over how thoughtful Jeff Sabatino was when it came to his mother.

It reminded her just how empty her own upbringing had been. It had never occurred to either one of her parents—when they were still together—to do anything even remotely thoughtful for her or for their spouse. And once their divorce was final, the idea of maintaining any sort of family unity, much less behaving thoughtfully, never seemed to occur to either one of her parents.

Mikki reiterated what Sophia had already told her son. "I'm afraid your mother can't have anything solid to eat yet."

Sophia didn't hesitate speaking up. "I can't, but you can."

Mikki looked at her blankly. "Excuse me?"

"Why don't you take my serving of chicken parmesan home with you?" Sophia suggested. "It's a shame to let good food go to waste, don't you agree, Doctor?"

"Yes, of course," Mikki agreed. "But I don't think—"

"Then the matter's settled," Sophia declared, bringing her hands together in what passed for a commanding clap—at least until she got stronger. "Jeffrey, give the doctor the dinner that you brought for me."

Mikki tried to talk the woman out of giving away her dinner to her one last time. "Oh, no, Mrs. Sabatino, I couldn't just—"

"Of course you could," Sophia insisted. "This isn't a bribe. We're still going to pay your bill," she told the young doctor.

His mother was a master when it came to talking faster than anyone else could think. "Mom, stop rail-roading Dr. McKenna and let her talk," Jeff said. He turned toward Mikki and apologized. "She has a habit of talking right over a person, so you have to speak up for yourself or you're a goner."

"Jeffrey," Sophia protested. "You make me sound like a cartoon character."

"Not a cartoon," he amended. "But definitely a char-acter," he said with affection. "But she does have the right idea," he continued, turning toward Mikki. "Why don't you take this home with you?" He held the bag out toward her.

"Don't you want it?" she asked him.

He grinned. "I have more than my fill, trust me. This way, maybe if you like it, you'll change your mind about having dinner at my restaurant."

"It's not that I don't want to have dinner at your restaurant—"

Jeff wasn't his mother's son for nothing. He'd picked up some things along the way, including seizing oppor-tunities when they presented themselves. "Great, then how about Thursday night at eight o'clock?"

Mikki didn't see how she could gracefully turn him down again.

So she didn't.

Chapter Nine

Mikki's landline was ringing when she opened her front door and walked in.

The old saying about there being no rest for the weary flashed through her head. After locking the door behind her, she quickly crossed the living room to the phone. She was afraid the call might be from her mother, wanting to discuss the possibility of her attending yet another party, cruise or some other function that she had absolutely no interest in going to. However, since she knew that it could also be someone from the hospital or one of her patients, she couldn't very well ignore it.

The caller ID made her smile even as she released a long, exaggerated sigh. Pulling the phone over to her, she sank down on the sofa and picked up the receiver. And relaxed.

"Hi, stranger. Haven't heard from you for a while.

What's up?" And then Mikki sat up, alert, as she answered her own question. "Wait, don't tell me. You're pregnant."

"No," Nikki Sommers-Wingate replied with a laugh. "I'm not. Although I have to admit that Luke and I have been thinking about it. Three is such an uneven number," she laughed.

"Unless you have twins again," Mikki pointed out. "And then you're up to five."

"Well, it's nice to know that at least your math skills are still good," Nikki responded, "which is more than I can say for your phone etiquette."

Mikki had no idea what her best friend was talking about. But it was really nice to hear the sound of her voice no matter what she was saying. Too much time had passed since they last spoke at length. "Okay, what are you talking about?"

"As in using the phone," Nikki prodded.

"Sorry. Still lost," Mikki told her.

"As in you haven't called me since forever," Nikki spelled out for her. Ever since she'd asked her mother to step in and find someone for her best friend, Nikki had had to sit on her hands to keep from calling Mikki to find out if there was anything new in her life. But curiosity had finally gotten to her, which was why she was calling her friend now—and doing her best to make it sound as if this was nothing more than just a friendly call. "How are things going?"

"Fine," Mikki answered, refraining from saying anything about her newest patient—and her good-looking, attractive son. "And the phone works two ways, you know. You could call, too."

"I *am* calling," Nikki pointed out. "And I repeat, how are things?"

Mikki shifted slightly in her seat, wondering if her best friend had suddenly become a mind reader.

"Okay. Mother's been calling, trying to get me to come to one of her parties. She's in between husbands and I think she wants a morale boost from me, of all people."

"Your mother's always done very well without any boosting," Nikki mused.

Mikki laughed softly. "Amen to that." She put her feet up on the coffee table.

"Anything else new?" Nikki asked nonchalantly.

Dropping her feet to the floor again, Mikki sat up. *Did* her friend know about her possible dinner out? "Like what?"

Nikki had wanted her friend to volunteer the story on her own, but apparently that wasn't going to happen, so she prodded gently. "Oh, come on, Mik. Word has it that someone sent you half the long-stemmed pink roses in Bedford."

"Not half," Mikki protested, then reluctantly corrected, "Just two dozen."

"Close enough," Nikki granted, then got down to the important part. "So who sent them?"

Mikki shrugged, even though her friend couldn't see her. "Just this guy."

"Okay, so far, so good, but I need more," Nikki prodded. This was like pulling teeth. "What guy?"

"This restaurateur," Mikki finally said. She didn't want to make a big thing of it. She knew her friend wanted to see her find someone and if she said anything about Jeff, Nikki would have her married off before the end of dinner. "I agreed to see his mother before office hours. Turns out she had a tumor plus some other complications. I operated. He sent flowers, end of story," she said with finality.

"End of story?" Nikki questioned. "And he's a restaurateur?" Those details she'd already gotten from her mother. She wanted to get to the meat, to find out how Mikki felt about the man. "Didn't he at least offer to give you a free meal for saving his mother's life?"

"Well, yes, he did, but—" Mikki stopped abruptly. Something wasn't adding up. "Wait, how do you know I saved his mother's life?"

"I know you," Nikki reminded her, brazening it out. "You said 'complications.' I extrapolated."

"Uh-huh." Okay, maybe she bought that. But there was still something being left out. "And who told you about the flowers?"

Nikki merely laughed. "I have my sources. So when are you going?"

The question caught her off guard. "To what?"

"To the restaurant. C'mon, Mikki, keep up here," Nikki stressed, trying to get answers out of her friend without Mikki getting suspicious.

Mikki felt herself getting warm and she pushed the feeling away, doing her best to remain aloof from the situation. "He said he'd reserve a table for me at eight tomorrow."

Finally, they were getting somewhere, Nikki thought. "So what are you wearing?"

"Nothing—"

"You're going naked?" Nikki teased. "That's a daring move, but you do realize that there are laws about that, right?"

"Very funny," Mikki responded. "I said 'nothing' because I'm not going."

There were times when her best friend made her want to tear her hair out. It was time for her to stop hiding, step up and become part of life. "For heaven sakes, Mikki, why not?" she cried.

Mikki blew out a long breath. "Because."

"*Because* is a conjunction," Nikki pointed out patiently, "it's not a reason. A good-looking man wants to express his gratitude by springing for dinner at a place he owns. Why would you want to insult him by not going?"

"Who says he's good-looking?" Mikki asked, suspicion creeping into her voice again.

Nikki never missed a beat. "You did."

"No, I didn't," Mikki protested.

So she explained it to her—and hoped the explanation would be enough to deter Mikki's suspicions. "Again, I know you. If this was a man whose face would stop a clock, or who was a wizened old troll, you wouldn't hesitate taking him up on his invitation— after all, it's a public restaurant. But you're thinking of *not* taking him up on his invitation and there can only be one reason for that. Because he's good-looking and you're afraid it might lead to something."

Listening, Mikki could only shake her head. "You know, you're letting all this talent go to waste. You should have been a police detective or a private investigator."

"And with that fancy footwork of yours, you should have been a professional dancer," Nikki countered. Maybe this was going to work out after all. "Now, as your best friend, I'm telling you to take this man up on his offer and show up at his restaurant tomorrow."

Mikki was honest with her—there was no point in telling her friend that she was wrong or imagining things. "I don't want to risk starting anything."

Nikki fell back on a play on words. "I have news for you—you've been eating for a long time now."

Mikki sighed. "You know what I mean."

Nikki grew serious. "Yes, I do, and you can't keep running like this."

"I'm not running," Mikki protested with a touch of indignation she did her best to pull off.

"Sprinting, then," Nikki corrected. "Look, I know how you feel. You're afraid of getting involved with someone, but that fear is keeping you from possibly finding more happiness than you could imagine. I was afraid, too, once—"

"You had the normal kind of fear that everyone has."

"Right," Nikki agreed. "Just like you."

"No, not just like me," Mikki contradicted. "I have a family with a history of making colossal mistakes." Scenes from her mother's multiple marriages did a slide show through her brain, and she shuddered. "Soul-destroying mistakes."

"Mikki, you're not your mother," her friend insisted. "You're smarter, sharper and kinder—and that's just for openers. What you're experiencing, oh beloved friend of mine, are cold feet."

Mikki laughed harshly. "Try frozen."

"There's one good way to warm frozen feet up, you know," Nikki said.

Mikki sighed. "You're just not going to give me any

peace until I wind up going to this man's restaurant, are you?"

"Good call. I always said you were brilliant. I intend to hound you forever," Nikki answered. "Or at least until you go and have that dinner."

"Okay, okay," Mikki cried, surrendering. "I'll turn up at his restaurant tomorrow."

"Wonderful!" Nikki declared, victorious. "Dinner's at eight, right?"

"Right," Mikki answered uncertainly, wondering what her friend was up to.

"All right, I'll be at your place tomorrow at six."

Mikki nearly choked. "Why?"

"To help you get dressed," Nikki answered matter-of-factly.

Okay, she needed to set limits here. "Nik, you might not know it, but I've been getting dressed by myself for years now."

"Right," Nikki agreed. "And you look very competent and authoritative, but that's not how you want to look on a date."

This wasn't a date, it was dinner, Mikki silently protested. Out loud she said, "No offense, but I don't need supervision."

"I've known you since elementary school," Nikki reminded her. "And in that time, you've never gone out on a date."

"And I'm not going on a date now," she insisted. "I'm just having dinner. By myself," she emphasized. Before Nikki could say otherwise or embellish on the situation, she told her friend, "I'm going to the man's restaurant and he's going to be working."

"He told you that?" Nikki asked. This was not what

her mother was supposed to arrange, she thought, wondering if signals had gotten crossed.

"No," Mikki admitted, "but I'm going there during work hours…"

Nikki suppressed a guttural sound of frustration. "How is it that you're so brilliant and so totally naive at the same time?" she asked.

"I am *not* naive," Mikki retorted.

Nikki merely laughed. "Right. None are so blind as those who refused to see. I'll be there tomorrow at six. And don't bother coming up with any excuses or stories why you can't go. You're going if I have to strap you to the roof of my car and drive you over there myself."

When had Nikki gotten so bossy? "Are you this dictatorial with Luke? Because if you are, he has my condolences."

Nikki ended their conversation by telling her friend, "You're going," and then hanging up.

This was a bad idea.

Mikki was convinced of it.

The phrase kept whispering through her head each time she thought about tomorrow night or about possibly eating her dinner while seated across from Jeff. And each time it whispered through her mind, her stomach tied itself up into knots. Big, fat, hard knots.

Nikki was absolutely right. The thought of spending any time with someone as good-looking as Jeff Sabatino made her more nervous than she could put into words. *Not* because he was handsome, but because he was handsome *and* nice.

It was his personality and the fact that he was good

to his mother that made her so nervous. Because it was precisely that nice quality that attracted her to him.

Attraction was the first rung on the ladder that would eventually lead to disaster.

Mikki frowned, trying her best to ward off a meltdown.

Nikki was right in one respect. Mikki wasn't her mother. She wasn't shallow like Veronica, falling for looks and hoping that things would work out. Though she was willing to admit that looks could be very compelling, they were also only skin-deep, and while it was nice to have a handsome face to look at, that didn't complete the portrait.

It was the person beneath the looks who counted.

But the bottom line was that she didn't want to fall for a person's looks, for his decency or his personality. Because inevitably, one or all three would lead to a place called heartbreak.

She'd watched her mother fall apart and carry on too many times. There was no way she would ever emulate that behavior. No way would she ever be in her mother's one-size-too-small shoes.

She was still giving herself that pep talk the next day. Half a dozen times she had reached for the phone, ready to call Dinner for Two to cancel her reservation.

She made her last attempt to pick up the landline receiver as Nikki was fussing with her makeup. She had gotten as far as saying, "Hello, I have a reservation tonight for eight o'clock—"

She didn't get the opportunity to give her name because Nikki very deftly, without missing a beat, terminated the call.

"Yes, you do," she said when Mikki looked at her accusingly as she hung up the receiver. "And you are keeping that reservation come hell or high water, remember? I'm driving you."

Mikki caught a glimpse of herself in the mirror. Nikki had gone all out, she thought, trying not to smile at what she saw. "I can drive myself."

"I have my doubts about that," Nikki replied.

Mikki made another attempt to dissuade her. "You can't drive me, because then I'll have no way to get home."

Nikki paused just before putting finishing touches on her hairstyle. "Well, maybe Jeff can drive you home."

"No," Mikki replied firmly. She knew what her friend was thinking. She wanted Jeff to bring her home because she was hoping there would be a natural progression of things after that. Well, that wasn't going to happen.

"All right, how's this? We'll compromise," Nikki suggested. "You can drive yourself to the restaurant— but just to be sure that you do get there, I'm going to follow you in *my* car."

"Don't you have a life?" Mikki demanded.

"A very full one, thank you," Nikki replied. "And that's why I'm doing all this, because I'm hoping to help you get a life like mine, too. I want you to have what I have."

Mikki rolled her eyes. "I never knew you had this matchmaking streak in you."

Nikki neither admitted to nor denied the accusation. "Life is a series of evolutions," she simply informed her friend. "There," Nikki pronounced, standing back. And then she declared, "Perfect, even if I do say so myself.

And now, Cinderella," she said, glancing at her watch, "if you don't want to miss the ball, I suggest you hustle yourself into that chariot of yours before it suddenly turns into a pumpkin."

"If there's going to be any pumpkin-turning going on here, my money's all on you, kid," Mikki said.

"Okay, stop stalling, grab your purse and let's go."

Mikki looked at her incredulously. "You're really going to follow me there?"

"Every inch of the way."

Mikki took another stab at getting her friend to reconsider. "Isn't Luke going to be annoyed that you left him with the kids all this time?"

"Only if I tell him that I let you go to the restaurant alone," Nikki answered.

Mikki just shook her head. "You're both crazy, you know that?"

"That's why we go so well together," Nikki said with a grin. "He wants you to be happy, too. Now, let's go!"

Resigned, wanting to get this over with, Mikki picked up her purse. She could feel the giant butterflies already climbing on for the ride.

Chapter Ten

Mikki glanced in her rearview mirror every few minutes. And each time she did, her best friend's silver-gray sedan was right there behind her.

True to her word—or threat—Nikki followed her all the way to Dinner for Two. Not only that, but when she parked in the restaurant's lot, so did Nikki.

Expecting her friend to accompany her into the restaurant to make sure she went in, Mikki braced herself. Much as she loved Nikki, she was going to put her foot down and tell her she needed to get back into her car and go home to her husband and kids.

But she didn't have to.

Nikki remained in her vehicle, giving no sign that she was about to get out. The woman did, however, stay and watch her, obviously waiting for her to enter the restaurant.

Mikki had no doubts that the pediatrician would remain in the parking lot for at least several minutes to make sure that she didn't slip back out of the restaurant and make good her escape.

Putting her hand on the brass door handle, Mikki turned and, with a smile frozen in place, she waved at her best friend.

What's the matter with you? Go inside already. You're behaving like some paranoid lunatic. This is just dinner, not a betrothal. The man's grateful to you for saving his mother's life and he's just trying to show his gratitude. He's not about to whisk you off to a Las Vegas wedding chapel on his private jet. If you even mentioned that to him, he'd probably turn pale and run for the nearest exit—while calling to have you committed.

Take a deep breath and get in there, Michelle Mc-Kenna.

She braced her shoulders and, still giving herself a pep talk, she entered the restaurant. The interior looked like something out of a painting of an old English manor. It even had a fire going in the redbrick fireplace. The words *warm and cozy* sprang to mind.

A hostess standing behind a tall desk looked her way the moment the doors closed behind her. "May I help you?" the young woman asked.

"I think I have a reservation for eight," Mikki told her uncertainly. Jeff had told her that he would reserve a table for her, but for all she knew, he might have gotten busy and forgotten all about it.

Or maybe he'd just decided to think better of the situation and hadn't made the reservation at all.

The hostess smiled pleasantly and asked, "Name, please?"

"Dr. Michelle McKenna," Mikki told her.

She watched as the hostess scanned the computer screen, running her well-manicured, light pink–polished index finger along it a total of three times. Finally, the young woman looked up apologetically.

"I'm sorry. I'm afraid I don't see you on today's list. Could the reservation be under someone else's name?" she asked helpfully.

"No, it was just for a party of one," Mikki told the hostess. She *knew* she shouldn't have come. Embarrassed, all she wanted to do was to leave. "I'm sorry, I guess there's been some sort of a mistake," she said, beginning to turn away from the reservation desk.

"The mistake was mine," a deep voice said. "I made the reservation in my name," Jeff explained as he came up behind the hostess. Coming around the desk, he greeted Mikki with a warm smile. "I'm sorry, I should have told you that I put it in my name. Force of habit." Plucking a menu from the desk, his smile widened as he looked at her. "You came. I had my doubts."

"So did I," Mikki admitted in an unguarded moment.

He liked her honesty, he thought. Among other qualities. "Well, you're here now and you won't be sorry. I had to do a little bit of juggling," he told her, leading the way to a centrally located table, "but we have the best table in the restaurant."

"We?" Mikki asked. Her stomach tightened. On the way over, she'd almost talked herself into believing that he just wanted to have her here for dinner, but he'd be busy elsewhere.

"Yes, I'm eating with you," he explained. Then, rethinking the situation, he said, "Unless you'd rather I didn't."

She couldn't very well tell the man that she preferred eating alone, not without insulting him. Besides, this was his restaurant.

But she made one last attempt at a reprieve. "I thought you were very busy here."

"Happily, I am," he confirmed. "But I always felt that there was no lonelier feeling than eating alone in a room full of couples and families. Even the best food has a way of sticking to the roof of your mouth in that sort of situation. After what you did for my mother, the way you put her at ease and took care of her, not to mention saving her life, I wanted you to have the very best experience possible here." He held out her chair for her.

"And that's dining with you?" Mikki asked. Despite the mounting butterflies in her stomach, amusement curved the corners of her mouth as she asked the question.

Jeff took his seat opposite her. "Now that I play that back in my head, that does sound as if I'm rather full of myself, doesn't it?" he admitted with a self-deprecating laugh.

Mikki laughed softly, doing her best to relax. "No, that sounds rather thoughtful of you, really."

Opening the dark green menu, she took a moment to look over each of the four oversize pages with their long lists of appetizers and main courses. There were two more pages after that, one with a full spectrum of beverages and one offering an array of sinfully rich desserts.

There was just too much to choose from. It would be tomorrow before she could make up her mind. So, closing the menu, Mikki decided to leave the choice up to Jeff instead.

"So what's good here?" she finally asked, setting the menu on the table beside her.

He knew every item listed, was responsible for having created most of them. And while she had been studying the menu, he'd been covertly studying her. The subtle overhead lighting all but made love to her, highlighting her high cheekbones and smooth skin like a smitten teenager. Making her so beautiful, it almost hurt to look at her.

When she asked her question, the first response that occurred to him was one that he wasn't at liberty to voice.

You.

Instead, he gave her a choice between three main courses, all of which he could personally vouch for. Lobster bisque, veal scaloppini and, just for simplicity's sake, prime rib.

Rather than the lobster, she surprised him by going with something he'd always considered to be simple, but elegant.

"I'll have the prime rib—the small portion," Mikki added, since the meal came in three sizes.

"Wouldn't you rather order something a little more exotic?" he asked, thinking that perhaps she was being conservative in her choice on his account, because she didn't want it to seem as if she was taking advantage of his generosity.

"Actually, I'm a meat-and-potatoes kind of woman," she explained. "My mother always tended to order things like escargots, and anything that's better said in French, but I never developed a taste for any of that."

Mikki didn't add that she'd always thought her mother was being pretentious, because she never finished eating any of the complicated-sounding things that she ordered. "Most of the time," she said, "between studying in medical school and then working double and triple shifts interning at the hospital, I ate on the run, anyway. Once I was finally able to slow down a little bit, my tastes were already set in stone."

Jeff smiled at her, enjoying the fact that she had shared something personal with him, even if it just pertained to her acquired food preferences.

The server approached discreetly and took their order. Jeff waited until the woman withdrew before he said to Mikki, "Maybe I can talk you into having something a little more unique next time."

"Next time?" she repeated uncertainly. "You want to take me out to dinner again?"

She sounded somewhat uneasy. He wondered if it was his imagination, or if she felt that he was coming on too strong.

Leaning forward just a little, he said, "Doc, I have no doubts that if you hadn't treated my mother the way you did, with understanding and kindness, not to mention kid gloves, she never would have agreed to the operation. And if she hadn't, I'm pretty certain that instead of sitting across from a beautiful, highly skilled physician, at this moment I'd be seeing to my mother's funeral arrangements.

"What I am saying to you in a lot of words and none too clearly is that there is a table reserved for you at Dinner for Two for the rest of your life."

"I think you're getting a little carried away here," Mikki said with a self-conscious laugh.

He surprised her by saying, "Maybe." And then he added, "But it feels good to do this, so humor me. My mother, who my brother, my sister and I all love to death, is, quite notoriously, a handful. She is stubborn as the day is long and I can honestly say that I have never seen her managed so well and so effortlessly before."

Their food arrived far more quickly than she thought possible, and Mikki refrained from making a comment on his observation as she waited while the server placed their orders before them and then withdrew.

"This looks lovely," Mikki observed. Everything on both plates had been artistically arranged to please the eye as well as the palate.

"Half of every dining experience relies on visual appeal," he explained.

"And the other half is taste?" She'd expected him to say that it was *all* about taste and was surprised that he hadn't.

"Definitely," Jeff agreed with a grin. "The food can be made to look as pretty as humanly possible, but if it doesn't deliver in taste, the customers are not going to be coming back."

Listening to him, she took her first bite of the prime rib and immediately felt as if she had slipped into heaven.

Raising her eyes to his, she couldn't help commenting, "The customers are definitely coming back."

She meant it in general, but he took her remark to be specific and smiled at her. "I'm very glad to hear that."

Needing to do something about subduing the growing flutter in her stomach, Mikki went back to their previous topic of discussion. "I think your mother knew

that something was wrong and she just needed someone to make her admit that, as well as make her feel
that she could be helped."

"Well, all that is to your credit, because before you
conducted your examination and talked with her, I had
talked myself blue in the face trying to convince her
to see a doctor. *Any* doctor," he confessed. "But time
and again, she summarily refused. Because, as I mentioned to you in your office, my father was misdiagnosed, and when his condition did come to light, it was
too late to treat him."

But Mikki had a different take on the situation.
"Your mother wasn't resisting seeing a doctor because
of what happened to your father. It was because, like
so many patients suddenly faced with their own mor-
tality, your mother was afraid."

"If she was afraid, wouldn't that make her *want* to
get checked out quickly so whatever was wrong could
be treated and taken care of?" he asked.

"You know how when a child closes their eyes, they
think the world disappears because they can't see it?
Well, it's kind of like that. If a person doesn't have that
test and doesn't hear the doctor tell them that they have
a specific disease or need to have something treated,
then they don't have to deal with having to face the possible consequences.

"As long as what your mother was experiencing
wasn't being given a specific name, she could go on
pretending it didn't exist. That all that pain she kept
having was due to gas, or indigestion, or just her imagination. Once a condition is given a name, it becomes
real. And it becomes scarier."

Mikki looked down at her plate and suddenly realized that she had talked while eating the prime rib and baked potato she'd ordered. Her plate was absolutely clean.

"I'm sorry," she apologized. "I just talked shop all the way through dinner."

He found her delightful. "First off, don't be sorry. I was the one who asked you questions, and I did find your explanation to be enlightening. And second, you didn't talk all the way through dinner. There's still a lot more dinner left to go," he promised.

"More?" Mikki repeated, her eyes widening as she looked at the man sitting across from her. "But I'm stuffed."

"Ah, but there's always room for dessert," he told her, laughing. "And," he qualified, "you certainly don't have to eat it right away. We can linger for the rest of the evening if you'd like," he assured her. And then, leaning in, he lowered his voice and said with a straight face, "I know the man who owns this place. We don't have to eat and run."

Sitting back again, Jeff asked her, "Would you care for some wine? Or a cordial? Or perhaps something light and fruity to drink?"

"Coffee," she told him automatically. It was an easy choice.

"Coffee?" he repeated uncertainly. At this hour, most people preferred to have a drink rather than something that would keep them awake.

Mikki nodded. "I need to keep my head clear," she explained, "just in case I get a call from the hospital."

"Are you expecting a call from the hospital?" he questioned, beginning to realize the full extent of the life she led. What she told him next confirmed it.

"I'm *always* expecting a call from the hospital," Mikki said. "Almost all doctors do—unless they happen to specialize in dermatology," she added with a touch of humor. "Dermatologists are the ones who get to keep regular hours."

"But I take it that you don't?" Jeff asked. From where he was sitting, it seemed to be a rhetorical question.

She didn't want him thinking she was trying to look like some sort of a martyr. "For the most part, I do. But there have been cases..." she allowed. "Like when a patient's ulcer decided to perforate just before midnight on Christmas Eve."

"Christmas Eve?" he repeated. "That had to be hard on you."

She didn't want him thinking that she had told him the story so he could feel sorry for her. It was just to illustrate how unpredictable her vocation was.

"Not really," she told him, backtracking. "I had no plans."

"Then you don't celebrate Christmas," Jeff guessed.

"No, I do. Usually with my best friend and her family," she qualified. "But for the most part, I usually sub for the doctors who want to be home with their families on Christmas."

"No family, then?" he asked, finding himself wanting to know things about this beautiful woman with the very sad eyes.

"I have a family—" Stopping abruptly, she looked up at him. "How did we get started talking about this?"

"One word led to another," he told her innocently. For now, not wanting to spook her, he backed off. "I guess I've got the kind of face that most people like to talk to."

That might very well be true, except that she didn't usually like to talk, Mikki thought. At least not about herself.

Still, she had to admit, she was enjoying herself.

Chapter Eleven

"Do you actually expect me to eat that?"

Mikki looked at the large slice of tiramisu cake on the plate in front of her. The meal she'd just consumed had been more than filling, and she doubted there was even a tiny bit of space left in her stomach.

"It's huge," she protested, adding, "If I eat it, I'll explode."

"It's not as big as you think," Jeff assured her, "and I can personally vouch for the fact that it really does melt in your mouth. But all I'm asking is that you try a single forkful to see if you like it. If you do, you can take the rest of it home with you. That's why God created doggie bags," he added with a grin.

She looked at the dessert, a light, fluffy serving of mousse and whipped cream trapped between several paper-thin layers of confection—and she had to admit that it did look absolutely delicious.

"I guess I can manage to fit in one small bite," Mikki speculated.

He held the dessert fork out to her.

After a moment, she took it.

"But if I explode all over you," she warned, "you can't blame me."

"I never blame a patron," Jeff told her solemnly. "It's bad for business and word like that gets around very quickly."

Mikki had never been the type to overindulge—and that included overeating—not even as a child. So despite the cake's very tempting appearance, she was ready for this to be a less than pleasant experience.

Bracing herself, she slid the side of her fork into the cake before her. Then gingerly bringing the fork to her lips, she opened her mouth and then closed it again around the sliver she'd separated from the rest of her dessert.

Mikki was prepared to become almost nauseated because she felt she was literally stuffing herself.

However, she discovered that Jeff was right. The sample was so light and airy, it was as if she'd closed her mouth over a thought, an impression, an illusion of cake, but not anything that was real and certainly not substantial.

She looked up to find Jeff watching her. He seemed like a kid at Christmas, waiting to find out if Santa was real, the way he believed, or not real, the way everyone else maintained.

She found the expression on his face touching almost against her will.

"Well?" he asked when Mikki said nothing.

A sigh of pleasure escaped her lips. "You're right.

This is fantastic. But I'm still taking it home with me—
if your offer still stands."

"Absolutely," he told her enthusiastically.

"Because I just can't do it justice here." She felt obligated to explain. "I *am* very full. More than full, actually."

"I understand perfectly." Turning, he signaled the
young woman who had served them their dinner. She
was at their table almost instantly. "Rachel, please box
this up for Dr. McKenna—and put an extra piece in
the box, please."

"Yes, sir," the young woman said, all but snapped
to attention.

The man was going over and above the call, Mikki
couldn't help thinking. "Are you sure I can't pay for any
of this?" Mikki asked him. She'd glimpsed the prices on
the menu when she'd perused it earlier, and they were
far from inexpensive.

"I thought I made it clear that your money's not good
here. And that you're welcome here anytime."

Was he issuing her a standing invitation? "I don't get
a chance to get out much," she began, about to demur
his offer.

But Jeff deftly headed her off at the pass.

"All the more reason to come here and eat. I know
you eat," he stressed with a smile. "Like a bird, but you
eat. And based on my own experience, I can testify that
getting out once in a while is good for the soul—not to
mention that it allows you to recharge your batteries."

"Well, my batteries—and my soul—are sufficiently
recharged, so I'd better get going and free this table up
for one of your other patrons. Your *paying* patrons," she
stressed. Turning, she looked past the reservation desk.

There were an awful lot of people there, all waiting for tables. "I can see a line forming."

Jeff laughed, rising to his feet. "They're not all waiting for *our* table. However, I'm happy to say that business is very good."

"Well, it should be," she answered, surprising him. "The food certainly is."

He executed a little bow. "Thank you."

Mikki returned the courtesy by inclining her head in a gesture of thanks. "And thank you for dinner."

"Anytime," he said, then repeated, "*Any*time." Picking up the boxed dessert, he told her, "I'll walk you out."

She wanted to tell him that he didn't have to do that, that she knew he had to be very busy. But for some reason, maybe because she *had* had a good time, the words didn't come out.

Instead, she decided to let Jeff walk her to the entrance of the restaurant—or the exit, depending on her viewpoint. Besides, this whole dinner had been a one-time thing, and as such, she'd decided to simply enjoy it for what it was and leave it at that.

Her life was a whirlwind of patients and the hospital, not to mention her volunteer work at the free clinic. She was always giving a hundred and ten percent of herself. Just this once, she decided to have a little me time, and as such, she intended to savor it—especially since it was almost over.

But like Cinderella holding her lone glass slipper after the ball ended, she had her souvenir of a surprisingly happy evening—she had her cake.

"Where's your car?" Jeff asked as they reached the double doors.

"Outside," she answered.

He laughed. "Considering the alternative, my insurance agent will be very happy to hear that. *Where* outside?"

She thought for a moment. She'd been in a hurry to park and have Nikki go on her way, she hadn't really paid that much attention to the exact spot. "Um, I'm not sure," she admitted.

"Well, then let's go look for it," Jeff offered, opening the double door and holding it for her.

She didn't feel right about this.

"I've monopolized you long enough," Mikki protested. "I can't take you away from your work any longer."

"Doc, it's dark out," he pointed out as they stepped outside. "I know this is Bedford and it's usually incredibly safe, but there's always that one in a million chance that someone might want to take advantage of a beautiful woman under the cover of night. Humor me and let me walk you to your car."

A rush of warmth came over her, and it had nothing to do with the fact that it was an early spring evening. She did her best to block it out.

"I know you don't do this for all your patrons," she insisted.

"No, you're right," he agreed. "But, like the name of my restaurant implies, most of my patrons come here to dine in pairs. And, in addition, none of my patrons saved my mother's life."

Mikki felt herself weakening despite her attempts to remain strong. "You make it very hard to argue with you," she told him.

Jeff's eyes appeared darker in this light, and they

seemed to almost sparkle as he smiled at her. "Good. Now, what color is your car?" he asked, looking around.

"It's a light blue Corolla. It's a two-door," she added.

"Right, I remember now. Two doors," he repeated. "That's why we took my car when we drove my mother to the hospital."

The parking lot was filled to capacity, and it took several minutes before they were able to locate her car. Ironically, Jeff was the one to spot it first.

"Is it that one?" he asked, pointing at a nearby vehicle.

She felt like an idiot for not having seen it first—and for forgetting where she had parked in the first place.

"Yes, that's it," Mikki told him. "Okay," she declared, taking the boxed tiramisu from his hands. Her fingers accidentally brushed against his, and something seemed to momentarily stir within her. "I can take it from here. Thank you again," she said, all but tossing the words over her shoulder as she hurried away.

She moved fast, he thought, wondering if it was because she was afraid that he would try to kiss her. He had to admit that it was a tempting thought, but one he would have never acted on unless she gave him some sort of indication that she wanted him to.

He stood there, watching her go, then waited until she got into the car. Not because he thought anything might happen to her. No, he watched just because he found the view to be extremely appealing from where he was standing.

Maybe what he was feeling *was* motivated by gratitude. At this point he really couldn't honestly say. But he did know that there was something about this graceful, beautiful woman with the appealing mouth that moved him and made him smile—from the inside out.

He stayed where he was until he saw her open her car door and get in. After Mikki pulled out of the lot, he finally turned around and went back inside. And that, Jeff mused, was the closest he'd come to a date in two years. Maybe he needed to begin delegating more so he could do this again—and this time bring his date home. After all, he'd been gone the whole day when his mother had had her surgery earlier this week and the world hadn't come to an end—and neither had his restaurant.

Pausing to take his wallet out of his back pocket, he fished through it. Nestled between the various business cards, he found what he was looking for—the card he'd picked up when he'd initially brought his mother to the doctor's office.

The woman's name was written in bold script. *Michelle McKenna, MD.*

The corners of his mouth curved as he stood looking down at the card.

Maybe.

Well, she'd survived, Mikki thought. She had gone to Jeff's restaurant, had dinner with the man and, if pressed, she was even willing to say that it had been a rather pleasant experience.

However, it had been a onetime experience and there was no reason to dwell on it, no reason to start daydreaming and fashioning castles in the sky, she silently insisted.

Most of all, she wasn't her mother, Mikki reminded herself. Her mother, who turned every minor encounter with a man into the greatest get-together since Scarlett and Rhett first met in *Gone With the Wind*.

Or maybe, she reevaluated, for her mother, every encounter she had actually *was* that sort of a get-together, because everyone knew how that particular love story ended. The same way all her mother's so-called love stories did: in total disaster.

"Your problem, Mother," Mikki said aloud to the thought of the woman who was undoubtedly letting her hair down at some party or other at this very moment, looking for her next ex-husband-to-be, "is that you never quit while you were ahead. Never called it a night, picked up your chips and went home. You weren't happy until you were on some man's arm—and eventually you weren't happy there, either," she murmured, parking her car in her driveway.

"My way is better. Lonelier, maybe," Mikki allowed. "But better."

Besides, she thought, letting herself into her house, her mother's liaisons never lasted and Veronica wound up alone anyway. Her own way was better. No false hopes, no brutal letdowns.

No one at all.

She had just enough time to kick off her shoes before her phone rang. Mikki approached the landline warily, like a lion tamer checking out his lion's mood before proceeding into the arena.

The caller ID told her that it was Nikki calling, undoubtedly to find out how everything had gone. Picking up the receiver, Mikki flopped down on the sofa, the way she had as a teenager.

"How did you know I just got in?" she asked without bothering to utter any cursory greeting first.

She heard her friend laugh. "Because I'm psychic, because you and I are spiritually connected—and because I've been calling every ten minutes and this is the first time that you've picked up," Nikki told her. "So, how was it?"

Pretty good, really. *Really* good. Out loud she answered guardedly, "It was okay."

"Just okay?"

Mikki heard the disappointment in her friend's voice. For some reason, seeing her go out with someone seemed to mean a lot to Nikki. And because it obviously did, she stopped behaving as if having dinner with Jeff Sabatino was no different than a quick, detached visit to the local hardware store.

"Maybe better than okay," Mikki allowed quietly after a beat.

But that wasn't enough for Nikki. "How much better?"

Mikki sighed. She might as well find out exactly what she was up against. "Just what are you trying to get me to say, Dr. Sommers?"

"I just want you to tell me the truth, Mikki," her friend answered. "That's all. Just the truth."

"All right," Mikki said. "The truth is that the dinner was fantastic, the restaurant was fabulous. And Jeff was very attentive. We talked all through the meal without realizing that time was just melting away and I want you to be the first to know that I'm having his baby."

"You're what?" Nikki cried, momentarily taken aback. And then she obviously realized that the other woman was putting her on. "Oh, right. Very funny, Mikki." She sighed, disappointed. "So I take it that you *didn't* have a good time."

Well, there was no point in lying. Their friendship was based on the truth and mutual respect.

"No, actually, if you must know, I did. Jeff was…" Mikki hunted for the right word, but in a moment of self-preservation, she finally decided to settle on, "Nice."

"Nice?" Nikki echoed incredulously. "Bacon and eggs are nice. Was that man just plain old bacon and eggs, Mikki, or was he more like caviar?"

"Neither," Mikki answered, then because Nikki was her best friend and had always been there for her through some very rough times with her mother, she found herself sighing before reluctantly admitting, "He was prime rib."

Nikki knew how her friend felt about prime rib. It constituted her very favorite meal in the whole world. A feeling of triumph flooded through her. Her mother had come through. "Even better," she declared, pleased.

"Can we drop this, please?" Mikki requested, uncomfortable with the way the conversation was going. "I have surgery first thing tomorrow morning and I'd like to get some sleep so I'm not bleary-eyed when I'm cutting into Mr. Miller."

"You're doing it again," Nikki told her. "You're coming up with excuses so you don't have to take a long, hard look at your feelings."

"My feelings are tired now, which means I might wind up saying things I shouldn't," Mikki warned her.

"Okay, I'll let you go for now. But we'll talk again later," Nikki told her.

Mikki groaned before hanging up. Loudly.

Chapter Twelve

The operation went without a hitch, despite the fact that her patient was nearly a hundred pounds overweight and that made removing his gallstones particularly challenging.

For the most part, Mikki preferred the surgical procedures that she undertook to be straightforward. She ordinarily liked her challenges to come in the form of difficult crossword puzzles.

However, she was grateful for anything that kept her mind occupied and off other things. Specifically off a strikingly handsome restaurateur.

The moment her gallstone patient was wheeled off to the recovery room, Mikki hurried to the locker room so she could change out of her scrubs.

Because of the patient's extra weight, the surgery had run long. What that meant was that she had exactly fifteen minutes to change and get over to her office before her office hours started.

She made it with approximately a minute and a half to spare. "Wow, just in time," Molly said, only moderately startled by Mikki's appearance. "So, how did Mr. Miller's operation go?"

Taking off her jacket, Mikki put on her lab coat. "It ran long, but I'm happy to report that both patient and doctor survived the ordeal," she answered.

"Well, I'm glad that *you* survived, because you've got a waiting room full of patients," Virginia told her, coming out of the third exam room. "By the way," she asked, dropping her voice, "how did dinner go last night?"

Mikki didn't bother asking her head nurse how she knew about the dinner. Somehow, Virginia always managed to ferret things out long before they ever became public knowledge.

Instead, Mikki merely answered, "Appetizing."

Virginia grinned wickedly. "Are you talking about the meal or the man?"

Mikki decided that it was best not to answer that question, or even acknowledge it. She focused on her patients.

"Who's first?" she asked her receptionist.

"That would be Mrs. Watters," Angela answered. "She's in exam room one."

"Got it," Mikki said, picking up the top file. And she was off.

The pace from that moment on was nonstop without a letup, partially because there had been two unscheduled patients wedged in, in addition to all the other patients already in her waiting room. Each of the two had called the office, pleading to be fit in. However, her day was jam-packed, predominantly because Mikki never moved on to the next patient until the one she was with was completely satisfied that all of his or her questions had been answered. Anything less was unthinkable to Mikki.

She didn't stop going until well after three o'clock, at which point she ate half a salad before resuming her examinations again.

By six thirty that evening, Mikki felt drained, but at least all of her patients had been seen to. Her *office* patients.

She breathed a sigh of relief. The finish line was in sight.

All that was left to do was to check in on her patient from that morning's surgery. If he was doing well, she'd be free to go home. No one had called from the hospital to inform her that there was any sort of a problem with Mr. Miller, but while hopeful, Mikki never took anything for granted.

"How do you do it?" Molly marveled just as she was about to leave the office herself.

"It's the glamour," Mikki deadpanned. "It keeps me going."

And then, telling her staff "Good night," she hurried off to see her last patient of the day. Mr. Miller, the nurse on duty on his floor told her, was doing very well. Quickly reviewing the man's chart to verify the verbal report, Mikki went into her patient's room and found him sleeping comfortably.

Satisfied, Mikki finally called it a day.

By the time she arrived home, parked her car and

got out, she felt so exhausted she could barely put one foot in front of the other.

Closing the door behind her, she was halfway to her kitchen when she remembered that she had never gotten around to going to the supermarket that week. The only thing in her refrigerator besides a third of a loaf of bread and a bottle of rosé, thanks to her mother's visit a couple of months ago, was a small basket of strawberries. The basket was half-full. Unfortunately for her, the strawberries had turned and were well on their way to becoming inedible.

Mikki tried to be philosophical about it. "I need to lose a few pounds, anyway," she murmured.

Besides, she needed sleep more than she needed food. She had just crossed the living room and was on her way to the stairs and her bedroom upstairs when her cell phone rang.

Muttering a fragment of a prayer, she sincerely hoped it wasn't her mother or someone calling because they had what they felt constituted an emergency. Hungry and tired, she was definitely not at her diplomatic peak right now.

She didn't recognize the number on her phone, and the only clue she had were the words *out of area* over the phone number.

Taking a chance, she picked up the receiver anyway. "This is Dr. McKenna."

"Did I get you at a bad time?"

The voice was deep, rich and she thought she knew who it belonged to, but just in case, she said, "I'm sorry, who's this?"

"Oh, I thought my name showed up on your screen. Sorry. This is Jeff Sabatino."

"Is something wrong with your mother?" she asked, immediately concerned. She struggled not to allow her heart to leap around wildly the way it had begun to do and forced her mind to focus on the practical reason for his call.

She had discharged Sophia from the hospital two days ago. It would have been sooner, but she had kept his mother in an extra day because of her age. She wanted to make sure the woman had fully recovered enough to go home safely.

Ideally, Sophia wasn't due for a recheck for another week, but Mikki knew that things didn't always go according to plan. Mentally, she crossed her fingers as she waited for Jeff's answer.

"No, nothing like that," Jeff quickly assured her. "Mom's staying at my sister Tina's house for a couple of weeks until she gets her strength back, but she's doing fine thanks to you. I'm calling because I was just wondering if perhaps you'd like to stop by the restaurant on Saturday for another meal, since apparently there were no ill effects from the last one."

"Saturday?" Mikki repeated to make sure she'd heard him correctly. When he didn't contradict her, she said, "I'm sorry. I'd love to, but I can't. Saturday's my day at the free clinic."

"The free clinic. You volunteer there?" Jeff asked. She hadn't mentioned that before, but it didn't surprise him. The more he knew about her, the more selfless this woman seemed.

"It's something I got into when I was in medical school," Mikki explained. "And I guess that I just never stopped going—except that now I'm a licensed doctor instead of just a medical student and they let me do doctor stuff," she added wryly. She heard him chuckle softly. The sound pleased her—more than it should have. Red flags went up. She needed to be wary, she told herself. "I'm sorry. Maybe some other time."

And then, unable to stop herself, Mikki yawned. Audibly. Embarrassed, she quickly told him, "Oh, Lord, I'm sorry. I didn't mean to yawn. That wasn't because of you. It's just that it's been a very, very long day.," she assured him.

"Well, then I won't keep you," Jeff told her. "I just wanted you to know that I was serious about that open invitation."

"I appreciate it," she told him. Then, because she didn't want Jeff to think that she was just trying to get rid of him, she said, "I don't know if I told you yesterday evening, but I think that you have a very nice restaurant."

"Thanks." And then he asked, "Can I quote you on that?"

He'd caught her off guard again. Was the man talking about getting her to give him an endorsement for his establishment? "Excuse me?"

He heard the nervous uncertainty in her voice. "I'm just kidding, Doc. Go to bed," he told her. And then he added, "Good night, Doc," just before he terminated the call.

She was a grown woman with medical degrees in several fields. There was no reason for her to feel this odd, giddy, fluttery feeling just because she'd gotten an unexpected call from a man she barely knew.

A nice man, she qualified, but still one she barely knew.

She went up the stairs smiling.

* * *

Over the course of the next week, Mikki found herself thinking about Jeff's call a number of times. More than once she caught herself wishing that her Saturdays weren't spoken for.

But they were, and she knew what she did was vital. She was performing a much-needed service because for some of the people she saw at the clinic, she was their only contact with the medical world.

As luck would have it, this particular Saturday the clinic was severely understaffed. Except for one retired nurse, Frieda Halpert, Mikki was the only medical person on duty at the clinic. The other doctor and the two other nurses who were usually there had called at the last minute to say they wouldn't be in. All of them had family matters to deal with. When it rained, it poured, Mikki couldn't help thinking.

As usual, the waiting room was filled to capacity when she walked in that Saturday morning. Appointments weren't necessary at the clinic. The usual procedure was that people came in when they needed to.

Mikki felt like the last woman standing two minutes after she'd walked in. Rolling up her sleeves, she declared, "Let's get started," to Frieda and she dived in.

Two hours into her day, she felt as if she had barely made a dent. For every patient she saw, it seemed like two more came in.

At this rate, she would be here into the wee hours of the night. And the noise from the waiting room, despite Frieda's efforts, just kept getting louder. One of the children had been crying nonstop for what seemed like an hour, growing progressively louder.

And then, abruptly, the noise stopped.

Completely.

Finished with the patient she'd just examined, Mikki looked quizzically at the veteran nurse. "Did they all leave?" she asked.

"We wouldn't be that lucky." Holding up her finger, Frieda went out into the waiting room to check. When she returned, there was a bemused expression on her well-lined face.

"No, nobody left," Frieda reported. "They're just being fed."

"Excuse me?"

Frieda jerked a thumb toward the front of the clinic. "There's a guy out in the waiting area and he's handing out a boatload of food."

"We're done here, Mr. Willis," Mikki told the older man whose bandage she had just changed. "That gives you any trouble—" she indicated his arm "—I'll see you here next week. Come in sooner if you need to."

"You gonna be here all week?" the older man asked.

"No, I'll be here on Saturday," she told him. "Same as always."

He nodded his shaky gray head. "Then I'll come back Saturday."

She accepted the compliment. "I'll see you then." And then, unable to hold back any longer, she hurried out to the waiting room to find out just what was going on.

When she walked out into the waiting area to look around, Mikki was convinced that her imagination had just run away with her. There was no other explanation for why Jeff was there, handing out a ton of boxed lunches he had apparently brought in using a large dolly.

"Jeff?" she asked uncertainly, coming closer.

He turned his head in her direction and flashed that unmistakable sexy grin at her. No doubt about it, the man was too good-looking for her own good. "Hi."

"What are you doing here?" she asked. Realizing that her question sounded almost hostile, she did her best to amend her tone. "I mean, not that it's not nice to see you, but—what are you doing here?" she asked again, totally confused.

A pint-size girl with curly blond hair ran up to Mikki and tugged on her lab coat to get her attention. When Mikki looked down at the girl—whom she recognized, because her mother had brought her in several times—Eva unabashedly asked, "Is he your boyfriend, Dr. Mikki?"

Blindsided, Mikki practically stuttered as she answered, "No, he's, um—"

"I'm a friend of the doc's," Jeff said, coming to her rescue. "She made my mother well a couple of weeks ago," he told the little girl. "The doc works so hard she keeps forgetting to eat, so I thought I'd bring her some food."

"But why did you bring so much food?" Eva asked, fisting her small hands on her waist as she surveyed the many boxes. "She can't eat all that."

"No, she can't," he agreed. "But she doesn't like to eat alone and she knew there'd be a lot of people in her waiting room, so she asked me to bring enough food for everyone."

"Oh." Eva thought the answer over and her face lit up. "That's good. Can my mom eat some?"

"Everyone can have some," Jeff replied. "That's why I brought so much. Would you like to help me hand the boxes out?"

The little girl bobbed her head up and down, her curls bouncing every which way. "Sure. I like helping. Don't I, Mama?" She looked toward her mother for backup.

A worn woman, looking far more tired than her years warranted, nodded and smiled at her daughter. "Yes, you do."

Mikki looked on in amazement, wondering what had possessed Jeff Sabatino to do this.

But very quickly, she stopped looking for a reason and was just happy that he had thought to do something so magnanimous.

Leaving the waiting room, Mikki got back to work.

Mikki expected Jeff to leave after he had distributed the last of the food and everyone had eaten. Instead, he came into the inner office and surprised her by asking, "Mind if I hang around until you close up tonight?"

Although she had to admit that she liked having him there, Mikki didn't want him feeling obligated to stay.

"It might be a while," she warned.

He shrugged. "That's okay. I left the restaurant in my assistant's hands and my mother is with my sister, so basically I'm free," he told her. "So, is it okay with you?"

"It's fine with me," she answered, wishing that she could think of something witty to say. But she came up empty.

Getting back to work, she wasn't able to quell the flutter in her stomach, so she decided just to ignore it, focusing on the patients waiting for her attention.

It felt like forever, but eventually, the last of the patients left the clinic and Frieda quickly closed the doors.

"Well, I've got a cat and a husband to get home to and make dinner for," she announced in her typical no-nonsense voice. "Nice of you to come by and feed the masses," she told Jeff, nodding as she picked up her things and made her way to the back door.

Then, passing Mikki, she said to the doctor in a low voice, "You want my opinion, he's a keeper."

"He's not mine to keep," Mikki quickly protested.

"Uh-huh," Frieda replied, sounding completely unconvinced.

Turning at the door, she glanced over her shoulder at the man who had come in and disrupted everything at the clinic, but in a very good way. "Hope to see you again, Mr. Sabatino."

"Jeff," he corrected her.

Frieda's uneven smile widened with approval. "Jeff," she repeated. "A keeper," she told Mikki again just before she let herself out.

Chapter Thirteen

"Looks like you have a fan," Mikki told him once they were alone. She saw Jeff raise an eyebrow as he looked at her. Afraid that he might have misunderstood her meaning, she quickly explained, "I was talking about Frieda."

"I see. But not you."

His expression was unreadable. Had she insulted him, or hurt his feelings? She didn't want to do that, but she didn't want to say too much, either. While she was attracted to him, she didn't want to encourage him, because that way lay trouble. She'd learned that by watching her mother.

"I like your food," she told Jeff. "And I admire your generous spirit."

He nodded, accepting her rather vague compliments. He didn't want her to feel as if he was crowding her. "I've been told worse things," he allowed.

"I'm just trying to figure out why you would come here and bring all this food with you."

"Well, it's simple," he told her. He watched as she began closing everything down. "I came here because you were here. I brought the food because you seemed to enjoy it the other evening."

"You brought way too much food," she told him and he knew it.

"Actually," Jeff corrected, "it turned out that I brought just enough. You had an awful lot of patients here, not to mention that most of them didn't come here alone."

"So you *did* plan on feeding all these people?" she questioned incredulously. Who *did* that kind of thing?

Jeff explained his reasoning. "I knew you wouldn't eat unless they had something to eat, too. Luckily, I'm in a position where bringing extra food with me is not a problem."

Mikki looked at this surprising philanthropist, still not a hundred percent clear about what had gone through his head—or how he would even think to do something like this.

"I don't understand. How would you even know—"

"My dad died when I was very young. I was raised by a single mom who sometimes had to work two jobs to make ends meet and feed all of us. And, as a kid, I wasn't a stranger to free clinics." He glanced around at the area that had been teeming with people just a short while ago. "Let's just say that this is payback—on a small scale."

She had just assumed that he had come from a comfortable background. To find out differently surprised her. "I didn't know."

He laughed. There was no reason why she would. "I don't have it printed on the back of the menus, but it's not a secret, either," he told her. "So," Jeff said, changing the subject. "Does this mean you're done for the day?"

"It's after eight o'clock. The clinic is officially closed," she told him. She began to turn off the overhead lights as she slowly made her way to the back.

"Considering it's strictly on a volunteer basis, you certainly put in long hours here," Jeff commented.

He was telling her that he thought she was being overworked. Right now, considering the way she felt, she couldn't really argue with him. But she felt she needed to tell him that it wasn't always this hectic here.

"There's normally another doctor here, too. We take shifts. I open the place and he closes up."

He nodded, taking it in. He'd been here for half the day and the only medical personnel he'd seen were Mikki and the dour-faced nurse. "And where is he?"

"He had a family emergency—same as the two other nurses who are usually here," she added.

He nodded. "I see. So in other words, it was all on your shoulders."

Mikki raised her chin somewhat defensively. "I managed."

"Yes, you certainly did," Jeff agreed. The last thing he wanted to do was offend her or get in some sort of an argument over the nature of her rather zealous work ethic. "Could I interest you in going back to the restaurant for a drink, or some dessert?" he asked her. He really wanted to spend some time with this compelling woman in a somewhat less harried setting.

She considered his offer. "Either one sounds good."

Jeff grinned. "Either one it is."

But just as she was about to turn off the last two lights in the clinic, there was a loud pounding on the front door. Surprised, Mikki immediately turned toward the front of the clinic.

But Jeff was apparently leerier than she was. He quickly moved in front of her, blocking her access to the door.

"Don't open that," he warned her. "Your hours are posted outside. Everyone knows that the clinic is closed now, and this isn't the greatest neighborhood," he pointed out.

Whoever it was pounded on the door again. "That sounds like someone who needs help," Mikki argued.

"If they need help, there's a hospital a few blocks away," he reminded her.

The pounding started again, even more urgent sounding than the last two times. Moving him out of the way, Mikki undid all three locks and opened the door just enough to be able to look out. There was a distraught woman on the other side, holding a whimpering little boy of no more than five in her arms.

The second the door was opened, the woman began talking. "Please, my son, I think he broke his arm. He needs help." The woman looked at Jeff, directing her words to him. "You're the doctor, right?" she asked breathlessly.

"No, she's the doctor," he said, indicating Mikki. "Here, let me help you," he offered, taking the bruised little boy from the woman.

At this point, the child, clearly frightened, began to cry and moan as he shrank away from Jeff.

"Bring him in the back," Mikki instructed him. She paused only long enough to lock the door again. "The first room," she called out to Jeff. "Put him on the exam table."

"I wanna go home," the boy cried.

Mikki was quick to follow in Jeff's wake. The boy's mother was one step behind.

"You will, sweetie," Mikki told him. "I just want to take a look at that arm."

Obviously anticipating more pain, the boy was wiggling as he sat on the exam table. It made things difficult and each time the boy moved, he whimpered and cried.

"Jeff, could you help him stay still?" Mikki requested. "Jeff's going to play statue with you," she told the little boy. "Both of you are going to stay as still as possible." She smiled encouragingly at him. "I bet you'll win, too."

"Mama?" the boy cried, looking toward his mother for help.

"Listen to the nice doctor, Henry," his mother told him, clearly on the verge of tears herself. Worry lines were permanently imprinted on her forehead.

"But she's gonna hurt me," Henry cried.

"Oh, you must be thinking of some other doctor, Henry," Jeff told the boy. "Dr. Mikki never hurts anyone." He winked at Henry. "*Especially* if you stay very, very still."

"Like a statue?" Henry asked, trying to look brave enough, though a few tears escaped and were sliding down his cheeks.

"Just like a statue," Jeff told him solemnly. He raised his eyes to Mikki's. "We're ready."

"All right, Henry," Mikki began in a calm, soothing voice, "I'm going to have to examine your arm—"

Henry immediately froze up. "No!" he protested.

"Why don't we have Dr. Mikki examine my arm first?" Jeff suggested. "Then you can see that she's not going to hurt you."

The boy looked at him uncertainly, as if trying to decide whether or not to trust him. Finally, he sniffed, "Okay."

"I'm ready, Doc," Jeff told her, pretending to brace himself for the boy's benefit.

Mikki went through the motions, slowly feeling up and down Jeff's outstretched arm. Henry was watching her so intently, she could almost feel his eyes on her.

"No break here," Mikki concluded. She moved away from Jeff and turned toward the little boy. "All right, it's your turn, Henry."

Henry stayed exactly where he was. Instead, he looked at Jeff. "Did it hurt?"

Jeff shook his head. "Maybe a little, but not too much," he answered, knowing that if he said no, the little boy would immediately balk at the first sign of pain.

"Henry, the doctor has to look at your arm," his mother told him. The woman turned toward Mikki. "He was running and he fell right on it. When I touched it, he started screaming. He's so delicate," Henry's mother added. "He's always been that way."

The woman looked as if she was very close to bursting into tears.

"Looks like a big, strong boy to me," Jeff observed. Henry gave him a grateful, brave smile. "What do you think, Dr. Mikki?"

"I agree," Mikki answered, giving the boy an encouraging smile. "This'll be over with really quickly," she promised.

She watched the boy brace himself. Very gently, she passed her fingers along the upper portion of his arm—the part she knew hadn't been hurt.

Henry watched her with huge eyes. And then, startled, he stifled a yelp of pain as she worked her way down his forearm.

"It hurts, it hurts!" he yelled. He would have pulled back his arm if Jeff hadn't been holding it down, keeping the limb immobile.

"I know it does, sweetheart, but you're being really, really brave and we'll be finished soon." She looked at Jeff, silently asking for his help. "I'm going to have to take an X-ray."

"What's that?" Henry cried, looking really frightened.

"That's a picture of your bones," she explained soothingly. "You've had pictures taken, haven't you, Henry?"

"Sometimes," he answered warily, watching her every move again.

"Tell you what, pal," Jeff said. "How about I take you to where the doc has her X-ray machine and she'll take that picture of your arm in no time?"

Henry looked up at him, clearly wavering. "You'll be there, too?"

"Wouldn't miss it for the world," Jeff told the boy. "Ready?" he asked, coming over to stand next to the exam table.

Henry nodded. "Ready."

As gently as possible, Jeff picked the boy up and,

with Mikki leading the way, he brought the boy into the room where the X-rays were taken.

At the hospital, this was something that was done by the technicians. But Mikki had watched it being done often enough to feel confident that she could operate the X-ray machine herself.

With Jeff's help, she managed to take two views of the break in Henry's arm. Development of the films went quickly.

"That doesn't look like my arm," Henry protested when Mikki showed him the X-rays he'd asked to see.

"That's what it looks like under your skin. See this tiny line here?" she asked, pointing it out to the boy as if she was talking to a colleague.

Henry leaned forward, squinting hard as he looked at the X-ray. "Uh-huh."

"That's called a hairline fracture," she told him. "That's what you have."

A terrified expression came over his face. "Is my arm going to fall off?"

Mikki congratulated herself for not laughing. "No, honey, we're going to put a cast on it and it'll be good as new in a few weeks."

"In the meantime, you'll have this cool cast all your friends are going to want to sign," Jeff told him.

Henry twisted around on the exam table to look up at his new friend. "They can't write."

Undaunted, Jeff switched gears. "They'll draw pictures."

Henry nodded. "Okay." Reassured, he turned so that he was looking up at the doctor. "Do it."

"You've got a brave guy here, Mrs. Hendricks," Mikki said to the boy's mother.

The woman nodded, blinking back tears of relief. "I know."

Working methodically, Mikki prepared the plaster for the cast and applied it, layer by layer, onto the boy's arm. She made sure she used a material that dried very quickly.

"It's kinda heavy," Henry told her when she was finished, gingerly lifting his arm up.

"I know, but that's to make sure your bone grows together," Mikki told him.

Turning away, she opened up the bottom drawer in the cast room cabinet. After some rummaging, she found what she was looking for.

"Here, let's put this sling on. It'll help distribute the weight for you." She slipped the sling, which had little cartoon characters on it, onto his arm and then up, onto the back of his neck. "There you go. You're all set." Turning toward the boy's mother, she told her, "I'm going to need to see him in two weeks. Depending on how it goes, we can put a lighter cast on in its place at that time."

"More casts?" Henry groaned.

"But it'll be lighter," Mikki emphasized, smiling at him.

"And your friends can draw more pictures," Jeff told the boy.

Henry glanced down at his cast. "Yeah, they can, can't they?" That seemed to satisfy him.

Jeff helped the boy off the exam table. His mother turned toward Mikki.

"How much do I owe you?" Mrs. Hendricks asked. The lines on her face seemed to deepen as she fumbled inside her purse.

Mikki put her hand over the other woman's, stilling it. When the woman raised her eyes in question, Mikki told the boy's mother, "It's called a free clinic for a reason."

Mrs. Hendricks exhaled a huge breath. "I don't know how to thank you," she said, tears shining in her eyes. A couple slid down her cheeks.

"Just teach him to walk, not run, and we'll call it even," Mikki quipped.

"Don't worry," she said, putting her arm around her son's shoulders—she had to stoop a little to do it. "I'm not letting him out of my sight."

"He was just being a kid," Jeff said, coming to Henry's defense. "Weren't you, Henry? Kids break things, sometimes on their own bodies. It happens. But you're going to try to be more careful, aren't you?" he asked.

The boy bobbed his head up and down. "Uh-huh. For sure."

"Good enough for me," Jeff responded, ruffling the boy's hair. "Can I drop you two off at your home?" he offered, turning toward Mrs. Hendricks.

"No, that's all right, really. It's just a few blocks away from here," Mrs. Hendricks told him. "We can walk."

"Yes, but riding in a car is faster. Besides, Henry here's been through a lot," he added. And then he turned to look at Mikki. "I'll be back in a few minutes. Wait for me?" he asked hopefully.

Truthfully, she didn't want to turn him down, but she felt as if she should. He'd already put himself out a lot today.

Motioning Jeff to the side, she waited until he joined her then asked in a lowered voice, "Don't you want to go straight home after dropping them off?"

"Not particularly. I'm going back to the restaurant. I thought you might want to follow me there for that drink or dessert we talked about," Jeff reminded her.

That had been more than an hour ago, and in all the excitement over Henry's arm, she had honestly forgotten that conversation.

"Are you still up for that?" she asked, surprised.

"More than ever." He grinned, his eyes washing over her. "I have to confess that watching you in action invigorates me."

Mikki's eyes met his. *Right back at you*, she thought. "Okay, I'll wait for you."

"Great," he told her.

He was tempted just to give her a quick kiss on the cheek, but he was afraid that might make her back off or change her mind about waiting for him. He still wasn't sure where he stood, so for now, he was taking baby steps.

He turned toward Mrs. Hendricks and her son. With a flourish, he bowed before the boy and said, "Mrs. Hendricks, your chariot awaits."

"What's a chariot?" Henry asked.

Very gingerly, Jeff picked the boy up. "A stagecoach without a top."

"Your car doesn't have a top?" Henry asked, his eyes widening. "Where is it?"

Jeff looked over toward the boy's mother. "I bet he keeps you on your toes, doesn't he?"

For the first time since she had pounded on the clinic's

door more than an hour ago, Henry's mother smiled as she followed her son and his new hero. "Oh, you have no idea."

Chapter Fourteen

"How did you get to be so good with children?" Mikki asked, sitting across the table from Jeff.

True to his word, Jeff had returned to the clinic less than half an hour after taking Henry and his very relieved mother home. As soon as he had returned, Mikki had locked the facility up again. And then, with his leading the way, she had followed Jeff over to his restaurant.

They were now sitting at a table for two that, unlike the table where they had first shared dinner the other night, was tucked off to one side, away from the other diners.

Because she had liked it so much the last time she'd dined here, Mikki decided to order another slice of tiramisu. Foregoing the wine Jeff had suggested, she'd asked for a glass of sparkling water.

"Well," Jeff answered, "I used to be one myself." When he saw her continue to look at him as if she was waiting for him to elaborate further, he explained, "And I had to look after my brother and sister while my mother was at work. I found that Robert and Tina didn't like having to listen to me, and yelling at them didn't get me anywhere, so I had to come up with a different approach."

A fond smile curved his lips as he recalled those days. Sometimes, it felt like a million years ago. At other times, it was as if it had all happened yesterday.

"I talked to them as if they were human beings— even though—" he laughed "—I had some pretty strong doubts about that at the time."

"Well, your method certainly worked on Henry," Mikki told him. "I don't think I would have been able to get a clear X-ray of his arm, never mind getting that cast on him, without you. Having you there, talking to him, was extremely helpful."

"Glad to be of assistance." Jeff raised his glass in a silent toast to their successful venture. "I did my best."

Taking a sip of wine, he set the glass down again. And then he looked at the woman he found himself growing increasingly attracted to, debating the wisdom of whether or not he should say something. He had a feeling that Mikki would probably prefer that he didn't say anything, but in all good conscience, Jeff really felt that he needed to ask—it had been preying on his mind ever since it happened.

Taking a breath, he pushed on. "You don't do that very often, do you?"

"You mean work late?" Mikki guessed. "About half the time. It's hard turning people away just because they happen to be sitting in the waiting room when it's time to close up."

It was a way out and part of him thought he should take it. But he found that he was worried about her. He didn't want anything happening to her just because she had such a kind heart.

"No," he persisted, "I mean open the doors after hours when everyone else has left the clinic."

Rather than look at the subject in general, Mikki was still focused on the specific. "Mrs. Hendricks was frantic. You saw her."

"I saw her," he agreed. "And I was with you so if there was any danger, I'd be there to protect you." He saw a somewhat skeptical look enter her eyes. Jeff doggedly pressed on. "But what I'm asking about is if you were there alone after hours—if I wasn't there and the nurse was gone—would you open the door?"

Very slowly, her lips curved into a small, touched smile. "Are you worried about me?"

"Guess my secret's out," Jeff quipped, and then he grew serious. "I'm just saying that it's a dangerous neighborhood—it's not like Bedford—and some punk might use a ruse, claiming to be sick, to get into the clinic when no one else is around."

Mikki thought she knew what this was ultimately about—breaking in to steal drugs. "You don't have to worry. All the drugs are securely locked up in the safe," she told him.

How could someone so sharp be so beautifully naive at the same time? "You know the combination?"

"Yes. I have to be able to open the safe in order to dispense the medication," she told him.

He hated having to state the obvious, but maybe if

she heard it, she'd think twice the next time someone was pounding on the doors, asking to be let in after hours. "A desperate punk would think nothing of doing whatever he needed to do to make you open the safe. Or he might not even be after the drugs," Jeff said pointedly, looking at her.

Mikki let out a long breath and inclined her head. "Point taken," she allowed. He wasn't saying anything that hadn't crossed her mind already. "And if it makes you feel any better, that was the first time I was ever alone after hours—and technically," she said, looking at him pointedly, "I really wasn't."

He nodded, but his mind still wasn't at ease. "Promise me that if you ever find yourself in that position again, you'll call me."

Mikki smiled as another forkful of tiramisu disappeared between her lips. "Right. And you'll come running over."

"Yes," he assured her seriously. "I will."

She could have sworn she felt a hot flash passing over her entire body, which was ridiculous because, at thirty-five, she was way too young for that. Mikki admitted to herself that it had more to do with the man sitting across from her than with her age.

"Oh," she finally said, forcing the word out of a mouth that felt bone-dry. She tried not to dwell on him coming to her rescue as if she was some sort of old-fashioned damsel in distress. "Well, lucky for you, I only work there one day a week and this has never happened before, so it shouldn't happen again."

"Yeah, lucky," he repeated in a monotone voice that said he really didn't feel that it was lucky at all. To tell the truth, he rather liked the idea of having to come to her rescue.

Seeing that she had finished both the cake and the goblet of sparkling water, Jeff asked her, "Can I get you anything else?"

"No, thank you." She picked up her purse from the floor next to her, ready to leave. "I think I'd better be getting home. I went in early today and it's been a really long, long day," she emphasized.

"Okay." Jeff rose to his feet. He pulled out her chair for her, then tucked it back up against the table after she stepped away.

When he began to follow her to the door, Mikki paused to tell him, "I know where I left the car this time. You don't have to walk me to the parking lot again."

"I'm not," he answered.

"Then why are you still walking with me?" she asked.

"Because this time," he told her, "I'd like to see you home."

It wasn't as if they were on a date, although she had to admit that maybe, at another time and place, she would have liked that. "There's no need to do that," Mikki told him.

He'd been more than a great help today, starting with all that food he'd brought to the clinic. She didn't want him to feel obligated to do anything more for her.

Then, recalling what he had said earlier about the clinic's location, Mikki reminded him, "After all, this is Bedford."

"I know," he answered amicably, still walking beside her, "but it would just make me feel better to see you to your door."

Well, she wasn't going to argue with him. "I guess chivalry isn't dead," she remarked.

Jeff supposed that was one word for it. But if he were being totally honest, chivalry didn't have anything to do with why he was doing this. He just didn't want the evening to end just yet.

But he had a feeling that if he said as much, that might frighten Mikki away. So he murmured, "I guess not."

Since they had arrived at the restaurant together, their vehicles weren't parked that far apart.

"Wait here," he told her. "I'll get my car and pull up behind you. Then you can lead the way to your house— or apartment," he amended, realizing that he had no idea if she lived in one or the other.

"House," she told him. "It's a house. I live in the Woodbridge development."

That caused him to stop walking for a moment. "You're kidding."

She looked at him, confused. "No, why?"

He laughed. "I live there, too. I guess that kind of makes us neighbors."

Mikki couldn't really explain why she felt that flutter in her stomach when he told her that, or why that flutter seemed to intensify by the moment.

She did her best to appear unaffected. "I guess so," she agreed. "I'm on Mayfair," she told him, then added, "It's a cul-de-sac."

"Alsace," he told her, giving her the name of the street where he lived. "That's on the other side of the development."

She knew that. She knew all the names of the streets in the development. And, considering the size of the neighborhood, his street wasn't all that far away from hers. It probably took ten, maybe twelve minutes to reach on foot.

"Small world," she commented. Belatedly, she noticed that she'd reached her car.

"I was just thinking that," Jeff told her. Pausing for a moment at her car, he nodded. "Okay, I'll go get my car. Be right back."

Her stomach continued to flutter as she watched him go to fetch his vehicle. For a brief moment she told herself that she should go now, while he was getting his car.

But she didn't.

Mikki had no idea why she kept glancing up into her rearview mirror every few minutes. Jeff knew where he was going. It wasn't as if she was going to lose him in the Saturday-night traffic.

It seemed like everyone and his cousin was out on the road tonight, determined to get to wherever a good time could be had. She supposed that she was one of the few people out on the road who just wanted to get home rather than to a club or a party.

The sudden sound of screeching brakes behind her had Mikki automatically tightening her hands on the wheel, instantly alert. Her heart had flown up into her throat and was throbbing hard there.

Straining to see behind her using her side mirror as well as the rearview one, she realized that the screeching sound had come from Jeff's car. He had slammed on his brakes, narrowly avoiding hitting a car that had flown through the intersection and a red light. The driver of the other car just kept going, either unaware or indifferent to the fact that he had nearly been the cause of an accident.

Mikki began to pull over, but she saw that Jeff just kept driving. So she righted her vehicle and continued driving to her house.

But the moment she pulled up in her driveway, less than ten minutes later, she leaped out of her car and quickly ran up to Jeff's vehicle. He was just parking at her front curb.

"Are you all right?" she cried breathlessly.

Getting out, Jeff closed his door. "Well, I'm a little shaken up," he admitted. "But no damage done."

She wasn't as cavalier as he was. "Only because you have quick reflexes. That guy was driving like a maniac. He almost plowed right into you," she said, clearly angry about the incident.

"The main thing was that he *didn't*," Jeff emphasized.

She was stunned that he could take it all in so calmly. "Do you always see the upside like that?"

He was sorry that she'd had to witness the near accident and that it had upset her, but he had his own way of handling things like that, at least when it only involved him.

"That's the only way I can keep things from getting to me. I dwell on the positive." It had been his philosophy in life for as long as he could remember.

Thinking that Mikki probably needed to get some sleep, he was about to say good-night when he took a closer look at her.

Without thinking, he took hold of her shoulders. "Hey, you're shaking. That guy didn't hit your car, did he?" he asked, glancing at the rear of her vehicle. But from what he could see, it was untouched.

"No. But I thought he was going to hit you. *Really* hit you," she stressed. She took a deep breath, steadying her nerves. "Would you like to come in for a drink, or to just pull yourself together?"

She looked like she was the one who needed to be pulled together, not him. He was not about to leave her like this. Dropping his hands to his side, he smiled at her and said, "I thought you didn't drink."

"I'm not on call tonight," Mikki told him. "Someone else is, so I can make an exception this time. Would you like to join me?"

He realized that his heart was not exactly all that steady. Whether that was because of the near accident or because of the invitation, he wasn't sure. But either way, he knew he was going to take her up on it.

"Very much," he replied.

Pointing his key fob toward his car, he pressed the button that brought all four locks down, then turned to follow Mikki to her front door.

"You know, odd as it is to admit," he told her, stopping on her front step, "in all the years I've been driving, that's the first time I ever came close to having someone hit me."

"Have you ever hit anyone—with your car, I mean?" she amended as she unlocked the front door.

"I'm happy to say I never have." And then he grinned. "Do you think that's going to jinx me?"

His question surprised her and she wasn't sure if he was being serious, or just teasing her. "Are you superstitious? Do you believe in jinxes and things like that?"

"No," he answered. "I didn't want to dismiss it out of hand just in case you were superstitious, but no, I don't. I believe in a lot of things, but I don't believe in superstitions."

"What do you believe in?" she asked.

"That's easy," he told her. "I believe in hard work and making your own luck. I believe in treating people the way you want to be treated. I believe in returning favors and sharing whenever possible—and in always taking care of your family and friends."

Mikki looked at him. The man sounded too good to be true. If her mother had come across him, she would already have him bundled up in her car and heading for Las Vegas.

Which was precisely why she was so leery of the feelings that were swirling all through her, Mikki thought. Feelings she had never even briefly entertained before about *anyone*.

Gesturing toward the gray sectional in her living room, she said, "Make yourself comfortable."

Leaving him there, she went into the kitchen and opened the refrigerator. There wasn't all that much to rummage through and definitely not a large selection of alcohol for her to offer him. Actually, there was only one bottle.

"I've got a bottle of rosé," she called out. "Is that all right?"

"Then you do drink," he concluded because up until now, he wasn't sure.

"No," Mikki answered, bringing the bottle and one glass over to him. "My mother does. She brought the rosé over to toast her new engagement."

"Well, then congratulations to your mother," Jeff said.

"No," Mikki corrected. "The wine lasted longer than her engagement. I'm afraid that husband-to-be number five is long gone without ever making it to the altar. But Mother kept the engagement ring—and left me with custody of the wine, which I will now gladly offer to you." She poured part of the contents into the glass she had brought over.

He looked at the lone glass, surprised. "I thought you said you were having some."

"That's right, I did say that, didn't I? Sorry. It's not something I'm used to doing," she confessed. "Let me go get another glass."

Returning from the kitchen, she set the second glass on the coffee table next to his. She only poured half the amount she'd poured for him into her glass, then raised it in a toast. "May you always have near misses."

Jeff raised his own glass. "At least when it comes to car accidents," he amended.

His eyes met hers just before he took a sip.

Chapter Fifteen

Belatedly, because she had been so mesmerized by the look in Jeff's eyes, Mikki came to.

Doing her best to seem nonchalant, she took a sip from her own glass of wine. Less than half a beat late, she could swear that she felt her head beginning to spin.

Granted, she wasn't accustomed to drinking alcohol on anything that even remotely approached a regular basis, but she certainly had had wine before on occasion. And this was rather a light wine at that. She sincerely doubted that the tiny bit she'd just imbibed was responsible for the light-headed feeling she was experiencing right at this moment.

Taking a deep breath, Mikki attempted to distance herself from the thoughts and emotions that were somersaulting through her right now.

She changed the subject. "Um, I've been meaning to

ask you, how is your mother doing? She's almost due for her second recheck," Mikki recalled.

After the seemingly nonstop day Mikki had just had, he appreciated her being so thoughtful and asking about his mother. The woman really was one of a kind.

"She's doing well. She's also thinking of adopting you," he confided.

"Excuse me?"

Jeff backtracked, starting from the beginning. "To be honest, she's surprised that she's feeling so well. I'm only just now beginning to find out that she'd been hiding just how bad she'd been feeling all this time. But now that she's feeling better, she's finally admitting the true extent of her pain."

He paused, letting that sink in, then said, "Since you, in effect, made it all better, my mother wants to show her gratitude. Best way she knows how is to adopt you."

Mikki laughed. "Tell your mother I'm very happy I could help her and I'm touched that she wants to make me part of her family, but I really don't need to be adopted. I have a mother." She paused as she took another long sip of her wine, nearly finishing what had been a very small amount to begin with. "I have to admit that she's more like a character out of a play, but I have a mother," she told him.

There was a lot of history behind that one sentence, Jeff guessed. He could hear it in her intonation. She had aroused his curiosity. "Tell me about her."

Mikki shook her head, dismissing the request. "You don't want to hear about my mother."

"Sure I do," he told her, sitting up. "She sounds colorful."

Mikki considered his comment. "That would be one word for her."

"What would be another?" he asked.

Other than confiding in Nikki, she had decided a long time ago to keep her mother's misdeeds and the way she felt about them to herself.

The glass was empty and she twirled the stem between her thumb and forefinger, searching for a way to frame her answer—or a way to deflect.

"Although neither one of my parents actually taught me this by word or example, I really, truly believe that if you can't say something nice about a person, you shouldn't say anything at all."

He read between the lines. "That bad, huh?"

Mikki shrugged. Why did she feel this overwhelming desire to share any of this with this man? It wasn't that her mother deserved her loyalty—if the tables were reversed, her mother certainly wouldn't keep any less than stellar details about her private. But Mikki just didn't believe in airing her dirty laundry in public.

"My mother has her demons," Mikki said tactfully. And then, because this wasn't exactly a secret, she said, "She's an insecure woman who is actively searching for a Prince Charming to simultaneously sweep her off her feet and worship the ground she walks on."

He raised his eyebrows, clearly trying to picture what she'd just described. "Sounds like that's a tall order."

"It's an impossible order," Mikki corrected.

Her childhood must have been hell, Jeff thought. With that in mind, there were a thousand ways her life could have gone awry. "Well, even so, it looks like you turned out all right."

An ironic smile curved her lips. "That was more in

self-defense than anything else," she told him. "Rather than spending my time getting all bogged down frantically trying to find happiness, I thought it was more important to try to get outside myself and help others."

There was a little wine left in his glass, and he raised it in another toast to her. "Well, on behalf of those others, I'd like to thank you for that."

She didn't like having attention focused on her. That was her mother's thing, not hers. "You're not exactly a slouch in that department," she countered. "You can't tell me that you always drive around with that much food in your car."

"Oh." Now he understood what Mikki was talking about. "That."

"Yes, that," Mikki laughed. She liked the fact that he was modest and didn't brag. She found it really refreshing, especially after having grown up in her parents' world.

"Well, I never got to be a Boy Scout, but I do believe in always being prepared," Jeff told her.

"For what?" she asked. "An impromptu banquet? Admit it, you brought all that food with you because you knew I wouldn't leave my patients to have lunch while they were stuck in the waiting room, hungry." Which, in her book, meant that he'd been paying close attention to the way she thought and behaved.

"I guess I'm guilty as charged," Jeff allowed vaguely.

"You're a very generous man, Jeff Sabatino," she told him.

"Maybe you bring out the best in me," he suggested.

He was sitting right next to her on the sectional. Because her hair was falling into her face, he gently moved it aside with the tip of his fingers. He wanted to get a better look into her eyes.

There went her stomach again, Mikki thought, feeling it do a somersault.

Breathe, damn it, breathe!

"I don't think it needs to be brought out," she told him, her voice sounding strangely low to her own ear. It was as if the words were struggling to emerge. "I think it's right there on the surface."

"Careful," he told her, his voice as low as hers. He set his empty glass down on the coffee table. "You'll turn my head."

It was as if everything around her had fallen into darkness. All she was aware of was him. "I wouldn't want to do that," she answered.

"I totally agree," he whispered. "Because then I might miss."

She didn't have to ask him what he meant by that, or what he'd miss, because the next moment Jeff went on to show her.

He lowered his mouth to hers.

Oh, no!

The words echoed in her brain in giant capital letters. This was worse than she thought.

She was really hoping that his kiss would be anticlimactic. That it would leave her cold and she could return to her isolated little world, none the worse for the experience.

But his kiss *wasn't* anticlimactic. It was, in a word, *delicious*. Delicious and it left her wanting more. So much so that she slid into not just the kiss, but somehow into him, as well.

Whatever space had been between them on the sectional was gone. Gone to the point that not even a well-worn dime could be wedged between them.

Everything she had hoped not to feel she was, in essence, feeling. Heat and desire, and everything inside her was churning and swirling.

He hadn't counted on this.

All he had wanted to do was kiss a beautiful woman—maybe several times—and then take his leave before desire had an opportunity to intensify, making him want to stay.

But desire had immediately taken on depth and breadth from the first moment of contact.

Jeff didn't remember enfolding her in his arms, didn't remember deepening the kiss until it was completely fathomless. Just like that, he was lost in an ocean of heated emotions.

He found himself not just wanting to kiss her, but wanting to make love with her.

Now.

And although he didn't detect so much as even mild resistance on her part, he wasn't about to overwhelm her in any manner, shape or form. It wouldn't be right.

And more than that, it was no way to repay her for what she'd done for his mother and, thus, for him. She had performed a selfless act and he was behaving, in a word, selfishly.

But he couldn't.

Exercising more strength and self-control than he'd ever had the need to before, Jeff ended the kiss and then drew away from this woman who lit him up.

There was a look of surprise on Mikki's upturned

face. Surprise and more than a little confusion. Her eyes were wide as she looked at him.

"I should go home," he told her, stringing the words together with effort.

She wasn't sure what Jeff was actually telling her. Was he rejecting her, or had he changed his mind? In either case, she went along with it.

"I guess it's my turn to walk you to the door," she said with a smile, congratulating herself that her voice didn't crack.

"You don't have to do that," he replied, trying to keep the situation light. "The door's not that hard to find."

"I have to lock it when you leave," she pointed out.

"Oh, right." He felt awkward about the whole situation. About giving in to his desires, and then about having to stop. "All right then," Jeff said, gathering himself together.

He had to admit that he was rather surprised at the impact she'd just had on him. The woman was absolutely intoxicating, far more than the wine he'd just had. Even more than straight whiskey. Yes, she was beautiful, but in no way had he been prepared for her having such a lethal mouth.

"Let's go," he said, leading the way to her front door. He reached it in several steps. Turning around to face her, he said, "Well, we're here."

"Yes," Mikki answered, her heart hammering wildly as she contemplated her next move, "I guess we are."

He was about to say something further, but he didn't get the chance. Because the very next moment, instead of saying "Goodbye," Mikki was saying "Hello" in the most basic way possible.

Almost on automatic pilot for the very first time in

her life, Mikki had threaded her arms around his neck and raised herself up on her toes until her mouth was less than a breath away from his.

And then it wasn't away at all.

It was hard to say, when she tried to analyze it later, who had moved in first. Whether she had completed the move or if he had beaten her to it.

Either way, it didn't matter who was first.

All that mattered was that when contact was finally made, fireworks went off, sealing them to one another and guaranteeing that they would remain that way, at least for the time being.

He had both wanted this, and he hadn't. Wanted it because the very feel of her breath aroused him to such heights, it caused him to become instantly dizzy, instantly hungry.

But he didn't want her to feel that this was because he had come to the clinic today. Didn't want her thinking that this was his endgame and once he reached it, the game would be over.

Because whatever was happening right now, it was far from over. And while he couldn't be accused of being a saint, or even remotely close to one, none of the women he had been with and enjoyed had ever caused this extreme, instant reaction within him.

He could barely contain himself.

And he didn't want to.

What he wanted was to make love to every single part of her—simultaneously. Wanted it so much, it nearly scared the hell out of him.

This was something completely brand-new, and he had no idea how to react to it.

* * *

She shouldn't be letting this happen, Mikki thought.
Shouldn't be letting it happen because the firm ground
she'd thought she was standing on had vanished underneath her.

And the worst part of it was that she didn't care.

The only thing she cared about was that she didn't
want whatever this was to stop.

Ever.

The only kind of hunger she had ever known was
the kind that was satisfied by food. But this hunger was
something entirely new, entirely different. She could
honestly say that it was frightening in its insatiability.

Since they had come together at her door under the
guise of saying goodbye, she hadn't even stopped for
air. All she wanted was to feel his hands along her body,
his lips devouring hers before they ultimately moved
on to leave their imprint along every throbbing inch
of her skin.

Between the door and the sectional, clothes wound
up vanishing, both his and hers—Mikki really didn't
remember how and when. When they were on the sectional, she was only aware of the heat radiating from
her body, heat mingling with his.

Their bodies tangled together, and it was as if they
were both bent on mutual pleasure while bringing one
another up to heights that caused mountains to look
small by comparison.

Mikki didn't want to feel this way, didn't want to feel
as if she could touch the very sky. Because that meant
that the eventual *lack* of this exhilarating feeling would
bring with it an inconceivable pain. It would consume
her and then spit her out. In pieces.

She didn't want to become like her mother—not even close.

And yet, she couldn't help herself. Couldn't stop reacting to Jeff. Couldn't stop these passions, these longings, from taking hold of her and keeping her imprisoned in their grip.

All right, all right, if this was her fate, Mikki decided, then she was going to make the most of it. And when it was gone, when *he* had gone on with his life and left hers, she'd force herself to accept it.

But right now, it wasn't gone. *He* wasn't gone. He was here, bringing her to the very brink of explosions time and again.

Unable to catch her breath, she was determined not to be the only one to remember this night for years to come. So for every sensation Jeff created within her, she reciprocated, mimicking his moves and then, going on instinct, creating some of her own. Each time his hands passed over her, caressing her, stimulating her, she did the same to him.

When she heard him moan, she knew she was succeeding and that spurred her on.

The woman was a veritable wildcat.

He'd had no idea that she was capable of this. Talk about still waters running deep—Mikki was an ocean. What he had discovered about her was utterly mind-blowing.

To think he had been worried about taking advantage of her. Hell, he could barely keep up.

With what amounted to the last of his strength, Jeff sealed his mouth to hers after reanointing every part of her body with that same mouth. And then, bringing himself up along the length of her, he united their two bodies.

An urgency mounted within him even though he managed to go slowly at first. That quickly evaporated as she moved beneath him, fanning his desires. Making him go faster and faster.

He seized the moment, driving her up further. He felt her nails digging into his back, heard her breathing growing more and more rapid. When she arched against him, uttering a muffled cry, he knew that they had reached the ultimate peak together.

When the explosion came, he clung to her and the moment, his heart pounding as hard as hers was. He could feel it against his chest. It blended with the sensation of the incredible rush that was passing over him, enfolding them both.

And though it seemed impossible, at that moment, he knew he was in love with her.

Chapter Sixteen

"That was incredible," Jeff whispered. His breath ruffled her hair as Mikki lay with her head on his chest. "I have to admit, you turned out to be a complete surprise."

Mikki raised her head and looked at him. "Why? What were you expecting?"

"Well—" he laughed softly, running his hand along her back, caressing her skin "—certainly not to have my shoes and socks blown off."

"What shoes and socks? You were naked," she pointed out with a grin.

"All the harder to do," he replied, then laughed again. "I just want you to know that I had absolutely no intentions of that happening when I came over here tonight."

"Are you apologizing or telling me that you're having regrets?" Mikki asked him, drawing away and wondering just how she was going to execute a retreat at this point without feeling like a complete idiot.

"Neither," he answered, tightening his arm around her. "I just want you to know that I didn't have any ulterior motives coming over." Jeff played with the ends of her hair as he talked. "To be honest, I guess I was kind of in awe, watching you in action today, especially when you were with Henry. You're really something, you know that?"

She shifted slightly, feeling somewhat self-conscious. Compliments had that effect on her. Especially in this situation. "You don't have to say things like that after the fact."

"After what fact?" Jeff asked her. With his forefinger, he raised her chin so he could look into her eyes.

"You know." When he continued to look at her, obviously waiting for her to go on, she forced herself to explain. "I'm saying we've already made love—you don't have to try to soften me up."

Mystified, he told her, "I'm not trying to soften you up. I'm just telling you what I'm feeling right now. Just what kind of men have you been out with?"

"None," she answered. And then, shrugging, she added, "Not in a very long, long time."

"Then where's this coming from?" he asked, wanting to know why she seemed so insecure. If anyone had a reason to be confident, it was Mikki. "A bad experience?"

She thought back to her first—and only—experience with a man. She'd been a sophomore in college and he was a TA. "Maybe," she admitted. "A very long time ago. More like a mistake, really."

Even though Jeff had a lot of questions he wanted to ask her, he knew it wasn't his place to pry.

"Well," Jeff began slowly, his voice soft, low and deliberately soothing, "I don't know how you feel about what just happened, but for me, it definitely wasn't a mistake." Ever so lightly, he ran the back of his hand along her cheek, stirring her. Stirring himself. "On the contrary, it was as close to heaven as I've ever been."

"Are you trying to seduce me?" Mikki asked incredulously.

His mouth curved in a teasing smile. "Maybe. How'm I doing?" he asked.

"Keep going," Mikki encouraged him. "I'll let you know."

"Nothing I like better than a challenge," Jeff told her, leaning over Mikki just before he brought his mouth down to hers.

It was just at that very heated, intimate moment that the phone suddenly rang. It was the landline rather than her cell phone, and the shrill sound shattered the air as it wedged its way into what was the beginning of another beautifully romantic interlude.

Jeff drew back. He looked at the landline accusingly. "Can you ignore that?"

Mikki sighed. "No."

He moved aside, resigned, as he allowed Mikki to sit up so that she could get to the telephone. "I didn't think so."

Reaching for the receiver, Mikki picked it up and brought it to her ear. "Hello, this is Dr. McKenna."

As he watched, Mikki transformed from the desirable woman he was about to make love with for a second time to the very efficient doctor he'd seen in action earlier at the clinic.

Mikki listened in silence, then said, "Yes, of course, I'll be there as soon as I can. Watch his vitals," she instructed the person on the other end of the line just before she hung up. She looked at Jeff. "I have to go."

"I kind of figured that out," he said wryly. And then he remembered something. "I thought you had someone covering for you."

"I do. But this is an extenuating circumstance," she explained, getting up from the sectional. She saw that Jeff was waiting for an explanation. "I operated on this man a little over a week ago. He was discharged."

"What went wrong?" he asked as they both began picking their clothes up from the floor and getting dressed.

Jeff could tell by her voice was she was trying not to sound irritated. "My patient decided he didn't have to take it easy for a few weeks the way I told him to. He was in his garage, trying to fix something, when he tripped over a box of tools and fell. He ripped open some of his stitches, and his wife panicked and drove him to the ER. He asked for me, telling the doctor on duty that he wouldn't let anyone else touch him."

Mikki sighed as she pulled up the zipper on her jeans. Finished dressing, she looked at Jeff, disappointment suddenly welling up within her. "I'm sorry."

"For what?" Jeff asked. "For being you? Hey, I understand." He knew exactly what he had signed on for when he had begun thinking of her in a romantic light. She was a doctor, and this came with the package. "I have a feeling that my mother probably feels the same way about you that this guy in the ER does." Jeff put his shoes on and stood up again. "Want me to drive you to the hospital?"

"That's really nice of you to offer," Mikki answered, "but you should go home. At least one of us should get some rest. Besides," she added, "until I see the amount of damage he's done to himself, I have no idea how long this is going to take."

"And no one else can sub for you?" Jeff asked in one last-ditch attempt to prolong their evening.

"If I was incapacitated or unreachable, they could probably come up with someone. But a doctor-patient relationship is really important to me, and it takes time to build up. Since he specifically asked for me, I wouldn't feel right about letting my patient down."

Jeff nodded, making his peace with the situation. "I guess I should just be glad that the hospital didn't call any sooner." Leaning over, he lightly brushed his lips over hers. "Sure I can't drive you?"

"I'm sure—but I really do appreciate the offer." She realized that she was guilty of rushing him out. She didn't want to come across that way, not after the wonderful evening she'd just had with him. "You can stay here if you like."

But Jeff shook his head. "I'm afraid that it just wouldn't be the same without you."

He stood there, waiting for her to get her purse. When she was ready, he walked out with her and waited as she locked her front door. "I'll call you," he told her.

Mikki nodded, telling herself not to cling to that. It wasn't a promise. It was just something guys said after an evening was over, even a wonderful evening. If she held him to that and he didn't call, she ran the risk of being crushed, just like her mother.

Besides, Mikki reminded herself as she drove to the hospital, *you don't believe in commitment, or happily-ever-afters, remember?*

As far as happily-ever-after went, she had absolutely

nothing to base it on or refer to as an example. None of her mother's marriages had lasted. Not to mention that Veronica certainly hadn't been happy during those marriages' short lifespans.

Maybe this was all for the best, Mikki told herself. One really fantastic night and now she was going back to life as she knew it, doing what she was really good at and was meant to do: be a doctor.

She forced herself to loosen her death grip on the steering wheel as she drove into the hospital's parking lot.

Mikki found it difficult to refrain from being curt when she spoke to Mr. Miller, the returning gallstone patient who had inadvertently cut her evening short. She wanted to lecture him, not just because of her shortened evening, but because the man had wantonly ignored her instructions.

The repercussions for that could have been very serious. Luckily, they weren't.

However, she found that it was difficult to be angry with her patient when he appeared so utterly relieved to see her.

"You were supposed to take it easy, Mr. Miller," she told him as she pulled on a pair of rubber gloves.

Drawing back his hospital gown, she closely examined the extent of repair that needed to be done.

Miller, a heavyset man in his sixties, shifted uncomfortably at the admonishment. "I didn't mean to trip over that toolbox and fall down," he said, as if that absolved him of his part in this.

Mikki raised her eyes to his for a moment. "I'm sure you didn't," she answered.

Miller's wife cut in. "I *told* him not to go into that garage. I *told* him to sit in his recliner and watch that movie with me, but would he listen?" Mrs. Miller lamented. "No, he had to go try to fix the heating unit. Said he needed to feel 'useful.'" Mrs. Miller laughed harshly. "I ask you, what do you do with a man like that?"

Mikki could see how uncomfortable her patient was becoming as his wife harped on his less than sensible behavior. She smiled at the man before answering his wife's question.

"Just love him, I guess. And stitch him up," Mikki added. Finished with her preliminary exam, she told her patient, "You didn't do as much damage as you thought. You do need some stitches. But I need to clean this up first," she said, nodding at the broken stitches and the dried blood around them.

"I don't have to stay here overnight, do I?" Miller asked, concerned.

"What, you don't like our accommodations?" she asked, doing her best to look serious.

"It's not that," her patient assured her quickly. "I just want to go home."

She could understand that, Mikki thought. Who wanted to stay overnight in a hospital? "I think we can arrange that. Wait here while I have the nurse get a fresh suture kit."

Although everything went off without a hitch, it was close to three o'clock before Mikki walked back through her front door again.

The first thing that struck her was that the house felt oddly empty, even though there was never anyone else here when she got home. She didn't even have a pet dog or cat, or a parakeet, to chase away the silence.

Given that, why the emptiness seemed to seep into her this way tonight didn't make any sense.

Because she felt so drained, Mikki paused to sit down on the sectional to kick off her shoes.

She knew she was probably imagining things, but she could have sworn that she detected the scent of Jeff's aftershave lotion. She was undoubtedly just punchy. Even so, she leaned over the cushion and took a deep breath.

And then she smiled.

It *wasn't* her imagination, she thought. Picking up the cushion, she held it for a moment and took in another deep breath. It smelled just like Jeff. She could even feel things stirring within her.

C'mon, get a grip. You're a respected physician surgeon, not a twelve-year-old with her first crush.

She was acting like some kind of an adolescent, Mikki upbraided herself. Worse than that, she was behaving like her mother every time her mother had been on the brink of yet another "love of her life" adventure. An adventure that always seemed to turn out to be another huge disappointment.

Well, she wasn't her mother and she didn't need or want that, Mikki silently insisted, tossing the cushion back where it belonged.

Come Monday morning, she would have the cushions dry-cleaned, she promised herself. As for now, she was going to go to bed and sleep—maybe even until Monday morning.

The idea heartened her.

Getting up from the sectional, she was about to head for the stairs and her bedroom when she saw a flashing light out of the corner of her eye. It caught her attention.

It was the light on her landline—someone had left a message while she was at the hospital.

Her first thought was that the hospital had called again, alerting her about another patient. But then, she decided, someone would have undoubtedly said something while she was there.

Reevaluating the situation, she sincerely doubted that the message on her answering machine had anything to do with Mr. Miller and his stitches.

Maybe it was her mother, calling to tell her "wonderful news, darling!" which was the way all Veronica's announcements about a new man in her life started out.

Well, if that was it, it could wait until morning, Mikki thought. She wasn't in the mood to try to humor her mother.

The next moment she realized that the message on her phone couldn't have been from her mother. While the woman still stayed up until all hours of the night, she had never known her mother to call after midnight.

"Stop guessing, idiot, and play the message," she ordered herself. "Maybe, if you're lucky, it's a wrong number or some prince, offering to leave his entire fortune to you—all you need to go is send him a cashier's check for a nominal sum and the rest will all be yours."

Lord, she was beyond punchy. Sitting down on the sectional again, she pulled the phone over to her and pressed the play button.

At first, all she heard was jarring static, followed by a spat of nothing. And the metallic voice on the machine informed her in a formal tone that was the end of the message.

As she started to push the phone back to its original position on the side table, she heard the answering machine go through the motions of queuing up a second call.

There had been two of them?

As she stared at the device, a second message came on.

"Sorry, that last call was me. I hung up because I didn't want you to get the idea that I was, well, stalking you."

Mikki straightened, at attention and hardly breathing.

That was Jeff's voice.

"But I really want to know that you got back safe. I know, I know, you've been doing this forever, but well... I just want to make sure you got in all right. Am I being out of line? Yeah, probably, but in my defense, I'm my mother's son and there's this recessive gene she passed on to my siblings and me. It's called the worry gene, and sometimes it kicks into high gear. When it does, the idea of getting any sleep goes right out the window.

"I'm rambling," he apologized. "Ignore what I just said. Except for this part: I had a really great time tonight—or more accurately, I guess, *last* night. I just wanted you to know that. Hope everything turned out okay with your patient—how can it not, right? You're his doctor.

"I'd better hang up now before I put my other foot into my mouth or say something even more stupid. Oh, and this isn't what I meant when I said I'd call you. It just happened." He sounded as if he was uncomfortable with the way he had to be coming across and cleared his throat. "Good night, Mikki. I hope that you managed to get some sleep."

The dial tone followed after the message ended. And

then the metallic voice informed her that there were no more messages.

Mikki smiled to herself as she looked at the now silent answering machine.

She changed her mind about going up to her bedroom. Instead, she curled up on the sectional and pulled the cushion closer to her.

She rested her cheek against it.

In a few minutes, she'd fallen asleep that way.

Chapter Seventeen

It was a first.

Ordinarily, she was a very light sleeper. But the sound of ringing slowly registered in Mikki's head in small increments. When she first became aware of it, she thought it was just part of her dream.

Eventually, she realized that it wasn't and she reached for the telephone on the side table next to the sectional. It was only when she heard the dial tone against her ear while the ringing continued that she realized it wasn't her phone.

Someone was ringing her doorbell.

Mikki was on her feet before she managed to completely banish the fog from her brain. Maybe she was getting old, she thought, struggling to focus. There was a time when she could go almost two days straight without any sleep and still function.

As she made her way to the front door, Mikki dragged one hand through her hair in a semiattempt to somehow neaten it a little.

Reaching the door, she looked through the peephole—and then blinked to make sure that her eyes weren't playing tricks on her.

Stunned, she didn't open the door immediately. "Jeff? What are you doing here?"

"Right now, standing on your doorstep with groceries that are getting progressively heavier." He shifted the bags to get a better grip. "Mind if I come in?"

Rather than answer his question verbally, Mikki unlocked the door, opened it and stepped back so he could enter.

"Thanks." Shifting the bags again, Jeff walked in.

"I'm sorry, did we talk about this and I forgot?" she asked, confused.

Jeff headed straight for her kitchen. "No, but I thought you might be hungry after going back to the hospital last night. Don't forget, I got a glimpse of the inside of your refrigerator. There was nothing in it except for that bottle of rosé.

"I can't stay long," he told her, unpacking the four bags of groceries he'd brought in, haphazardly placing the items on the kitchen table before organizing the contents according to type. "I've got to be at the restaurant early today, but I thought I'd make you breakfast before I went."

When he turned around to look at her, he saw the expression on her face. Mikki didn't appear to be upset, but she did look rather conflicted. "Did I do something wrong?" Jeff asked.

"No," she answered a bit too quickly. "No, you

didn't." What was wrong with her? She should be happy that he was being so nice. "You're being kind, and caring and, in a word, *terrific*." She paused, running her tongue along her lips, searching for the right words. "And that's just the problem."

He was doing his best to understand what she was trying to tell him. "I can scowl while I'm making breakfast," he offered. "Better yet, I could burn the toast. Would that help?"

He must think she was crazy. Not that anyone would blame him. She tried again.

"I'm sorry. It's just that this whole thing is wonderful and I know what happens when things are wonderful."

Jeff waited for her to continue. She was obviously having trouble expressing what was bothering her. He couldn't pretend to understand, but after last night, he was certainly more than willing to try.

"I'm listening," he told her. It was getting late and he didn't have all that much time. "Would you mind if I put the groceries away while I listened?" he asked, not wanting her to think that he wasn't paying attention to her, or that he was just humoring her by saying he was listening while he was doing something else.

"You probably think I'm crazy," she told him, at a loss as to how to explain any of this to a man for whom most women would kill to have in her life.

"No," Jeff answered patiently. "I think that maybe you're having ambivalent feelings. And I'm probably contributing to that by coming on so strong. I have a habit of doing that when I feel so keenly about something."

He didn't want to crowd her or risk losing her because she felt smothered. He wanted her to take all the time in the world—as long as she eventually came up with the right answer.

"Look, why don't I just make you breakfast and then go so you can eat in peace?" he suggested.

"No," Mikki protested. This wasn't turning out right.

Jeff opened one cabinet after another, looking for a couple of frying pans. "You want to eat in chaos?" he deadpanned.

"I don't want to chase you away—" she protested. However, he deserved to hear the truth. "But I don't want to fall in love with you, either."

Finding the pans, he almost dropped them before he finally put them on the stove. *Was* she falling in love with him? He tried not to react to that and instead said, "Mind if I ask why?"

"Because if I fall in love with you," she said in despair, "it's all going to fall apart."

He glanced at her over his shoulder. It was really getting hard trying to keep the conversation light. But he was determined not to frighten her off and to get to the bottom of what she was trying to tell him. "You read the fine print?"

"Stop making jokes," Mikki lamented. "I'm being serious."

"That's why I'm making jokes," he told her. "Because that's my way of coping with something I don't understand." He sighed as he rolled the matter over in his head. In a way, he kind of understood what she was trying to say. "Okay, how about this. I'll make breakfast, then you eat that breakfast while I go to my restaurant to catch up on some things and also get the place ready for the Strausses' fiftieth wedding anniversary party. And after I'm finished—and you're finished—we'll take things as slow as you want. How's that?"

"You're willing to do that?" she asked, surprised. She'd been afraid that she'd ruined everything.

"Yes. I'm willing to do whatever you ask—as long as you don't ask me to walk away. Not from the best person I've found in a very, very long time."

She took a long breath, feeling like someone who had come perilously close to falling over the brink—and then stepped back.

"I need to explain something to you," she said.

"No, you don't," he told her. "You don't have to explain anything."

"Yes, I do," she countered.

He heard the almost desperate note in her voice and that made him change direction. "Okay then, I'm listening. But I really do have to leave soon, so I'm going to be making your breakfast while I'm listening."

Mikki laughed, shaking her head. "You really are something else."

"And I hope to prove that to you—slowly," Jeff added, mindful of what he'd just promised her a few minutes ago. "Go ahead," he urged as he began to whip up a ham-and-cheese omelet along with a serving of French toast.

She wasn't proud of what she was about to share, but he needed to understand why she was so leery of having a relationship. She knew she'd already touched on this, but he had to be made to understand the full extent of how much this had affected her.

"When I was a kid, I thought everybody's parents argued all the time because mine did. But despite the arguments—and there were some knock-down, drag-out ones—we were a family and I thought we'd always stay that way. But we didn't."

Afraid of seeing pity in his eyes, she stared at the napkin holder in the center of the kitchen table.

"My parents got divorced before I was twelve. My mother fell wildly in love with Albert. They were married before her divorce papers were dry. I didn't realize it then, but that was the start of a pattern.

"My mother would fall head over heels for some 'absolutely wonderful guy,' and they'd get married, but before too long, Mr. Wonderful would stop being wonderful and just become another albatross around her neck. An albatross she'd shed the moment she found her next Mr. Wonderful."

She'd mentioned some of this before, but he hadn't realized the extent of it, or how much it had traumatized her, Jeff thought. "How many times has your mother been married?"

"Four," Mikki answered, then corrected herself. "Five if you count the annulment."

He put the diced bits of ham and cheese into the egg mixture, whisking everything together. "Annulment?"

She nodded. "Harvey," she said. "I'm not sure about the circumstances. I was in medical school at the time. All I know was that by the time I received her announcement saying she'd married Harvey Winthrop, Mother was already getting the union annulled." Mikki sighed. "From that point on, I learned not to ask any questions," she confessed. "It was a lot less stressful that way."

She paused, allowing the import of her words to sink in. "What I'm saying is that my mother taught me by her example that nothing ever lasts, no matter how fantastic it might seem at the outset."

The omelet was ready. He slid it onto a plate, then placed it on the table in front of her. He set the slice of French toast he'd prepared at the same time right next to it.

Clearing off the counter, Jeff picked his words carefully, not wanting to scare her or make her think that he was making light of what she had gone through. "From what you just told me, I can see why you'd feel so leery about entering any sort of a relationship. But I'd like the opportunity to prove to you—slowly," he underscored, "that it doesn't have to be that way.

"But right now," he went on, drying his hands on one of the kitchen towels, "I've got to go and start preparations for that fiftieth wedding anniversary celebration. That's fifty years," he emphasized, his eyes meeting hers. "With the same person." Having made her breakfast and having said what he'd come to say, Jeff paused to kiss her quickly. "It happens more often than you think."

When she rose from the table, he looked at her. "Where are you going?"

She gestured in the general direction of the front door. "I thought I'd see you out."

"Eat the omelet," he told her. "It tastes better warm than cold." He winked at her. "I'll call you."

Mikki sank back down in the chair. After a minute, she began to eat the omelet and French toast he had made for her. While she ate, she wondered if she had just managed to ruin the best thing that had happened to her—or if she had just carried out a preemptive strike, saving herself from experiencing devastating heartache in the near future.

Jeff didn't call.

Not that afternoon and not that evening. When he didn't call the next morning, she tried to tell herself that he was busy. Busy with the restaurant, busy with the party, both before and after, and busy with life in general.

And since it was now Monday, her own routine began all over again, a routine that kept her almost too busy to breathe. And almost too busy to think.

Almost.

Every time her phone rang, whether the landline or her cell, she expected it to be Jeff on the other end.

And when it wasn't, she upbraided herself for thinking—hoping—that it was.

Obviously she'd been right to put the brakes on, Mikki thought, struggling to keep the hurt at bay. She would have felt that much worse if this happened in the future, after she'd invested a lot of time in Jeff. Time and emotions.

Right, like you didn't do any of that already, she mocked herself.

When her phone rang as she walked in her front door at the end of the next day, Mikki flew across the room and grabbed the landline receiver with both hands, simultaneously praying that the person on the other end was Jeff.

But it wasn't.

It was her mother. She'd been in such a hurry to answer the phone, she hadn't bothered to look at the caller

ID. She was slipping again, but then, she supposed she could be forgiven. She was still dealing with the fact that when Sophia Sabatino had come in for her second postsurgical exam, her daughter, Tina, had come with her.

Mikki had expected to see Jeff.

It was over, she thought. Over before it actually began.

Her mother's voice jarred her back to the present.

"Sweetheart, I wanted to you be the first to know," her mother gushed in that familiar voice she knew all too well. "I'm getting married."

Mikki pressed her lips together to suppress the sigh that had instantly risen in response to her mother's news. She was supposed to feign happiness, then ask about the groom-to-be and wish her mother well. But she just couldn't do that. Not again.

So instead of dutifully playing her part, Mikki sank down on the sectional and braced herself. "Why?"

Instead of being annoyed by the challenge the way Mikki had expected her to be, Veronica giggled.

"Well, it's not because I have to, not in *that* way," she heard her mother laugh, "if that's what you're asking me."

Her mother was well past childbearing age no matter how many times she fudged the date on her birth certificate. They both knew that.

"No, Mother, I'm asking why are you going through all this again?"

"Why, because I love Randolph, that's why," her mother answered, sounding surprised that she was even being asked such a question. "It's what people do when they're in love, darling. They get married."

Mikki closed her eyes, searching for strength. "Mother, you have been in love with enough men to form a small army—and each of those men has turned out not to be the soul mate that you thought they were."

Undaunted, her mother said, "I know that, but Randolph—"

This time, she wasn't going to back away. This time she was determined to talk some sense into her mother. She needed to stop this insane cycle of fall in love, marry, divorce, repeat.

"—is probably going to wind up disappointing you, too," Mikki pointed out.

"What would make you say such a thing?" her mother asked, sounding shocked and appalled.

Mikki dug in. Her mother's recurring pattern of behavior was what was responsible for destroying her optimism. She needed to make her mother change. "Because I'm tired of watching you be disappointed time after time."

Her mother was quiet for a moment and Mikki thought that, finally confronted with the truth, maybe her mother had just hung up on her.

But then she heard her mother's voice. "That's very sweet of you, dear," she said patiently. "But I think you're missing the point."

This was where the double-talk came in. This was where her mother started building castles in the sky.

She felt as if she was banging her head against a brick wall.

"And what is the point, Mother?" she asked.

"That's really very simple, dear," her mother said, talking to her as if Mikki were just becoming an adult. "The point is that if I don't go out and seize the moment, if I don't believe that this next union will be the right one and the man that I'm exchanging vows with is going to be the one destined to be by my side for the rest of my life, well, then I might as well just give up on life entirely.

"You have to understand that things don't happen if you sit the game out on the sidelines, Michelle. Things only happen if you have enough courage to go out there and fight for your happiness. *Really* fight for it. If you don't try, you don't win. Do you understand what I'm telling you, Michelle?"

Yes. You're spouting every single cliché out there, Mikki thought, feeling like she was engaged in a losing battle.

But she also remembered reading somewhere that clichés only existed because, at the bottom, they were rooted in the truth.

Besides, maybe her mother was right. Maybe *this* man was going to turn out to be the right one for her. Who was she to say no?

"Yes, Mother," Mikki answered. "Where there's life, there's hope."

"Exactly!" her mother exclaimed. "You *do* understand! So you'll come to the wedding?"

"I'll come to the wedding," Mikki promised.

"Wonderful!" her mother cried. "I can't wait for you to meet Randolph—your new stepfather."

Oh, Lord, Mikki thought, closing her eyes as she searched for strength.

Chapter Eighteen

Mikki felt as if she couldn't find a place for herself. Tension resulting from the last few days, especially after she'd weathered the disappointment of not having Jeff accompanying his mother for her second postsurgical exam, was beginning to tie her up in knots.

With all that going on, who would have thought that her mother could actually say something sensible?

Maybe she should be looking out her window, waiting for the arrival of the four horsemen, Mikki thought, because obviously the end of the world was coming.

She was happy for her mother, happy that her mother felt that she had finally found the right man. Chances of that proving true were slim, but if Veronica could still believe in miracles, why shouldn't she?

But meanwhile, her own life suddenly looked as if it was in complete disarray and she had no idea how to fix it, or even if it *was* fixable.

Maybe she should call Jeff.

Or maybe she shouldn't, because the two of them just weren't meant to be.

When the phone rang again a little more than five minutes later, she looked at the landline accusingly. "Give me a break, Mother," she muttered under her breath.

It rang again and she knew her mother wouldn't stop calling until she answered.

Crossing back to the landline, she yanked the receiver from its cradle.

"I said I'll come." It was an effort not to snap the words out. After all, what she was going through really wasn't her mother's fault. This was all her own doing.

"I haven't asked yet," the deep voice on the other end said, "but good to know."

The receiver almost slid out of her hand. Was she getting a do-over? "Jeff?"

"I take it that response when you picked up the phone wasn't meant for me."

Relief at hearing his voice temporarily made her mind go blank. It took Mikki a second to pull herself together and answer him. "I thought you were my mother, calling back."

"Oh, if you're expecting her call, I'll just hang up," Jeff offered.

"No!" she cried. If he hung up, he might never call back again. And then she realized how desperate that plea had to have sounded to him. Embarrassment all but saturated her. "No," she repeated in what she hoped was a far more subdued voice.

She heard him laugh softly, and a warmth bathed over her.

"If you don't want to talk to your mother that much, you can always take the phone off the hook," he told her. "Although I wouldn't advise it, because she'll probably catch up to you sooner than later, and in my experience, it's best to deal with things head-on, even if you'd rather avoid them."

Was that a veiled message about her approach to things?

Stop it, stop reading into things. Just be happy he called.

"I don't want to talk about my mother," Mikki told him.

"All right," Jeff responded gamely, "we can talk about something else."

It sounded as if he was leaving the choice of subject up to her. She didn't want to say anything that might wind up pushing her back to square one, so she asked about the first thing she could think of, even though she was afraid that she might accidentally bring up a sore subject.

At this point, she was totally unsure of herself—but not saying anything was even worse, so she began slowly. "How did the party go?"

"Party?" He'd been all but counting the minutes until he felt he could safely call her again. For the last few days—for the first time since he'd started in this field—it was all he could do to keep things going at work. What for him had always been a labor of love had been strictly labor since he had left her house on Sunday. His mind kept wandering back to thoughts of Mikki at the most inopportune times, causing him to lose track of things.

Work had taken a complete back seat in his thoughts. Consequently, he drew a total blank at her question.

"The fiftieth-anniversary party at your restaurant on Sunday," Mikki prompted. Had it gone badly for some reason? Had she raised a subject he would have rather left alone? She felt as if she was verbally all thumbs.

"Oh, that." How could he have forgotten the Strausses' anniversary celebration? Pulling it off had been a huge deal, and he had outdone himself. "That went well. Very well," he told her, adding, "The couple was totally surprised."

Now it was her turn to be confused. "They didn't know they'd been married fifty years?"

He laughed, and the sound went straight to her stomach, causing it to really tighten this time. She'd forgotten how much she really loved the sound of his laugh. Just hearing it was immensely comforting.

"No, they knew," he told her. "But what they didn't know was that their kids were throwing them a big party. The Strausses thought they were just being taken out for dinner."

She could picture the couple entering the large banquet room and the surprise on their faces when they saw that everyone they loved was in that room, celebrating them. That was a family scene she had longed for her whole life.

"Sounds nice," she told him, a wistful note in her voice.

"It was." Jeff paused for a moment, as if debating whether or not to say the next thing. He didn't want to risk scaring Mikki off, but keeping away from her like this was really getting to him. He decided to go for it. "Mikki, could I come over?"

Her heart practically did a backflip. She hadn't ruined it. He wanted to see her.

Almost afraid that this was too good to be true, she asked, "You mean tonight?"

"Yes—unless you want to go slower," he qualified.

Mikki had wanted to see him even before her mother's phone call had gotten her thinking that she had made a huge mistake. She had behaved in a manner that she had always detested—she'd been cowardly. Her fear of giving her heart away and having it broken could have very well cost her the experience of a lifetime: love.

When Jeff had called just now, she had been debating calling him—and praying that he wouldn't just hang up.

Having him ask to come over was an answer to a prayer.

"No, no, tonight's fine," Mikki told him, hoping she didn't sound too eager. She didn't know if that would make him step back.

Just then the doorbell rang.

Why now, she thought. Of all the times she didn't want to see someone...

Determined to tell whoever was there to either go away, or that she'd get back to them, Mikki made her way across the room.

"Hold on, there's someone at the door," she told Jeff. Reaching the door, she closed one eye and looked through the peephole with the other.

"I know," Jeff said. He completed his sentence just as she opened the door. "It's me."

She knew she'd been the one to put up the boundaries, the one who had honestly thought she'd wanted to go slow, but right at this moment, none of that mattered or held true.

Rather than hang back or maintain decorum, or even express surprise at seeing him on her doorstep, Mikki skipped right over that and went straight to throwing her arms around his neck.

Before he could say a single word of greeting, she was kissing him.

Kissing him with all the pent-up passion she'd been denying, passion that had been brewing within her for the last few days and was now tottering on the very brink of release.

Jeff kissed her back, relieved that she wasn't standing on ceremony or telling him that she still wanted him to keep his distance.

Relieved to just be holding her like this again.

And then, just for a moment, he drew back and looked down into her eyes. "I'm sorry, is this what you meant by 'slow'?"

He'd scared her just now. She'd thought that he'd suddenly changed his mind and realized that he'd rather be without her after all. When she saw he was only teasing, she could have cried.

Instead, she raised herself back up on her toes, her heated body pressed urgently against his. "Shut up and kiss me!"

"Yes, ma'am," he answered dutifully, amusement dancing in his eyes. "But I think we should close the door first before your neighbors start talking about the hot doctor who lives at 2712 Mayfair Circle."

The very suggestion of that happening made Mikki start to laugh. Laugh so hard at the image he'd created of gossiping neighbors that it caused every drop of tension that had invaded her body to totally dissipate and disappear.

The sound was infectious, and Jeff wound up laughing right along with her.

Mikki relaxed. It felt wonderful to laugh, and even more wonderful to have Jeff standing here, in her house, being part of her life.

Regaining some of her composure, Mikki finally locked the door. Turning back toward Jeff, she asked, "Can I get you anything?"

He shook his head, almost amused by her question. "I just spent an entire day at the restaurant. I didn't come here to eat, Mikki. I came to find out if I could start seeing you again or if you still wanted me to go slower."

Since it had been eating away at her, she had to ask. "Is that why you didn't come with your mother when she came in for her postsurgical checkup?"

He was honest with her. "I thought if I brought her, you'd think I was using my mother's condition as an excuse to see you."

Mikki shook her head, reviewing the myriad thoughts that had gone through her head when Sophia came in, accompanied by her daughter rather than Jeff. She couldn't remember ever being that disappointed before—not even when her parents had divorced.

She debated keeping that to herself, but then she decided if this relationship was going to work, it had to be based on honesty. No more hiding emotionally for self-preservation purposes.

"When your sister brought your mother in instead of you, I thought I was never going to see you again."

"I was just trying to do what I thought you wanted me to do," he told her simply. Jeff studied her face now, fighting the strong urge to pull her back into his arms. But he needed to get some things cleared up before he could allow himself to move forward. "What *do* you want me to do?"

She didn't want to waste any more precious time. "I want you to forget everything I said before. I want us to go forward."

This was a complete 180 from the wishes she'd expressed when he'd been here the last time. It sounded too good to be true, and that had him feeling just slightly leery.

"Why the change of heart?" he asked her. "What happened?"

"My mother's getting married," Mikki told him bluntly.

He tried to remember what she'd told him when she'd mentioned her mother's unions the last time. "This is husband number five?"

"Maybe six," she allowed.

And then he remembered. "Right, the possible annulment." But why had her mother's pending marriage made her change her feelings about commitment? "Help me out here. Aren't all your mother's marriages the reason why you wanted me to back off?"

Mikki flushed. "Yes."

He shook his head, still not able to make sense out of the change in her attitude. "I'm confused."

She tried her best to explain what she was feeling. "When my mother called to tell me she was getting married and to invite me to the wedding, I finally confronted her and asked why she was going through this again, especially since we both know that her track record when it comes to marriage is less than stellar. Why get married if there's the very real possibility that she'll just divorce this one, too?"

It was a legitimate question. So far, he followed her. "What was her answer?"

"She said that if she didn't keep on trying, then she'd never be able to find the happiness she was hoping for. That she knew it wasn't just going to fall in her lap. And that this latest guy to enter the marital sweepstakes just might be the one. As long as that possibility existed, she was going to go for it."

Jeff laughed shortly. "You know, in its own way, that makes sense," he told her. "If you don't try, you don't stand a chance of winning."

She looked up at him, her eyes meeting his. "I know," she replied.

He ran the back of his hand along her cheek. "You know what else?"

She could feel desire spiking within her. "What?" she asked almost breathlessly.

"You're not your mother. You haven't been frantically going through men, trying to find Mr. Right behind every rock and tree. You've been much too busy, saving the world one patient at a time."

It was a wonderful thing to say, but she knew he wasn't into empty flattery. What was he basing this on? "How would you know?"

"I looked you up," he told her simply. Seeing the surprised look on her face, he quickly assured her, "I wasn't trying to spy on you. I just thought that the more I knew about you, the better my chances were of winning you over."

He touched on a couple of the highlights he'd learned. "You have an awful lot of accolades written about you, not to mention that you've gotten a lot of awards for your 'selfless service,' I think the wording was."

She nodded. That was all well and good, and once upon a time, that had been enough.

But not anymore.

Not after she'd met him. "None of that matters when I come home to an empty house night after night."

"They say pets help fill up the emptiness," he told her, doing his best to keep a straight face.

Seeing the glimmer in his eye, Mikki doubled up her small fist and punched his arm.

"Wow, you have a violent streak. Who knew?" he teased.

And then he kissed her long and hard. When he drew back, he saw the look of surprise on her face. Jeff wasn't finished reviewing the ground rules, because this time around, he wanted to get it right.

"So, if I promise to go very, very slow, can we start seeing each other again? *Really* start seeing each other again?"

"I don't know," she answered, and for a moment, he thought he was back on shaky ground again—until he heard her ask, "Just how slow is slow?"

Drawing her into his arms, he smiled at her. "As slow as you want."

"What if I don't want to go slow at all?"

"Even better," he answered, tightening his arms around her.

There was a look he could only describe as mischievous in her eyes as she asked, "Does this mean that you'll make love with me tonight?"

He was already pressing a kiss to the side of her neck, igniting her. "Twist my arm."

"Why would I ever do that?" she breathed, tugging at his shirt and unbuttoning it.

"Beats me," he replied, the words all but burning along her skin.

"Only if you stop," she warned.

"Then I'd say we've got nothing to worry about," he told her as his lips covered hers again, taking what was already his.

Epilogue

"Well, ladies," Theresa Manetti told her two best friends happily, "this is one more in our plus column."

Theresa slipped into the pew next to Maizie and Cilia after double-checking with her staff to make sure that Mikki and Jeff's specially designed wedding cake would be arriving at Jeff's restaurant in plenty of time for the reception. She had put her best pastry chefs on the job.

"You mean two more, don't you?" Cilia asked. She glanced knowingly in Maizie's direction.

Totally in the dark, Theresa questioned, "Two? Maizie, what is she talking about?"

This was a topic for future discussion, not in church right before the wedding ceremony was about to begin. Maizie's expression was one of pure innocence as she said, "I really have no idea."

Theresa thought otherwise. She turned her attention to Cilia. "Tell me," she ordered.

"Apparently, our friend has taken it upon herself to freelance without telling us." Cilia's smile was triumphant. "You forget," she told Maizie, "our daughters talk."

"Well, *somebody* talk," Theresa insisted. She hated being kept in the dark.

"All right," Maizie relented. "My daughter came to me after talking to Mikki to see how things were going. She was afraid Mikki was never going to risk getting married no matter how wonderful Jeff was—not until her mother finally found someone stable she could really settle down with. If that happened, that would encourage Mikki to say yes to Jeff."

"And so Maizie found someone for her," Cilia said, taking over the narrative. "Honestly, Maizie, sometimes you just talk too slowly—the wedding's almost starting."

"Wait," Theresa interrupted, still trying to get the story straight. "So you played matchmaker for Mikki's mother?" she asked Maizie. "Without us?"

Maizie nodded. "I'm afraid I did," she confessed. "I knew a gentleman who was just perfect for her mother—and Nikki helped," she added proudly.

"Nikki? Your daughter, Nikki?" Theresa questioned, surprised.

"The apple doesn't fall all that far from the tree," Cilia told their friend.

Maizie quickly filled her friends in. "Randolph is a retired army doctor. Kind, intelligent and not the type to be intimidated by a forceful woman. I think he's just the influence that Veronica needs in her life. Her mother marrying Randolph also showed Mikki that the right one *can* come along if you don't give up. And Lord knows, that woman never gave up."

Theresa laughed softly. "My, the lengths we go to in order to help our unsuspecting clients find happiness," she marveled.

"Well, it worked," Maizie said proudly. "The happy couple had their reception at Jeff's restaurant. And during the celebration, Jeff worked up his nerve to propose to Mikki." Maizie's smile went right to her eyes. "I hear tell that she couldn't say yes fast enough."

"You are one devious woman, Maizie Sommers," Cilia told her friend.

Maizie exchanged glances with her two friends. "We all are." Then, before either one of them could say anything in response to her comment, she said, "Shh. It's starting."

A moment later, Cilia looked at her closely. "Maizie, you're tearing up."

"Nikki is her matron of honor," she pointed out. "Isn't she beautiful?"

"Always," Theresa and Cilia both agreed, although it wasn't clear if Maizie was talking about her daughter or the latest young bride.

Right about now, she'd expected to be nervous—to the point that she would be contemplating bolting from the church. Instead, Mikki realized that she had never felt more confident in her life. Marrying Jeff, committing herself for the rest of her life to this man, was not just the right thing to do, she knew that it was the *only* thing to do.

And here she was, slowly walking down the aisle toward the man of her dreams.

She couldn't believe it.

And to think that she had almost thrown it all away out of fear because she didn't want to emulate her mother's mistakes.

Mikki glanced over to where her mother was seated with her new husband. Her *last* new husband, her mother had whispered when she'd introduced Randolph to Mikki, and she'd felt her mother actually meant it. More important, she felt that this man was going to keep her mother happy.

Love was possible in this turbulent world, Mikki thought happily—and *she* had found her love. Thank goodness he hadn't given up on her.

As she slowly made her way down the aisle behind her best friend, her eyes were focused on the man at the altar. The man who had been patient enough to wait out her craziness.

The man she was meant to be with forever.

When she finally reached the altar and joined Jeff before the minister, Jeff leaned in and whispered to her, "You came," as if he had been harboring some doubts.

Mikki smiled warmly at him. "Wouldn't have missed this for the world," she whispered back.

And then they both turned to look at the minister, who began to say the words that would, in the end, join them for the rest of their lives.

The way they were meant to be.

* * * * *

MILLS & BOON

Coming next month

BABY SURPRISE FOR THE
SPANISH BILLIONAIRE
Jessica Gilmore

'Don't you think it's fun to be just a little spontaneous every now and then?' Leo continued, his voice still low, still mesmerising.

No, Anna's mind said firmly, but her mouth didn't get the memo. 'What do you have in mind?'

His mouth curved triumphantly and Anna's breath caught, her mind running with infinite possibilities, her pulse hammering, so loud she could hardly hear him for the rush of blood in her ears.

'Nothing too scary,' he said, his words far more reassuring than his tone. 'What do you say to a well-earned and unscheduled break?'

'We're having a break.'

'A proper break. Let's take out the *La Reina Pirata*—' his voice caressed his boat's name lovingly '—and see where we end up. An afternoon, an evening, out on the waves. What do you say?'

Anna reached for her notebook, as if it were a shield against his siren's song. 'There's too much to do . . .'

'I'm ahead of schedule.'

'We can't just head out with no destination!'

'This coastline is perfectly safe if you know what

you're doing.' He grinned wolfishly. 'I know exactly what I'm doing.'

Anna's stomach lurched even as her whole body tingled. She didn't doubt it. 'I . . .' She couldn't, she shouldn't, she had responsibilities, remember? Lists, more lists, and spreadsheets and budgets, all needing attention.

But Rosa would. Without a backwards glance. She wouldn't even bring a toothbrush.

Remember what happened last time you decided to act like Rosa, her conscience admonished her, but Anna didn't want to remember. Besides, this was different. She wasn't trying to impress anyone; she wasn't ridiculously besotted, she was just an overworked, overtired young woman who wanted to feel, to be, her age for a short while.

'Okay, then,' she said, rising to her feet, enjoying the surprise flaring in Leo di Marquez's far too dark, far too melting eyes. 'Let's go.'

Continue reading
**BABY SURPRISE FOR THE
SPANISH BILLIONAIRE**
Jessica Gilmore

Available next month
www.millsandboon.co.uk

LET'S TALK
Romance

For exclusive extracts, competitions
and special offers, find us online:

 facebook.com/millsandboon

@millsandboonuk

@millsandboon

Or get in touch on 0844 844 1351*

For all the latest titles coming soon, visit
millsandboon.co.uk/nextmonth